MIDNIGHT CREEPS

JEFF MEDEIROS

Copyright © 2017 Jeff Medeiros
All rights reserved
First Edition

PAGE PUBLISHING, INC.
New York, NY

First originally published by Page Publishing, Inc. 2017

ISBN 978-1-68409-943-6 (Paperback)
ISBN 978-1-68409-944-3 (Digital)

Printed in the United States of America

CONTENTS

1. Homunculus 5
2. The Clayton Boneyard..................................27
3. The Sea Pod 41
4. The Will to Die 49
5. Night Things 59
6. Bowen's Burden 63
7. Scraps for the Crows 71
8. Through My Eyes 77
9. The Shelter of Thorns 92
10. Killerpillar 108
11. The Eye of Cy 138
12. The Minions of Neath 151
13. Flicker of Fear...177
14. The Orbs 182
15. Shark on the Shore 196
16. In the Chair of Nightmare........................212
17. A Day Above Ground...............................231

HOMUNCULUS

I WAS IN MY STUDY enjoying a pipeful and a glass of fine Irish whiskey. Sleepily I gazed, trancelike, through a cloud of dancing smoke, out through an open window at the thick, wet fog that curled and crawled in toward me. My state of tranquility was suddenly shattered, not by the sudden swing of the door, but by the look of worry in the intoxicating brown eyes of my lovely wife, Alyssa. She stood in the dim light of the doorway, pinching a letter in her trembling fingers.

"I had to stop myself from burning it," she muttered.

"Burning what?" I asked impatiently. Her slender, freckled hand reluctantly stretched out across the heavy night air in my direction and threw its dense, snake-like shadow at my feet. I rose, creaked across the squeaky floor, and pried the envelope from her retracting hand. When the name in the upper left hand corner caught my eye, I understood my wife's concern as I gasped for breath, as if I were being pushed underwater by a monstrous wave. Alister Graves, 122 Oakwood Lane, London, England. Alister Graves! Suddenly, the thin package I was holding felt as if it weighed fifty pounds. Then it felt as if it were warm and growing hotter. I knew it was all in my head, which now began to spin and ache with anticipation. I wished she had burned it.

Dear Dr. Edward Harris:

I understand that you have recently hung up your stethoscope. It has also come to my understanding that you are the most sought after and respected doctor in all of the UK. I will keep this message very brief for I am writing to you with an infected hand. Each letter pains my every knuckle, every joint. I have seen many doctors, none of which have been able to help me. They cannot tell me of what I am suffering from. You are my last hope, Dr. Harris, for I am afraid whatever afflicted my fingers and hand is not only seemingly incurable but it is spreading slowly up my arm. I beg of you to see me at once, Doctor. You will be rewarded handsomely for your troubles. Enclosed is ample fare, an advance, and directions to my estate. Please find the time and heart to help me, for I have no options left, save for a slow and agonizing demise.

Yours: hopelessly doomed,
Alister Graves

The contents of the letter shook me enough indeed. For his very name alone was enough to send my imagination hurling through the vastness of space, collecting any oddities it might come into contact with along the way like a hungry, dragging magnet. There was no shortage of rumors that followed the name Alister Graves. To start with, they called him the mad alchemist. Everyone took him for a madman, and they whispered words like witchery, black magic, and deviltry when they spoke of him, and they crossed themselves and quickened their pace whenever they would pass by his stone abode. I myself had heard many a speculation concerning Mr. Graves, but the one that disturbed me the most was the one about him murdering his own wife. Now I, being a man of medicine, had to confront this situation as any before: with a clear and rational mind. I did not know what to believe or even what to think at this point. But I was afraid I must put all superstitions and my wife's warnings aside and pay a visit to this ill man of alchemy.

"We're coming up on the manor now, Doctor," spat the whipper of the horses as he lashed them again, and they ran and they ran. Now and then, the sliver moon would peek out through the rivery clouds and the ever-consuming fog. "Doctor, sir," spoke the coachman suddenly, "is madman Graves ill?"

"Yes," I replied. "Do you know this Graves?"

"No, sir," answered the man as he flogged the horses again, "but I know of him. Many people talk of him, but no one actually knows him. He is a complete hermit. He never leaves his house. His servant does that for him. He doesn't have a single friend, and his own family won't go near him. They say he's working for the devil. Some say he's a witch, a powerful witch who practices black magic. They say he sacrifices animals and… and… well, sir, some folks say he offered up his own wife, sir! And then there's those who say he steals up babies in the night and sucks their very souls out through tiny holes in his two front teeth."

"Well, you don't believe in all of that, do you?"

"No, sir, maybe not all of it is true. I'm only telling you what I've heard. You asked, sir, I don't know what to believe. All I know is I'm glad I'm the one dropping you off on his doorstep and not the other way around."

As I tapped out the ash from my pipe, I noticed that the dirt road we had been traveling on had turned to cobblestone. Although it was impossible to see, the extreme bumpiness and the rhythmic noise of the wheels and hooves told the tale. Soon, the snorting steeds pulled us through two tall stone pillars, one of which held the weight of a large open gate. Suddenly without warning, they stopped simultaneously, throwing me headlong into the opposite side of the carriage. They would go no further. I paid the apologetic driver, and off they bolted into the deep night without the crack of the whip.

As I climbed the steps, the front door creaked open slowly. The soft, inviting voice of a dark figure spoke. "Dr. Harris?"

"Yes, miss," I responded.

"Please come in. Mr. Graves is waiting." I noticed as she led me in that it was just as dark, perhaps even darker inside. An exotic Asian woman whose pale face was aglow in the flame of a single candle she held started elegantly up the stairs. Halfway up, my ears were filled with the muffled sound of agonizing moans. *He must be in bad shape,* I thought.

Down the lonely hallway, our footfalls echoed until at last I found myself at the door of Graves's chamber. Knocking softly on the hard oak with tiny knuckles, the servant woman announced me. "Enter!" a shrewd voice answered. There in a large bed lay an old man with unkempt long white hair and a long beard. His beady gray eyes seemed to burn through my own as they fixed themselves upon me. "Dr. Harris, thank you for seeing me. It's a great honor to meet you." As he stretched out his long right arm, I stepped forward and said, "Likewise, sir, now let's get a look at that hand."

The servant lady began lighting candles on either side of the alchemist's bed to brighten the room. As the last of the wicks were set alight, I noticed while shaking his feeble hand that it was extremely discolored. In fact, it was a disturbing gray. I had never seen anything like it in all my years of practice, except, of course, among the dead. I began to thoroughly examine the eerie gray hand and wrist. Then I noticed two tiny holes between his thumb and forefinger that were surrounded by a vague purple hue. "Tell me everything you can about what you think could have caused such a baffling condition," I said.

"Well, Doctor, all I can tell you is that I've been bitten," said Graves with reluctance in his eyes.

"Bitten by what?" I wondered.

He grew uncomfortably silent before he finally muttered, "I don't know, Doctor."

"You have no idea?" I questioned.

"No, sir, I was working in my lab two weeks ago when I dropped my stirrer. I reached under the table to retrieve it when I felt a sharp pain in my hand. It was very dim under my workbench, and when I looked to find the cause of my pain, I saw only a fleeing blur scamper out of sight."

"It looks like the bite of a snake, if anything, Graves, although I must confess I know of no known snake venom that will cause such colors to manifest. And although the partial crippling of the affected area does somewhat fit in with that of a snake bite, there are many things that don't add up. Have you experienced any pains in your chest, a shortness of breath, perhaps?"

"No," replied the ill old man.

"And as of the other doctors that have examined you, what have they learned?"

"Completely baffled they are," he replied solemnly.

"We must take some blood and conduct some tests," I said as I pierced the large needle into his bicep. "I shall stay up late tonight with my microscope and tools."

"Don't stay up too late," the man replied. "I need your mind fresh in the morning."

"Don't fret over me, Mr. Graves, there is little time to waste. You get some rest."

"Thanks again, Doctor," he said in a weary voice. "Ms. Ling, show the kind doctor to his quarters."

That night, I studied the strange old man's blood as it spread out on the glass 'neath the lens of my microscope. If I didn't extract it from his veins myself, I would not believe it were human, or any other animal, for that matter, for his reds, whites, and platelets made about as much sense as the color of his hand. I felt at once as if I were studying an alien life force. It simply could not be. And as tired as I was, I knew that I was indeed awake although it all seemed like a terrible dream. Exhausted and puzzled, I laid my head down to rest. Again I heard the distant, haunted moaning worm its way into my weary bones.

For three days and most of three nights, I studied the mysterious old man in a newfound state of unyielding confusion. I stayed with him and his only servant, Len, the beautiful Asian woman who was his only human connection.

I longed for my wife, especially when I looked into Len's dark eyes. I thought about how I had to pry myself away from her loving arms when I left to cure Mr. Graves. How she clung to me and begged me not to go. I could not turn such a desperate man down, or anyone, for that matter. But now, for the first time in my long career, I felt utterly helpless to even figuring out what ailed poor Graves, never mind cure him in what seems such little and dwindling time. For the grayness and stiffness has spread to his elbow in three days. And for once in my life, I felt like I was fathoms over my head, and no one could help me help him. Although I was glad I tried to help him, I almost wish I had listened to my wife in the first place, for I seemed to have wasted his precious time like the ones before me. I felt my brain would explode if I didn't undo it from the knot that could not be untied.

I remembered her last resort to make me stay was to ask me why I felt so obligated to cure a man of such evil. I said to her, "How do I know he's evil? I do not know him from anyone." I could not simply believe such rumors and superstitions, and so far, I'd seen nothing that would bring light to their far-fetched accusations, which pained me all the more. I guess deep down in the darkest region of my mind, I'd hoped that he truly was evil. Maybe then I wouldn't feel so bad about not being able to help him. But the worst part of all I feared was that I, perhaps one of the most sought-after doctors in all of London, his only hope, had failed. And even worse, I had to look him in his expectant eyes and tell him so. As much as it weighed on me, this I must do. I would break the news to him in the morning before I headed back to Alyssa. I would waste no more of his time. Perhaps someone else could save him, perhaps not. Either way, he should waste no more time on me. Again I sank my perplexed head into a stranger's pillow. And again, the tortured moans floated across the dead, empty hall into my pitiful ears. Perhaps it was the moans that disturbed me the most.

I must have only been blessed with a few hours' sleep last night, for the moans and groans, like usual, kept me awake hours after I turned in. Mrs. Ling knocked on the door to tell me she was about to put breakfast on. As hungry as I was, I politely declined.

Slowly ascending the stairs, I tried to gather myself, assemble my words. When I reached the end of the hallway, I was surprised to see that his chamber door was open. "Mr. Graves," I called as I stepped up to the threshold. "Yes, Harris, come in, my good man."

"Mr. Graves, I must be frank, sir. I'm afraid I've done all I can for you. I'm sad to say your suffering is beyond my understanding, therefore, beyond my help." With my words, he stared at the blank space on the far wall behind me. The silence seemed to last forever until he finally spoke. "Doctor, perhaps you will bear with me a bit longer, for I have not told you or any of the other doctors the truth. Perhaps it will help the outcome. Maybe it won't matter at all, but this, Dr. Harris, is truly my last hope. The truth… for it was no snake which bit me…"

"Lies will not help me help you, Mr. Graves. I need your complete honesty. I'm in the dark here, and we've wasted enough time."

"Doctor," he interrupted, "I am about to show you what has never been seen by human eyes other than mine. You must vow complete secrecy. I mean your own dear wife mustn't know."

"Yes," I promised, "now let's see the culprit which has brought this horrible plague upon you."

I could not begin to imagine what he was about to unveil to my curious eyes. Questions began to pour into my mind like water into a ship that struck a rock. I helped him out of bed and followed him slowly down the stairs. His decrepit-looking gray hand swung limply at his side, while his left hand, still strong and reliable, gripped the rail. As we passed the room where I had tried to sleep for the past four nights, a sound quite terrifying filled my ears. My heart began to thump with great speed and heaviness. And although the sound was hauntingly familiar, it filled me this time with fright, not pity. The maddening sound, which grew slightly louder with every step, took on a whole new meaning. For what tortured my ears was the disgusting moaning I mistook for Graves's pain. I found myself walking slower and slower.

At the end of the dim hall stood a door with a large lock. By the time he undid it, I had caught up with him. As the alchemist pushed it open, he gazed at me with his sharp, piercing eyes. Not a word left his hair-hidden lips. As the whining door opened, the moaning ceased. However, it did not comfort me. Graves fumbled across the dark room and drew back the curtain of a single window, revealing a dusty laboratory full of beakers, glass tubes containing colored liquids, melting pots, dusty books strewn about here and there, and small curious mounds of gold- and silver-colored metals.

I put up my arms and shrugged my shoulders as if to ask, "Well, what?" Looking back at me with stern, twinkling eyes, he said, "Turn to your right, Doctor." With those words, I suddenly felt as if an entity worse than death himself were looming over me. And within that intolerable instant, I felt utterly frozen. As if fire from the mouth of a beast would scorch my side and I would not be able to run or turn my head and—oh god! When I finally forced myself to, although my split-second instinct was to turn away, I could not. For there, gazing back at me through a glass cage bulged the biggest beady eyes of a small, grotesque creature that I'd never envisioned in my most terrible nightmares, yet as I stood before it speechless, I beheld its sunken chest heaving and its solemn lips breathing! I noticed before I blinked that it had no irises or lids to cover their wild, blank, tortured stare. Its left eye seemed slightly larger than the other. The head was enormous in relation to the body. I wondered how its tiny frame could support its ugliness. Its veins, like tributaries on a moonless night, were a darker gray, almost black, and many of them protruded from its cracked-looking flesh. Then my eyes were drawn to the curled claws at the ends of its stumpy limbs, whose sharp tips jolted and convulsed. So too did I notice that there were only four of them twitching at the end of each paw. But perhaps its skin spooked me most of all. For its covering was so gray it resembled decay. Rough, scab-like tissue, scratched and withered, which displayed the absence of nose and nostrils. And despite all its threatening wretchedness, it only stood an approximate fifteen inches tall. Such a fragile, freakish, pathetic-looking creature. Yet it seemed to hold such enormous power within its haunted stare. I didn't know how long I stood staring in awe at the unbelievable thing before Graves's voice woke me from its hypnotizing spell. "What do you think, Harris?" He said condescendingly.

"I don't know what to think," I said with much silence between. Nor did I know what to say.

"I guess I can refrain from locking the door from now on," he spoke, "as long as you can give me your word that you won't try to take it out."

"You don't have to worry about that."

"Oh... and don't feed it," he continued.

"What does it eat?" I asked. "Is it a he?"

"Can't tell what the hell it is myself, but I call it the homunculus. It loves meat."

"Where did the homunculus come from?" I demanded.

"It... why, it came from those."

With his trembling gray forefinger, he pointed to the empty glass tubes at the end of the room.

"So you are saying that you—"

"Yes!" he interrupted. "Yes! I am to blame for this monstrosity." In that very instant, I thought of the things I'd heard all along, the warnings from my wife's tender lips.

"Sir," I pleaded, "I must know, for we spoke of the truth earlier."

"Yes, trust me," said he.

"Then tell me, Mr. Graves, what is your reply to accusations of Satanism?"

"Satan! Satanism! Ha! Ha! Ha! Ha! Ha! Ha! Ha! Doctor, foolish doctor, alchemy, and in this rarest of cases, this vile product you see before you is not the work of the devil, nor, I must admit, is it the work of God."

"Then what is it the work of?" I asked.

"The work of a madman, perhaps, a foolish madman."

"I have a million questions for you, Graves. I'll need a blood sample from this... this thing that bit you. It has few slightly human features, is it at all human?"

"Perhaps a tiny, insignificant percentage, Doctor."

"What else is it made up of, and how did it come to be?" I asked.

"No time for all that now, Doc. Maybe you should take a sample and see what that tells you."

"Yes," I said, "but is there a way to restrain him without the risk of another bite or scratch from those claws?" The claws were thick and over an inch long. Their shadow resembled an alligator-like jaw that snapped and crunched behind the beast on the table the glass cage rested on. "Get ready with the needle." The old man said as he picked up a long rod with a hook at its end and inserted it into a slot in the side of the cage. I then noticed that there were ventilation holes drilled in the side of the cage near the slot as well as the ones on the top piece. The thing tried to maneuver away in a nervous panic, but there was little space to run. Soon it was hooked around its scrawny, gray neck, and Graves pulled the thing tightly into a corner. Nervously I stuck my needle through a hole and into one of its dark veins. It arced its back, tensed every tiny muscle in its sickly looking body, and clenching its claws, hissed like a threatened viper in response. My overwhelmed mind whirled with the mysteries of the darkest night as I watched the cylinder fill with black fluid.

I knew from the start that this was no ordinary house call, but now this! The whole experience had become too much to take in. Yesterday was the longest and strangest day of my entire life. I felt euphoric, as if I were part of some wicked dream, although I knew all too well I was not lying beside my Alyssa. I spent the day in a somewhat hypnotic daze, in utter awe before this awful being, noting its behavioral patterns, watching it breathe through its corpse-like lips. Watching it scamper around in that claustrophobic cage, twitching its claws as if to sharpen them as it returned constant, unforgiving glares back at me, which held as much curiosity for me as I had for it. And when I wasn't poisoning my own mind with its vile image, I sat at the mad alchemist's bench, studying the poor creature's mysterious black life juice under the microscope's scrutinous eye. And what I beheld within the tiny dark pool was one single type of cell that would expand and contract in size with rapid speed. These crazy cells would grow and stretch to almost twice their original size until they would finally vanish with a burst. It resembled a night sky full of dying stars. This disturbed me greatly as I thought of the infected creator of... of whatever it was that was moaning and existing in that gleaming cage of glass. And although I'd been exposed to all this new information, I only grew more and more baffled as the situation seemed all the more hopeless.

"What have you learned, Doctor?" Graves asked as we sat down for evening tea.

"All that has come to my realization in an entire day of study is that its cells are self-destructing, and again, Graves, I'm afraid I've wasted another day of your dwindling time, and I can waste no more, for I'm sure I've just told you what you already know and nothing more." Before he could respond, I offered my deepest apologies and told him I would be leaving in the morning. "As you wish, Doctor, for I should have never burdened you, a healer of man, with such a mountainous, unholy task. Thank you for all your help, Dr. Harris, you will be paid gladly for your efforts."

"Oh no, Mr. Graves sir, I could not accept under the circumstances. Besides, your hospitality is ample fare."

By now the grayness had spread beyond his elbow up to his shoulders, and he could no longer ball a fist or summon his finger to rise. Now and then he would stop in midsentence to wheeze or groan in pain. "Edward," he spoke grimly, "my days are numbered, and the rumors of strangers who only mock and misunderstand me have always been an eroding force upon my spirit. I feel I must clarify a few things, for what it's worth."

"I'm listening," I responded as I looked across the table at him through the dancing, twisting steam.

"Doctor, I need you to understand that my intentions were good although the outcome was quite evil. You see, I've discovered some time ago an astonishing property in a certain neutral human cell. I have learned that these cells can in essence be taught how to act, told how to grow. They can be manipulated like the shape of a finely pruned bush. These cells can be modified to take on the properties of certain tissues.

"I have grown within my tubes steamy, veiny flesh, teeth that never chew. Teeth that have no jaws to hold them, still they grew and grew. A lone eye afloat in preserving solution, an unconnected ear, which pulsated every time a loud enough noise would disturb its slumber. I produced a kidney in a Petri dish, Doctor, can you imagine the boundless possibilities? We could virtually create on demand parts for needy patients. Now do you see where I was going with my experiments, Harris? I, like all alchemists, only wanted to help mankind. To cure their ailments, and I'm sure you can relate, but I know now all too well that it is far too much of a task to ask of any man, even a man as skillful and extraordinary as yourself. Perhaps it was a stone which never should've been overturned, for some way, and I can't completely tell you how that thing was the final outcome.

"My wife warned me not to dare so many steps, but I knew I'd already gone too far not to keep on."

"Tell me about your wife," I mustered up the courage to ask. "Tell me what became of her, Graves."

"Yes, Doctor, I did murder her, if that's what you're hinting at, is it not?" Here I felt a lump in my throat that rendered me silent, and I stared down at my teacup. "Yes, I did, Edward, but believe me when I say I loved that woman with my every fiber. She was my closest and only true friend. I cared for her more than a mother cares for her firstborn, and I never stopped loving her. She was everything to me, Ed, but you see, because I loved her so, I had to put her out of her misery."

"Her misery, sir?" I whispered.

"Yes, for she was the first to be bitten. I opened the door of the cage to feed that... that thing, and it somehow managed to flash past me and leap to the floor. Before I knew it, I was alone in the room, for I watched it scurry and scratch past the door and down the hall. I ran after it in a panic, but it was too fast to see where it went. From room to room I searched frantically until I heard my wife screaming from the kitchen. There she was, lying on the floor, bleeding severely from her ankle, a pool of blood stretched out rapidly around her. She let out one last scream that split my soul in two before she fainted mercifully.

"There above her ankle spewed a hole as large and as deep as an apple. I ripped off my shirt and began wrapping her crimson leg when that wretched thing caught my eye. There it sat beneath the dinner table, gnawing at my poor wife's missing flesh. She woke, trying to flail her limbs around, which I had bound. As I cauterized the wound, she expelled muffled shrieks through a gag while she bit down on a piece of wood I had placed between her teeth. She fainted again, and I carried her to bed.

"The next morning, I awoke to a nightmare. My wife's skin was the gray of death. It covered her entire body and her once beautiful face. Her eyes were dull and sunken and surrounded by pitch-black rings. There was a violet ring around her wound, and she appeared to have aged fifty years overnight for her once soft, young skin was shriveled, dry, and wrinkled beyond belief. Her veins had blackened, and she was foaming from her stiff lips as she moaned and convulsed in agony. Yes, Doctor, I did indeed destroy her."

"I'm sorry, Mr. Graves, you have my deepest sympathy. May I ask how old your wife was when…?"

"She was twenty-five, Edward."

"Twenty-five!" I exclaimed. "And what was your age? You must have been over twice hers."

"Ha! Ha! Ha!" He laughed madly. "You assume odd, sick things like they do, Doctor. You see, this atrocity occurred thirteen years ago, sir!" he revealed as he reached with his healthy hand for his teacup, which was dry.

His eyes sharpened as they again fixed themselves upon me, and his pale gray hand began to tremble. I began to grow impatient with the disturbed old man's revelations and lies. "It doesn't add up," I said while my mind raced. "I thought you said you'd give me pure truth from now on, Graves."

"The truth is what I speak!" he shouted. "You see, I only fibbed before when I gave my age, Doctor, for you are looking into the weary eyes of a thirty-eight-year-old man."

"But it still makes no sense, Graves, what you speak. Tell me, when were you bitten?"

"That very day," he said.

"The same day as your wife?"

"Yes, the same."

"Are you telling me she didn't last through the night, but thirteen years later, you still live to tell the tale?" I said sardonically.

"Yes, Doctor, its victims react in different ways to its bite. Some were destroyed instantly, somewhat mercifully, while others suffer greater periods and exist longer to learn new horrors, but all its bites are fatal. Yes, I have survived the longest, but sometimes, I contemplate sticking my hand in that cage just to get it over with."

"Yet it does not seem to harbor any venom in those fangs," I interrupted.

"No, it does not. My theory is that my homunculus was born without a soul, Doctor, and when a person has been bitten, I think, in essence, the soul of that person begins to drain from the body, perhaps through the two tiny holes. Perhaps it sucks part of it out through the holes in its fangs to sustain its own existence. Either way, the outcome is the same—the evaporation of the soul, whether rapid or slow."

Graves stood from the table to fetch some brandy. As he filled two glasses, he went on with his story. "I finished wrapping her leg and grabbed for the monster as it swallowed my wife's meat. With twice the swiftness of a scared rat, it scurried out the open door. I searched the yard for hours in vain. Besides, I could not catch it in the house, what chance did I have even if I spotted it outside? I decided to leave a few traps around the yard baited with chicken heads. Later in the afternoon, I was disturbed in my laboratory by a muffled commotion. Upon hearing what sounded like a panicking crowd, a certain figure entered my head. After a solid five minutes, it finally died out. The next day, Len returned from the drugstore with deplorable news. A quarter mile from here stands the steeple of a church, Doctor, and it seems that five women and four men were mysteriously bitten as they sang prayers to their god. At first, it was attributed to hungry vermin running beneath the pews, until they all fell gravely ill. Then they thought it was the black plague, until they witnessed the way they grew dead. For as horrible as the face of the plague was, this new, unknown threat made its victims seem attractive. And for this, they blamed Satan, for they said it was the devil in the house of God! Sometimes even now I wonder, for all I know and as little as they do, that maybe they were right. But I know better. Some things are worse than the most terrible thing your wildest imagination could possibly conjure from the deepest, darkest depths of the forest of your mind.

"I also learned that an infant was found lifeless in its cradle with skin of gray and two tiny purple-colored holes on its chubby left thigh. Fortunately, this was the last incident, for normality soon crept back into the monotony of this small village. But not for me, for although my traps were untouched, my sick creation came back to me like a frothing dog. When I picked it up to put it away, it buried its fangs into my hand."

That night I laid my troubled head to rest. It began to ache. I felt as if my puzzled mind could not possibly absorb another fragment of information no matter how familiar or far-fetched. I couldn't take the insanity anymore. I certainly could not make sense of it. And as rotten as I felt for abandoning Graves in my powerlessness, it helped, although only little, to think that he brought this on himself, in his genius ignorance. There I went again trying to justify my inability to save him. I only wish I knew how. Tomorrow I would return to my sweet wife's lips and try to forget the terrors that had summoned me to the stench of their festering hide.

That night I was awoken by a piercing pain on my nose. I woke up swatting my face in a fury. And although my mind was mostly still adrift, I was sure I had knocked a solid object off my open mouth. I heard a loud thud followed by what could've been footfalls tapering off.

Groggy and dazed, I sat up in the night and gasped for air as horror set in. My wide eyes searched vainly in the blackness for answers. I tried to convince myself although the pain was throbbing that I was only dreaming, until I felt a warm sensation trickle down my nose and into my lips—the unmistakable taste of blood! My heart pounded wildly while I listened to a mocking silence that somehow seemed worse than a hissing, scratching, or moaning that I was now waiting for. After an endless moment or two, I began to fumble for the candle on the nightstand.

Blood was now streaming off my chin as I fumbled for a match. For a while I held it in my trembling fingers, too frightened to strike it, while the blood oozed down my chest and began to pool in my navel. Finally, I lit the candle. I shined the light over my bed and all about the room. I looked around for a possible weapon, but the only thing I could use was the small candleholder I was holding. I checked the dark corners and turned my attention to the bed. Underneath… I must look underneath. I dragged my feet to the side of the bed and slowly folded to my knees. I could hear the bright-red drips as they hit the hardwood floor one by one.

Holding my breath, I tore back the bed skirt violently, stuffing the flickering glow 'neath the bed frame. There was nothing but cobwebs. Rising, I turned my attention to the door. How reluctantly I crept up to it. I put my ear to it and listened. Again I heard the dreadful silence fill my empty ears. Slowly I wrapped my fingers round the knob, and the coldness seeped into their tips as I cringed at the thought of what was on the other side. When I realized I was counting the droplets as they ran off the point of my nose, I finally wrenched the door open.

As the light spilled out into the hallway, I looked to the right and then to the left, yet I saw nothing. Suddenly, I found myself running down the hall though I wasn't being chased. I didn't stop till I was before the door of Graves's lab. It was open, and the room was dimly lit inside. "Please come in," an all-too familiar voice said. Pushing the door aside, I entered the den of that wicked creature, and there it was in its cage, licking its dark, dead lips with its two brown wormlike tongues. "Why?" I shouted as I turned my stare at Graves sitting in his chair. "Why?"

"Ha! Ha! Ha! Ha! Ha! Ha! Ha! Ha!" He replied, "Think about it, Doctor, you're a man of intelligence. Give your exhausted mind a chance to wake up." Then it came to me like the lone candle that broke up the darkness 'neath my bed exactly why he had hung that foul thing over me while I dreamed and let it bite my face. "If you think this will change the hopelessness of the situation, you're sadly mistaken, Graves."

"Ah! But I think it will, Edward, for as I have nothing to lose, maybe this will give you the incentive you need to find a cure, Doctor!" he said with a look of newfound security in his piercing eyes.

"No, Alister!" I barked. "No, for I will kill you before I try to help you now."

"Ha! Oh, I think not!" He sneered. "Do you know what it's like to take a life, Ed? Do you? No! You've spent your entire life trying to save lives. I bet you cried your little eyes out the first time you lost a patient. You wept like a mother, didn't you, Edward?" While I stood taking in his words, he went on. "You can only imagine what it's like… to press a feather bag over your lover's lips as she kicks her legs at the air and digs her fingernails into your neck. I really don't think you have it in you, Doctor."

"Maybe you're right, Graves, still you can't force me to help you."

"Oh, I really don't think that will be necessary, though. I believe you will help me all the same."

I then realized I was no longer leaking, and running my fingertip along the numbest spot on my nose, I felt two tiny swollen holes. "It's grown late, Doctor, and although it's been entertaining, I must say good night. I suggest you get all the sleep you can. Tomorrow you can resume your quest for a cure." With that, he rose and slowly walked past me, disappearing through the doorway, his limp arm dangling at his side like a scarf. Again I found myself alone in the presence of a pestilence with eyes and teeth. As I stared at it, my head became heavy and dizzy. A weariness shadowed over me like a rain cloud. I felt too tired to stand. My legs began to wobble. I turned my heavy eyes away from the gray death and staggered toward my bed.

I woke up to the sound of rain knocking at the windows. What a nightmare I had last night; it was so vivid! This whole ordeal must be taking its toll on me. An eerie instinct told me to check my nose anyway. I felt nothing unusual. No holes. *Ah! It was just a disturbing dream. Thank mercy!* I thought to myself. But then I recognized the taste of my own crusty blood upon my lips. *Maybe I bit my lip in the night, maybe I scratched myself.*

I rose and stepped out into the hallway. There, Len, like usual, had left me fresh water in the washbowl. I began to scrub my face, and as I did, I saw a small ash-colored object splash and float in the light-pink water. I couldn't tell what it was, but all the same, it engulfed me with unexplainable fright. Picking my head up, I gazed into the looking glass on the wall. My eyes swelled as they fell upon a gaping hole in my face where my nose used to be.

With this, my fear turned to rage. I punched the mirror and knocked the washbowl over as I stormed down the hall toward the being in the glass. Before I knew what I was doing, I picked up the heavy glass box and was struggling with it up the stairs. The creature ran in circles, its claws clicking against the glass floor as I carried it down the dark hallway, grunting and hissing all the way to the evil alchemist's chamber door.

Kicking it aside, I rushed in to greet my former patient. And among all the commotion, he lay there in a deep sleep. "Graves! Wake up, Graves!" I yelled. He did not respond. I raised the cage above my head and smashed it down over his. The homunculus fled out of the room in a hail of shattered glass. And still Graves lay motionless on his bed of shards. Had I killed him? How could I have done this? No matter what led me to this deplorable act, I still couldn't believe what I had done. My mind raced as I stood over a man I had just murdered. The very man I came to save. The reality of it all began to chill me like a sudden winter breeze. I felt the wrist of his good arm. There was no pulse. But his arm seemed rigid, and his face felt cold. Flicking back the lid of his right eye, I saw only white. I hadn't killed him after all, for he must have passed in his sleep last night. Relief began to thaw the frost in my bones, but only for a minute. For the cold wind returned again as the shine of the scattered glass caught my eye.

The thought of that thing getting loose again sickened me. I thought of the poor people in that church—and the baby! And this time the blame would be my own. Then my worries turned to the soft-spoken Len, the beautiful little servant girl. She was probably down in the kitchen, preparing breakfast for me and Graves, who was at last ready for his own to be dug.

I moved cautiously through the hall and down the stairs, searching along the way 'neath tables and drapes. As much as I loathed the thought of locating it, I knew it had to be captured. I only hoped I saw it before it saw me. As I walked, I could almost feel its huge beady eyes following me. Those eyes! Those lonely black holes, which never knew the embrace of colored irises. Those terrible, uncovered eyes, which polluted both my dreams and my days. Finally, I reached the kitchen, dreading the worst. There she stood at the table in a stained white lacey apron, cutting a grapefruit. My eyes still swept the lazy shadows on the floor as I walked toward her. "Len, are you all right?" She turned to face me and shrieked like a banshee. I quickly turned and looked behind me, expecting to see that hungry little fiend creeping on me, but it was still elusive. She screamed again as I turned back around to feel the harsh pinch of a knife. The terrified black-haired woman plunged it into my chest. She ran out of the kitchen, panting and chanting something in Chinese. I looked down at the knife that was hanging halfway out of my chest and, with it still dangling, headed after her. Suddenly I felt a strange sensation. A rush of cool air had swooped down into a cavity in my face. With all that was happening, I had forgotten what made me snap in the first place. No wonder she stabbed me!

Still, I pursued her, leaving a trail of red blotches on the boards behind me. As I ran, I wrenched the knife out of my flesh and dropped it to the floor. Although my shirt was soaked with blood, I thought the wound not fatal. As I reached the front hall, I heard her scream again. This time it was not for me, for there blocking the door twitched the homunculus! She turned around only to scream again at the sight of my disfigured face.

She made for the stairs in a frenzy. Falling halfway up, she crawled the rest of the way, as if the use of four limbs would carry her faster, as if she couldn't waste a second to rise to her feet. There it stood, looking up at me with the boldness of a great beast. It stood, heaving and twitching those filthy claws as it watched me bleed.

And out came those wretched, hungry worms from its shriveled lips. And they squirmed and they stretched out for me through its horrible hollow fangs. Suddenly, the reality of it all slapped me across the side of my face like a wave from nowhere. It struck me then that I was already doomed. I realized I may never see my beloved Alyssa again. I knew the nightmare had to end. I leaped for the thing like a leopard on a hare, but it did not flee. Instead, it hissed as I clenched my fingers round its coarse frame. The tips of its claws sunk into my wrists as it opened its jaw wide for a bite, but I shook it and strangled it with all my might. Its teeth snapped at the air as it flailed its oversized head violently. Still, I felt the sting of its fangs piercing into my hand. I slammed its head into the floor again and again and again till it finally stopped moving. Its thorny fangs still embedded in my hand like the stinger of a dead bee. Freeing myself from the teeth of the tiny terror as I had with the knife, I felt the dark, swollen veins of its gray neck. It was still alive.

I carried the thing down the stone steps to the moldy cellar. There I located a web-covered crate and placed it inside. I took one long last look at the face of evil. That tiny, sinister creature that had caused so much disaster. Suddenly, it sat up in its makeshift coffin and hissed at me; its two brown forked tongues licked my face as I shrieked. Leaping backward, I had to fight the instinct to run. My pounding heart began pumping blood through my shirt faster than before. I looked back down into the dimness of the box. It lay as still as I had placed it there. Its empty eyes seemed hazy and unseeing. It was still unconscious.

Now I became aware that my encumbered mind was weaving illusions on my tortured eyes. I placed the lid on and nailed it shut. Carrying the box up the steps, I went to check on Len. By now she may be far from this house of gloom and madness. I found her lying in the hallway. She must've fainted. After I bandaged myself up, I scooped her up and brought her to bed.

I dragged my feet into the den and began to fill the fireplace with dry logs. Soon, I was sitting in a daze, warming my bitten hand before the twisting flames. Hours must have snuck past as the dance of the blaze mesmerized me. I only turned my gaze away periodically to peer at the silent crate. I decided it was time to check on poor Len.

Halfway down the hallway, my ears collected a disturbing sound. Not screaming or crying or moaning but laughter. As it grew slightly louder, I looked through the doorway of the servant's quarters. Her bed was empty. But the insane laughter still filled the room. There she was, sitting in the corner beside her dresser. Her clothes were hanging from the opened drawers, and some were strewn about the floor, stained with crimson blotches. Her lips appeared to be bleeding, and I saw two frayed wounds in her right bicep and one torn into her hand. "Len, Len, my god, what happened to you?" I shrieked with my hand over my nose hole to spare her pretty eyes. *How was she bitten by that thing?* I wondered. *It's impossible, but how?* Again she began to laugh, but this time, it was a muffled laugh, which squeezed through her bloody lips. She laughed and laughed while she chewed on something. I froze before her, searching my hiding thoughts to come out from the dark shadows of my traumatized mind and tell me what to do. She chewed and she laughed as she swallowed something down. "Ha! Ha! Ha!" She laughed as she raised her bloody hand and bit it. She ripped a hunk of flesh from her palm and laughed as her molars began to grind it to bits.

That was the final straw. I ran down the hallway from the laughter that only seemed to follow me. I heard it echo ever louder in my head as I ran toward the room aglow at the end of the hall. The box was still there where I had left it. The lid was still secure. Picking it up, I said aloud, "Sorry, little one, but I've got to put you out."

Slowly I stepped to the fire and tossed the crate in. The curling flames rose and hissed as they began to consume the box and its ferocious contents. Soon I heard a sizzling sound followed by a piercing shriek, which turned into a long, violent hiss. A scratching was heard as the burning box thumped about on the blazing hearth. Then, as quickly as it started moving, it again became still. The sizzling commenced and chorused with the crackling of the hungry fire.

I sat and watched it burn to nothing. I wondered how bad it must've smelled as it melted. As I reached in with an iron rod to stoke the fire, I beheld the odd-looking skeleton. I poked it, and the remainder of its crispy flesh flaked off the hot bones. Suddenly, it stood up in the blaze, and I dropped the pointed iron. Its freakish skull turned its empty eye sockets upon me as I trembled in disbelief. *Wait!* I thought. *It's only my mind playing rotten tricks on me again like down in the cellar. Perhaps I've gone mad like Graves and poor Len.*

I blinked my heavy eyes. I looked away and back again at the sooty figure as it stepped from the fire. Its black skeleton smoked as its bony feet clicked across the floorboards toward me. I could not scream. I could not rise. I could not turn away. I batted and rubbed my eyes, and still it came my way. Up into my face, it stared without eyes as I sat glued to the floor. Smoke poured through its charred jaw as it hissed in my face once more. I could feel its hot breath slither into the hole where my nose once was. Here I covered my eyes with my hands and said out loud, "This isn't happening! This isn't happening! When I open my eyes, it won't be there." But I knew it was all too real when I felt its hot fangs burying themselves into my hand.

> Within the glass, the miserable mass
> stretched and scabbed and bled, alas!
> It was there contained, that the tortured brain
> of the abomination was created.
> A sickly, grotesque thing sprouted from the rotten root of madness,
> which gasped and grew and slithered like a thorny vine
> in the dark shadow of blasphemy.
> A wretched, damned subcreature,
> haunted by every breath and every day it should've never known.
> The thing that should have never screamed.
> The poor, horrible freak born without a soul…
> the homunculus.

THE CLAYTON BONEYARD

I'M NOT THE KIND OF grave robber that will waste my night on the gamble of unearthing any old random grave. Most of the people in this profession are usually classified as uneducated, low-life scum. That's not me at all, for I am not only literate, I'm known as a relatively intelligent man. And as far as the low-life part, well, I guess I can't argue too much with that, for defacing the homes and disturbing the rest of the dead is an unavoidable part of my work night, and I've never had a problem with that. Only a few choice people know how I'm able to buy my bread. Most grave robbers don't spend a lot of time in the library, but I've been seen there many days, researching history in the hunt of the well to do in the neighboring towns. And while others in competition may break their backs to expose a poor, naked old skeleton who was buried with everything he had only to come out with nothing at all, or maybe a lousy silver ring if they're lucky. Me, I don't like digging for nothing. My approach has made me quite successful. Besides, I've never been a huge fan of silver. I like gold, diamonds, rubies, and emeralds. No, I've never been much of a gambler.

When I stumbled on the name of Erwin Clayton, it was as if a candle had been lit in my brain. Here was a man who spent his days in the trade of shiny yellow, red, and green little beauties. Here was a man who had it all. A great estate, only two towns to the north, built with the fortunes he acquired by selling ill-gotten treasures, which he purchased at a fragmented price. Here was a man who was apparently suspected of doing business with pirates. Ah! Pirates! No wonder he was so successful. Sea dogs have been credited with making many a businessman happy and bloated, for the booty, undoubtedly could not be sold by the pirate for top quid. They would only walk away with a portion of its worth, and oftentimes they would trade precious gems for medicine, rum, or ammunition. But Erwin Clayton could ask and did receive full price, and when profits are high, business is good.

So seeing this Clayton fellow as a very worthy client of mine, I set out with my trusty shovel, lantern, mallet, and bar in a dirty burlap sack hung over my shoulder. The moonrise was magnificent. A barren, lifeless mass that, on this night, seemed unusually vibrant. Although it was three or more days until it would be deemed full, its enormous, glowing girth seemed to tug at me as it loomed like a watchful eye above the gently swaying pines.

The dust gently settled on miles of dirt road that lay behind me. Owls called out among the drone of crickets in the lonely fields. Shadows leaped and bushes stirred, and it made me think of all the night creatures whom I could not see, but I could feel the heaviness of their eyes on me. On the northwest edge of the field stood a stone wall, and if my calculations are correct, that wall should be the boundary of the Clayton estate. Climbing the wall and pushing my way through blue spruce trees, I felt a sharp bolt of excitement hit me before my feet met the ground. Ever since I was a young lad, I've had a certain fascination with graveyards. It all began at the age of eight, late one afternoon, when I disobeyed my parents and walked my dog past the reach of their prying eyes and found myself walking up a dirt path that led to an open iron gate. Beyond that rusty old gate surrounded by wall of stone stood winged statues, skulls etched in tombstones, and slanted crosses sticking out of the ground. Tall grass and weeds covered the names and words below them. The ancient dates and eroded words on the marble and bluestone slabs that sometimes briefly sum up the lives of the people who lay beneath them. Beautifully carven angels with sad lips and solemn eyes. The great mounds of earth and stone, where behind frozen doors, someone sleeps in his eternal home. The strange excitement I felt that day as I strolled among the dead never fails to return to me every time I visit a boneyard. But tonight, it was stronger than it had ever been.

The first thing that caught my eye was the ivy-covered ruins of the old Clayton manor. The few walls still standing looked as if it were only the vines that were holding them up. But that wasn't what interested me. I had come to visit his more recent home. A square patch of trees off in the distance was the next to draw my attention. Undoubtedly, this patch of trees formed the border of my interest. Two slanted cedars in front of an opening in a stone wall intertwined together to form a gloomy arc, which creaked in the breeze above my head. Upon entering the moonlit yard, I suddenly felt a cold chill wash over me. I felt as if the seasons had changed in an instant. The midsummer air, which was fairly warm, now felt unbearably cold, wintry cold. Tiny bumps began to appear on my arms, and my legs began to tremble. Some digging would warm me up, I thought, and began to read the stones. Ivy Clayton, Benngermin Clayton, the daughter of… the son of… Ah! Here we are! Covered in yellow spots of fungus, carved in dingy, weathered white marble, the name of Erwin Clayton gleamed at me in the twilight. Erwin Clayton, born 1369, died 1423.

Without reading the rest of the epitaph, I pulled my shovel from the bag and began to break the ground. The sudden, intense cold was incentive to work fast. Heaving the sod upon the grave of his wife, I fell into a trance and commenced to dig a rather sloppy hole in a state of frenzy. Soon the grass was dancing above my head, and the rusty blade of the shovel struck the wooden coffin. I was sure I had exposed this one in record time. When I scraped the last of the dirt off the lid, I realized that although I was sweating and my heart racing, the frantic exercise had not warmed me up in the least. I then fumbled in my bag and retrieved a pry bar and a wooden mallet. The sound of my labor set a pack of coyotes crying and yelping as it echoed out of the hole I had made. But I did not feel threatened, as they sounded quite far off, and I carried tools that could be used as weapons. Ordinarily, a casket so old would be terribly rotten and might not require any prying at all, but this one was made from cedar and was quite thick. It showed very little signs of decay. I am well aware that bugs hate the smell and taste of such lumber, and I've dug up cedar boxes before, but none so old that it seemed to grin in defiance of time and the elements.

As I yanked another spike from the lid, I suddenly felt an overwhelming sensation of being spied on. Looking up above the edge of the hole, I thought I saw a fleeting faint white light disturbing the darkness. *It's my weary mind and my eyes being tricksters,* I thought and commenced working. Two nails later, I felt a cold wetness touch my bare neck, and gasping for a breath of air, I dropped the bar and spun around. There was nothing behind me but a wall of dirt and the emptiness which hung before me returned me to my regular state of mind. My breathing and pulse began to slow back down, and just as I was thinking of how ridiculous I was being, I felt it again. A cold, clammy fingertip tickled the back of my neck. This time I whipped myself around twice as fast, and again I saw only that wall of earth looming behind me. My pulse again began to race, and I dropped my mallet and brushed my neck with my palm as a dog might set his leg to scratching a flea. Even as I continued pawing at my neck with rapidity, I saw a small blur drop on the coffin's lid. Bending down to get a closer look, I saw the object of my mere panic and utter fright was only the half of an earthworm wiggling a pattern in the dirt on the coffin's lid. With that, I began to laugh aloud in the night. I laughed madly with relief as my thoughts again returned to the safe zone of how silly I was being. *What's wrong with you, Sid Grimes?* I asked myself. *Have you lost your touch, old man?* I have always prided myself on how hard I was to spook. My friends have always said that I didn't know what fear was. In this profession, you must have a strong stomach and a spirit that does not scare easily. I could not help but notice that the pattern the worm made as it writhed about all too much resembled the letters *d, g, r*! It disturbed me greatly for a moment, but then I thought that if they were the letters *e, d, c*, I'd really be concerned. It couldn't be more than a creepy coincidence, I thought as I gathered my tools and began once more to work the lid free.

As I pulled another iron splinter from the box, the ill feeling of being watched from above slowly wrapped itself around me like a damp fog. This time I thought little of it, so little in fact that at first I did not bother to look. I almost felt like laughing again, but laugh I could not, and the grip of that fog contracted round my guts like a snakeskin around a rat. Still, I did not stop to look up. *Only a few more nails and I can claim my prize,* I thought. I'll climb from the grave, walk home before the sun comes up, and sleep the day away. But the grip of that sick sensation soon became too much to ignore, and when curiosity came into effect, I had to look. Standing upright, I gazed above the edge of the grave and beheld the figure of an ancient, dreadful woman. Her wild white hair danced eerily around the ugliness of her wretched face. Her skin was tan like old leather, her lips thin and sunken, spoke not a word, but her stern eyes said a million disgusting, taboo words as they pierced through the night air, through my own, and into my brain. Around her decrepit neck, there hung a silver heart-shaped locket. Her white dress fluttered like ripples in a pond as she stood silent above me midst a pale, silver glow. I'd never seen a human being so disgustingly ugly. Hell, I'd seen prettier corpses! All that was dark, mad, and vile in the world seemed to pour from her sharp eyes. If evil had a face, I felt as if I were gazing into it.

Time stood still as we stared at each other like two different animals discovering each other's existence for the first time. She stared at me with malice and disgust, while I stared at her with awe and fear. "What!" I finally barked. For I could not stand the silence for another unending second. "Who are you, and what do you want with me?" I muttered aloud. But still she stood unyielding, without answering, her stare cutting through the night and jabbing into my soul. "Answer me!" I barked again. "Answer me, or I'll throw a rock at you." But my threat did not make her gray lips move, nor was there a difference in her eyes or her posture. "Okay then," I yelled up to her, "have it your way!" With that, I dropped my mallet and took the bar in my right hand and brought it over my head ready to throw. "Last chance, witch!" I warned. But she stood her ground and retained her silence. I hurled my pry bar up toward the wretched woman, expecting her to duck, but she did no such thing. Instead, I watched in horror as the spinning piece of metal passed through her body without a flinch. It pealed out against the silence of the awful night like a bell from the belly of hell as it must've struck a headstone.

Now the feeling of horror intensified tenfold within me. I began to tremble, and I could hear my own heart thumping within my scrambled head. I suddenly thought of my bed and wished I was home, lying in it, but I knew all too well where I was. Then she lifted her right arm and slowly twisted her frame to the left. She lifted a shriveled, ashy finger on her right hand and pointed to the cedar arc. She stood pointing for a moment. A moment that seemed like five. Then she simply disappeared before my eyes.

Get a hold of yourself, Grimes, I thought. *You act as if you've never seen a specter before.* Indeed, I had. I had seen white blotches of light materialize and vanish before me. Once I followed a shadowy figure. I watched him walk in through the iron door of a crypt. I had seen figures appear off in the distance. I had seen them slowly walking between tombstones, and each time I felt a strong chill, but never like this. This was different. This was close, almost personal. And as I've said, I followed spirits before with both my feet and eyes, but this one came to me with more than curiosity. This one did not flee when I stared back. This one wanted something, and I knew exactly what. She wasn't happy about my actions. She clearly wanted me to leave, and ago I shall, but not empty-handed.

All I could think of was that woman's horrible face as I pulled the last nail. Nothing that was lying beneath this, or any other lid, no matter what state of decay, could have sickened me half as much as that sorry burden that she wore on the front of her skull. Nothing I'd ever envisioned in my darkest dreams had ever disturbed me so. For the first time ever, I genuinely felt the creeps.

With great reluctance, I gazed up again over the edge of the six-foot-deep hole, almost expecting to see her standing there. I was quite relieved to see only waving leaves 'neath twinkling stars. With cold, trembling hands, I pried off the lid of Erwin Clayton's coffin. *What? What's this?* I asked myself. For there was no skeleton wearing a large emerald ring. There were no bones at all, only dirt. *Surely, for whatever reason, he must be under that dirt,* I thought. I didn't even want to ponder the riddle; I only desired to finish the job and get home to my warm bed. My teeth began to chatter from the unnatural cold as I picked up my shovel and began to remove the dirt that lay within the oblong box. When more than half of the dirt had been shoveled out, I climbed into the bed of death and fumbled around with my hands in the soil. But I felt no rib cage. I felt no skull, only earth, and the bottom of the box did my fingers scrape.

Now I was utterly perplexed. I had never seen anything like this in all the years I had dug up bones. Sure, I'd seen boxes full of dirt before, but only ones that were badly decayed. Rotted boxes that had caved in, but which still contained their resident. I stood there, shaking and wondering, trying to make sense of it all. And as I made a move to climb from the coffin, I heard a creaking sound like the rubbing of branches, which turned into a sound that of the snapping of wood, and I pictured a falling limb in my mind. And before I knew it, I was falling! Slipping down through the dirt-laden floor of the casket. As I fell, I saw the stars going out one by one above me. Utter blackness enveloped my soul as I fell. Down, down I went, scraping and clawing at the edge of a vertical tunnel while desperately trying to stop my descent. Clawing and kicking and screaming as I fell farther and farther still. The echoes of my helpless scream shattered my soul as I fell, and the silence that followed a heavy thud that knocked the breath and the scream from my lungs as I finally hit solid ground was all too much to bear. I lay there on the moist ground, too petrified to move, with pain in my chest and a buzzing in my ears, while the hopelessness of my situation began to grasp me like a spider's web grips the weary wings of a fly.

I didn't know how long I lay there, but it was long enough for the ringing in my ears to subside to a dreadful silence. I lay there with my eyes wide to the complete, empty darkness. It was a void so black it was too dark to be shown. It was the deepest dark I had ever known. Then I thought of the dancing grass above and wondered how far away it was. I longed to pet it, to caress it. I then in that very moment began to realize its beauty. I saw each tiny blade as an individual flower stretching out toward the glow of a silver moon. Then without further hesitation, I stood up. I knew that if I didn't push myself up in that very instant, I might lay there on that cold ground forever. Feeling around with my arms outstretched, I began to take tiny steps forward. Soon I felt the moistness of a dirt wall with my probing palms. I felt my way slowly and blindly along the wall of earth and nightmare.

The wall stretched out above my reach; how high, I could not tell. Perhaps if I closed my eyes, I could forge a better guess. Slowly I inched my way along the wall, patting it, molesting it, trying to draw a picture of it in my mind, trying to understand its shape, searching for a possible route of escape. But it wasn't long before I realized I had groped my way around an odd-shaped room, for I recognized a pointy rock jutting out of the dirt wall about chest high. Who had dug this out, and what all for? I asked myself over and over again. Nothing in all my experience could possibly prepare me for this. I felt consumed by doom.

Round and round the room I went, feeling and searching for a way out. High and low, I felt every inch of the worm-infested boundaries that imprisoned me deep within the skin of the earth. As time unmeasured passed slowly before me, I hoped my eyes would soon adjust to any light there might be, but there wasn't so much as a spec of light to behold. So I sat down in the darkness. I sat down on the floor of clay and imagined the bottoms of the roots of the trees stretching downward toward me, high above my head. I thought of the living world above and figured it must be half a world away. I could not find the hole from which I had dropped, and I pictured all the tombstones so far above the dirt that lay between this sleepy lair and that dancing grass of life so far away from my own.

I sat there, pondering, listening, shivering on the cold, damp floor. I wondered if any light could penetrate these depths when the sun did rise. I wondered if it would be any help to me at all if it could. How long I sat there, I could not tell. The minutes, the hours, the seconds all blended into one mass of confusion. I sat until I could sit no more. *I must find a way out. I've got to get out of this ungodly place*, I thought. I stood up and began again to feel around in the darkness as before, and just when I thought I had covered every inch of the dank pit, I took another step forward, but there was no ground to catch my footfall, and I tripped into another hole. Again I found myself falling down a tunnel. Deeper and yet deeper I descended, pawing and kicking, dirt in my mouth and stinging eyes. Falling and scraping and scratching and screaming. Down, down, down I fell farther and farther away from the living world above. My mind whirled and ached as I fell. Down to the bottom of the pit of darkness I dropped. This time I fell faster and hit harder. All the breath in my lungs was forced out by the impact, and I heard a crisp snap. Instantly, a severe, throbbing pain was evident in my right ankle. I was sure it was broken. My head began to ache as well as my gut, my hands, my knees, and my back. Then the pain in my ankle began to worsen. My head began to spin, and I blacked out on the dirt.

When I awoke, the cold, moist soil under my palms reminded me that I was not home lying in my bed. I felt like crying, but I was too horrified to do so. All at once, a hunger so potent and undeniable swelled in my aching gut. I'd never been so hungry in all my life. I thought of screaming for help, but I knew it was of no use. I began to crawl along the ground, feeling my way around. This time, I was careful to paw along the floor as well as I slowly felt my way around the circumference of the dirt wall. The smell of mold was thick and choking, and the wall was slimy and cold.

Just as I had figured I had gone around the room twice, exploring the ups and downs of it, my hand found a hole in the wall about chest high. I felt around the edges of it. It was the same width as the tunnels I had slid down. What beast had built this place? How far did the tunnel stretch, and where did it lead? Something told me it did not lead up or out. I dreaded the thought of climbing in, but the thought of rotting down here in this pit of despair was less comforting. Still, I could not bring myself to climb in. Again, I sat down and released a hopeless sigh. The complete silence was eerie and disheartening, and to gaze on the thick emptiness of the pitch-black depth of night was quite maddening. The more I pondered my situation, the more I felt the swelling pressure of great despair. The hole in the dirt wall above my head offered me no comfort. It couldn't possibly lead out, I thought, nor did it give me the impression that it might lead to a better place. Did it lead farther down? I asked myself. I decided I didn't want to find out at all. My body was numb, and my scratchy throat was hoarse and dry. The taste of dirt was foul on my tongue, yet I could not work up a spit.

Suddenly, the thick, wet silence was disturbed by a deplorable sound. A low-pitched, clicking, belching sound that set my soul ablaze, and I could feel tiny hairs in my tortured ears rising like well-trained soldiers to the call of war. This vile, abominable sound roared and echoed out of the hole above my head, and I froze in the thralldom of fear. A short silence followed but soon was shaken by the low roaring, belching, beastly call as it poured threateningly out of the hole. Soon I heard a rustling from deep inside the tunnel. A scratching, dragging sound that clearly grew louder as it inched closer toward me. I broke my stillness abruptly and leaped to my feet. I ran blindly to the opposite edge of the pit's boundaries. I clasped my hands and knocked my head against it. I fell to the ground and cowered like a rat in the corner, trembling and gasping for breath. And as hard as I drew, I felt as if there were no air to take in. *I must be calm*, I thought. *I must be still and stealth*. But even if it couldn't hear or see me, it would surely sniff me out. My mind became as dark and empty as the pit was as I tried to put a face on the thing in the hole.

That terrible noise grew louder as the thing lumbered toward the edge of the hole. I had realized for the first time since I blacked out that my eyes were closed. Hell, they might as well have been shut the entire time. Louder the thumping and dragging grew until I thought I heard the creatures snorting breath. I heard then a loud thud as it dropped from the hole, and I felt my mind and my body would simultaneously implode. I could not move, I could not scream, and it hurt to try to draw a breath. My eyes popped wide open, and my poor ears were pummeled by the sound of feet shuffling their way toward me. Closer and closer it grew, until a rotten smell assaulted my nose. I felt like running, but I knew it was of no use; besides, the fear had overwhelmed my muscles. I only wished that my end would come quickly and painlessly as I cowered in the utter darkness, too frightened to shiver. Long before its movement seized perhaps three yards before me, my nose cringed to the indescribable stench of its breath. All the feces in the stagnant sewers and all the festering corpses I'd known combined could not produce such a ghastly, choking odor. Again the silence began to torment me as I waited for it to pounce.

"Welcome!" The heavy voice of ages whipped like a cold, violent wind across my face, which was both human and beastly. It was an ill combination of the English language and the animalistic belching that I had heard from within the hole. I could not speak, I could not think, and I could not bear to answer. I felt dizzy and faint, and although I did not blackout, I wished I would. "Is that any way to treat your host?" the stern, low-pitched voice belched at me. Still, I could not respond; I only sat there, shaking. "I know you're there, digger!" it continued. "I don't know your name, but I know why you came. And know this, that you may acquire what you've been sniffing around here for, but you will not leave with it."

"Is there any way I can leave without it?" I asked suddenly, with much humility in my voice.

"Now you speak, digger!" it roared. "Now you are willing to give up your search for precious gems which belong to others who sleep in their beds and search instead for your freedom, for the happy grass above, for the life you left gleaming in its dew. Well, know this, digger, you are right to feel doomed."

"I must find a way out. There must be a way out," I said in a brewing panic.

"There is no way out, thief, only a way down."

"What are you?" I begged. "Tell me what you are!"

With that, the demonic voice broke into an insane fit of laughter, which filled my bones with frost. "I am Erwin Clayton, boy!" it responded. "The very one you've come to see." As the words sunk in, my battered brain denied them. For surely it was a demon who growled before me in the blackness. Surely it was a demon sent to trick me, torture me, and who knew what else. "Believe it, digger!" It growled. "Believe my words, or think what you may, but either way, they are the truth. Eons ago I woke to total darkness to find myself laid out in a wooden box. My mind was not my own. I did not recognize it for a coffin. I did not realize I had died, perhaps because I was moving and thinking. It did not even dawn on me that I was human, and I could not even recall what one was. Upon instinct I began scratching at the base of the box which held me. I clawed at it until the flesh fell from my fingertips. I clawed my way out of that box and began to claw at the dirt beneath it. I pushed the dirt past my chest and with my legs did tamp it into the coffin. I scratched and clawed and scraped but could dig no more, for there was nowhere to put the dirt once the box was filled.

"I remember the second time I awoke. I recall the insatiable hunger I felt, but there was nothing to eat. Before I knew it, I was consuming the earth. I ate and ate some more. I ate as the days, months, years, and the centuries slowly crept by. I hollowed out that hole you slid down, digger! I ate the dirt that should still be there, just as I should still be in my coffin. Over time, I consumed enough earth as to acquire a small living space. I ate away the walls till my chamber of darkness grew larger and larger. Over time, I grew bored and began eating another tunnel, chamber and so on. So now do you see, digger, can you see with your eyes shut?"

"Why is your voice so inhuman, Clayton?" I asked with much disbelief. "And what became of the waste your body produced from eating so much dirt? Where did you tamp that?" I asked sarcastically. "And how did you not suffocate down here in the pit? And what did you wash it all down with? Hmm, Clayton." The response was abrupt and full of rage. "That's what eons of consuming dirt does to a human's vocal cords, digger!" he roared as I sunk further into a ball shape. "I do not defecate, nor urinate, nor perspirate. I do not grow. I thirst not for fluids, yet my hunger lives on, for the hunger is the life. And as far as running out of oxygen, my heart, it is as hard and as still as a stone, and my lungs are shriveled-up sacks. I need not water, I need not the air, only the earth, digger, only the earth."

"My name is Grimes, Sid Grimes," I said somberly. I had come to believe those words from the darkness. As unbelievable as they were, in the strangest of ways, it all seemed to fit. My mind then pictured the specter. Her piercing eyes and sunken lips. "Your wife, Mr. Clayton," I went on, "did you give her a silver heart-shaped locket?"

"Why do you ask me this, digger, are you trying to enrage me?" he barked with magma in his words.

"No, I only ask because I saw the spirit of a woman who wore such a locket in the graveyard," I said with a shaky voice.

"You saw the ghost of my wife, digger!" he belched forth. It was then I realized she wasn't trying to frighten me out of my claim; she was only trying to warn me. "My wife, my children, my children's children, all who have died and were buried in this unholy ground have woken to suffer the endless torment of the undead. Even now they sleep in their coffins. Sometimes I still can hear their cries, their moans ringing out in the ever-night. She found her way to me. She dug her way out of the coffin and into the hole 'neath my own. She dragged her feet up to me, her skin wrinkled, veiny, and decrepit. So ghastly was her appearance in my mind's eye while my hands felt her face like a blind man does. Her skin was hard and withered and pieces of it flaked off as I groped her. Her lips were flat, empty, and frayed. As I took my hand from them, she spoke to me. She wanted a kiss."

"What did you do?" I asked with reluctance.

"I showed her mercy, I destroyed her," he said. "I clawed at her. I ripped her to pieces. I forced her spirit from her crusty shell. I could not let her share my fate. But now you, Sid Grimes, are doomed to do just that. Hell, I could use the company." Again he began laughing madly.

"No!" I yelled. "No! I must not die down here, I must escape, I must find my way back."

"There is no return to where you came from, nor to what you were." He growled sardonically.

"What do you mean by saying what I was?" I asked, like a child looking up at his teacher.

"I mean you are not the same as you were when you came here to disturb my grave, digger."

"Yes, I admit, I'm on the verge of going mad, Clayton, is this what you mean?"

"No, you fool," he continued. "I am not referring to your sorry state of mind. Tell me this, Sid, when was the last time you were thirsty?" I began to ponder this question, the relevance of it. I tasted the stale dirt in my mouth and wondered exactly how long I had been down in the subterranean world, and I realized that although my mouth was as dry as dust, I did not crave water. "And what of your ankle, Grimes, how does it feel?" With those words, it dawned on me that I was standing and had been running on it earlier without problems, and the pain was gone completely. "And what of the cold you felt digger? When was the last time you felt it? I feel your vibrations as you shiver, but it is not from the cold nor from a specter's presence. It is only from fear. And what of your pulse, Grimes? Tell me, is it racing, is your heart throbbing in your head, thief?"

With that, my mind raced. I realized that the cold I had felt so long was gone, and I did not hear that beating in my temples, and that I was not breathing rapidly or heavily. And then I heard the sound of a small object rolling on the ground toward me. I flinched out of my fetal position as it touched my right foot. With little hesitation, I felt around for it and picked it up. It was cold, smooth, and solid. It was a ring of some kind, with a large stone, but ruby or diamond, I could not determine. Then I suddenly realized as I held it between my fingertips that it didn't matter at all.

"Happy now, digger?" he roared again. "Since you like digging so much, perhaps you can stay with me and dig some more tunnels, maybe a few chambers of your own."

"No!" I screamed, and the echo pulsed throughout the lair and poured up the tunnel. "No, I must leave this dreadful place."

"Ha! Ha! Ha!" He laughed. "You still don't get it, do you, digger? You still do not accept the sapro that has transformed your flesh. Do you have any idea how hard you hit when you fell down the second tunnel? Do you know how long you laid there in the dirt?"

"I have no idea, Clayton, I'm going bloody mad," I said, on the verge of both laughter and tears. "Tell me!" I pleaded as I shook in the pitch-black depth of endless night. "Tell me! Help me, help me!"

"I thought I told you that you were beyond help, digger," he continued with his guttural voice. "I cannot help you, nor can anyone, but tell you I will. You were blacked out upon the ground of my lair for over three years!"

THE SEA POD

THE ROAR OF THE WAVES boasted of power and dominance as they curled toward a happy black dog on the shore. Charlie was his name, and he had been my loyal companion for over twelve years. Nothing made him happier than to run free on the miles of sand or to swim in the calm, cool water of the Atlantic Ocean. But Charlie's fur would not be soaked with the salty sea today, for as long as I have been his master, I'd never seen him wade into the water when it was not still and calm. He seemed to have a fear of waves. And on this bright morning in June, just after dawn, it was anything but calm. For the fifteen-foot swells that rose and crashed with might and clamor were only the dwindling, dying offspring of the monsters that towered and swept across the high dunes to ravage the road the night before, which was now littered with foul-smelling seaweeds and shellfish.

Large clams, starfish, and jellyfish lay dying on the edge of the dunes, even among the reeds in the marshlands across the road, a testimony to the ultimate power of the sea. And just as I decided to stop and head back home, a peculiar object pulled at my eyes. There, before my eyes and half-hidden in a wrap of kelp at my toes lay a shiny jet-black capsule shaped like a small watermelon, with two long, thorny appendages on either end. Picking it up, I noticed it was quite heavy, and when I shook it about, I determined it was hollow, for there was something of bulk rolling around inside among the muffled swishing of thick liquid.

Never in my life have I seen or heard of something of the like. And so, being naturally intrigued, I tucked the thing under my arm and began to carry it home. Charlie seemed to disapprove, for as soon as I started back with the pod, he began to growl and bark obsessively at my feet. And although I commanded him to be silent, Charlie, who was always completely obedient, barked and snapped at my ankles the whole way back.

I chained Charlie to a tree in the backyard, and soon, he stopped his annoying protest. I began to try to break the crust of the black seed, first by battering it with my fist as it lay atop my desk. Although it seemed soft, almost rubbery to the touch, I found the shell to be harder than a coconut's. With my fist sore from pain, I decided to try a different method. I began to beat upon it with a mallet to no avail. I whacked it till the handle snapped, and the head flew across the room. I then found myself hacking at it with a large serrated blade. But my arm grew tired long before my useless, sweaty efforts began to leave even the slightest scratch. I chiseled and chopped at it for a good part of the day. I even tried burning it. But it would not crack, chip, or submit to my endeavors. The thing seemed harder than steel and stone. And as it shined on my desk, surrounded by knives, mallets, saws, and a hatchet, I fancied as if it were laughing at me in my frustration.

That night, my sleep was disturbed by a horrible nightmare. I dreamed I saw Charlie being scooped up off the shore and swallowed up by a hungry wave of enormous girth. It was an angry wave with several rows of teeth like a giant great white, and as it dragged him under, I saw the sea itself as a colossal, breathing beast. Next I found myself in the midst of that beast, sinking slowly down to the ocean floor, while sharks of every shape, size, and breed swarmed in to circle around me, their teeth and murderous eyes gleaming in the sunken moonlight. And as I descended closer to the bottom, I saw that its sand was black, jet-black, and just before I hit the bottom, I saw the sand for what it really was. It was not sand at all, for the floor of the ocean was encrusted with countless pods huddled chokingly together, all of which were half-rooted in the sand and standing upright with two of their four long sharp thorns jutting out and up in all directions. And as I screamed, all the air left my lungs in the form of bubbles, which rose between the fins and fangs as I was impaled upon the floor of thorns.

I woke the next morning with the sting of the sun in my eyes. Usually I am awoken just before dawn by Charlie tugging on the sheets or barking to be let outside. As I rose to my feet and called for him, I felt a sinking feeling in my gut, for he did not come. Walking around the corner, I saw a trail of yellow-and-red slime on the floor some eight feet in length. It was a trail of slime that led to the open jaws of my dead pet. His tongue was spread out of his mouth, his eyelids frozen back to show only the whites of his eyes. He was stiff and lifeless.

He must've been sick, I thought. I'd never seen anything vomit so far. It would make sense if the trail had stretched out behind him. Had he gone mad with rabies and been walking backward before he expired? These questions and more began to disturb me. Charlie seemed perfectly healthy the day before.

Then my mind was invaded by a single image, and I found myself running toward my writing desk. There I found it, dripping with bright yellow slime. Atop it, the uncrackable pod lay open and frayed like a black autumn rose, and inside oozed the thick bright-yellow liquid, which slightly resembled egg yolk. Something had hatched from this wretched thing of mystery. The black sea egg of death had been torn by some vile thing in the night. And that thing that crawled from its shell killed my dog, and it was still somewhere in the house.

With the fog of madness swirling in my mind and the heaviness of fear on my head, I began to search the house. With hatchet in my trembling hand, I slowly wandered about, checking under furniture and piles of dirty clothes scattered on the floor. Under the bed and beneath the table. Behind the cluttered books, both of documentation and fable. Behind the curtains that swept the floor. In the dusty corners behind the doors. Every square inch of the house did I search, and still I could not locate the thing that took my poor Charlie from me. And as frightened as I was with the thought of coming face-to-face with the thing, it horrified me tenfold not to know where it was, not to see it. But I could feel its vindictive presence begin to erode my dwindling composure.

Hours of frantic search revealed nothing. I had to stop looking, for I could feel my sanity evaporating from me. I looked down at my beloved canine lying rigid on the hallway floor, flies crawling on his open eyes.

When I had finished burying him in the backyard under the willow tree I had always chained him to, I headed back inside. Slowly, cautiously I opened the door, my eyes fixed to the floor, expecting to see some freakish creature snapping its sharp, powerful, lobsterlike claws at me, but I saw no such thing. Shutting the door behind me, I decided I could use some wine. Instead of pouring it into a glass, I began chugging from the bottle. I needed to numb my nerves and my aching mind from the things I had seen. I found myself looking down, always watching the floor. Then, a sight that brought me sadness filled my eyes. There, against the baseboard in the kitchen, was poor Charlie's water bowl. I decided to throw it away for the sight of it only brought me sorrow. I didn't want to be constantly reminded that Charlie would no more wander up to it and lap up the liquid of life so thirstily. I wished to only be reminded of him from time to time, thinking of our happy excursions.

As I bent down to pick up the bowl, my heart began pounding madly, as if it wanted to break free from my rib cage. For there, submerged in dog water, was a fist-sized sphere beautifully colored in vibrant violet and adorn with tiny bright-yellow dots. I knelt down, leaning over the water bowl in a hypnotic state of awe. This thing from the secret niche of the sea seemed innocent enough. No eyes, no sharp teeth, no appendages snapping insanely about. It sat submerged, utterly still as I gazed childlike with curiosity and fascination. It was truly a thing of beauty. A strange flower plucked from its nautical habitat.

But I knew better, for as delightful to the eye as it was and as harmless as it appeared, I knew it was not so for it killed my dog. My awe and fear soon turned to rage, and I choked the handle of the hatchet. I nudged the bowl, and the water rocked to and fro, but the thing did not budge. And as I thought of the flies crawling on Charlie's eyes, I raised the hatchet above my head and brought it back, ready to swing. And just as I was ready to split the thing in two, a strange sensation seized me. And as I tried to bring the hatchet down on the culprit with anger and intentions of revenge, my hand, instead, suddenly opened up, and the tool slipped from my grip and clanged its metal blade on the floor with the sound of a cracked bell.

Why had I dropped the small ax? Was my subconscious feeling pity on the little creature? Was I growing soft because it seemed so harmless? Every part of me wanted to destroy it. My brain told my hand to pick up the hatchet and do the deed, but as I reached for it, I found myself, quite against my own will, reaching down and submerging my hand into the water bowl. Now a dread dampened my soul as I realized I had no control of my own actions. I picked the thing up and pulled it from the water. It was soft and lay dormant in my hand. And as the slimy water dripped between my fingers, I stared at it intensely, expecting it to move. But it only sat there in my hand.

And just as I felt I could put it on the floor and stomp it out of existence, a lightning like flash of movement forced my eyes to blink, and a second later, the pain set in. Cactus-like needles over two inches long pierced through my hand and fingers. As I moaned in agony, I flailed my arm around, trying to fling it off my hand, but every movement only sharpened the pain. The thing was embedded in my flesh, and I could not throw it down.

Then a pain so sharp and intense brought me back to my knees. It hurt so bad that my ears began to ring, and I tried to scream but could only gasp and grunt. My mouth cramped wide open, and saliva poured out steadily to the floor. It was a piercing, sucking, stinging sensation, which pulled at the flesh of my palm. It was a pain of such magnitude, the like of which I'd never felt, which reverberated through my entire body, and I writhed upon the floor like a drowning worm.

The pain that was eating away at my hand was also consuming my mind. For a while, I could not drudge up a single thought; my mind only focused on the pain. The first thought that came to me was to grab the hatchet with my free hand and chop the thing to bits. As I wrapped my left hand round the wooden handle, I realized I was not thinking rationally, for it was still connected to my right hand. I felt my sanity slipping away like the blood that ran down my arm. Finally, a thought came to my burning brain, and I quickly acted on it. I put my stinging hand back into the water bowl, which instantly turned red as I submerged the spiked orb. It took all my nerve to hold still, to resist the urge to flail around and scream, but somehow, I froze with my hand in the dish.

Soon, the sucking and tearing ceased, and the quills retracted with lightning speed. I pulled my hand from the bowl with a splash of bloodstained water and gazed into a gaping absence of flesh in my crimson palm. My throbbing hand swelled to almost twice its size, and its skin had turned a faint, sickly yellow. Soon my vision became blurred and hazy, and my muscles ached and began to feel stiff as though they were seizing up.

When I was done washing and wrapping my wound, I returned to Charlie's water bowl. To my astonishment, I found that the water was as clear as crystal. I imagined that the thing had sucked the blood from the water as I stared down on it lying as silent and as still as a barnacle on a rock. Again my troubled mind was consumed with thoughts of its destruction, and again I gripped the hatchet with my good hand and raised it behind my head. When I tried to bring it down, my grip only loosened, and again I dropped it to the floor. Why could I not control my body's movements? Or was it my mind I was losing control over? All I knew was that I had to destroy it even if it killed me in the process, for I could not allow this thing of menace and doom to be unleashed on the territory of grass and sand.

Wait, that's it! How simple the solution was all along! Why hadn't I thought of it sooner? I searched the entire house, only to find it soaking in my dog's water bowl. After all, it was a dreadful creature of the sea. If I could not, for some reason, take it apart with my hatchet, perhaps I could kill it with a simpler and less violent method. All I had to do was deprive it of water. The water that it needed like we need to breathe air.

I laughed as I kicked the clay bowl over. I laughed madly as I held my belly with my swollen, bandaged hand. I continued laughing hysterically as I watched the water disappear slowly through the spaces in the floorboards. The purple and yellow sphere sat motionless on the floor of my kitchen, and I went on laughing till my stomach ached. But I wasn't laughing when I saw the thing rolling toward me. I leaped to my feet and began to run, but I slipped in the puddle and smashed my chin as I fell. My teeth grinded together, and a dizziness engulfed my head. It was in that moment when my dying vision failed me completely, and a black veil of darkness misted down slowly before my open eyes. I scurried to my feet and began running blindly across the room. I held my arms out before me to prevent myself from running into a wall. The way the thing moved, I was sure it was close behind. My only hope was to find the front door and flee from the house.

But an object, possibly a chair, tripped me, and I tumbled feet over head before I was thrown again to the floor. I quickly got back on my feet but soon realized that I now had lost my sense of direction. I knew not where the front or even the back door was, and even worse, I was clueless to the whereabouts of the sea fiend. I stood there, listening for it, motionless in the absence of light and sound. It made no movement to aid me, and I wondered if it were still pursuing me at all, for I did not hear the wet, squishy sound I'd heard before as it rolled toward me. Then I wondered if it were still alive at all. I wondered how long it could live out of water. Maybe it choked on the air, for it should've reached me by now.

I don't know how long I stood there, listening in vain, but I decided to feel around for a door. I knew that once I felt a familiar object, I could determine my own location and feel my way out. As I took a single step forward, I felt the piercing of its many quills sinking into my foot. It was a pain so agonizing that it brought me back to the floor. I began kicking and shaking my leg, trying to break free from the thing that was stuck securely to it. And again, the more I moved, the more it hurt. But this time, I somehow ignored the additional agony and kept on kicking. Still the thing would not let go. I thought of the water dish, but this time, the solution would not be so simple, and even though I might not be able to locate it now, I still wished I hadn't poured it out. Then I had a sickening thought. I thought of the sucking, tearing pain that I knew would come next, and I had to kick it loose. Realizing the shaking about of my leg was useless, I stomped my foot onto the hardwood floor. The extra pain was intense, but pain or no pain, I had to free myself from the thing that hungered for my flesh, and do so at any cost. I screamed as I stomped on the floor, driving its thorns deeper into my foot with every stomp till they poked through the top of my foot altogether. I slammed the spiked sphere into the floor over and over again, and finally, its needles retracted, and I heard a slight sloshing sound as it rolled away.

I turned around and tried to walk away. My right foot was useless, so I decided to crawl, and soon I felt a wall. Feeling along the wall, my face was brushed by the leaves of a potted plant, and I remembered that it was the only plant in the house. The plant was kept in the den, and I knew I wasn't far from freedom. In fact, now I knew exactly where the front door stood. Frantically I made my way for it, knocking over the rubber tree. Crawling through the topsoil half-mad, I heard myself laughing. But my breathing became labored, and I felt a prickly sensation running up my leg as if I had stepped into a patch of seven-minute itch. The feeling intensified, and as I crawled for the door, I felt it spreading through my entire body.

As I felt the door with my one good hand, a smile came to my face, and as I wrapped my fingers round the knob, I felt that smile freezing up below my nose. A sense of undeniable doom wrapped around my numbing frame, and as I dropped back to the floor, I certainly felt like losing that smile, but I could not cover my teeth with my lips. I tried again to rise, to reach for the knob of the door that stood between death and the life I heard calling on the other side, the squawking of the gulls, whose shadows circled the grassy dunes.

I tried again with all my strength to reach that door, but I could not move a muscle save for the tiny ones that controlled my now useless eyes, the eyes that would see no more the happy black dog running on the beach. I lay there paralyzed upon the floor, and soon I felt the moistness of the sea creature against my cheek. Next I felt the sharp stinging of its ghastly quills stab abruptly into my face. And the horrible, merciless sucking that ensued bit down into the very core of my poor soul. The ripping and the slow tearing of the flesh delivered me to madness as the toothless mouth fed leisurely upon my face.

THE WILL TO DIE

The first time I woke up to find myself lying on my back in the tall grass with a tombstone behind my head, I thought I was still in the midst of an awful dream. The sun was burning my eyes, and as I sat up and looked about me, I found myself in the middle of a gloomy sea of slanted slabs and musty tombs. Before long, I saw far off in the distance the steeple of the church on Chaney Hill, which stood not far from my house. I knew then that not only was I not in my bed, where I laid my sober head down the night before, but I was quite awake.

The second time it happened, I wondered if it was not the result of drunkenness, but I soon realized that I hadn't had the money to buy a single drink in nearly three weeks. The third time I woke up in the boneyard, I figured myself mad. Had I been sleepwalking? I'd never before been known to, and if so, why did I always end up here in this dreadful, lonely place of sleep and decay?

It wasn't until the fourth time when I realized that I had always woken up lying before the same gravestone. This, for whatever reason, frightened me all the more than finding myself sprawled out on my back in the dry weeds of a cemetery. For I knew not of this man who in life was called Jarvis Stone, who had been carried to this accursed place some 312 years before my birth.

I found it somewhat strange too that I was always lying on my back with my arms crossed over my chest the way that men are buried, for I usually slept on my chest or on my side, half curled up, my arms wrapped round my pillow. As time went on, the mornings I awoke in my bed between my morbid awakenings were fewer and fewer still, until they became a daily occurrence. I can't remember the last time I woke up in my soft, warm bed. And every time, I lay neatly stretched out above the grave of Jarvis Stone.

Oh, the dreams I dreamed in that land of bones! The ghastly nightmares that tortured and poisoned my sorry soul, I dare not relay for fear of reliving them. But he of the shadowy figure and fiery eyes is in all of them. He is the very embodiment of doom and woe. His is the face of emptiness and despair, of sorrow and regret. His is the face of suffering. He is the cold darkness of dread and the echo of sighs, who is condemned to dwell forever in the dust of a tomb. His eyes are the fire of immortality, the merciless, undying torture that burn without rest. All of these things I had come to learn, for I was told by a deep voice that spoke from inside the house of dirt and death in my most troubling nightmares.

I could not take the madness of waking in that place nearly two miles from my home anymore. I could not bear another chilling dream of the shadow man, as I had come to refer to him as. My body ached from the hard ground, and many times I awoke with unexplainable bruises and lashes on my arms and legs. I knew too that the winter was not far away. Every evening grew yet colder, and I was horrified by the thought of freezing in the night before that ancient tombstone. I had begun to respect death and cringed timid and humble beneath the weight of its shadow. And in turn, I also began to appreciate life for the first time ever and looked upon the living world with eyes not quite young but new. I wished that I had never wished aloud to die.

I had an idea one cold morning as I woke shivering in the graveyard. I would make sure I woke in my bed the next day. I took a rope and tied it round my right ankle. The other end, I secured to one of the bed posts. I chuckled lightly before I dozed off. Why hadn't I thought of this sooner? I thought. The next morning, I awoke to a new horror. Even before I opened my eyes, I felt the grass tickle my neck, and the dew was cold under my feet. I knew too well where I was, and as I sat up and opened my tired eyes, I saw the rope was still tied round my leg. How did I manage to make my way here last night? I asked myself. Had I untied the knot from the post in my sleep? As I stood and turned around, I gasped heavily at the sight of the other end of the rope tied loosely round the marble marker of Jarvis Stone.

That was it! The fear and puzzlement had reached a new level. The sight of the rope tied round that tombstone made me cringe. It told me that other forces were at hand. Was someone playing a cruel joke on me? If so, who, and for what purpose? Had I been carried here night after night? And if so, how had I not been woken in the process? All these questions gnawed hungrily at my brain, and the imprint my body had made in the weeds before the gravestone repulsed me.

This time, instead of making my usual way out of the cemetery via the shortest and quickest route, I found myself wandering off aimlessly through the maze of stones and statues. Why I did not leave that dreary place and what I was looking for, I knew not, but I found myself standing before the rusted iron door of a dirt-mound tomb. The very tomb I had heard the voice of the shadow man emit from in my tortured dreams. And as I stood before it, I felt the spell of vertigo intoxicate me, and I moaned drunkenly as I fell backward to the ground. Then, a great hollow, rumbling sound echoed out, scaring off the monotonous silence. A heavy, creaking, scraping sound, as of the grinding of metal and stone. And I beheld as I stood, frozen in fear, the great iron door of the tomb slowly swinging open. As I stared into the thick, stale blackness of the tomb, I wanted to turn and run madly. Instead, I found myself walking slowly through the arced entrance, out of the warm sunlight and into the cool, dank lair of sleep. Into darkness thick and heavy with age, the ancient, immortal darkness that knew not the piercing of light. And as the scraping sound commenced, I realized the door was now closing; however, I did not make my way for it. Instead I stood there, emotionless, and watched it shut before me.

Unmeasured moments passed as I gazed wide-eyed upon the nothingness, till at last two tiny red flames disturbed the unholy darkness and flickered fearsomely at the far end of the tomb. The demon eyes entranced me as they burned with intimidation, watching me with patience from the opposite end of the dank tomb. My limbs began to tremble as if I were standing out in the cold as I waited for the shadow man to speak. And still he spoke not. Finally, I could not stand the silence anymore, and somehow I found the strength to address him. I think the strength I found to overcome my fear came from my thought of it all being nothing but another nasty nightmare. But it felt so real. "What do you want with me, fiend?" I barked as I took two steps backward to feel the cold, coarse rust of the door at my back.

"It's not what I want," he grumbled in his deep, godly voice. "It is what you want, you jaded old fool! I am no fiend." He continued, "I wish you no harm, however, it's what you wish that concerns me, and sometimes a man lives to see his wish granted only to discover that he was better off had it not come true, but by then it's too late to wish it away."

As I stood there, watching those two red flames dance as they burned, I understood all too well exactly what he meant, yet I did not want to let on that I did, nor did I want to admit that I had wished so many times aloud to die, especially here and now. "What do you mean?" I asked.

"Don't play ignorant with me, you know exactly what I speak of, and pretending you don't won't buy you any time. You see, here, all there is is time, and I'm here to make sure you get what you want. All I want is out of this wretched place. All I ask is to wake up in my bed."

"Did you not wish you were dead?" he interrupted sternly. "Did you not ask aloud of the low gray clouds time and time again to be done with this life?"

"Yes," I said with regret and sorrow in my voice.

"Yes!" he snapped. "And something heard you, and forces invisible united to satisfy your desire."

"The same forces which carried me here night after night?" I asked with conviction. With that question, the shadow man burst into maniacal laughter, and when he was done, he continued. "No one carried you here, you fool. Nothing but your own two feet!"

"Then how do you explain the rope?" I asked.

"The same hands that tied it to the bedpost untied it and looped it round the headstone."

"Impossible!" I shouted. "You speak lies!" With my accusations, the flames grew larger as he shouted back, and I flinched with every word. "The truth is what comes out of this dry jaw for I have nothing to gain with lies. You are the liar! And now that you know the truth, you still refuse to believe." After a short pause, the flames died down to their normal size, and his voice was again calm as he continued. "You see, although you changed your mind, even you're outlook on life, still a part of you remains stubborn and loyal to your suicidal thoughts. A part of you which lies dormant, sleeping while you roam about in your daily doldrum of insignificance. A part of you which wakes when your tired mind reaches the state of REM. The part of you which remembers and serves your will to die. That part of you brings you here each night."

As his words sunk in, so too did a new, potent dread as I came to accept the thought that I alone continually brought myself to the cemetery in my sleep and lay down willingly among the weathered slabs. "Who are you?" I asked.

"I have already told you in dreams who I am," said he. "I am the face of solitude, regret, despair, and suffering. Here, take this candlestick, light it so you can gaze upon the face of emptiness." I heard a small object roll toward me across the dusty floor, and I felt it stop at my feet. I bent slowly to retrieve it, and I watched his eyes burn intensely as I fumbled in my pocket for a match. And as I felt each end of the candle to find the wick, I wished I hadn't asked that question, for he already told me who he was, and now he wanted to show me his face, and I did not wish to look upon it. But still I struck the match and lit the wick and stretched the tiny flame of the red candle out before me. And as the small glow of the candle shone upon that face, if you could call it that, all the horrors of hell could not have inflicted more fear into me, nor could any foul, taboo words describe the crusty, rotted mask that peered eerily back at me. A merciful dizziness again engulfed me before all went black.

When I came to, the day was old, and the shadows of the gravestones stretched long on the moss before the sealed iron door of the tomb. My waking mind began slowly to warm up to a state of relief as I realized it was all a twisted dream. As I drifted through the crosses and the arm and handlike appendages of dead trees, I heard a scraping sound before me. I followed the sound as it grew steadily louder to a curious movement between two stones. A shadowy apparition seemed to jump up and down two feet high from the weedy ground. My desire to flee in the other direction was strong, but still I could not resist inching slowly toward the nightmare vision. With each ending moment, the dwindling daylight was elapsing into shadows, and I knew I had to leave this place before it got too dark. Still the hopping blotch of thicker darkness captivated my interest, and I moved closer still. My squinting eyes focused on the maddening movement, and with a few steps closer, I realized that it was dirt being shoveled out of a rectangular hole in the earth.

"Hello there," I said as I stepped cautiously to the edge of the pit. It was incredibly dark in the hole, but I could barely make out the figure of an old man hunched over as he shaped out the floor of the grave. As he turned round to face me, his eyes gleamed oddly, terribly in the moonlight. "What can I do for you?" he barked miserably.

"I was wondering if you had any knowledge of a man buried here centuries ago, sir, named Jarvis Stone." His face was ancient and disturbing, and his eyes seemed to shine yet brighter as they widened at the mention of the name. He stretched out a shaky, wrinkled hand covered with sweat and earth, and I noticed it was unusually cold as I gripped it to pull him up. "Jarvis Stone was a very well-known man back in his time," said the old man as he sat cross-legged at the mouth of the grave. His voice was cracked and low, and I imagined that the deep, stern intensity of it was partially due to its echoing in the hole he had dug. "Ah, the story of Jarvis Stone was told to every young child on the island for well over two hundred years after his death. Everyone knew his name, and woman and man alike cringed when it was spoken.

"Jarvis was quite a lot like me, you see, that is to say that he too was a grave digger. In fact, he dug the very first grave in this boneyard, and he laid many a man and child to rest in this ground. Jarvis, in spite of his morbid job, was a happy man. He gained a resentment and a fear of death as the years went on. But his occupation taught him to appreciate life. He loved life, as he loved his wife, that is, until one day when he came home early to find her in bed with another man. He was a kind and gentle man up to that point. But when he opened the door of his chamber on that fateful night and saw his beloved wife entangled with the stranger, something inside of him was awoken. Something ghastly and terrible, which devoured in that instant the light, the sweetness, all that was good in his heart. With his rusty shovel, he murdered his wife and her lover in a blind fit of rage. He chopped them to bits with an ax and burned the remains in his fireplace. Not to get rid of the evidence, rather to make sure that they did not receive a proper Christian burial. He felt that they did not deserve to be buried in his cemetery.

"Of course, when his wife was discovered to be missing, Jarvis was suspected of her murder. He was brought to trial, but they never could prove his guilt. As months passed slowly by, the townspeople shunned and loathed Jarvis Stone. They began to fear him as well. Needless to say, he quickly lost the desire to dwell on this planet, and one night, he took two red-hot coals from his fireplace with his naked hands and pressed them into his eyes! The horrid scream was heard by every living thing on the island that awful night as he burned his eyes from their sockets for he wished not to look upon the world again.

"That poor man dragged his feet around the dirty streets for months afterward, bumping into tree trunks and fences as he felt about the town in blindness. No one witnessed him partake of food or drink, and one night, weary and delusional, he found his way through the utter blackness to the place he knew so well. Using his shovel as a cane, he lumbered around the graveyard till he found his favorite nook. There he dug himself a shallow grave, no deeper than two feet. He crawled into the hole, and lying on his back, he pulled the dirt over his body and then over his face. Yes, Jarvis Stone buried himself alive!"

With this revelation, I squirmed in my skin as I thought of one of the reoccurring nightmares I'd had as I lay stretched out above the grave of Jarvis Stone. Perhaps one of the most haunting ones of all, I remember a set of bony arms and hands rising out of the ground and wrapping themselves around me, and I cringed as I thought of that corpse, which was lying directly under me, barely covered by dirt at all. By the end of the gravedigger's chilling tale, it had grown darker, and I thanked the old man for his time and told him I had to go. "Leaving so soon?" he asked sardonically.

"Yes, I must be going," I said nervously.

"Don't you have any more questions for me, young man?" he said. "For example, aren't you curious to know whose grave I'm preparing?"

"No," I responded hastily. "I must be off."

"Somewhere not far, a man is chiseling a name on a slab of white marble. If you listen, in fact, you can hear his mallet ring." He began laughing madly at that, and I began to walk faster, half running through the boneyard. And when I put enough distance between us, the laughter died out, and it was replaced by the clanging of what I fancied to be a mallet striking a chisel.

When I got home, a weariness settled on me, and I went straight to bed. This time I tied myself to each post with a separate rope. First my legs and then my wrists. Knot on top of knot I tied till I was sure that I would wake up in my bed in the morning. That night, I dreamed of a man in a dimly lit room who was chipping patiently away at a marble headstone. His hair was white, and his back was to me, and try as I might to peer around his broad shoulders to read the epitaph, I could not see his work. When I asked for a peek, he told me, without turning his face toward me, that I could only see it when it was completed. And when I begged him to show me, he spun around toward me and shouted, "Not till it's done!" His eyes were ablaze with fire, and his voice like thunder shook me from my slumber.

When I awoke, it was dark, and the night was cold. I felt for the knots that were around my limbs, and they were gone save for one that was still tied around my right wrist. Figuring that I must again be lying over the shallow groove of the ancient grave digger, I gasped as I recalled the old man's story. Before I rose to my feet, I felt the ground beneath me and realized it was not matted weeds or grass, instead it was moist, soft dirt. As I stood up, I realized I was not dreaming, and so too I came to the realization that this was the first time I woke up in the cemetery in the middle of the night, which disturbed me greatly. And as I realized I was not before the stone of Jarvis the grave digger, I wondered where I was. I began walking in no particular direction, but after only three short steps, I banged my face into a wet wall of dirt. The horror of it all began to sink in, and I could feel a thousand unseen eyes watching me from the darkest of shadows. I began breathing heavily, and just as I began to panic, a tiny feeling of relief came to my distraught mind. The rope! Thank God! The rope! I pulled it taut and found it to be secured around something above ground level. "Thank God!" I said again aloud as I began to pull my way out of the grave. Finally, my struggling paid off, and I reached the dry, dead weeds on the surface. I saw then that the rope was tied to a headstone. A headstone that was not there earlier, for this was no doubt the fresh grave I sat by and listened to the story of Jarvis Stone.

It horrified me to be in that barren place alone with the darkness wrapped around me, and I thought of running out of there as fast as I could. But oddly enough, it was not my only thought as I unhooked the loop from the tombstone, for my curiosity had the best of me, and I had to read that stone. Quickly I reached in my pocket for a match, and to my surprise, I felt a strange object. An object that I was sure I had not put there. It was about six inches long and cylindrical in shape. I pulled it out of my pocket and struck a match. The flickering flame between my thumb and forefinger revealed to me what that object in my left hand was. It was a red candle! This horrified me even more than reading my own name on the white marble slab, my birth date, and the first three numbers of the current year.

I found my way out of that accursed place in the deep, thick blackness with the help of that candle. And I found my way back into it night after night despite how many knots I tied. And every time, be it day or dark, I found myself, instead of lying before the marker of Jarvis Stone, asleep on the floor of that newly dug grave. I prayed that I would not wake there anymore. I shouted aloud daily my newfound desire to live. I cursed the times that I wished to die, but I knew it was of no use. For my bones ached more each time I woke in that grave with my arms crossed above my chest. My teeth chattered and my hands trembled. Not just with absolute fear but also from the cold. This morning I woke up with frost on my beard. I fear it won't be long now, for the winter's fast approaching. Perhaps I'd soon get my wish after all; I won't wake in this wretched place anymore. But when the frost claims me and the dirt seals me, I know I will, and that's what terrifies me most of all.

NIGHT THINGS

The campfire hypnotized all who huddled round it as it danced and twisted magically. All who were talking and laughing loudly before were now mute and still as darkness crept up slowly. No one said a word, no cricket or bird, no frog call was heard, just the hissing and crackling of the fire. The dead, still silence was odd, almost disheartening. All our moods seemed to suddenly change from glee to somberness as it grew yet darker. No one moved much, save to raise a bottle to their lips. An hour's time drifted slowly by, and still not a single word was spoken. I'd never seen my friends like this. It seemed that we all sensed the same thing: a lurking, inescapable doom.

I kept telling myself that it was all in our heads. For what young man that's spent the night in the woods has not felt the creeps? It was a somewhat expected sensation, and being deeper in the woods than we'd ever been, I was sure, was a factor. Seeing my friends in utter silence was not what disturbed me most of all; it was the way I too was somehow unable to speak every time I felt like doing so. And each time I tried to speak, before I opened my mouth, all the words evaporated from my mind, leaving it empty and confused. So we stared at the orange-and-yellow flames like a pack of mindless zombies for hours, which felt like nights.

Finally, an owl's call echoed out in the empty darkness and seemed to break the spell we were under. Someone began talking, and we started to laugh and feel at ease. But the feeling of comfort was short-lived as we heard a stick snap. It sounded like a large branch broken by a large animal. It sounded too loud to be broken by the weight of a fox or a skunk. We all exchanged wide-eyed glances across the fire's glow. We had no use for words. Again we heard a loud, crisp snapping, but this time from the opposite side as the first. Some of us began to gather rocks, and others grabbed sticks, frantically searching for one that was thick and not rotten. For by now, we had regretfully burned up all the strong sticks in the fire. And it disturbed us greatly to grab a large limb that turned to mush in our hands. Suddenly, a rustling was heard. Twigs were snapping all around us, and it was so dreadfully quiet that you could hear dried leaves crumbling.

"Coyotes? Do you think?" asked one of us, squeezing the end of a club. At first I was terrified by the idea of a pack of coyotes surrounding us, sniffing and prancing closer, salivating through their teeth. But when I saw those unbelievable eyes piercing at us through the brush, the thought of coyotes seemed like a warm and welcome one. At first I thought I was hallucinating, but the alcohol we consumed and the herbs we had smoked had nothing to do with what we saw that fateful night. I continually tried to blame the horrible visions on the herbs, but try as I might, I knew I was fooling myself in order to comfort my poor, battered brain. I was searching in vain to explain away the mysteries of the deep night that were upon us, sniffing loudly and scratching about. They were so close now you could hear their wheezing breath.

But it was the eyes that aroused our fear the most. Those terrible eyes! Some were yellow, and some were red. They lit up all around us like tiny faint candle flames. They infested the bushes, and many were now leering at us from high in the trees. I searched my mind for a logical explanation, yet nothing tied to logic or normality settled on my brain. Coyotes, wolves, birds, nothing could come close to explaining what we beheld. And still the yellow and the horrible red eyes glared back at us from the brush, watching, learning, waiting.

I looked about me for a weapon, something, anything to provide protection, for I seemed to be the only one without a stick or rock. My friends became impatient in their fear. They began pacing madly around the fire, some beating their palms with sticks, others waving rocks in their fists in the night air. For some reason, a rock or a wooden club would not suffice, and instead I looked to the fire as it curled and hissed and popped.

Dan hurled a rock at a dense crowd of eyes, and before we heard its thud against a tree, we watched those eyes vanish, only to reappear yet closer to our circle. They were hideously fast and surprisingly wise for it seemed as though they perceived our every move long before we executed it. We threw many a rock and bottle, and each time the eyes would shut only to reappear even closer. Now many of the disgusting beasts were no more than a leap away, and I could feel that our end was near. I prayed it would be over quickly. Still, a spark of hope was burning. I found myself gazing at the fire, while others focused on the glowing eyes. Was this the answer? I wondered. Could we at least keep them away till morning? Grabbing a club from my friend Jim, I immersed it in the blaze to set the end alight.

All at once they came crawling from the shadows. They crept freakishly into the flickering light. Their bony gray bodies in great horrible masses came lumbering toward our circle. I somehow gathered the strength to raise the burning torch in their hideous faces. They only sneered and howled and hopped about mockingly. They showed clearly that they were not afraid of fire, for one of them grabbed the burning end of my torch and wrenched it from my hands with immense strength yet little effort. It then began dancing madly with the burning club amidst the insanity of the battle, only stopping briefly to set Jim's hair ablaze. And as he fell to his knees, screaming in panic and terror, the thing began dancing in circles around him. My friends hurled rocks at them and swung their clubs as they advanced, but they were much too fast to comprehend. They jumped and ducked and fled, only to return again within an instant, snapping and growling and slicing with their claws.

My face was splattered with the blood of my friend. I grabbed a stick from his limp fist and swung it in a frenzy of anger and rage. All was chaos. A blur of screams and growls, of howls and claws, of yellow and red eyes, and flesh-tearing jaws. From the trees they descended like a fright forgotten and swarmed upon us like biting flies. As the gruesome, snarling hoard pried the stick from my hands, I felt the soul-snuffing sting of many teeth tear into my thigh and ankles. I could hear the crunching of my bones among the horrible din of beastly grunts and the screams of my peers as I was pulled to the ground.

The stars hung low in the dark sky like frozen tears above the scratching branches as I was dragged away. I gathered all the strength I could summon to lift my head enough to gaze back at the campfire. I saw those wretched night things carrying the limp bodies of my friends off into the dark wood, past the border of our circle of light. I watched as some of them gathered bottles and our paper garbage before they crawled off into the night. The few of them that remained seemed to be gathering dirt and sprinkling it over puddles of the blood of my friends. And I watched in disbelief as they clearly were brushing away footprints with their green-and-gray paws. As they gathered yet more dirt, I watched them snuff out the fire we had made. With numbing pain in my useless limbs and unnamed horrors from unspeakable places dancing madly in my brain, I watched as they dragged me away into the cold night, the flames turning to sparks and fluttering away like fireflies.

BOWEN'S BURDEN

"Ahhh!" screamed the horrified Bowen, with his jaw stretched to the limit, his tongue folded in his mouth, his dark, tormented eyes overflowing with the heavy burden of a dreadful past. His hairy chest heaving in and out as he gasped for breath, sitting upright in his bed of straw. Sweat dripping from his scarred forehead and his saturated burly black beard.

It had been over twelve years now that he lived in seclusion in a thickly wooded area, miles from any form of civilization. He could look all around his makeshift cabin and see nothing but trees as far as his vision permitted. But he knew all too well now that although he ran and hid from his demons and put so much distance and time between them that they would not let him alone or let him forget. He was a haunted, disturbed man plagued by vivid, ghastly nightmares of pain and morbidity. He had come to loathe the thought of laying his tired head down to rest when the moon was high. Only by the light of day could he find peace and control of his own thoughts. For in the depth of night, his mind was pierced by the clutches of the bloody claws of nocturnal fiends.

Wiping his jaded face dry, Bowen stepped out into the welcoming morning light with the songs of birds soothing his ears. The weight of a shadowed mountain was lifted from his head as he watched hummingbirds buzzing among lilacs and bleeding hearts. He expelled a long yawn before he started on his short walk to the nearest stream to bathe and quench his thirst in the cool, clear water.

Kneeling down on the mossy bank, Bowen sunk his arms to the bed of the stream. He began gulping the water as it sped by. Suddenly he felt the grip of hands wrapped around his throat, and as he tried to stand and confront his attacker, he was pulled beneath the surface of the gleaming ripples. He was a barrel bodied man of great strength, yet he could not, for the life of him, pull his saturated head from the water. He wasn't necessarily being choked, rather held beneath the surface. He tugged and pulled and tried with all his might in utter desperation to tear his head from the curling stream. And just as the thought of unexpected oblivion as a blessing in disguise had stirred in his brain, and just as he stopped resisting and began to wait for that uncontrollable reaction, that final gasp for air where there is none, he was released.

He came up sucking air yet ready to fight. He could hold his breath for quite some time, and he had an unnatural knack for resisting the urge to panic. He sprung from the water and spun around open palmed, like a black bear rising to his hind paws with rage, water pouring from his matted hair and beard. But there was no one before him, no one to seek revenge upon. He looked all about him, yet there was no one to behold. He could not understand it. "What just happened? This cannot be!" he said to himself aloud. *I finally lost my mind,* he thought. *This time I've finally lost it for good.* But he knew when he gazed into a small pool on the side of the stream that he hadn't lost his mind. For he saw in the reflection red marks around his neck. He sat down in that muddy puddle and rested his weary head in his hands. He knew then that his nightmares had begun to bleed into his days. And worse yet, they had begun to become real. The torturous nightmares were now more than a maddening mental strain. Now they were developing into a physical threat. He knew then that they not only had found him but they were ready and willing to deal out their punishment.

Just then, he was reminded of one of the ill dreams he'd had the night before. Skeleton hands were groping him. Six or eight little bony pairs of them all scratching and clawing at his chest, while the playful laughter of little girls echoed throughout the dark chamber. He then ripped open his shirt, and his dark eyes bulged at what they saw. Sure as sin, his chest was covered in deep, swollen red scratches that stretched out in all directions. There were hundreds of them. They looked like overlapping red spiderwebs.

This disturbed him greatly, for he had been long tormented by the awful nightmares, and he had heard the laughter of the young girls many times before, but now there were traces of the dreams becoming real. As disturbing as the laughter was, it was the screams that horrified him the most. The terrible, piercing screams of many little girls. The screams he could never get out of his head even in the day. It was the screams, alas, that drove him mad. The screams and the laughter and the voices.

Yes, they spoke to him. Clearly and calmly yet swiftly and stern. Whispering eerily aloud in the night. "How could you do it? You'll pay for what you've done to us! We were just little girls!" Yes, the voices and the screams sunk like swords into his soul. Many times he had entertained the thought of suicide. Each scream, each dream, each night drove him closer to the edge. And now there was no solace even in the light of day. The day was all he had. Each time he laid his head down late at night, the only comforting thought in his head was that of the sun rising over the cedars and pines. But now, somehow his demons were no longer frightened away by the blinding light of dawn, and they were getting stronger.

As he turned his eyes from his mutilated chest back to the puddle, he saw not his own reflection but that of an old, wrinkled face of a puritan man staring back at him from his black robe. The disgusting expression on the man's face did not change, and his lips moved not, but Bowen could hear the man's voice stomping and smashing around in his battered brain. "Sinner! Heathen! Blaspheme! Child of the devil!" He stomped the face in the puddle with his huge right foot. But the voices still raged on for a time.

That night, he dreamed he was suffocating. The dream was one of many that was vivid enough to shake him awake. As he opened his eyes and came out of the dream, he found it hard to draw a breath. His mouth was wide open, and his nostrils uncovered, and yet his lungs strained for air. When he started to rise, as he usually did upon waking from the dreams, he found that he could not sit up. A monstrous weight then became apparent as he reached with both hands for his chest. Cold and rough, hard and porous were the objects that rested heavily on his belly and chest. In a panic, he began flinging them off himself, and he gasped for breath as they crashed to the floor.

Sweeping the last of them off his concaved stomach, he sat up abruptly in the night. Wheezing and choking with fear, he fumbled on his bedside table to set a candle alight. As the small glow flickered on the floor, his troubled mind began chasing itself in circles. "Stones!" he said in between gasps. "Stones!" He searched the house for an intruder. The door was still locked and the windows boarded up tight. There were no footprints or any other traces of entry. He knew he wouldn't find them anyway. Still half asleep, he started to wonder if what he had just experienced was all just another dream altogether. He made his way back to bed and cursed as he stubbed his toe on one of the rocks. He did not return to sleep that night. Instead, he sat up, yawning, staring at the dancing candle flame while he waited for dawn.

Bowen was losing more sleep now than ever before. He would now go two or three nights without lying down at all. He was terrified of the dark and the dreams. The voices in the night and the awful screams. And now he was hearing them by day, and even when they were silent, they echoed in his head. He was sluggish and weak. He became delirious. He found himself staring like a madman with an empty head at the candle flame, mostly silent yet sometimes laughing hysterically at the candle glow. By day he would wander through the trees like a lost dog. Sometimes he would collapse and sleep by the stream. But the dreams he suffered by day were no less frightful.

As he drifted off into dreamland, the peaceful sound of the singing stream was drowned out by a dreadful one. At first it was faint and distant. But soon it grew loud and overwhelming in his poor ears. It was a hissing sound as that of an immense fire crackling, popping, and hissing in his head. Then among the sound of the awesome blaze was heard a screaming. It was a shrieking louder and more disturbing than any before it, and added to the horrible screaming was a chorus of crying girls. Before long, most of the sobbing turned into screams, and a hellish vision, sickening and deplorable, emerged from the darkness of Bowen's mind. As if the fire had suddenly glowed to break up the blackness of deep-buried bones to show a pretty young girl in a white gown and bonnet tied to a pile of branches and logs. Her beautiful little face, which was shrouded in smoke and aglow with the blaze, was frozen and twisted into the mask of ultimate horror and doom. Her tiny hands flailed about beneath the knots of the hemp braids, as if she were trying to sweep the heat away. Her slender fingers curled up into her palms and a scream so loud and piercing split through the evil night like a thunderbolt as the fire rose.

Bowen expelled a piercing shriek of his own as he broke from the grasp of the nightmare. Sitting up abruptly, he looked around as if he expected to see someone or something lurking about him. There were squirrels hopping and birds buzzing, but now even the hummingbirds and the warmth of the sun's rays, not even the song of the stream could bring him peace. He sighed as he looked at the lilacs and bleeding hearts. They were withered and gray and hung like old cracked bells. The leaves were all dried and crumbling in the midspring sun. All the flowers were dead, and the berries were all shriveled. The colors were all gone save for brown and gray. He could not decipher whether he were dreaming or not, although he was somewhat sure he was awake, but the withered flowers made his mind want to think he was still asleep. Nothing made sense anymore. Somehow, someway he knew he had to get some sleep.

For the first time in three days, Bowen laid his tormented head down on his feather bag. As frightened as he was, he knew he could not force his eyes to stay open any longer. After all, he thought, that daydreams were just as wretched as the nightmares. He knew it was inevitable, and so he lay down. Again, the cracking and hissing of an enormous bonfire filled his ears. Louder and louder it grew and roared. The dream was so real this time that he could smell the smoke and even feel the heat of the awful blaze. Louder it hissed like a thousand threatened snakes, and soon it was accompanied by a chorus of maddening screams, all of little girls crying and screaming and pleading to the empty night.

Now, the dreadful black souls in puritan garb danced mindlessly around the pyre. They shouted out disgusting words at the little girl as she began to burn. Expressionlessly they mocked her as she sizzled. "Blaspheme! Sinner! Child of Satan!" Then came a whisper among the screams: "I'm just a little girl!" Bowen woke at those whispered words for they seemed to trouble him the worst. He sat up, gasping for air in his bed of straw. But the air was thick and choking, and his nose felt like it was stinging with smoke. He was sweating more than he ever had from the dreams, and he wondered if he was truly awake, for he could feel an intense heat on his body and face. An orange glow was now apparent behind him, which slowly broke up the darkness before him. Although he could barely think, on instinct he made his way to the cabin door. He looked back before he opened that door, and he saw his bed light up. He noticed then that he was holding his breath. He flung the door open and stepped out into the clear night air. While he began to suck in that cool air, he gasped again at the sight of a little girl standing before him silently.

He fell to his knees and struggled for breath. He was afraid to look up at her, but it was more horrifying and draining not to look. When he expelled the last of the smoke from his lungs, he looked up, hoping she was gone. But she was still there, staring down at him with a look of hatred that seemed to include a small drop of pity. As he looked at her, her face began to change. It began to blister and bubble. She was melting before his eyes. And as the flesh dripped off her little skull, her bony jaw opened, and she said to him, "I was just a little girl." With those words, she vanished to the dreadful night, and Bowen, for the first time in his life, began to cry. The tears did not fall for the gloom of his own dreadful situation but for the regret and remorse he felt. Then he heard a huge crumbling sound, which turned him around, and he knew he was not dreaming, for his cabin was burning to the ground. He thought of the candle he had watched burn night after night. He remembered perfectly how he watched it burn down to nothing and snuff itself out. He wondered how his cabin caught fire. He wondered for a while as he watched it burn. He knew it was no fault of his own, but still it was burning. It was no dream, for the next morning, he returned home, and sure as sin, his cabin was reduced to a pile of smoldering ashes.

It was not the loss of his home, however, that brought him to his grisly conclusion. He'd had enough of the torture and suffering, and he had endured more than his fill of the whispers and screams and the punishment, which reached him in the form of dreams. He could bear no more the horrible visions that now followed him even through the sunlight. He knew he could never escape his demons no matter where he went, and still he knew deep down he deserved his fate and all the torment he swallowed along the way.

Bowen went for a last walk to the stream he had drank from and bathed in for so long. He climbed the beautiful oak tree he had spent so much time underneath, basking in the warm sun and hiding from his fiends. He knew that spot would conceal him no more as it now cast its sickly shadow on the withered lilacs and fragile flowers. He tied the hemp braid around a thick bough and slid the noose around his thick neck. Bowen had faith that the noose would not fail him. He was a master at such things as tying nooses. And just such a reason it was that he leaped from the bough and swung silent in the midspring sun.

The merciful, silent darkness was short-lived. He wondered again if he was dreaming, but he looked at his thick hands and saw they were covered in the soot of his burned-out home. He wondered then if he had not tied the noose properly, but when he gazed up at the old oak, he saw his own body still swinging from it. He knew then that he had passed, and he saw the lilacs and bleeding hearts were vibrant and full of color once again. Green leaves played happily in the spring breeze, and he smiled when a tiny hummingbird caught his eye.

But the smile fled from his spirit's face as he saw the white forms close in on him. Beautiful they were, the little girls, perhaps more beautiful than they ever were in life. They moved so daintily and majestically, all aglow with a warm, radiant silver light. Their white dresses and bonnets flowing in the spring breeze. But this did not bring Bowen joy. He realized then that even with self-annihilation, he would not escape his destiny. His destiny was their judgment and wrath and even more so their revenge.

Soon they began to dance around him playfully. They were laughing and giggling with delight. Some began to float about his spirit with ease in the enchanted air. He wondered how they would treat him now that things were different, now that he paid for his sins. He wondered if he had suffered enough. The laughing went on for some time. It was not comforting. It was creepy, even disturbing. And soon his tormented ears were filled again with the sounds of screams. The laughter had all turned into screaming as they danced and floated around him.

He covered his tormented ears, and still he could not block the sound. And as he gazed at them, some of their pretty little faces flashed at him with clean skulls. Some of their little faces were bubbling and blistering and melting as they screamed. And oh, how they screamed! The piercing screams that cut through his soul were a thousand times worse than they had ever been in his miserable existence, and it was not over now, for he thought he could escape it by taking his own life. He realized then that it was the end of one aspect of retribution yet only the beginning of a whole new form of suffering.

For they danced about him madly, some laughing, some screaming their horrible screams. Some whispering words among the voices he still heard in his head. "Blaspheme! Sinner! Child of Lucifer! Burn, witch, burn!" And still the soft whisper that had always chilled his spirit the most, inflicted on him the dread of doom and eternal torture. The words that will forever be ringing in his tormented ears: "How could you? I was just a little girl!"

SCRAPS FOR THE CROWS

MERCY? THERE IS NO MERCY for me. For if there were, I wouldn't be around today, breathing, existing, writhing in fear, staring at the blank white walls of this madhouse, this chicken coop for insane folks. And although they think me completely mad, and I admit I am quite disturbed after what I've beheld and lived through, I am surely still mentally competent. I see myself not as a crazy man but as a traumatized man, and likely so, for I know what I've been through was real. They've tried to convince me with their therapy and pills that I have been the victim of either hallucinations or an overactive imagination, but let me assure you, I've never had much of an imagination. My mind doesn't roam off the page much. I am a simple man who always focused on his daily duties, and as for the hallucination part, I've never touched drugs until they brought me here and forced them on me.

As much as I despise this place, I wonder how I would get along on the outside now. Farming was all I've ever done. And although I don't feel completely safe in here, I would feel like a wounded fish out there, waiting, floating in the open sea like so much bait. Even if they let me out, I could never again milk a cow or scare a crow from my corn or fork hay for a horse. I cringe now when I hear the caw of a crow, and a chill runs through me at the thought or mention of a horse. Milk, I cannot drink. They relentlessly persist on serving it to me with my meals, and although I used to love it, the sight and the smell of it now makes me vomit. I will never be the same. And I say there is no hope or mercy for me because I know what I've seen was real and mostly because I'm alive to tell the tale.

It all started on my farm one spring night in 1829, just seven years ago. I was awoken from sweet dreams by a stirring of my animals. I huffed and cursed as I pried my tired bones from the bed and fumbled for my trusty Adeline. Adeline was my shotgun. A beauty of a weapon, her stock was made of the finest cherrywood, and her chamber and barrels were polished brass. It was a unique, custom weapon that I bought at an auction. I wish I had her now. I'd splatter my poor brains all over the walls, add some color to the place, liven it up a little.

Anyway, as I walked across the field toward the barn and pens, furious for being woken again, it occurred to me that this time, all my livestock were in a panic. Usually it was the chickens being threatened by a fox or a coyote, and sometimes they'd get the hogs going, but never the horses and cows and all. I had an odd feeling as I got closer to the frightened animals. The cows were huddled in a far corner in the pen. The horses were neighing frantically and jumping about the corral like their tails were on fire. The hogs, hens, and goats were all in a frenzy. I'd never in all my life seen my animals all behaving this way. And the oddest thing was, I saw no fox or coyotes. Maybe all the noise scared them away, I thought, and went back to bed.

The next morning, I went out to tend to my animals like I'd always done. But this was the start of something cataclysmic and the end of the dependability of monotony. For a murder of crows on the ground of the horses' pen captured my curiosity. I made my way toward them to scare them off, and I got a scare of my own. As they flew away, I became mortified to see what they were feeding on. I dropped the basket of eggs and screamed like a schoolgirl as I beheld the white-spotted brown head of Bessie, my favorite thoroughbred. I stared down at the bodiless fright for some time, wondering who would've or what could've done such a deplorable thing. Her shiny black eyes were wide and drying in the sun, and her tendons and frayed muscle extended outward like the tentacles of a beached jellyfish from the crows ripping and pulling at them. But what horrified me most of all was not the head itself but the body. The body!

For search the corral as I may and cover the ground as I did, I only found frustration and confusion. I even searched for miles outside the perimeter of my land, and I could not, for the life of me, find a trace of the body, no mane or bones of that horse.

    I spent the whole day wading through the weeds, looking for the rest of Bessie. I wouldn't be content till I found the remains, but as the sun hung low, I realized that if I hadn't found her by now, I probably wasn't going to. As I headed back, a feeling of nausea and uneasiness seized me. I knew that something was dreadfully wrong, but pondering what only brought me more questions. The mystery of it all intensified that awful feeling. The feeling never for a moment went away, and it haunts me till this day. I buried Bessie's head 'neath the apple tree she'd always fed from. I didn't want to give the crows the satisfaction of picking clean her skull. Oh, how they hop and crawl about fighting over dead things! The blackness of their feathers and the nasty, threatening, sinister look in their dark, beady eyes. And each time I hear that loud, wretched cawing, it fills me with fear and the urge to vomit.

    I had a hard time falling asleep that night. I lay there for hours, trying to name any enemies I might have made, though none came to mind. I could not for the life of me even begin to explain what had happened. When I finally drifted off about two in the morning, I soon fell into the clutches of a wicked dream. I saw my own head lying in the horse's pen, surrounded by a crowd of the ghastly birds. They were pecking viciously at my frayed flesh. Some were burying their heads deep within the gory cavity, while the rest fought over my eyes as they dangled from their sockets. Their heads, beaks, and wings were wet and shiny with my blood. I wasn't asleep long before I was awoken from the nightmare by my livestock crying out in a mad chorus of panic. This time, I was frightened as well as furious. With slight hesitation, I grabbed Adeline and headed out into the night.

    The same unusual scene played out before me. The moon was shrouded by clouds, and the terrified beasts neighed and mooed and hopped around wildly, their dark figures, like shadows moving through shadows, were hardly visible. My straining eyes scanned inside the pens, looking for the culprit among them. I searched the barn, the coop, and all around the grounds and found nothing to blame for the disturbance of the poor animals. Long after they had quieted, I sat on my porch, waiting, listening with Adeline under my arm. After an hour or so, I went back to bed. The rest of the night was uneventful. But I wish I could say the same for the morning. For when I went out to milk the cows, I saw them all huddled together in the far corner. They were frozen and silent. As I walked up to the fence, I realized that my rooster, although he was quite alive, hadn't crowed the past two mornings. I was awoken instead by the call of the crows. What an ugly sound to wake to. As I entered the pen, I saw at the opposite corner of the mass of cows a black flapping mess. There must have been a hundred of them cawing and snapping at one another. At that moment, everything seemed surreal. I felt as if I were dreaming as I slowly made my way toward the nasty birds. There came a ringing to my ears, and the awful commotion was muffled as it felt as though I were high on a mountaintop. My limbs were weak, and I became dizzy as I got close enough to send them fleeing to the treetops. As they flew off like dark blotches of midnight, they slowly revealed the contents of their breakfast. For there, lying in the dirt, were not one but two dusty, eyeless heifer heads!

When I calmed down, I began again to search the farm, and when I found nothing, I started to sift through the fields and forest all around the property. The rest of the day was a haze of fear and maddening questions. Something unexplainable yet undeniable was abound. I felt the overwhelming weight of something powerful and horrible lurking, hovering over me unseen. And I carried that weight through the trees and brush and corrals as I searched in vain for the bodies of those poor cows. Not a trace of them did I discover. No footprints or carriage tracks did I come across. Nothing unusual, save for the half-pecked heifer heads. I gave up the search sometime before the sun went down. I went to the gun cabinet and filled a sack with shells. I did not eat, for hunger did not beckon me. I spent the first three hours of darkness polishing my shotgun, with my mind in a state of emptiness. When I snapped out of my hypnotic mode of polishing over the shiny polished brass, I decided I would not retire to bed that night. Instead, I walked with Adeline to the apple tree beside my barn. Strapping the weapon around my neck, I began to climb the tree. I walked along a sturdy limb near the top and jumped onto the roof of the barn. There I crouched and waited, watching for movement among the dark brush. Waiting and watching above the corrals of sleeping beasts.

I must have drifted off for once again, I was awoken by the cries of my animals. I sat up and fumbled for Adeline, while my mind began to slowly waken. The horses were running in circles around the edge of their pen, neighing and huffing and kicking high their hooves. The heifers were mooing as they huddled in the corner. The fence creaked with the stress of the cows backing themselves into it as they thought they could hide themselves there. The hogs belched as they sunk themselves into the mud. The chickens flapped about the coop in confusion. White feathers floated against the pitch-black night.

I waved my shotgun hungrily down at the chaos. My weary, squinting eyes were begging for the satisfaction of their curiosity. All at once I beheld one of the heifers being lifted high in the night air, while the rest of them moaned and bucked in fear and torment. My mind was consuming itself as I watched that twitching heifer jerk and cry as it hung in the twilight some twenty feet above the roof of the barn. What deity of evil could spawn such a thing? What force of darkness could possibly hide it? My mind raced to catch up with the fleeing reality as I witnessed in terror the body of the cow vanish to the deplorable night with a loud, horrible crunch.

It was then, as I saw the head fall above the huddled heifers, that my poor eyes made out the silhouette of a colossal figure of some giant, dreadful fiend. I could barely distinguish the darker outline of the head, shoulders, and limbs blending into the night. Within an instant, I was trembling. So much so that I could barely hold the barrel straight. For I saw then two thin horizontal slots of dim white glow, which appeared to be the thing's eyes. Without hesitation, I squeezed the trigger. Two light-blue sparks trailed out before me. My eyes were stinging with the smoke from the powder as I watched its eyes go out. I fumbled through the sack for two more shells and reloaded Adeline faster than I'd ever done. As I did so, I was hoping to hear the sound of the beast crashing to the ground. To my dismay, I saw the white slots glowing again. I fired again at the white eyes, and I was sure either time I hadn't missed, but this time, they didn't so much as blink. A roar like thunder shriveled my ears and blew back my hair as I struggled again to reload. The next thing I knew, I was flying backward through the air, gripping Adeline. A hot, foul wind blew me off the roof amid a whirlwind of shingles that slapped and scraped my face as I fell.

When I came to, the sun was burning my eyes. My whole body was sore and bruised. The rosebush my grandfather planted broke my fall, yet it's still a wonder that I survived. When I stroked my aching head, my hair fell, swirling to the ground like dry, crusty leaves in the late-autumn breeze. I wondered if it were all a nightmare as I walked up to the gate still gripping Adeline. Upon inspection of the pens, I found two noisy groups of crows cawing and pecking at one another. And I knew when I saw those dreadful fowls that I was not dreaming. And I knew I didn't have to scare them off to know what their feathers were covering as they fed. Without much thought, I opened the gate of the heifers' pen. I set free then all my beautiful steeds as well. The goats, the hogs, the chickens too. I laughed as I watched them wander off into the wilderness.

Not long after I had emptied all the pens did I begin to wander off into the trees. I could not stay at that farm anymore. I left my whole life behind that day. Everything I'd ever had and worked my whole life for. I knew not where I was going; I only hoped I was getting away from that... that thing. I only knew one thing for sure. I could run from my fear, but I could never leave it behind. For no matter where I might roam or end up, I knew I'd never escape from the sight of those nasty, vile crows. And shrivel as they might, I could not spare my poor, haunted ears of that god-awful cawing.

THROUGH MY EYES

The elixir always burned my eyes terribly, yet it did not improve my vision. At least, that is, for the first few weeks. Anyway, it was not my eyes that needed improving. In fact, I'd always had perfect vision. It was my father who was rapidly losing his sight, and I feared his sight wasn't the only thing he was losing. I feared his sanity was slipping away, perhaps faster than the light from his shadowed world.

For the past year and a half, he had been consumed with the unbelievable task of not only stopping but reversing his condition. He had become obsessed with finding a solution, as he was completely horrified by the thought of walking into a world of permanent, utter darkness. He would toil tirelessly both day and night in his makeshift laboratory. No, he was no scientist or a doctor, although he excelled in chemistry when he was my age. He also was a master herbalist. He had a special knack for knowing the ins and outs of almost everything that grew leaves. He was a man of great intelligence who could've been just about anything he desired to be, but he did not end up with a doctor's prestige. He somehow became a winemaker. A humble occupation, yet it brought in ten times what a doctor could annually, for Tilden Holt knew how to make wine. Everyone who tasted it said it was the best they'd ever sipped. Many begged for the recipe, but of course, he would never tell. He would not even tell his own son, although I have a feeling he added an unorthodox ingredient. Perhaps some little-known herb or root; only he knew for sure.

Night after night, day after day, he would tinker with his potion down in the damp wine cellar. The thick wooden door was always locked whether he was behind it or not. No one was allowed access to that now-taboo area deep below the manor's dusty floorboards. Not his own wife, not the maid, not even me, no one but the workers who made the wine, while he searched frantically to find a cure for the blind. So too were we forbidden to trespass on the glistening beauty of the vineyards. This was a great disappointment to me for I'd always loved wandering around beneath the purple clusters of hanging grapes. The huge waving leaves and curly vines expelled a tranquil, surreal atmosphere. But one day, he told us of his new rule, and he ordered his workers to construct a great wall to tower around the vineyards. I hadn't seen those grape vines or the workers since the wall's completion. I always wondered why he would not allow me in his lab, yet every so often, he would fumble his way up the stairs with a newly improved batch for me to sample. It frightened me to be his guinea pig, yet I had complete trust and faith in him. He was greatly horrified by the approaching blackness, and so I drank from the beaker many times without question. Every new concoction tasted and smelled fouler than the one before, just when I thought I had inflicted upon my palette the suffering of the harshest, most disgusting thing a man has ever choked down.

When I did question him, he would tell me little. He said it was a harmless solution, completely herbal, whose most vital ingredient was extracted from a wildflower that he'd come across on his journey to Africa. He would tell me no more, just like he would not tell me why he would not drink his own purple remedy when it was he, not I, who was losing his sight. It was that day he told me about the strange, foreign flower that brought a new revelation. For it was on his return to Africa that everything began to change. He seemed more troubled than before. He had returned with a complete head of gray hair while there were only a few strands before, and there was a blankness in his eyes. It was that very day I noticed a change in his way. He seemed paranoid, untrusting, and sneaky. He seemed as though he'd been knocked on the head. He'd left a sane man and returned half mad. Not long after the lock was put on the wine cellar door, the monstrous wall was erected around the vineyard, and the workers moved about unseen.

One day, my father lumbered up the stone steps with a twinkle in his dying eyes and a crooked smile on his face, which disturbed me greatly. "I think I've got it this time, boy!" he said in an uncharacteristically sinister voice. "Come, son, drink this and lie down for a while so that when you wake, I may see through your eyes." He had been speaking in riddles for some time now. His vision was getting rapidly cloudier, but his hope seemed restored. I wish I could say that I shared faith in his success, for the light in his mind seemed to be slipping into darkness quite rapidly as well. His words now made little sense to me, and although he hadn't been happy in a long time, he was laughing madly as he ascended the dim staircase. The beaker in his outstretched hand was full of that familiar purple liquid, but this time, it was alive with peculiar bubbles that formed at the bottom of the glass and slowly rose to the surface.

This time, I was slightly reluctant to partake of the tonic for I had only seen bubbling in fluids that were boiling or in chemistry experiments. "Is it hot, Father?" I asked.

"Don't be silly, boy, just drink."

"Why does it bubble so?" I asked. "Is the new ingredient a chemical?"

"No! All natural it is, now drink. Drink it!" he shouted madly. I took the beaker in my hand. It was cold. To my surprise, the taste of it did not make me cringe. It was almost pleasant; however, it still stung my eyes. It smelled slightly of carrots and other things I could not place. I drank it quickly, and within five minutes, a weariness came over me, and so I dragged myself to bed.

When I woke, I felt strange, almost as if ill from a night of heavy drinking. My head was heavy, and my limbs were bathed in the oddest sensation. It was almost as if I could feel the blood flowing through my veins. My eyes were still stinging, and my vision was slightly blurred. *Great,* I thought, *his potion is making me blind like him.* As I descended the stairs, I recalled a strange dream I'd had during the night. It was more like part of a dream, or maybe it was the only part I could remember, but an image flashed in my head of a beautiful grape leaf. It was a single humongous leaf that hung motionless in the warmth of the sun. Then the vine, like a curly vain, turned red, as if it were being filled with blood. Slowly from top to its end, it turned from green to red as if crimson liquid were flowing through it. Then the glow of the sun became brighter, and so did the leaf, which revealed to me its system of veins, which slowly became filled from top to the end of the pointy leaf with the bright-red fluid. I pondered over the strangeness of the dream, over its possible significance with reality. *It's only a dream,* I thought and made my way to the kitchen for a drink. My throat was dry and acidic. It burned the way my eyes did. When the grape juice was gone, so too was the blurriness. The clearer my sight grew, the more relieved I became. I yawned as I stretched my arms. I was starting to feel like myself again.

The maid returned with news that my fiancée was at the door. Elizabeth was a real beauty, inside and out. Her pale skin and her soft red lips. Her wavy red hair and her emerald-green eyes. Oh, the way they looked at me! They seemed to see through to my soul. Her face and figure were a work of art. But her beauty was not purely physical, for she was kind, sweet, and loving. She had a heart of gold, and that was why I wished to make her my wife.

Brushing my hair with my fingers I walked through the kitchen toward the parlor beyond. There she stood in a white dress that glowed with the morning sun. She looked like a wingless angel. Her back was to me as she gazed out the window. The smile leaped from my face as she turned around. Within that instant, I could feel the worms squirming beneath the ground. For as she faced me, I could not see it, that is to say, that her beautiful face I could not behold. Instead I could see only muscle, veins, and bones. The roots of her teeth were exposed and grinned at me wildly. Her eyes were huge white bloodshot orbs that pierced through my flesh. I saw her heart beating within her rib cage. A heavy, tingling dizziness washed over me, yet I did not faint. Instead, I stood there speechless, staring through her skin at all that lurked beneath. I stood on weak legs and watched the blood travel through her veins in systematic spurts, down the streams and tributaries of her elegant frame.

"Johnny, is something troubling you?" she said with concern.

"Ah... ah, no, I... I... ohm..."

"What's wrong, Johnny? Are you all right?"

"Yes, Liz, I just woke up. Pardon me if I seem a little groggy."

"Oh, don't be silly, John, there is no need to apologize. Well, aren't you going to kiss me?"

"Ah, ohm, of course, my sweet," I said with delayed response. As she moved in to kiss me with those long teeth, I felt a weakness and repulsion seize me. The last thing I remember was watching the ceiling fly away from me as I fell backward to the floor. When I came to, I figured it was all a dream. The huge grape leaf, my girlfriend's skinless body and face. For a second, I imagined my father's blindness and queer potions were also a figment of the deep, asleep subconscious mind. But I could picture him down there, sitting at the bench, mixing strange-colored liquids in a simmering beaker, surrounded by dozens of flickering candles, while his eyes slowly betrayed him.

As I sat up in my bed, my head began to pound and ache. Suddenly, my aching mind became infested with many ill images of some of the vivid nightmares I'd suffered through in the night. I then felt a large lump on the back of my head. Had I fallen? Was it a side effect from the new potion I had consumed? My head hurt too much to think, yet these questions continued to scratch around in my brain. As I looked out my window, I saw a crow dart across the glass. For a second, I thought I saw its bones, but I could not be sure. Although it flew past me swiftly, I was certain it was a crow, yet I was also sure I saw a lot of white among the black feathers. It almost looked striped.

What's happening to me? I thought. Was it the potion playing tricks on my mind? Or had I been knocked on the head? As I made my way slowly down the stairs, I became dizzy. My head was swirling as I grabbed for the rail. I made my way to the washroom to splash some water on my face. I jumped back as I looked in the mirror. I jerked my head away from it in terror. Slowly and reluctantly I turned back and gazed yet again into the looking glass. "The mirror never lies," I heard a woman's voice whisper in my head as I beheld the sight of my own skull and uncovered eyes staring back evilly at me. I could see the muscles and the veins within them also, stretched around the skull. On trembling legs, I beheld the cartilage of my nose and the dark cavity behind it. My teeth were long, for I could see their roots embedded in my jaw. So too could I see the blood traveling within my exposed veins. I held my hand before my face. I could not see my skin, yet I squirmed in horror as I watched the muscles flex around the bones as I opened and closed my palm.

I stared into the glass at the gruesome vision of my own skinless face till I could look no more. I blinked my eyes, I rubbed them, yet the image did not change. *What was in that potion?* I asked myself. *There must be some hallucinogenic drug which is having this wicked affect upon my eyes.* I looked at the table to my left and noticed that I could only see its surface. It was the same for the painted vase that stood atop it, yet the flowers it contained were oddly transparent. The leaves were more veiny than ever, and the petals were thin and bright like stained glass. Again I turned my gaze to the mirror. My full round white eyes stared back at me eerily. I moaned aloud as I turned away.

As I walked down the stairs toward the wine cellar, I thought of Elizabeth. It wasn't a nightmare after all. I cringed at the thought of seeing her that way again. Hell, I couldn't stomach looking at myself without skin. The horrible elixir had worked after all. What a pity it worked so well. My father had, without a doubt, stumbled onto something. Why had I let him experiment on me so? My vision was perfect. It needed no improving, yet that wretched juice did exactly that. It amplified my already perfect sight beyond even my father's wildest expectations. And now I was the sufferer of his success.

I banged on the thick wooden door with the wrath of a man betrayed. "Father, I must see you!" I yelled. And see him I did, indeed more then I'd ever wished to. I heard a chain clanging. He squeezed through the jamb and the door, which he opened just enough to squeeze out, and he kept it closed enough as to not make it possible for me to see in. Although I knew it was the man who called me son for twenty-five years, it gave me an awful chill when I saw the bones of his hand wrap round the edge of the door like a creeping spider and his bulbous, piercing eyes turn themselves on me from the sockets in his naked skull. His long teeth chomped like dreadful fangs as he spoke. With his wild silver hair waving about, he looked like some demon spawn.

"John, are you all right?"

I gasped before I answered. "No, I'm not right at all. What have you done to me?" I sneered.

"What do you mean, son? Tell me how you feel," he answered with concern.

"I can't begin to describe how I feel. Mortified, to say the least, but it's not how I feel, it's how I see. How I see now."

"Tell me," he said with great interest. "Tell me what you see!"

"I'll tell you what I can't see!" I said in anger.

"Son, your vision, is it blurry? Did the potion not work?" he said with more concern than ever. But I could see it in his uncovered eyes that his concern was more for his own fate. It was almost as if I could read his mind. Hell, I could see his brain. "Oh it works all right. I'd say too well," I responded condescendingly. "And it's not only what I see but also what I cannot see."

"Explain yourself, John."

"I can't see your skin!" I said slowly, with much conviction. "I can't see mine. I can't see Elizabeth's soft, pale skin, yet I can see her bones! I have seen her red, slimy muscles laden with her veins, and I've even seen the blood that flows within them!"

"Ah, ah, glory be! Ha, ha, ha! Son, do you know what this means? All my hard work and dedication has finally paid off. And what a success my elixir has turned out to be after all. I can restore my vision. I can wake dead eyes and make them work! I can give sight to the blind! Ha, ha, ha! And think of all the money to be made. A fortune, and some of it is yours."

"Money is no concern of mine right now. I'd give all the money in the world to look upon it the way I did before. Do you have any idea what it's like to look at your beautiful lover from the inside out? Can you stop thinking about yourself for a second and try to imagine how I feel?"

"Forgive me, son, perhaps I've gotten caught up in the excitement of my sudden success."

"Success! You call this success? I call this deplorable, maddening. I call this the infliction of a disgusting new torment. You have turned me into a misfit, a freak!"

"Wait a minute, son, don't get hasty. I'll fix this condition of yours. Somehow we'll get you back to normal."

"Normal," I repeated like a child learning to say a new word while pondering its meaning. "Yes, normal would be nice."

For the next two weeks, my father worked feverishly in the makeshift laboratory, trying to find a way to reverse my wretched condition, while he took small doses of the potion that had poisoned my vision. He was careful not to take too much, for he was just as horrified of becoming like me as he was of going blind. He figured that since I had perfect vision to start with and he had given me such a heavy dose of that vile demon drink that his vision would be restored normally if he took it in small amounts, seeing as how he was almost completely blind. I did not speak with him the whole time for he vowed he would not leave the wine cellar until he had an antidote worthy of testing. Great, I thought, more experimenting.

The next few weeks were the most horrible, agonizing period of my life. I spent my time locked away in my chamber night and day. I told that skeleton maid of ours that I would see no visitors until further notice. My stomach ached when I thought of what Elizabeth was thinking. I sent word to her that I was ill. I hated to be away from her for so long, but I could not bear to see her like that.

The floor sparkled by day and glistened eerily by night for I had shattered my mirrors in a fit of rage. Oh, how the moonlight made them twinkle. Like strange stars in a lonely unknown region of deep black space. Many lonely, empty nights I sat up in my bed and fancied I was afloat on a meteor in that forgotten, barren galaxy. I was slipping further away from reality with every horrible night. And there wasn't much solace in the day, for they were equally as lonely and deplorable. And although I spared myself the madness of gazing at anyone, my condition could not be denied or forgotten, for there were always the birds. The skeletal animals and bony, beady-eyed birds. They hopped and swooped and flapped about with mocking conviction. Even if I ever gained my normal vision, I fear I'd never look at them the same way. The huge willow outside my window had been infested with crows lately. It was almost as if they knew I couldn't bear to view them. Day after dreary day there were more of them in the tree. The limbs and leaves were black with their wings and shadows. The hollow white bones made freakish patterns among the thick clusters of the birds of death. I had always thought the cawing was obnoxious and slightly loathsome, yet now their odd silence seemed much more dreadful. Perhaps it was the way they looked at me. Perhaps I was losing my mind.

One morning, there came a knock at my door. "Who is it?" I asked.

"Open up, John," spoke the familiar voice of my father. There was joy in his tone. His long-toothed grin was enormous. But then again, they all seemed to have that same sickly smile. Like the smile of a madman whose intentions you couldn't quite guess, still you knew better than to trust. To see those uncovered teeth grinning their permanent, sinister grin was too much to bear or describe. In his gory hand he held a beaker full of bright-green liquid. "Try this, son, I'm confident it will reverse the effects and bring your vision back to normal." The last thing I wanted was to be experimented on further, but at this point, I was desperate enough to try anything. After all, he was my father. He meant me no harm. When I was done drinking, he told me that his sight had been returned. And he told me how appreciative he was for all that I had done for him. He was overwhelmed with happiness, and still I detected in his manner that he was sorry about what he had put me through. The sight of him was so grisly that I had to remind myself that he was human, that he was indeed my father, and that he was trying to help me. It was then I regained faith in him. "Go to sleep, son," he said. "I will visit you in the morning." Soon after he left, I became groggy. The room began to spin, and I collapsed on the bed.

When I woke up, my head was heavy. My throat was scratchy and dry. And as I began to pull the blanket past my legs, I became overwhelmed with relief and joy for I realized that I was able to see the skin on my hands and legs. I saw not the veiny muscle tissue or the bones, only the skin with its wrinkles and prints. I was excited and happy beyond belief. The sudden inheritance of an unexpected fortune could not bring me near as much pleasure. I turned my hand slowly before my eyes as a prospector might do with a large gold nugget 'neath the strong noon sun. I praised the gods aloud then and thanked them for blessing me with the eyes I once had. Then I got dressed so I could go down to thank my father. Suddenly there was a knock at my door. "Who is it?"

"It's Mary, sir. Elizabeth is here to see you."

I finished dressing and made my way down to the den. I was excited to see my sweet Liz again the way I had known her. The faint freckles on her pale skin. Her soft, rosy cheeks, her tiny nose, and her full, sweet lips. How I longed to feast my once-burdened eyes on her beauty again.

As I walked through the archway into the den, my poor eyes were once again splattered with the horrific vision of a waking nightmare. For my lovely Elizabeth stood in the center of the room, gazing back at me with those huge peeled-back, bloodshot eyes. A horrendous grimace stretched across her bony jaw. Her long teeth, roots and all, glimmered menacingly in the morning sun. Her branch-like veins were pulsing within her slimy red muscles. "I just had to see you, Johnny. Are you all right?"

"No, I'm not, Liz, I'm very sick and extremely contagious. I'll send for you when I'm better. Now you must go," I said with haste.

"I don't care if you're contagious. I want to see you," she said pleadingly.

"No!" I responded louder and more sternly. "You must leave now!"

"Johnny, please, I need to be with you. Tell me what's wrong with you."

"I can't say now, Liz, just trust me. I'll be okay, just go now!" But she did not obey my wishes. Instead she moved in toward me with her arms outstretched as her bony hands reached out for my face. "Touch me, Johnny. I don't care if I catch it, touch me," she pleaded. But I couldn't bear to touch her in my condition. The vision was simply too ghastly, so I took a step backward. "Touch me and I'll go, Johnny. Hold me!" she begged.

"No!" I yelled. "You'll go now. Mary!" Within a moment, Mary entered the room. "Mary, kindly escort Elizabeth outside, and do not let her in again until I give word," I barked at the nervous servant. I told her I loved her as she was shoved out the door, and I became filled with anger and hopelessness as I heard it shut.

I banged on the thick wooden door of the taboo wine cellar. I was furious with the madman who lurked behind it in secrecy. Soon it began to crack open, and my father began again to squeeze sideways through the opening. But I mashed my hand into his face and pushed my way into the cellar. Caught by surprise, the old man gained his balance and quickly pushed the door shut and locked it. Putting the key back in his pocket, he said, "What's the matter with you, John? How dare you push your way in here, I told you—"

I cut him off and began yelling back. His bulbous eyes lit up with shock as I had never spoken to him that way. "That goddamn antidote is a failure! It only works for a few moments, and then it's back to this hellish sight. You said you'd fix it, but apparently, you couldn't care enough to put more than a fraction of the work into a proper antidote than you have into your sick elixir you made to fix your sight. You made me a guinea pig! A freak! Your vision is back to normal. Ha! Normal! You said you'd make me normal again. You lied!" He tried to respond, to get a word in, but I did not give him the chance. And all the time I yelled at him, my face was right up in his, and his face showed fear, and so did his body language, for he was taking slow backward steps away from me. Slowly his trembling legs fumbled up the small stairs onto a platform. I went on stepping toward him as I yelled. The gruesome-looking workers went on toiling, oblivious. "You don't know what you've subjected me to. You haven't the slightest idea what it's like to see what I see. To feel the nonstop torture and morbidity of looking through my eyes! You've become a madman down here in this dungeon. And now you're infecting me with a far worse form of madness. You were willing to sacrifice your own son for the sake of your sight. I hope you're happy, Tilden Holt!" I yelled and finally stopped to catch my breath. He was still walking backward across the platform.

"You have no idea what I've sacrificed," he said in a low and humble voice. There was regret in his tone. And as he said it, he took a last step backward over the edge of the grape-smashing trough. It was that very instant that my blind rage had subsided like a dark cloud sliding back off the sun. For I noticed as he fell backward into the pit of mutilated grapes that I could not see his bones or his muscle. I could only see his skin. I then checked my hands, and I could no longer see through my skin. My mind began swirling with confusion. Was the horrible vision fading in and out like the sunlight behind drifting clouds? I gazed back at the winemakers. They were bony and veiny. My father's head resurfaced from the thick knee-deep mashed grapes only to be pushed back under by the feet of the ghastly looking workers, who went about their business as if nothing unusual had happened. I stood at the edge of the platform, frozen in confusion. My head was a battlefield of conflicting emotions. I stood and watched as he struggled several times to keep his head above the mash. Every time he opened his purple mouth to call for help or to gasp for breath, it became filled with crushed grapes.

The workers continued to emotionlessly stomp his body and face with their bare, bony feet. I stood and watched as if it were all a dream. I made no attempt to save him. In that moment, I could not move, nor could I think. I was numb and gripped with the confusion of madness. I could not believe any of this was happening. Finally, my father failed to resurface. When I realized he was dead, I snapped out of the daze that held me.

The next thing I knew, I was standing at his workbench. It was covered in mounds of melted wax and loose papers. There were measuring spoons and glass vials. Beakers full of strangely colored liquids and all kinds of queer instruments that I could not name or decipher their use were strewn about the bench, surrounded by candles. A notebook then caught my eye. I opened it and sat at the table. Expecting to see it full of scribbling and equations like those scratched on the loose pages all around, I was surprised to find it was my father's journal. I began thumbing through the pages. Every entry captured the maddening process of experimentation with his many formulas. I kept flipping through the pages till I saw the Africa entry. This was where I began reading thoroughly.

January 15, 1782, Within the jungle of Zimbabwe, Africa

I have been experimenting with many unknown herbs, plants, and berries. But today, a beautiful pinkish-purple flower caught my eye. I have done many tests on it. It has a strong concentration of a substance which appears to have visual enhancement qualities. I have been warned by our guide not to tamper with the flower. He told me that the natives use the extract of this flower, which he called datura, to bring people back from the dead. He said it opens the eyes of the dead, and with the aid of voodoo rituals, it can give them new life. Of course, I laughed at his absurd superstitions. This flower is without a doubt the answer to my prayers. I have faith that this beautiful flower will reverse the effects of blindness.

February 9, 1782

The flower has a strange effect on me. It is a powerful hallucinogenic drug, yet I feel it can be used wisely in small amounts. No wonder the African natives believe in all that voodoo nonsense! I discontinued the ingestion of the extract for now. Today I will administer my new concoction unknowingly on one of my workers. This way, I can keep a clear head and keep track of progress and effects through experimentation.

February 20 1782

Bradford, my worker, has been stricken with a strange illness. The effects of the drug administered were nothing less than dreadful. He seems to have slipped into a permanent hypnotic state. I have not heard him respond vocally in days. His eyes have become glazed over with a disturbing emptiness. However, he is quite able to function otherwise. He goes about his work as if nothing has changed. I will try and find a new solution.

March 10, 1782

Bad day for medical science! Bradford, although shockingly not bedridden, has developed an unusual condition. His flesh has turned an awful ash color. His grisly skin is dried and extremely course. It is cracked and withered like the floor of a desert. It is flaking off his body! However, he still goes about working, completely oblivious to his condition. I will experiment on James in the morning.

It was then that I was filled with a new horror that made me writhe in its vile clutches. It was then my mind began to piece the morbid puzzle together. My father's last words then echoed in my brain with a frightening new understanding. All of a sudden, I felt the heavy presence of the silent, dreadful hoard that moped and lurked about hideously behind me. Mindlessly stomping the grapes with their bones and veiny muscles. Brewing the wine in the dank, shadowed cellar. Then too did I think of the other poor souls working unknown behind the immense wall of the vineyard.

I turned my poor eyes to the thick, heavy door and its huge lock and chain, and I felt the weight and the burden of doom hanging over me like a thunder cloud. The wretched mass of skinless freaks toiled and slaved behind me without emotion in dreadful silence. Then, for a second, I stopped thinking about my own dread. And once again, my hopelessness and horror was intensified. For a sickly vision flashed in my tormented mind. It was a vision of Elizabeth.

THE SHELTER OF THORNS

It was no accident that I came into temporary possession of the book, with its dark, mad ramblings and its hideous illustrations. Normally, I would never dream of invading someone's privacy by sneaking into their bedroom and searching through their things the way I had done to my tenant Harold Jennings. But my curiosity eventually consumed my guilt, and I found myself going through the papers of his desk the day he left for Charleston to attend his sister's funeral.

Harold was a mason by profession; he was no writer. In fact, he didn't even enjoy reading. He did not do well in school, and so it was that he ended up with the back-breaking job of hauling and stacking stones. It wasn't long after I noticed many changes in his actions and personality that I came to realize that he was writing a book. He would not tell me of the subject matter, nor would he release a single hint or clue no matter how much I pried. Harold was usually in bed by eight or nine, yet now he stayed up late every night, sketching and scribbling in his notebook by candlelight.

I found it more than strange that such a man who was in his midforties and had never so much as sat down to write a letter would suddenly become obsessed with the brain-draining task of writing a book. It was especially odd too that Harold, a man who never displayed any interest in art and never seemed to have much of an imagination, would suddenly be writing such an impressive work of fiction and illustrating it so wonderfully. Perhaps I would not deem it so queer had he been writing a do-it-yourself book on masonry and sketching crude pictures of stone walls.

His book was by no means a keen work of literature in the classic sense, yet it was his choice of words and his wild and detailed display of imagination that impressed me so. I found myself captivated in the clutches of his writing. It was almost as if I were reading Poe yet without the use of long, intelligent words, and it was of completely original design. The effect it had on my spirit was shadowy and chill. It was the stuff of which nightmares are made of. The kind you wish not to remember yet you can't forget. And all the while, those dreadful images and fearsome words were covered in only a thin layer of dust, waiting for a weak breeze to be recalled. I could feel those words worming their way under my skin, as were the claws of those horrid beasts Harold had sketched. So too could I feel their yellow eyes upon me as I read. I wished I'd never snuck into his room and found that accursed book.

That very night, my mind was invaded by the disgusting images of those unmentionable beasts Harold drew. So too was my sleeping mind disturbed by not only his words but by full passages of his book. Word for word, line after line, as if someone were reading it to me as I slept. Each sentence felt like the poke of a needle or the sting of a whip. Each morbid paragraph bit and bruised my soul like some strange torture as I writhed in my bed.

As the narrator spoke from the darkness with a voice deep and low:

> Behold! The horrors of the night! No living eye but mine has seen. Save for their victims, red with blood, whose dry bones have been picked clean. They lie, scattered deep beneath the dirt and the tall grass green. Beware the ancient, hungry, nocturnal ones, no man has ever dared to ween. Well hidden are they from human sight, who sleep by day and rule the night. Much like piranhas, they gnaw and bite. They prowl in the shadows cast by the moonlight. Human meat

> they crave to taste. Never a speck do they save or waste. The eyes, the guts, the feet, the face. Wise are they who leave no trace. For the scalps and clothes and teeth and bones are buried deep beneath their homes. It is they and not the wind that moans. They hunt and breed and thrive unknown. Down in the burrows so dank and deep, where the sun's rays cannot penetrate, they do sleep. The burrow holes surrounded by thorns and thistle, this secret they keep. Out from the blackness of prickly bushes they creep!

It must have gone on for most of the night, for when I woke sometime before dawn, I did not feel rested. My body was, but my mind was sore and disturbed. I felt odd, almost ill, as if I had lived through a traumatic experience. Almost as one might feel while walking through a battlefield in the aftermath of warfare, counting smoking corpses. The morbidity of those vile images and the dark, gruesome words left their mark on me. It was hours before I felt normal again, and even then, my mind kept slipping back to those dreadful sketches throughout the day no matter how I tried to forget them.

That night, again I would not find rest. Again the deep, low voice filled my mind as I dreamed. Once more, the nightmare images of those shadowy beasts scratched about in my brain. Their fangs and teeth gleamed beneath the moonlight. Their catlike eyes pierced at me through the blackness that was enveloping my mind and my soul. And the voice said to me:

> Some of them have eyes almost like a cat, yet their irises, as well as their pupils, are vertically slanted, and they are mostly yellow or red in color. They display vague canine features, mostly in the jaws and pointy ears. But there seems to be many different species of them. Some have scales and reptilelike qualities, while others are covered with fur. Some are laden with long, sharp quills,

while many of their muscular bodies are bare. Others have long, thick spikes running down the length of their backs. Some of them are green, some are brown, while others are black or gray. Some have horns, some of which are short and straight, while others are long and curled like a ram's. Some have tails, while most do not. Some have long fangs, and some double rows of teeth. Most are the size of a fat raccoon, while some are slightly larger. Some have paws like a bear, yet others have hands much like a human, all of which bear long sharp claws. Some crawl like wolves, yet others walk effortlessly on their hind legs. Their feet are all unlike any known animal. Most have only three toes, and some have long clawlike appendages pointing backward off their heels. This is why they seem to be afraid of muddy areas and do not trod on them. In fact, they have little fear. They stay away from mud and soft ground so as not to leave a print. They are keen enough to keep themselves unknown to humans, who could cause a major threat to their existence. But exist they do, as they have for eons. For all these things I have seen.

The first time I saw them, I stood frozen in awe and fear for a few minutes before they noticed me. I turned and ran faster then I'd ever run in my life, but they were soon growling at my heels. I thought for sure they had me, for I was still quite a distance from civilization. I felt something scraping at my leg as I ran, which almost tripped me. Over a brook I leaped, and I heard them splashing behind me as I fled. Then I found myself slipping and sliding, almost drunkenly, through a muddy clearing. I thought they'd have me without fail then, as my heart and hope sank like my shoes in the sucking mud. Once I slipped in the mud and expected to feel them pouncing on me, but when I looked back, they were gone. It was then I assumed foolishly that they must have had a superstitious fear of mud. Perhaps one of them had been consumed by it once, but now I knew better. And it struck me with fear all the more to discover how smart these beasts really are.

No wall, no matter how thick or tall, can keep them away. This I learned the hard way. I was able to watch them and study their behavior for a short time. I came up with the idea to build a twenty-five-foot-tall stone tower that would protect me from their claws and jaws, while I could observe them safely through slits in the walls. Of course, I had constructed the tower by the light of day, and I made sure I was out of the woods long before sundown. I would never walk through the wilderness at night again, knowing what I knew now. Hell, I was not sure I'd ever again enter the woods even by day.

When the tower was finally completed and I felt safe enough, I spent my first night locked in and taking notes. The outer surface of the cylinder I purposely made smooth so as to make climbing impossible. The spaces between the stones were filled flush to their edges with mortar, leaving no possible foothold. The ground around the tower was muddy well before its completion due to my feet killing the grass and softening the dirt as I worked. This, I thought, would be extra protection.

For the most part, they lurked about unseen, and even when I could see them, it was blurry at best. But the moonlight did reveal them quite clearly from time to time. And when I could not see their bodies, the eyes always gave them away. I studied them successfully for four nights. But on the fifth night, everything changed. It was an uneventful evening for the first few hours. It was quite creepy how I saw not a single one of them for quite some time. Then the silence was disturbed by the churning of the ground beneath my feet. I jumped back and looked down. The dirt was moving and caving in. I knew then that they had tunneled under the tower walls to get in at me. Neither the ring of mud nor the thick high tower of stone could protect me.

My mind began to race. How could I stop them now? I had become trapped in the very structure I worked so hard building for my protection. My only hope was to reach higher ground. Luckily, I made the tower quite narrow as to save time building. I pressed my back and hands against one side and my feet against the other. Slowly I began to push my way little by little up the shaft. I was maybe five feet up when they broke through and began jumping and clawing at my back. A few times I felt myself slipping, but I pressed even harder, and somehow I kept my position. Halfway up, my limbs grew weak and numb. I don't know where I found the strength, but I inched my way slowly up to the top. Perhaps the sniveling and growling that echoed from below provided incentive to endure the pain and the difficulty of the situation.

When I neared the top, I was at a loss as of what to do to make my way over the edge. I knew I could not stay in that position for long. My limbs were weak and shaking. It was then my imagination found a possible solution. I wasn't sure it would work, but I had to try something, for I was about to fall into the horde of hungry beasts below. I pushed with my feet up and away from the wall and somehow hooked my forearms around the edge of the tower. My legs and back slammed against the other side, and I hung there by the inside of my elbows for a time. Finally, I summoned a last bit of strength to twist my body around with my right foot while unhooking my right arm. As I did so, my left arm was ground into the edge of the tower as it held most of my weight. But the pain was numb, and somehow I managed to grab and kick and pull myself halfway over the edge, where I lay on my belly and rested.

But my rest was short-lived, for I heard their claws scratching against the stone as they were climbing the inner walls. The mortar joints provided enough of a foothold for their claws to grab. Now I felt the hopelessness of doom as they drew closer. Their eyes were bright as they snapped at me. All I could do was to kick and swing at them. One by one I knocked them off as they reached me. Some fell no sooner than they had slashed me with their claws. After a while, they retreated back into the hole they had dug. I lay there on the top edge of the tower, exhausted and cold, trying to stop the bleeding. It was the longest night of my life, but I made it through to the morning. That night brought an end to my observations, but I had already gathered enough information to write this book.

These tales within a story tormented me as I slept. Night after night, the narrator inflicted his horrors upon me. Not once did I wake during the ordeal. I was held firmly 'neath the speakers influence. The words captivated as well as tortured me, as if I were under a spell. And every morning when I woke, it was the same. I felt tortured and disturbed, even violated. I was not losing sleep, yet I was losing rest. I found no peace in my bed or my dreams for close to a week. I was beginning to feel like I was losing my mind, losing myself. I wished I'd never opened that book. I wondered if I'd ever be the same. *It's only a work of fiction,* I told myself repeatedly. A well-told story written by a stone stacker. "Get a hold of yourself," I said aloud in the mirror. Yet as tired as I was, I dreaded lying down again.

I could not wait for Harold to return from his trip. I had so many questions, most of which I could not ask, for he would know I snuck in his chamber and read his book. But there were a few I could ask him that might bring peace to my mind. On the day of his expected return, I made it a point to stay home and wait for him; however, he did not show. That night, the wind came out of nowhere. The chimes that hung from the apple tree were dumb, yet it howled and moaned. And without fail, the faceless voice spoke over me and painted grotesque pictures on the cave walls of my dreaming mind. *Everything has a purpose,* the narrator began.

> The little things we deem useless, even absurd, all have a meaning and a job to do. Mosquitoes, for example, why were they created? What purpose does this disease-infested bug serve the planet earth? Why does it extract blood from its victims only to use it to breed and bring more vampire bugs into the world? Perhaps they are for population control. Maybe these beasts were created with the same purpose in mind. Perhaps without them, rabbits, raccoons, deer, and other animals would be as rampant as gnats. They are not evil in my eyes, the more I look upon them. They are no more evil than a coyote ripping a hare apart. They just are.
>
> Thorny plants and bushes, poison ivy, these things too have been seen as useless and only

menacing. And true, they are to us, but what about them. I believe they were designed with the things of the night in mind. For they specifically dig their access tunnels in the middle of the thorny bushes, mainly the ones which are intertwined with poison ivy. Again, they are smart enough to do this. Is it just the instinct the creator installed in them, or was it their own idea? Either way, these creatures have thinking minds. They know how to survive and endure, even outwit humans, as they did to me in the tower. As I sleep, I dream of them tunneling upward beneath the house, scratching their way through the dirt cellar floor to get in at me. As I will never traverse the woods again, I fear I will never again sleep soundly. For they infest and pollute my dreams. And the nightmares do not end come the dawn. In fact, they only climb to a new level, for unlike most nightmares, which are fantasy, you find relief in such a revelation upon waking. But each morning I find no solace, only the continuation of ill feelings of terror and doom. I cannot deny in dreams or by day the things I have seen that lurk in the night.

By now I must have heard in my head, each page three or more times in the night. It was never in order, yet I was sure not a single page was left unnarrated by the voice in my dreams. I could not take any more of the madness. The lack of rest and peaceful sleep was taking its toll on my health. I had to speak with Harold. Maybe then the nightmares would leave me be. But on the second day, he still did not return. But every night, the deep voice did fill my tired mind with its madness.

It had been a week now since Harold was expected back, yet there was no sign of him or a letter of explanation from him or his family. I had developed a habit of only sleeping every other night.

Only when I could no longer fight the urge to sleep would I lay my tortured head down. Every night I relived the same familiar nightmares, and each day that followed, I found only temporary escape. I was still sane enough to realize that I was losing my mind.

One day I thought of retrieving that evil book from his desk and destroying it by fire. It was a childish and superstitious thought, but I hoped it would work. Maybe it was all a psychological problem that demanded a simple psychological solution. If it would make me forget the book and all its morbid contents, I was willing to try anything. Anyway, I knew it couldn't hurt. With the book under my arm, I set out into the woods to burn it. At first I was going to rid myself of it in my fireplace, but I felt, as I held the match in my fingers, that it must be taken out of my house as soon as possible. I did not want so much as its ashes lying upon my hearth. So I walked through the trees and the brush with the source of all my anguish in the pit of my arm. The sun was bright and the air was warm, and for the first time in weeks, I felt rejuvenated. I felt confident that the destruction of the book would restore peace to my life. Even if it was only a symbolic gesture, I thought it might work. I had nothing to lose. Either way, I knew I'd feel better knowing that the book was destroyed.

When I had reached the place I had intended to do the deed, something suddenly compelled me to keep on walking. And so, without much thought, I pressed on. I wandered through parts of the woods I'd seldom explored since I was a youth and kept on walking. For the first time in weeks, my mind was completely empty. It was a feeling I'd longed for all that time yet could not have. Perhaps that was why I kept on walking without a care.

Suddenly, it occurred to me that I should go no farther. I was not past the point of familiar ground, yet if I kept walking, I might become lost. I decided to burn the book on the spot where I stood. I looked around for some stones to circle around the book as it burned when something caught my eye. Something of substantial mass, which was light gray in color and seemed out of place, was standing out between the trees. I began walking toward it with curiosity. As I got close to it, my mind struggled to understand it. I could only see parts of it among the leaves and branches. It wasn't until I was right up to it that my heart started throbbing, for I suddenly saw the whole structure as I stepped out into the clearing.

There it was, standing before me, so tall and so real. All at once it struck me like a lightning bolt. It was the smooth-faced stone tower that Harold had written about. I stood in its shadow dumbfounded with awe. I felt then a new kind of fear crawling over me like an army of spiders as I looked up at the structure. There were tiny slits all around the base at eye level, just as it was written in the book. None of which were large enough for a rifle or gun to poke through like in so many castles and forts, yet the slots were perfect for spying through. As I slowly circled around it, I began to search my mind for a logical answer. I found myself reaching out to touch it, as if I expected not to feel it on my open palm. As if I were going mad and seeing some sort of mirage. After all, I have been in a strange and disturbed state lately. Surely, with all the things I'd been subjected to, my mind and eyes were beginning to play tricks on me. But the stone was smooth and cold as my hand pressed upon it.

Surely Harold hadn't built it, I thought. *Yes, that's it! Harold didn't build it at all. He simply stumbled upon it and worked it into his story.* My pulse began to return to a normal rate as I thought of this rational explanation. But still, an eerie chill pervaded slowly through my tingling chest as I noticed the obvious youth of the tower. There were no vines or moss or any fungus crawling on it, and it also occurred to me that although it had been a few years since I had visited this part of the woods, I certainly had never noticed it before. As I pushed on the thick, crudely made door, it became clear that it was locked from the inside. Without realizing the ignorance and haste of my overwhelming sense of curiosity, seeing what was on the other side of that door became my new obsession. I was foolishly determined, the same way I was when I snuck around in Harold's desk. Soon I was beating on the thick door with a large stone, and the echoes of the commotion crashed up the shaft and rang out into the clear blue sky.

It was well over an hour before the door gave way to my relentless efforts. Its splintered edge finally swung in as I hurled the stone again at the same strategic spot. As the sunlight poured into the tower,

I stood before the open door and took slow, deep breaths, trying to calm my pulse. I was weary and soaked with perspiration. When I was relaxed enough and my thoughts were gathered, I went inside. I stepped into the center of the tower and slowly turned myself in a complete circle. It was cramped inside and quite empty. I looked above me. There was nothing secured to its curved walls, no stairway and no upper level, no bell hanging. No ceiling, only a circular cavity at its tip, which opened up into the sky above. It was a peculiar tower indeed, for it clearly did not serve any of the purposes that a normal tower would be constructed for.

It chilled my spirit again when I thought of the similarities of the structure I stood within and the tower in which Harold had written of. I looked down then as I recalled a passage from his story that involved the tower. It was a story that was told to me countless times in my twisted, flinching dreams. I examined the earth beneath my feet. Slowly and meticulously my eyes passed over it. It seemed undisturbed. The dirt was flat and hard. There was no evidence of the ground being dug or churned. This revelation brought me great relief as it went against a vital part of Harold's story. *I must be losing my mind,* I thought. I stood there, chuckling for a moment. Now I became all the more impressed with Harold's style of fictional writing. *Look at the effect it's had on me!* I thought. No story I'd ever read, no matter how disturbing or gripping, had ever left such an impression upon me. Oh, how it sucked the rest from my sleeping and molded my dreams into nightmares. And how I could not stop those words from infecting my days with their potent poisons. Once more I began laughing. Laughing with relief, with joyous tears streaming as I thought of how preposterous I had been. After all, I was never a man of superstition or gullibility. I'd always been of clear mind, rational and factual.

When I ceased laughing, I thought again of the book that lay on the ground within the tower. I pondered in a new light how influential it was. I felt quite confident that this new feeling of peace and relief, which was brought on by this new revelation, would put an end to my nightmares. I thought about how Harold hadn't returned in over two weeks. Perhaps he'd met some ill fate in South Carolina.

I thought of the overwhelming hold his writing had on me and wondered how other readers would respond. I thought of all the things I might obtain, both material and metaphysical. The admiration, glory, and perhaps wealth. Although I was no writer, if I could only come up with a climactic ending to his merely completed book, I could take all the credit and reap all the benefits of such a work of art as his. After all, Harold himself was no writer by profession. I decided not to burn the manuscript then, with this newfound peace and satisfaction I welcomed so eagerly. I reassured myself too that if the nightmares persisted, I could always burn the book. But the more I thought of its value and what it could bring me, it was the last thing I wished to do.

I took another look at the circle of blue sky that hovered dreamily above the opened peak of the tower before I started outside. To think, I almost burned what could bring me fortune and recognition! But all such warm thoughts were swiped from my head as I was tripped to the ground. My mind was a whirlpool of darkness and nightmare illusions as I felt a gripping around my ankle. The breath was forced from my lungs as my chest struck the ground; therefore my scream was unheard. I clawed at the earth as I groaned and flailed my free leg about. I kicked wildly and tried with all my strength to scamper away, yet I was held firmly by the foot. I felt a stinging pain pierce into my ankle as I tried in vain to crawl out of the tower. I was terrorized by the idea of twisting my head to look behind me. This time, my curiosity was not as strong as my will to escape with my life. I was too afraid to glimpse my captor. I clawed and scratched at the hard ground, trying to pull myself away from the thing that seized me, yet no matter how or what I tried, I could not move forward an inch.

I soon realized that I was moving in the opposite direction despite my efforts. Backward I was dragged along the ground that I mauled and pawed. I screamed with hopelessness as I watched the golden glow of the sun, which sparkled in the doorway, slipping farther away from me. Then my eyes fell on the stone that I had used to beat the door in. It was my only hope, I thought, as it was not far from reach. Still I thought about how I was unable to advance a single inch forward with all my strength. Again, I felt hopeless as I crawled and kicked, and still I was being dragged past it. Then I thought quickly; perhaps I could reach it after all for it was not ahead of me but to my side. I switched my efforts then from clawing at the ground to using my arms to push my body to one side. Somewhat like a crab, I scuttled sideways toward the stone while still being dragged backward. With a last, great effort, I reached the rock, and an overwhelming feeling of hope rekindled my spirit as I felt it in my hands.

Then I felt my legs sinking beneath the dirt as my arms embraced the stone. I had no time to think as I had no time to fear to look upon what I wished not to see. I twisted my body around till I was lying on my back with the stone nestled on my chest. I raised it high with both hands and prepared to smash it on whatever was pulling me down. But when I looked for my target, it wasn't there to be seen. I only caught a quick glimpse of a ghastly gray clawed hand before it disappeared with my legs up to my knees into the ground. As I was being pulled farther down, I let go of the stone and twisted myself around again till I lay on my chest. Once again, I clawed and mauled the ground in a last attempt to save myself. Now I was almost up to my waist in the hole, and as I screamed, I realized how deep in the woods I was, and I knew my cries of terror would be inaudible. One last object grasped my attention as I was being sucked into the earth, and I grabbed it without thought. I clenched that book in both hands as if I were holding the end of a rope.

Down I went into the hole, and the light dimmed rapidly as my head was pulled beneath the surface. At this point, I must have been too frightened to scream for I became as silent as the dirt as it slowly claimed me. Down I slid through a slanted, jagged tunnel. The darkness was thick and heavy, and the rocks tore at my flesh. Dirt was spraying in my mouth as I slid, and I struggled to breathe through my nostrils. Once my body came to rest with a thud as the tunnel curved, but soon I found myself being dragged again along a lesser pitch. Before I knew it, I was sliding down yet again while clawing at the earth as I descended.

When I opened my eyes, I saw not a thing. For a while, I tried to convince myself I was having yet another nightmare. And even when I knew I was not so lucky as to be lying in my bed, being tortured with macabre words and gruesome images, I still tried to convince myself that I was. I laid there for a while on the cold, damp earth and listened. There was nothing but silence. It was a silence so potent and vacant that it alone disturbed me. It was an utter lack of sound, the likes of which I'd never experienced before.

For a time unmeasured, I lay there, as still as a dead branch on the ground. Finally, I could no longer handle the suspense of my surroundings and my newfound situation. I sat up slowly and fumbled in my pocket for a match. As the tiny flame lit up a small area around me, my eyes struggled to focus. Slowly a white figure before me began to emerge and stand out against the blackness. It took a second match before I realized what was there, only a few feet in front of me. My eyes must have popped out of my head, and my mind began to swirl as I was face-to-face with a human skeleton. Before the match burned my fingers, a new realization struck me like a thunderbolt. For there, sitting upright at arm's length in front of me rested the bones of Harold Jennings! His remains were unmistakable, as his short black scalp was still intact, and atop it was perched the old brown top hat he always wore.

Once again enveloped in pure darkness, I sat and shivered. I had but a few matches left, and each one was precious. Besides, there was no need to look upon the skeleton again for I knew it was no doubt my former tenant Harold. I wished to get away from his bones. I could feel his presence, his empty black eye sockets staring back at me. But where to crawl away, I knew not. Perhaps it would prove to be a worse place, and so I sat still and silent. I had noticed that the ceiling was quite low, but as for the direction out or away, I saw no clue in the tiny flickering flame. I dared not to move. The only sound was the faint wheezing of my own breath. I was surprised I could not hear my heartbeat, for the air was so quiet, and it was still thumping rapidly.

Suddenly, a voice pierced the silence. It was a human voice that tore at my soul. A voice that brought with it no hope, only damnation. A voice that I was all too familiar with. And then I recognized the voice although it did sound out of its normal tone. It was a louder, deeper pitch of a known voice purposely disguised. It was the voice of my former tenant Harold!

My manipulated mind, sore and deprived of reality, searched for a sane explanation. The lurking, shadowy images of those wretched beasts began to infest my mind as I listened, against my will, again to those eldritch words. But this time, it horrified me all the more as I realized again that I was awake. And the voice spoke unto me in a tone deep and low, stern and slow: "Behold! The horrors of the night, which no living eye but mine has seen. Save for their victims, red with blood, whose dry bones have been picked clean. Lie scattered deep beneath the dirt and the tall grass green. Beware the ancient, hungry, nocturnal ones, no man has ever dared to ween…"

As the dead man's words echoed in the vacant cavity that was once my mind, they tore through me like a violent storm, devastating everything that was once solid and rational. And as I cringed with the sharp lash of each word, a disturbance of the darkness became apparent to me. In the time it took for my straining eyes to focus on one pair of the tiny gleaming orbs, several more had begun to appear. Suddenly, there were dozens of them then hundreds of glowing eyes, some yellow, some fire red, all peering at me through the nothingness. The consuming eyes were like that of a cat, save for the fact that their retinas, as well as their pupils, were slanted. And still, yet more appeared as the dreadful voice continued: "For the scalps, and clothes, and teeth, and bones are buried deep beneath their homes. It is they and not the wind that moans."

KILLERPILLAR

Finally, we reached the top of the cliff, and we pulled ourselves over the grassy ledge. The land atop was flat and choked with thorny brush and thick vines that hung from evergreen trees. Tall weeds and reeds swayed dreamily in the breeze. We sat down on the edge to catch our breath and take in the view. And what a view it was! The Atlantic Ocean stretched out forever below and before us and sparkled fantastically in the late-afternoon sun. Far off to the right, we could see tiny bumps on the landscape, which we knew to be houses. The roads stretched through the town like brown veins, and on them we could see a few carriages inching along them like beetles. We were far and high above our homes, well over a hundred and fifty feet high!

The face of the cliff was vertically flat. It was an enormous challenge to behold this view, and we sat, hanging our feet, proudly grinning while we rested our muscles. There weren't many footholds or protrusions to get a grip on, and any footholds we found at all were very narrow. Seldom came the opportunity to feel rock beneath our heels when our toes were facing the cliff, and so we had to either climb on the tips of our toes or with our feet turned sideways. When I was halfway up, I came across the thinnest foothold of all. I did not think I would make it then, but when you're that high, there's no turning back. For as impossible as it seemed to reach the top, I thought about going down, and that to me presented an even greater challenge. There were quite a few loose rocks that tumbled 'neath our feet, and there were a few close calls, but somehow we made it.

We rested for over a half hour, till Jimmy finally spoke. "Hey, let's go check this place out." As we waded through the dense vegetation, a potent, barren loneliness dampened my spirit even though I was beside two of my closest friends. As excited as we were to be up there, I noticed that none of us was saying much, and when we did speak, our tones were low. We wandered aimlessly, dreamily through the waving green growth of the plateau. Once I fancied I was a deep-sea diver walking along the ocean floor amid a forest of dancing sea grass. My head felt light and dizzy, and my ears were ringing. It certainly felt as if I were underwater. Everything felt strange and new, and perhaps it was a fitting feeling, for we were exploring an unfamiliar land, yet my emotions extended beyond the excitement of discovery. I felt wary in my steps, and with each step I took, I felt all the more disconnected from my friends although they walked close beside me. I felt torn away from the little ants I knew, which toiled and scratched about down in the village. I felt as though we were trespassing on soil that should not be tread upon. I wondered if my dumbfounded friends felt the same.

At long last, Jimmy spoke. "Look over there!" We followed the direction of his shaky forefinger until our eyes fell on a stone wall whose surface was barely distinguishable among the vines and shrubs. As we drew closer, we could see that the wall was rectangular in design, about ten by fifteen feet and four feet high. We parted the thick, thorny brush and bled a bit to get to it, but we soon found ourselves peering in baffled awe over its edge at what it embraced. For what was within the confines of the rectangle-shaped wall seized, stunned, and amazed us all. The area was filled with weed-choked earth three quarters of the way up. There were strategically placed stones that resembled the markers of graves, and on some of the moss-covered stones were perched small weathered gargoyles, their stone teeth frozen in a timeless grimace. Their dusty wings spread and ready to leap into flight. Their claws curled in a pose of power and threat. Their empty eyes watching all who may stare back. Upon the center marker sat a stone sea turtle faced curiously in the opposite direction of the ocean.

"What on earth is this?" I uttered. "What could it all mean?" Of course, no one had an answer to my questions, and the only way Jimmy could respond was to express his desire to possess at least one of the gargoyles. "Mine!" he shouted with glee and fascination. "They're mine, I saw them first."

"There's five of them, Jimmy," interrupted Dave. "Don't be so damn greedy. You can have three, and that leaves only one a piece for me and Sully."

"All right, Davey," Jim agreed. "I get three, and I get first pick."

"Wait, fellas," I said reluctantly. "I don't even want one. This place looks like a cemetery, and it's not wise to take things from dead folk."

"Shut up, Sully, you crybaby, you're just like my grandfather, so superstitious he's scared of his own shadow. If you don't want one, that leaves four for me and one for Davey. Have it your way. If Davey boy feels lucky enough, I'll let him have the stupid turtle if he's lame enough to want it. Besides, this doesn't look like any cemetery I've ever seen, Sull."

"I know it doesn't look like a regular cemetery, Jim, but I tell you, I have a feeling it is. Just look at those square-cut stones, they look like the headstones they give poor folk who can't afford a real head slab with their name carved on it."

"Yeah, Sull, they kinda do, but that don't mean they are headstones just because they look like them, and even if they were, who's gonna stop me, a pile of muddy old bones?"

"It's not right, Jim, and you know it. If this is a cemetery—"

"Shut your whining trap, Sull, and let me take a few souvenirs. We'd better stop wasting time arguing. Can't you see the sun's getting low?"

Now I became less concerned with Jimmy's actions and what was moral or what this place really was built for. I was now concerned with the low-hanging sun. It seemed we had spent more time than expected climbing the cliff and even more time exploring it. I wanted to get back down to the beach before dark more than anything I'd ever wanted before. Jimmy jumped the wall and began looking over the gargoyles, deciding which ones he liked the best. Dave jumped in with him, and I watched him staring silently down over the turtle. He picked it up slowly with swollen eyes and began stroking it as if it were made of gold. By this time, Jimmy had three gargoyles cradled in his arms. A sinister smile stretched crookedly across his face. His eyes were glazed over and lit up with an insane fire. I had never seen that look in his eyes before, nor had I ever seen it on anyone's face. It disturbed me greatly.

But suddenly, the look on my friend's face was my least concern. For all at once, my eyes beheld the figure of a wrinkle-faced old woman standing behind Jimmy, who had his back to her. Her ugliness was potent, and she had a fire of her own in her dull gray eyes. It was nothing like the look on his face; she was clearly enraged. Her long white hair hung down and disappeared behind the wall. Before I could yell, I saw her raise her arm above her head in a swift motion. Her hand, which was hidden behind the wall before, now revealed a long, wide knife that gleamed 'neath the setting sun. The muscles in her jaded face tightened and curled up into a sadistic smile, exposing her gleaming teeth. "Jimmy!" I shouted with panic. All I could do, besides shout his name, was to show him the mask of horror that must have manipulated my face and point at the woman behind him. Upon shouting his name, I became mute. I tried to warn him further vocally, but the terror seized my ability to speak. As Jimmy turned around, his head jerked backward, and he shrieked like a threatened animal. Still the woman held the knife above his head, ready to bring it down swiftly. He was so close to her if she were to speak, he would feel her breath brush across his face. Finally, Jimmy made his move. He took a few desperate steps backward quickly and awkwardly, and he tripped over a stone. He fell swiftly, backward, expelling a horrified groan as he dropped to the ground, smashing his head on another stone marker. The gargoyles rolled across his face as his hair turned red. His eyes were vacant and staring at the darkening sky. His blood poured out rapidly, staining the stone and pooling around it. There was no doubt; Jimmy was dead.

Hearing the commotion, Dave reluctantly turned to face its source. I heard him gasp as his stinging eyes fell on the wretched woman wielding a large knife and then downward onto our mutual best friend, who lay still among the bloody weeds. A long moment had elapsed as our horrified minds tried to ingest the wicked happenings. Finally, he broke out of his frozen state and dropped the turtle on the very stone it was sitting on when we found it. I heard it shatter as he turned and leaped over the wall. He was running madly through the thorny brush, and I called to him to wait. He did not turn to acknowledge me. He kept running for his life. Dave had always been the swiftest sprinter among us, and showed tremendous skill as he fled across the vicious terrain. The fear propelled him through and over obstacles that must have torn at his flesh the way it did mine as I pursued him. Still, he seemed unstoppable as he ran through thorns and shrubs. Many times I tripped and stumbled, which made me lag behind all the more. I called out to him in vain to stop, yet he did not respond. He ran like a scared rabbit, not once looking back. I shouted to him to stop, as loud as I could, and I was sure he heard me, but still he kept on running. Then I saw him trip. He folded forward fast and hard. I thought then maybe I could reach him, but all hope was gone when I heard his scream tapering off and fading into silence. I realized then that the worst had befallen him. He had run completely over the edge of the cliff! Perhaps in his fear, he forgot exactly where he was.

Soon I reached the edge and stood before the very spot where Dave had fallen off the face of the earth. I had to make sure that he wasn't hanging on to a root or something, waiting for rescue. There was no such luck left for my friend; he too was gone. I kept looking back to see if that horrible woman was pursuing me, yet I saw nothing but weeds and trees. I could feel her crushing presence among them as they swayed and danced eerily. I stood trembling with my back to the ocean, watching branches shaking their vines as the shadows grew long. I gripped a large rock in my hands as I watched for her. If she came for me, I would open her skull the way she did Jimmy's.

Finally, I snapped out of it. I wasn't sure how long I stood there, watching for her, but I figured she wasn't coming for me. By now the sun was low, and I realized what I was up against. It was a hell of a task climbing with the help of my friends in the light of day, but now I had to descend the cliff alone in the dark. I loathed the thought of it, but it was better than spending the night up there with the body of my best friend and a knife-wielding madwoman. I knew there was probably about thirty minutes of dwindling light at best, so I made my way down slowly and cautiously. The surface of the cliff was no more than twelve feet above my head when a sudden voice almost shocked me off the edge. I clung to its side and looked up. There she was, looking down at me with those awful gray eyes. Her long white hair flowing out before her in the wind. Both her wrinkled hands hung by her side. The knife was not in sight, yet it did little to soothe my nerves. "No!" she shrieked. "You mustn't go now. You have to fix what you've done. You and your terrible friends have made an awful mess."

"Leave me alone, you wicked beast!" I hollered. "You killed my friends, you crazy old hag!"

"I am not crazy," she sneered back, "nor have I killed anyone, and besides, you, young boy, don't know the meaning of the word *beast*!" Her fists clenched, and her eyes bulged in her wrinkled head as she emphasized the word *beast*.

"You did so kill my friends. Even if you didn't lay a hand on them, you scared them to death. It's because of you and your knife they're dead."

"That may be so, boy," she responded with a lower tone. "I never meant any harm. All I wanted to do was scare you off."

"Yeah!" I yelled back. "You practically scared Jimmy's head off, and as for Dave, you scared him right off the cliff!"

"What's done is done, boy," she continued. "Although it is not what I wished, it can't be changed."

"It isn't what you wished, witch!" I shouted back. "If you had it your way, you'd have gutted us all."

"Not true, boy, I never hurt anyone in my life. Do you think you were the first kids I've ever scared out of my graveyard before? I've scared hundreds of people off this cliff over the years. Why do you think my gargoyles are still here after all this time? Besides, I had more than a chance to stab Jimmy, and did I?"

"No," I said as I gazed up at her. She was right, she could have stabbed him three times before he turned around.

"Now listen to me, boy, you have to come back up here and fix this mess you've made." She may have been right about stabbing Jimmy, but there was no way in bloody hell I was going back up there.

"No way in bloody hell!" I shouted as I continued climbing farther away from her.

"You must overcome your fears, boy, forget me, forget the darkness. You must come up here and fix this." Ignoring her, I continued to make my way down. "I'm warning you, boy, you don't know what you've done. You speak of hell without knowing that you and your beloved friends have brought it upon the land. But it still can be fixed. I beg of you, come up here and make it right. I've kept it safe forever, I can do no more." I went on ignoring her. Soon she was out of sight, yet I could still hear her mad ramblings among the wind and the crashing of the surf below. The last thing I thought I heard her say was "I'm glad I'm dead." What the hell was she babbling about? I'd talked to some crazy old folks before, but she was beyond crazy, I thought as I inched my way down the cliff. Now that I could no longer hear her gibberish, I started to feel a bit safe. As safe as I could possibly feel climbing down the cliff in the dark, anyway.

By now it was too dark to determine where the footholds were. I knew it was a bad idea, making my way down when I did, but it didn't seem so bad when I thought of staying up there. The half-moon was all I had to aid me, yet the clouds kept sliding over it, leaving me in periods of blind darkness, at which point I would keep utterly still, leaning my chest and face against the cold stone. My legs were growing weak, and the longer I stood in one spot, the more they would shake. The night air was chill and breezy, and I felt hopeless at times, as if I would soon meet the same fate as my friend Dave, who was lying below on the jagged rocks. The maddening events that unfolded on the plateau clawed and gnawed at my spirit, yet the sobering sound of the surf curling and crashing to the shore below me brought peace and sanity to my distraught mind.

As I stood on shaky legs, embracing the cliff face, I heard a scratching sound above me. I didn't want to look, but I had to see if it was that crazy old woman climbing down after me. Pebbles were bouncing off my shoulders and head, and as they fell, I thought of what a disadvantage I had being on a lower level, for she could soon drop larger stones. When the pebbles finally stopped raining down on me, I forced myself to look up. "What do you want with me?" I yelled in horror. I heard no answer, yet again the scratching filled my ears as dirt misted down over my face. When it stopped, I opened my eyes again, and peered into the darkness above me. Suddenly, the moon shone as a cloud passed, and as my eyes slowly focused, I saw that there was no one on the ledge above, yet the scratching commenced. Knowing how short and rare the periods of moon glow were, I continued my descent, wishing to waste no light. Just as I had made a few yards of progress, the moon hid itself again, leaving me again in the frustration of darkness. This time, it was a longer period of moonless night than ever. The sky had become much cloudier than earlier, and I found myself wondering if I could hang on the face of the cliff throughout the night.

By now, the scratching sound was louder and closer than ever. Whatever it was, it was coming my way. Closer and closer it drew, pawing in the darkness, knocking small rocks off the ledge as it moved in toward me. I stared vainly in its direction, yet all I beheld were vague outlines of rock formations. What would it do when it reached me? I thought. How could I defend myself while hanging on a ledge in the darkness? It was all I could do not to fall off the edge, how could I swing a kick or a punch? Then I remembered how the woman appeared out of nowhere behind Jimmy. The grip of panic began to seize me as I searched my mind for a safe means of defense, yet I kept coming up empty. My eyes scanned the black face of the cliff, and I saw nothing but rock, yet I heard the scratching halt before me. My nerves began to settle slightly as I noticed the outline of a small animal at my feet. Soon it began to move again, and I prepared myself for its attack. I felt much relief knowing it was not the mysterious knife-brandishing madwoman, yet I was still afraid. Preparing myself to maintain my balance while on one foot and give it a kick as it came near, I was shocked to watch it moving down below my feet. My pulse began to slow as I realized it wasn't after me at all. Then I realized there was a ledge stretching out diagonally to the left that I had not seen. Suddenly, the moon shone down on me again, and I saw the animal for what it was. It was a turtle! Ha! Imagine, a young man frightened of a turtle! For the power of darkness! I chuckled aloud then and began to follow it down the ledge, for the ledge I was on was half the width. Animals have a keen sense of direction. His shell was the same width as my shoes, if he could make it down safely, then maybe I could as well. I could still see his outline as the clouds surrounded the moon again. His shell almost seemed to shine in the blackness. It was a dark-gray, glossy shine, which vaguely stood out among the black. Anyway, if I lost sight of him, I could still hear him. I decided to put all my faith in him. He was now my new best friend.

    I followed the turtle through the darkness, closely behind, feeling my way along the ledges with one foot, for the footholds, while slowly and gradually distributing my weight to the new rocks. By now the darkened sky was choked with clouds. It had been a long while since I was blessed with a single flash of moon glow. The darkness was so thick that I could only hear the ocean, nor could I see the shore below me, so I could not determine how far I had to go to reach it. I think that was more frustrating than descending the cliff blindly. But the shelled animal was my salvation, and when I could not see him, I'd feel around for his tail. Luckily, he was one of the slowest animals ever created, and so I could always keep up with him no matter how meticulous I was with my movements. Once again I could not see the outline of his shell, and I stooped down and began to feel along the ledge for him. Every so often he would stop, and I couldn't hear him either. Patting my hand blindly on the course, cold stone, a sudden horrid sound that called my name leaped swiftly at me from the awful black night. It was a voice I would have sold my soul to never have heard again. "You have to fix this mess, boy!" The moon peered out from the mass of clouds just long enough to illuminate her horrible face as she said those words. Her long scraggly hair danced about her wrinkled face; her piercing gray eyes stabbed at me across the cold night and sent me jumping backward in panic and fear.

    Before I realized what was happening, I found myself hanging off the ledge with hands that were quite numb from the cold. My grip was already loosening as my weight worked at my weary hands. I felt the jagged rocks slicing at my palms and fingers as they slowly slipped across the edge. My feet were desperately searching for a foothold, but there seemed to be nothing there to support me. I could only hear her now, as the moon hid away again. The muscles in my arms began to tremble. "Listen to me, Sully!" she said from the blackness above me. I cringed when she called my name. "You must undo what you've done. It is a simple fix, but there is little time and much at stake. I know you think me mad, even evil. However, most of my life has been devoted to keeping this land and its people safe. There's no time to explain now, but you and your friends have disrupted the order of things up here in my graveyard. You've done much more than desecrate and disrespect the dead, and your friends have done worse than rob the dead. Now you have to make it right again. You, Sully, have to fix it."

"What can I fix?" I said in a straining tone. "Soon I won't be able to do anything. Can't you see I'm falling off this godforsaken cliff? Help me. Pull me up, and I'll do anything you say, I swear."

"If I only could help you, I would, Sully, but I'm afraid I no longer have the means."

"You're a liar!" I responded. "You are evil! You say you didn't wish my friends any harm, and they're dead. You say you are not evil and you help people, yet you expect me to believe you as you stand over me and say you can't help me up?"

"I cannot help you. I can no more pull you up then I can lay a finger on you," she responded. "I could lay my hand upon you, and you wouldn't even feel it."

"You're a liar! You're a madwoman!"

"No, I'm a ghost, Sully," she said as my hands slid closer to the edge. "I'm a ghost. I cannot pull you up."

"Ghost or no ghost, you're still a liar! If you can't wrap your hands around my wrists, then why is it you could wrap them round the handle of a butcher knife?"

"I had that power before. Yes, I had the power to move objects for centuries, but the very moment your friend broke the turtle, the spell too was broken, and the blade fell from my grip. When I tried to pick it up, I could not. I can no longer pick up anything, including you. That is why I need you to fix this mess. Listen, Sully, all you need to do is carry the turtle home with you and put him in a locked cage."

"If I could pick him up, believe me, I would."

"No matter what happens, do not let him get back into the sea, Sully, do you hear me? Keep him out of the ocean forever. That is all you have to do to fix it. Keep the turtle out of the sea!"

"I'll do it. I'll do it if you save me!" I pleaded. I knew I could not hold on much longer.

"I cannot pull you up, but if you live, will you promise me you'll do as I asked?"

"Yes!" I screamed. "I promise, if I live, I'll keep the turtle out of the sea!"

"The task is simple." She continued. "And the fate of the village is in your hands, Sully."

"I have death in my hands," I said as my fingers slid over the edge, and I began to plummet.

"I know." I heard her say as I fell. The sickly vision of the woman's face flashed in my head as I fell, followed by the flash image of a gargoyle, then a stone turtle, and then… I slammed into the sand. The breath was knocked out of my lungs, and a migraine headache shot into my brain as fast as the breath was forced out of me. I heard a ringing in my ears, and a stinging pain began tingling all over my chest and limbs, but I was alive. I couldn't have fallen more than fifteen feet, and luckily, I landed between two rocks. The whole time I dangled off the cliff, I had no idea how close to the ground I was. If I did, I would've let go.

I lay on the sand for a while, gathering my scattered thoughts and resting my aching body. And just as I was about to rise, I saw my old friend the turtle pulling himself along the shore, slowly inching his way toward the curling waves. I thought then about my promise. I thought too about how lucky I was to be walking away. Especially when I thought about how I was leaving without my friends. I thought about that crazy woman and all her mad ramblings and how if it wasn't for that turtle, I would still be shaking on that cold, dark cliff with that insane, homicidal woman lurking over me. I thought about how that little friend of mine would not survive long outside of the ocean he was crawling toward. I was too grateful to deprive him of the sea he calls his home. Anyway, I already had a dog, and he was about all I could handle. I didn't need another pet. "Thanks, little buddy, couldn't have done it without you," I said as I watched his shell disappear among the waves.

"You expect me to believe all that, Sull? This is a practical joke, right?" said my grandfather, with skepticism overflowing from his bulging eyes.

"No gramps, I don't, and no, it's no joke," I answered. "I wish it were, my friends would still be alive."

"Davey and Jim are really dead, Sull?"

"Why would I joke about that? There's nothing funny about watching your friends die."

"Have you boys been drinking?" he asked.

"No, I drank half a beer once, but only that one time, I swear. I didn't much like the taste."

"Were any of you taking drugs?"

"No!" I hastily responded. "None of us has ever."

"Okay, I believe you, Sull," he said, cutting me off. Suddenly he was silent. He stared out the window with a look of grief on his old face. It dawned on me that he was looking out the window in the direction of the cliff. He stared out the window and said not a word for three long minutes or so until I asked him, "Gramps, are you okay?"

He did not answer; instead he asked me, "Why did you boys go up there?"

"I don't know, Gramps, we just wanted to scale the cliff to see the view."

"Then you and your friends had no knowledge of the graveyard up there or the gargoyles?"

"No, we stumbled on it."

"And neither you nor your friends have ever heard of the ghost that roams around up there, or the legend behind her?" he asked while his old eyes stared through me.

"No, Gramps, if I knew there was a ghost up there, believe me, I would have never let them talk me into making that climb. I'm no fool, I know enough to believe in ghosts." He sat staring silently out the window again at my response. He had a look on his face that made me feel that he was content that I was telling him the truth, but there was also a disturbed expression mixed in with the contentment. Perhaps he was distraught in knowing that I wasn't lying. I felt like there was something he didn't wish to tell me. "What legend, Grandpa?" I asked with reluctant curiosity.

When he was ready, he finally spoke: "When I was your age, Sull, my grandfather told me of the legend of Lone Plateau. He forbade me to ever go up there. Hell, after he told the story, I lost my desire to ever climb it. And believe me, I've lived a long life practically in its shadow, and I never have. I only wish I had told you before what I'm about to tell you now. It seems that not many, if any, still pass on the legend anymore. Over the ages, erosion has made the cliff almost impossible to climb, and the legend is so old all of the people that heard of it when it was new are long buried. It was passed on for many generations until gradually it petered out. Hell, I'd forgotten about it myself long ago. It's a shame how we lose hold of the ways and the stories of old.

"My grandfather Shamus told me of a woman who was murdered on the plateau when she was in her late seventies. That was over five hundred years ago now. Rumor had it that she practiced witchcraft, and certain folks who knew her said that she was harmless. They said that she was a good witch, that is to say that she supposedly practiced white magic. She belonged to this strange cult that she had started. They called themselves the Chelonians. They claimed to be saving people from some maniacal doom, but people just thought them mad and perverted. They thought that they worshiped turtles as a god, which is, of course, sacrilege and blasphemy in God-fearing eyes. Besides, they didn't care whether a witch practiced white or black magic. Good or bad, it was all evil to them.

"And so, one day, a meeting was held in Saint John's Church. The outcome was a good old-fashioned Christian lynch mob. A large group of men and even a few women climbed the plateau one

Sunday, knowing full well that the top of the cliff was where they held their ceremonies once a week. They carried knives, hatchets, and other weapons of choice strapped to their legs and backs. When they reached the summit, they found a small group of people, mostly women, sitting in a circle upon a mound of dirt, making unexplainable gestures with their hands. Most had bowls of odd-colored herbs, which they occasionally sprinkled on the ground while proceeding to chant in a riddled tongue. The lynch mob closed in on them, cutting them to ribbons. They left them there, where they fell upon the mound of Lone Plateau."

"They killed them and left them there like that, Gramps?"

"Yes, so the story goes."

"But how did the graveyard come about?" I asked with frustration.

"You see, Sully, they left them lying on the ground 'cause they considered them blasphemes. They refused to give them a proper Christian burial for that would be blasphemy in itself. So they left them as is. But strange things began to happen around the village, queer things, which only happened to members of the lynch mob. They found themselves having horrible nightmares, which they refused to discuss. And when they woke, they would find something odd placed upon their night stands. Some found shells and seaweed, some woke up to bowls of brightly colored herbs, yet all would eventually wake from slumber to find unidentifiable symbols in a circle, which surrounded the image of a sea turtle carved into the inside of their doors!

"Needless to say, a new meeting was held in the church, and all members of the lynch mob agreed to ascend the cliff again, but this time with shovels instead of weapons. They buried the cult members crudely in shallow pits where they had slain them. They left stone markers at their heads, which of course bore no names. It certainly was not a Christian or even a proper burial. They were laid to rest without coffins, but it apparently put an end to all the odd happenings the lynch mob participants were experiencing. There were no more herbal offerings appearing on their night stands. No more carvings on their doors. But still the nightmares persisted. Though they would not speak of the details, they complained that they were nautical in nature. They all refused to relay even one of their haunted dreams for fear the ghastly, nightly revelations would come true, perhaps. Perhaps it was the weaving of their own guilt. No one knows for sure. Anyway, years after the lynching, a hiker climbed the cliff and returned with disturbing news. Not only had the distraught climber reported seeing the ghastly apparition of the cult leader with intense, undeniable detail, he also spoke of the area in which she was seen. A small area of scattered stones which was enclosed by a stone wall. Upon some of the stones were small gargoyles, he claimed, and on one of the stones lay the stone image of a sea turtle. The man told the villagers how he picked up one of the gargoyles to examine it closely, when his attention was drawn to the sudden appearance of the old woman. He explained how he put the small statue back in its place and ran towards the ledge. The members of the lynch party only believed that he saw the cult leader's ghost, for she had visited each of them at their homes, but they had a hard time believing the report of the stone wall, and especially the gargoyles and the stone turtle which he said adorned the markers.

"A return trip to the cliff top was made by a few of the lynch mob. They could not believe it when they came upon the rectangular stone wall and saw what was perched upon some of the markers within. They began to whisper among themselves about the possibility of some cult members which were unknown to them that might have done this. It seemed a likely explanation. One of them began examining the gargoyles. Soon they were scared off by the cult founder's ghost. But they, as you know, Sully, weren't the only ones scared off in the same way. Now I know the legend is truth and not just a tale. To think, after all these years, she's still up there, warding off all who may try to make off with one of her gargoyles. Scaring away anyone who may tread upon her sacred ground." I sat in silence upon the ending of his story. So many vile images were still churning around in my heavy head. We sat together in solemn silence for quite a while before I started to come back to reality. I realized then that I too was staring out the same window at the monstrous, shadowy cliff.

I swore to the fires of hell that I'd never again climb that plateau. Anyway, why would I want to after what I'd been through? However, it was what I'd been through that would force me to return no matter how much I protested. The authorities insisted on my bringing them to the bodies of my friends. And as gruesome as the thought of gazing on the lifeless shell of my friends sounded, I had no problem bringing them to Dave's body. It was Jimmy's body that I was less inclined to bring them to, although I came to the morbid realization that Dave's body would probably be in much worse shape. I tried all conceivable means to talk the police out of my escorting them to the top of the cliff, yet they would not hear of it. I told them exactly where he was; I even drew a crude map. Still they insisted on my escort. So there I was, walking across the beach with two policemen in the shadow of the hellish formation, to show them the body of one of my closest friends shattered at its base. And although I swore I'd never again step foot on its summit, here I was, and so soon, returning to scale it in order to bring them to the body of my other best friend. The more I thought it all over as I kicked up the sand, the less I could believe it was all real. It all seemed like a horrible dream, and as I got closer to the spot where Dave's life had ended, I kept picturing the putrid image of that awful woman, that ghost that terrified me half to death and literally scared Jimmy and Dave to death. Soon I found myself plotting ways to get out of the climb, and yet I knew it wouldn't work. I once thought about running, yet I knew that even if they didn't catch me, they eventually would, and if I didn't produce the bodies, I might even become a murder suspect. All these things grappled at one another while they swirled in my head as we drew closer to Dave's body.

Of course, I wasn't exactly sure where he had fallen; I was only sure of the general location. Anyway, I was confident that I could find him fairly easily, without much searching. However, we had walked up and down the entire length of the cliff's base, weaving in and out of rocks, without finding Dave's body. I knew he had fallen somewhere around the middle, though it was quite dark the night before, so we covered the entire area. Up and down again we slowly searched the shadowy base of the plateau to no avail. One of the policemen suggested that his body was probably carried out to sea with the high tide. It was the most plausible explanation. Still, the other officer had an expression on his face that made me wonder if I were lying about my friend's disappearances. It was the same look my grandfather had when I first began explaining the horrid events. Still, no matter what suspicions may have been crawling around in the policeman's heads, we were still going to make the climb.

Finally, with great effort, we reached the top, and I found myself resting with my legs dangling off the edge of the jutting mass of land that stood, towering high above the village and the treetops in the empty sky. I was glad it was a cloudless, bright, windless day, and we had set out much earlier than my friends and I had, and it helped only slightly to calm my nerves when I thought of the policeman's promise that we would be home long before sunset. So there I sat, breathing heavily, looking at a magnificent view, which I never thought I'd see again, this time, with two armed strangers instead of my friends. Yet this time, every five seconds, I found myself turning around to scan the untamed landscape for the nightmare apparition of the long-dead witch / cult leader. And when I thought about the billy clubs and guns that swung from their uniforms, it did little to soothe my fears, for bullets and other weapons are useless on spirits. They cannot be harmed, for they are already dead.

So once again I waded through the reeds and the thorny brush, in between two others, who also trotted in eerie silence. Even Sam, the policeman whose jaw was constantly flapping past the point of annoying his partner's badge off, was suddenly dumb. Once again, the spell of vertigo crowded my head as I struggled dreamily through the hanging vines and towering weeds. Poor Dave, I thought, he, like those unsuspecting cult members, won't even receive a proper burial. No body for the funeral service, no coffin, no lot of worm-laden earth with overgrown grass. Not even a lousy stone marker. Right about now, he was probably food for the fish. Hell, even the crazy cult members got better than that. Fear seized my legs in midstep as my eyes fell on the tip of the wall of stone that bordered the unsacred, makeshift graves where we first saw the terrifying apparition. The damnable spot where Jimmy lay lifeless, with a crack in his young skull. "He's in there," I said, disturbing the awful silence, pointing toward the weed-choked rectangular wall. "This is as far as I go," I continued. We had worked out an agreement that I would bring them to Jimmy but without having to look upon his corpse. I had already unwillingly subjected my eyes to enough visual torment. I needed normalcy to begin healing. The horrible image of the ancient woman was carved into my brain, and there were other ghastly images and happenings that kept recurring in my mind like segments of a play. I did not wish to see Jimmy in that state again.

I tried not to think about what the policemen were seeing as they climbed over the wall, but I knew all too vividly what they were seeing as clearly as if I were looking through their eyes. I may as well have climbed in there with them. I wondered if I could ever clear my mind of the morbid sights. But apparently, I was wrong about what they were seeing, for they began to call me to their side. "We had a deal. You promised I didn't have to see."

"I know, and a promise is a promise, now get over here."

I whined. "But you said—"

"Get over here!" he hollered sternly, cutting me off in midsentence. Slowly I dragged my shoes through the weeds and the thistle, up to the old wall. "Where the hell is he, Sully?" Sam shouted in aggravation. Looking over the wall among the stones and gargoyles and weeds, my mind began to swell and throb with confusion and disbelief. The swirling of dizziness elevated to just shy of the extreme of fainting as my eyes fell on the bloody stone between the two squatting policemen. Jimmy's body was gone!

The police were shouting all kinds of babble at me, yet I could not understand a single word they spewed toward my face. It was like we were underwater. The words were muffled, and my ears were ringing. I stared blankly at the flattened, blood-soaked weeds where Jimmy had fallen. Then I noticed something equally as strange. The stone that the turtle rested on, the same stone that Dave had shattered it over, was littered with thin fragments of stone. The remnants could not have consisted of more than one quarter of the statues mass. It must've been hollow, I thought, yet I recalled then how Dave struggled to pick it up. I stood there as if I were alone on Lone

Plateau with the officers interrogating me, trying to make sense of it all. Suddenly, a phrase Sam uttered slapped me in the face like a gale would upon turning a corner of a building. I did not hear the first part, yet I heard "Murder suspect, Sully! You better start talking, and tell the truth this time."

"I've been telling the truth, damn it! How could anyone make this up? Don't you see the blood on that stone? Maybe he didn't die right away. Maybe after we were scared off, he regained consciousness and wandered off to die somewhere else like a wounded animal does. I don't know any more than you do. Do you think for one second that if I killed my best friends that I would go to the police?"

"He does have a point, Sam," Harry said. "Let's search the rest of this place."

As we climbed over the adjacent wall, Sam gasped with excitement. "What do we have here?" he asked. It was the knife the woman almost stabbed Jimmy with. I thought then about what she said, about how when Dave shattered the turtle, she lost the ability to grip or move objects. Maybe she was telling the truth after all, for the knife lay where she dropped it. "This blade is quite a find indeed! Besides the fact that it's a clue, if I'm not mistaken, this blade is over half a millennium old!"

We scanned the landscape of the dreary plateau, yet we did not find Jimmy's body. The only notable find we stumbled on was the weathered statue of a woman, whose empty eyes seemed to gaze back at us. The artistry was nothing shy of perfection. It was incredibly, eerily lifelike. "Was this, by chance, the woman you saw, Sully?" Sam asked.

"No," I responded. "It could not have been her, even when she was young. Her features are different. I told you of her wretchedness, didn't I? No, this statue was chiseled in the likeness of a different woman."

"And a beautiful woman she must've been," Harry exclaimed.

"She is beautiful," I agreed.

"Beautiful is her shell!" A sickly voice bit our ears from behind. We jumped, we jerked, and we cringed at the sudden deplorable sound. "Beautiful, no doubt, yet ugly as sin inside!" By now, we were all turned around and face-to-face with the ghost of Lone Plateau. The police were dumbfounded with awe and fear. They did not move, nor did they respond as she continued with her verbal scorn. "You speak of promises broken, Sully McColgan, yet you could not keep your promise, a promise on which you staked your life." I was so horrified! I didn't know how I didn't drop down dead. How did she know my last name? "Yes, Sully, you staked your life on a promise you did not keep, yet here you stand, trembling, yes, but still breathing. You could have kept your promise easily. It was such a chore-less task to clean up your mess. 'Yes! I promise! I'll keep the turtle out of the sea!'" She mimicked me with shocking perfection. "A crazy old hag, ha? A wicked beast, right? Soon you'll all see that it is not I who is evil. Soon it will be revealed that it is you who are the crazy ones who choose not to believe my words. Soon you, Sully McColgan, and the whole damned land will understand the validity of my revelations. Soon too will you learn the meaning of the word you spit out so freely and so ignorantly. Soon, you'll understand the worth of the word *beast*!" I had no rebuttal. I, like the policemen, stood trembling, seemingly unable to speak or react physically. It was all we could do to stand and listen. "Perhaps now you have the time to stay and hear my explanation." She continued, "You were correct in the assumption of calling me a witch, Sully, yet you were wrong in calling me evil. I, as I told you before, have spent most of my life, and eons of my afterlife as well, dedicated to protecting mankind from impending doom. While that beautiful sculpture behind you spent her life in the dark devotion of unleashing it upon the land. This thing is the devourer of the sea, and she, in all of her marvelous beauty, wished only to make it the devourer of both sea and land. And now, thanks to you and your friends, Sully, she will get her wish after all this time.

"Yes, I brandished the very knife I was slain with for well over five lifetimes. Yes, I kept the spellbound sea turtle from baiting the beast and feeding him the power to breathe air. Yes, I am the one who froze the immortal, evil witch in cement, putting a halt to her torment and plagues. And it was also I who froze the sea turtle whom she put a spell on. Not only the same spell of immortality, but also the magic spell of amphibian transformation. You see, the sea turtle was perfect for such a task. Not only is it an amphibian, it is one of the favorite morsels of the beast. That is why they are endangered. In the nick of time, I discovered her evil intentions. In an epic confrontation, it was white magic which barely prevailed. Yet as I was sure she was dead, she kept rising to destroy me. It was then I realized that she had discovered the ingredients of immortality. I used my magic to place her in a temporary coma-like state. It was all the time I needed to gather a batch of cement, and I did the same to the poor hexed sea turtle. I could not kill her, nor could I put the innocent animal to death, so it seemed a likely solution. And for eons, my gargoyles and I protected my graveyard from trespassers and thieves like your friends. But you three have managed to make quite a mess of things, haven't you? And now, the beast will feed upon the magic turtle, and it will be blessed with the breath of amphibians! You see, you have done the work of the black witch for her. Thanks to you and your friends, Sully, the territory of land will come to know the terror and the hunger of the beast!" Upon her final word, she vanished among the weeds and spruce trees.

The police were dumbfounded. They looked at each other with horror and confusion on their faces. They spoke not a word, yet I somehow got the impression that although they didn't take the spirit's mad ranting story seriously, they now had little doubt in believing mine. Sam, who boasted on the way up the cliff about how he did not believe in ghosts, was now quieter than ever. "We've got to head back now if we're gonna make it down before dark," Harry finally suggested.

"Yeah!" Sam and I shouted simultaneously. There weren't many more words spoken on the walk back to the edge, just a lot of surreal thought and questioning going on in each of our heads.

"Let's take a breather before we start down," Harry said as we reached the edge. As much as I loathed being up there, I figured that taking in the beautiful view one last time wouldn't be a bad idea. We sat down at the edge of the cliff and gazed out on the vast, sparkling ocean. We rested there for a good twenty minutes or so, all the while, without a single word spoken, until Harry asked if we were all rested enough for the climb. Sam and I were both very anxious to sink our shoes back into the dry, hot sand again, so we stood up and prepared to make the descent. The way Harry sprung to his feet, I could tell he was not heartbroken to leave Lone Plateau.

Just as I was about to turn my back to the sea and make my way down, a bewildering movement in the water caught my eye. It was a queer wake or a wave that was moving not as they normally moved, horizontally with the shore—this wave was moving in a straight line that crisscrossed all the others. I had never witnessed a phenomenon of the like in all my life. It filled me with excitement and wonder. "Look!" I yelled, pointing down at the unorthodox disturbance in the water. Sam, who was already on the lower ledge, slowly turned around yet quickly noticed what I was shouting about. He hopped back up to the peak of the cliff and spun around to view the strange, swelling current. All at once, a wall of water sprayed high into the air as a blurred mass slid onto the shore, sending people, who looked as small as ants, scattering in panic and confusion. A muffled roar of screams and cries echoed up the face of the cliff as the crowd trampled themselves. A cylindrical grayish-green mass lay beached on the sand among the terrified villagers. "What... What!" said Sam with a long stutter as his trembling finger pointed at the beached monstrosity.

"Is it a whale?" I asked.

"Yes, Sully, it's a whale, all right. No need to worry, it's just a whale," Harry said nervously. His shaky tone did not convince me that even he believed what he was saying. I wondered too why all the people down on the beach were so frightened of a beached whale.

Then, suddenly, it moved. It pulled itself slowly, awkwardly out of the surf. We watched, seized and silenced by horror, as it revealed itself from the cover of the waves. It dragged itself along the beach as the people screamed and fled. I wasn't positive from the great height, though it appeared as if the thing was swallowing up some of the people the way I'd seen a lizard snatching up crickets. It was somewhat slow and uneasy the way it emerged from the water, yet it could turn and jerk its head and neck to one side with surprising speed and agility. It snapped at the people, as they tried to run, like some gigantic sea serpent. I swear it was scooping them up in its mouth, yet I could not be certain. As we stood and watched the inconceivable insanity, ghastly images began to flash in my mind. I recognized them as the terrible, mythical illustrations depicted in a seafaring book belonging to my grandfather. It was a whole chilling chapter of individually comprised captain's logs, mostly from whaling vessels, which spoke of eye-witness accounts of and even confrontations with horrific sea monsters. Giant scaly beasts that resembled sea serpents, many of which would boldly attack large ships.

The illustrations of these monstrous sea beasts towering above the waves continued to flash in my mind as we watched in disbelief as the people scampered away, screaming as the enormous sea beast crawled farther up the shore to the dry sand while still sliding out of the water. I kept expecting to see its hind region. "That thing's gotta be fifty feet long!" Sam exclaimed. Its head was now close to the dunes by the base of the plateau, and still there was no sight of the tail end of the thing.

"Try seventy-five feet, Sam!" Harry uttered with awe.

Then it began to turn its head around, facing the ocean. "Is it going back?" I asked.

"Pray that it is, Sully," Harry responded solemnly. It began moving back in the direction of the surf, yet soon it moved, much faster than before, in a crescent-shaped path, curling out to our left-hand side and then closer to the wet sand, and all the while, it was still pulling its gray-green body out of the surf. "Holy smoke!" Sam hollered. "How long is it?" Suddenly, the intentions behind its odd movement became clear, for it appeared to be corralling a crowd of people with its cylindrical, cyclopean body. The crowd became caught in a sandy circle between its coiling frame. It then buried its head into the trapped crowd, whose terrible whaling tore at my miserable soul. By now there was no doubt: it was feeding on the poor villagers. Some of them tried desperately to climb over the immense creature, and some of them did manage to climb on its back. From the plateau, it resembled a worm with ants crawling on it.

Suddenly I found myself hunched down, vomiting over the edge of the cliff, for I had recalled some of the words the spirit had spoken to me of the mess we'd made and how I could have so easily fixed it, but I didn't believe her. How could the mad riddle-like babble she told me be the truth? How could the madness I was witnessing be reality? Now I had no choice but to believe in something that was undeniably real. Something that stung my eyes to look upon, yet I could not close them to. And it was just sinking in, among all the chaos that it was me and my belligerent friends who brought about this hellish whirlwind of doom.

When I was done being sick, I wiped my watery eyes and looked back down. The thing was now devouring people toward the other side of the beach. "How did it get over there so fast?" I asked. I had heard the police yelling while I was losing my breakfast over the cliff, yet I couldn't make out what they were saying. "You should have seen it move, Sully!" Sam exclaimed. "I thought they might be far enough to get away as slow as it was before, but you should have seen it move! As much as this place gives me the creeps, I'm glad we're up here," he continued. "Yeah," Harry responded. "To think, we couldn't wait to get down there earlier! We should be safe up here." I wasn't sure what the police were thinking, but I wasn't thinking about my own safety. Those poor people!

By now, the cries of the bewildered villagers were fading off, for many of them had fled in either direction, far down the beach. Soon, there was a shift in the sea thing's movements. It had stopped the twisting of its neck and the downward snatching of its head. Perhaps there were no more ants to feed upon. I prayed silently that it would return to the sea. Now it began moving toward the dunes again. Closer it drew to the shade of the plateau. Maybe there were people hiding behind the rocks and the reeds, I thought to myself. There was nowhere else to hide on the blistery beach. They should've ran for it.

But I was wrong in its sniffing around between the rocks of the dunes, for all at once, the maddening sea beast began scaling the cliff! "Oh no! Oh god!" Sam uttered frantically. "No! Please, God, no!" He continued hopping around like a frightened child.

"Sam!" Harry shouted. "Sam! Get a hold of yourself! Sam, listen, we've got pistols, remember? Don't panic, Sam, please, we need to all try to stay calm and fight this thing."

"Fight this thing? Fight this thing? F-F-Fight... that? Harry, this thing is gonna have us for dinner, and you want me to be calm? You want to fight it? Ha! Ha! Ha! Ha ah ha ahh!" Now Sam was laughing madly. It was clear he was losing touch with reality. Me, I had begun down that path the day my friends and I climbed this cliff.

"Yes, we might become its dinner, Sam. Hell, we might be sucked up through its nostrils, and that's what'll happen, no doubt, if we don't fight." Harry spoke, as the voice of reason among madness. "Listen, Sam, this thing may be colossal, but we have an advantage." Finally Sam stopped laughing his sickly laugh and stopped his frantic movements. He looked like his eyes were welling up. "Okay, Harry, I'm listening." He said quietly, even calmly. But as he went on, he began to raise his voice to a holler, and he began shaking and pacing around again as he continued. What advantage could we possibly have against that... that thing?"

"Listen, Sam! We have pistols, not only that, but it's in a bad position. It is below us, scaling the cliff. I figure if we aim for the eyes, we can at least blind it, maybe even knock it off the cliff. It'll be in bad shape after a fall like that, maybe even dead," Harry said, cocking his pistol. Now Sam stood still, shaking, but still. He thought it over for a moment. "Let's do this!"

We stood boldly at the edge of the plateau. I thought that if this was how I was going to die, then at least we lived to see such an epic, fantastic creature. To gaze on something so mystic, so hellishly gruesome and glorious in its own right, might be worth it to die in its jaw. I got the feeling that maybe Harry and Sam were thinking the same thing. Even so, I was not ready to die. And it was not bravery that kept me standing there; it was more the grip of awe and absolute fear that kept me from running. Not only that, but I had faith that Harry and Sam's pistols could knock it off the rock.

As it climbed Lone Plateau, its features slowly became clearer. The body was less like that of a serpent, for we could now see that its cylindrical framework was made up of round, hump-like segments, each of which displayed undetermined numbers of circular suction-like pads, which gripped the jagged rock quite effortlessly. So too did it become painfully obvious that the body of the beast was covered in long, thin, sharp spines, on some of which were impaled the limp and bloody bodies of men, women, and children! I could not help but notice that many of them were not blessed with the mercy of death. As the beast got closer, I noticed that it was not laden with shiny scales like the sea serpents drawn out in the book I had read. In fact, the closer it got, the less it looked like any of the creatures in the illustrations. As well as the thousands of padded legs that marched swiftly up the side of the cliff like a line of odd, enemy soldiers, off both sides of each circular segment hung limply long gray fishlike fins. And the eyes! Oh, the horrible, empty yellow eyes! Larger than carriage wheels they were! No pupils, no irises, no covering, only a faint, sickly yellow. I could not be sure exactly what the ghastly thing was gazing at, yet the emptiness in its eyes was hypnotic. I stood, wobbling on the edge with a sudden dizziness filling my head. It took all my strength not to fall off into its gaping jaw. Its mouth was packed with jumbled rows of teeth. Teeth that were curved and as long as cutlasses. The ugliness of the thing was maddening, indescribable. I stood there, teetering on the edge of insanity, as the vacant eyes and the cave-like mouth crawled closer. All the while, as it neared the peak, incredibly, its hind region was still submerged within the waves!

Then, as if I were shaken from a nightmare that spilled into reality, Harry's voice broke me out of my trance. It was almost upon us now. "Get ready, Sam. Aim for the devil's eyes!" he hollered. "Ready… ready… now!" In unison, the first shots were fired. Together, they emptied their pistols successfully into the ugliness of the hallow eyes of the unweenable beast. Twelve balls in all were seen sinking into the huge yellow targets, yet it did not flinch or even slow its ascent. "Oh no! Oh god no!" Sam cried with bulging eyes. "Oh god no!"

"Reload, Sam! Reload!" shouted Harry. Sam was on the verge of another panic fit, but he came to and reloaded his pistol with trembling hands. Harry was firing again at the eyes of the wretched beast, while Sam fumbled with his gun. Harry was done emptying his pistol successfully into the eyes. Every shot hit, yet again, the thing kept climbing up undeterred. Sam began emptying his pistol, while Harry reloaded. He too was right on target with each shot, despite his shaking hands. By now the beast was upon us. It was too close to miss a single shot, yet Sam, instead of reloading, dropped to his knees and began muttering undistinguishable words and grinding his teeth, as Harry boldly stood his ground and fired again at the eyes of the gargantuan predator.

Up and over the edge of Lone Plateau, the face of ugliness and destruction rose, with a monstrous flapping, wheezing sound as it breathed through its vibrating gills. Sand and blood were crusted beneath its jaw, which was now spreading apart slowly. Then came a sound that shot from its mouth like the roar of a hundred lions. We were slapped to the ground by its rancid breath, which smelled so horrible I could only compare it to a beach covered in rotting fish. My ears rang and throbbed as I lay, gasping among the thistle. With the speed of a lightning bolt, the beast snapped down at Harry and Sam as they quivered in the brush. In a flash, they were both within his massive jaw. A thundering crunch split through the air. Although half deaf from the roar, I could hear the beast snapping trees and pounding the ground behind me as I ran. I knew not where I was running to. I could not think; I could only run. All I was sure of was that it was in close pursuit. The trees that I ran through did little to slow the beast down as it tore across the plateau after me, snapping them the way I did the reeds. From out of nowhere, the spirit of Lone Plateau appeared before me. She was facing me, floating backward in front of me as I ran. "Where are you running off to in such a hurry, Sully?" she asked mockingly as she drifted like mist on the wind. "It's funny, you're usually running away from me!" she said laughingly. "Now, have you learned your lesson? Now do you understand the true meaning of the word *beast*?"

"Yes!" I said in between heavy breaths. "Yes, but tell me, how did those people get stuck to its back?" I asked as I fled.

"Sometimes he rolls over his prey. Sometimes he picks them up and puts them on his spikes."

"But how?" I asked while gasping for breath.

"When his bellies are full, he sticks them there, you see… to save them for later. And as for how, you'll find that out. The question is, Sully, will he snatch you up with his jaw, or will he save you for later? Ha! Ha! Ha! Ha! Ha! Ha! Ha!"

"Help me!" I pleaded. "Help us, help me fix it. Tell me how to make it go away."

When she stopped laughing, she said, "You had your chance, Sully, but you didn't listen. Now the turtle is in the belly of the beast with about a thousand of your beloved townspeople. And soon you shall join them! I hope you're happy. I know the black witch would be." As soon as she had appeared, she vanished before me as I ran, while the briars tore at my ankles.

Half-blind, half-deaf, half-mad, I pushed my way through the towering weeds till I struck an immovable object. Luckily, my head did not hit it as hard as it would've if my arms weren't stretched out before me. I lay on my back, confused, nauseous, dizzy, and weak, looking up at the object I had run into. It was the beautiful statue of the black witch, as the spirit spoke of her. There were cracks all over her surface from the collision, and as I sat up wearily, I watched segments flake off piece by piece. As the pieces fell, I began to recall more of the spirit's words. About how it was she who knew about the sea beast and desired to bring it to land and give it the gift of amphibian breath. And about how she wished to use the beast to control man and make them worship her and do her bidding. And as the chips of cement fell to the ground and began to reveal the sickly ivory-white flesh of the evil woman, I felt the ground shaking beneath me as the beast gained on me. The woe of inescapable doom seized me. Still, more flakes of cement fell to the ground, and finally, the half-hidden body poured limply from its stone cocoon to the weed-choked ground. I experienced then an overwhelming will to black out, which I fought off with all my strength and will to persevere. A spiraling dizziness still plagued me, and like before, I felt as if I were underwater. I thought I would faint at any second, but the cracking of the snapping trees kept me from slipping away, and I raised myself to my wobbly feet.

Just as I began to run, a horrible sound seized me. It was a wheezing, moaning sound coming from the ground where the scattered cement lay piled. She was breathing! She was stirring! She lay there, writhing in the weeds. Her disgustingly pale skin, ripped and torn from the fall, began to bleed. Then, bright-crimson streams began trickling slowly down her ghostly flesh. She moaned again as she slowly rose to her feet. Her beautiful brown hair hung at her side as she stood. Her closed eyes were crusted with remnants of the cement, yet I felt undoubtedly that she was aware of my presence.

The crushing, snapping sound grew louder. Birds flew in fear as the trees folded abruptly to the ground. Suddenly, her eyes popped open. They gazed into mine as if she were reading my thoughts. A long moment passed as the crashing sounds grew closer, and her blueish lips moved. "Yes! Yes, you did it, boy! You did the deed! Now the land of men will come to know my name, and they shall worship at my feet! Finally, the people will collaborate to do my bidding! That's him, isn't it, boy? Isn't it? Together we brought him from the sea. He's coming to claim you! You and all who will not submit to me. And all the while, I cannot be killed, nor can my beast be destroyed! Ha! Ha! Ha! Ha! Ha!"

All at once, the top of a huge tree folded down before us, and the head of the majestic beast emerged from the shaking leaves. Slowly it rose, while the witch gazed upon it approvingly. Arrogantly it hung its ugly head into the air. A wicked smile came to the woman's face as she looked it over. She then raised her hands above her head and said, "Now, it shall be done!" She then began chanting. Chanting aloud words I'd never before heard. Words that did not resemble any language I'd ever even read about. "Doomah ote ladnog, nif gin! Nif gin! Doomah ote ladnog, nif gin!"

The beast snorted a heavy spray of both air and seawater through his gills. Still she went on chanting: "Doomah ote ladnog, nif gin! Nif gin!" Suddenly, out from the tops of the trees behind the woman rose a grayish-green serpent of a thing laden with quills and fins. *Oh god!* I thought to myself. *This cannot be! More than one?* But as it grew closer, I saw no yellow eyes or swordlike teeth; instead, I saw two pointy appendages that resembled the pinchers of a colossal ear wig. "Holy smoke!" I screamed as I thought, *Is that its tail?* All at once, the claw-like tail of the beast swooped down toward me. All I could do was freeze in absolute terror. I thought it was all over. When

I opened my eyes, the woman was in the grasp of the great pincher. She screamed, "No, not me! No! Doomah ote ladnog, nif gin, nif—" She was silenced as the pincher brought her to its open mouth.

When I heard the crunch, I took off running. I ran through the tall weeds that blocked my vision and the thorns that tore at my flesh. Soon I heard the dreaded crashing and thumping on the ground and the horrible snapping of trees close behind. I ran like a scared rabbit through the reeds atop Lone Plateau. I ran faster than any man had ever run before me. I ran with the abominable beast snapping and roaring behind me, shaking the ground as it followed with people in its belly and impaled upon its back. I ran, and I ran till I could run no more, for suddenly there was no more ground beneath me.

THE EYE OF CY

I HAD GOTTEN A GOOD deal on a small, humble house that I recently purchased with most of my life savings. It was quite old and weathered and needed some fixing up, but it was perfect for me. The scraping, the painting, and the minor carpentry tasks were nothing I couldn't handle, and I was quite relaxed when thinking of the renovations. For I had plenty of time to do the work, and besides, the roof was in good shape, and I was more concerned about starting a vegetable garden. All my life I dreamed about owning my own home and a nice chunk of land on my beloved birthplace, the beautiful and majestic Isle of Crete. And on that land, I always pictured an elaborate garden curling, hanging, and dancing in the breeze.

I had a large rectangular plot dug out in the area that absorbed the most sunlight. Of course, I had taken into consideration the enormous, heaping mass of grassy earth and jutting stone that stood well over a hundred feet in the sky and stretched out for miles away from the boundaries of my backyard. It worked out well that with the way the sun rose and fell that my garden would not be consumed by its dark, heavy shadow.

Although the work was strenuous, I worked at a slow but steady pace, humming a tune as I overturned the soil. This was one of the happiest moments in my life, and so I toiled in the soil with a smile. But my tune was interrupted midway when my pitchfork unearthed a peculiar shiny object. Suddenly, as if a dam gave way, I was overwhelmed by an overflow of mixed emotions. Curiosity, fear, and awe churned with the burden and dread of discovery. The discovery of something both baffling and disturbing, which instantly held me firm in a groggy, hypnotic daze. I found myself crouched over the frightful object, which leered back at me. I almost felt as if my limbs were carved from stone, for quite some time, I had seemingly lost the will to move. It was long after my weak, sore limbs began shaking that I finally reached down and plucked the curious object from the freshly disturbed earth. I had no idea then how long I gazed on it before I snatched it up, or how long I had contemplated its origin or its worth, its meaning or its make. But the eye that gazed silently back at me from the now-dried ground shined as if it were made of glass. Strangely too, it was the size of a large cantaloupe. As I walked back toward my new house, I realized that although I had started not a long time after dawn that the sun had already gone down. It seemed it took me all day to do two hours' worth of work. Exhausted and drained, I threw myself on the bed without eating dinner.

That night, I was frequently snatched from peaceful slumber by a reoccurring fragment of nightmare. I kept seeing that awful eye emerging from the swirling blackness, staring at me with conviction and contempt. But much worse than the loathsome feelings of disapproval it conveyed was the utter lack of privacy I began to encounter in my new home. My first night was spent without any valuable rest, while the enormous glossy eye watched over me as I tried to sleep in my darkened chamber.

Early the next morning, I went out to finish preparing my garden. My head was groggy, and I wandered wearily across the damp grass. When I took a good look at the small amount of work I had accomplished, the events of the previous day began to surface in my half-asleep mind. I remembered then, how I had been in the garden plot from dawn till dusk without leave, and it perplexed me greatly to see in the light of a new day how little I had accomplished in so much time. Suddenly, it sunk in. The image of the mysterious glass eye. In my mind, I saw it surface from the churned earth, just as my pitchfork had lifted it. Then I saw it peering at me through the darkness as it had in my dream. Recalling the fresh and disturbing memory, I went back inside to further examine the object of wonder and confusion I had accidently unearthed. Apparently, I had left it on my bedside table before I leaped into bed. Sitting on the edge of my old mattress, I picked up the gleaming thing and nestled it in my palm. A hundred questions flashed through my brain as I slowly turned the sphere. Although it looked like frosted glass, I noticed that there wasn't a single bubble trapped beneath the surface. So too did I realize that although it was as smooth and shiny as glass that there was a peculiar pattern of red and blue dots that formed a small circle on the opposite end of the retina. What this meant, I could only guess. Maybe it was an identifying mark left by the maker. Perhaps the colored dots were a signature, place of origin, and date in code.

But as much as the mystery of the colored dots befogged my mind, it was the iris that intrigued me most. For when I turned its brown ring to face me, I suddenly felt powerless and frozen. The ring consisted of more different shades of brown than I had ever noticed in my life. The strange ring was a kaleidoscope of all earthly brown hues and other unknown cosmic browns. The ring, which encompassed a hole so black, so deep and vast that when I gazed into it, I became entranced. I felt as though I was floating on a gentle current to a far-off galaxy. I felt as if I were melting, pouring like liquid into the empty black hole that so eagerly and so blatantly wished to consume me.

A toxic and powerful vertigo soon engulfed me. A swirling, drifting sensation pervaded my spirit. I felt as if my body were a puddle of muddy water afloat in the air. A small mass of dirty water that was slowly breaking up into large droplets, all of which were heading off in different directions. It was a strenuous task to gather a somewhat rational thought, and almost impossible to mold it, for the mind kept switching to different concepts long before any conclusions could be made. And when I tried to look away, to twist my neck to one side, each time, just before I tried, my thought pattern became distracted. I wanted nothing more than to turn away, yet it was like I kept forgetting to do so. And each time I closed my eyes, it did not help matters for the dizziness became immense. Within the instant of closing my eyelids, I lost track of which was up or down. I felt as if I were spinning madly through the darkened, starry void. Colors so vibrant and unexplainable flashed like lightning in my brain. Colors yet undiscovered by man swirled in my hollow head. Strange colors so intense and insanely beautiful, that I could not bear to witness them for long. And when I reopened my eyes, the horrible hypnosis of the iris continued to grip me. With all the strength within me, I could not look away.

It was a different day when I awoke. I couldn't fathom what had become of the previous one or what became of me, for that matter. Still, no work had been done in the garden, and the horrible eye was found lying on the floor. I did not recall retiring, yet many ill dreams I could distinctly remember, all of which consisted of being closely watched by a shining eye among the darkness. My stomach was rumbling, and as I stood, I felt weak. When had I eaten last? I could not recall. As I thought of food, I thought too of my garden. Was it ready for planting? Yes, I was sure that it was. As I made my way across the chamber floor, I paused and stooped down to fetch the eye. I did not wish to gaze upon it. I don't even know why I bent to pick it up, but gaze into it I did, and a dizziness swiftly washed over me.

That night, my dreams were more elaborate. The ever-present eye, which continually made its menacing presence known, went beyond the captivating reach of surveillance, for a powerful voice from the darkness behind it said to me in a tone that cracked and roared like a dozen lions: "Behold the features of my face! In this dark, dank, lonely place. Amongst the dusty layers of ages lie sleeping the forgotten horrors of time." Upon the last word spoken, I was shaken from my slumber. I was trembling and soaked with sweat, and the sun was rising once again.

My weary muscles were aching for sustenance. My head was dizzy and light, and my stomach rumbled like a distant thundercloud. After I had finished with breakfast, I headed out back. My belly was full with bread and eggs. I had eaten twice as much as I usually did, and although my stomach now ached from overeating and not from hunger, I felt better. Just as I had reached the back door, I realized I did not have my seeds, so I went into the kitchen to fetch them. As I gathered them, I felt as if there was something I was forgetting, yet I could not, for the life of me, recall what it could be.

Something told me that whatever it was, was in the bedroom. As I wondered what I could possibly need for gardening that was kept in my chamber, the image of the awful glossy eye flashed in my mind. The last thing I wanted to see then was the eye, yet I kept walking toward the bedside table where it lay on its side. It surely wasn't anything I hadn't already seen, yet part of me wished to look upon it, even for a moment and no more. As I came closer to the thing, I came to my senses. Something told me not to touch it, not to look on it even for an instant, and I stopped in front of the table with the sole intention of wrapping it in a blanket and putting it away somewhere out of sight. The cloth that draped over the table would be perfect, I thought, and as I gathered the edges and pulled them up, the cloth moved the eye, and it rolled upright and stared angrily into my eyes.

It seemed to look at me as though it felt betrayed, and as I pulled the cloth up to cover it, I beheld colors between the shades of brown I had not previously seen. The emerging of these new colors intrigued me and filled me with uneasiness. These were the strange and unidentifiable colors I had seen only in my mind when I had closed my eyes to the enormous shining eye. As the cloth slipped through my fingers and hung again from the table's edges, I felt my thoughts, my will, even my mind slowly drifting away from me. The sphere seemed aglow with a faint purple hue, and the many insane colors swirled slowly out of the iris like a maddening nightmare fog reaching out to caress me. I tried to turn away, and I felt as though I could, yet the whole dreamy experience was too beautiful and too unbelievably unique to miss. My head again was light and dizzy. My limbs began to tingle, and they became soaked with weakness. Fear overtook the sleepy sensations of awe as the unearthly colors swirled closer, yet I could not look away. Suddenly, the earth and its colors seemed a distant memory. I felt again as if I were drifting alone through the vast blackness of space. The dark emptiness of isolation that stretched and swelled all around me began to seep into my soul.

Before I realized it, the room was dark. I felt as if I were awakening from some frightful dream as the maddening, swirling colors became swallowed up by the night. Weak and dizzy, I collapsed on the bed, and the real dreaming began. This time, I did not see the eye staring back at me from the pitch-dark. I saw, instead, a hand pushing its way through the thick black fog. A hand that was balled up into a fist and its forefinger extended slowly outward. In my dream, I turned to see what the hand was pointing at. Turning around, I saw a gigantic round stone that rose over forty feet above me. I immediately recognized the land mass in which the stone was jutting out of as the tall hill formation that rose high and stretched far from the bounds of my backyard. I looked down at the base of the stone and saw a shovel whose handle and blade seemed to be made of gold. I picked up the shovel and began digging in the earth at one side of the stone, not in the ground beneath my feet, but in the vertical wall before me. As I dug away at the cliffside, a tunnel began to take shape, and soon a muffled rumbling sound was heard. The gold blade sparkled as I pulled it from the dark hole to see dirt and stones raining down in a large cavity within the enormous hillside. As I stood and watched the dirt rain down, the eye appeared within the hole and glared at me with threat and spite. The huge terrible, gleaming eye, which never closed or blinked.

    I awoke in the middle of the night at the end of the strange dream. I sat up at the edge of the bed and reached for the cloth on the table. Carefully I pulled it up and wrapped the glass eyeball in it and bound it with many tight knots. I knew I could never look on the dreadful object again, not even for a second, not for any reason. That morning as I got ready for work, I noticed an envelope on the floor in front of the door. Inside was a small stack of currency and note that read, "Since you can't even show up to pick up your pay, here it is. I don't know why after all these years of service and loyalty, you decided to quit without any word. Anyway, good luck with your new life. Sincerely, John."

    As I stood holding the letter, I tried to make sense of it. Why had my employer thought I had abandoned my job? Exactly how long had I stared mindlessly into the evil eye? It felt to me like two days, which both went by like two flashes of lightning. And here I stood with my last bit of pay in an envelope, from a job I had lost unknowingly. I was again incredibly weak and hungry. I could not recall the last meal I had eaten.

Weary and groggy, I stumbled through the house and across the high grass of my backyard. Confusion set in as I neared my neglected garden plot. Had I planted the seed after all? I could not recall exactly. I was almost certain that I never got the chance, yet here I was, staring at some stocky plants among tall weeds. I could not identify the plants. Some looked like weeds, yet others looked like they could be my vegetables. Neglect was surely obvious, and there was no order to the garden. There were no neat rows or grouping of the plants. Everything was jumbled and chaotic. And in the middle of the leaves and weeds, there stood a single sunflower, which towered above the rest of the greenery. I knew I did not plant it, yet a bird could be a likely explanation for its presence. Either way, the height of the flower was a spooky revelation. It was clear proof that I had spent a long time staring at that wretched glass eye. Not days or weeks, but perhaps two months or more! And as I stared at the sunflower in disbelief, I saw a sight that made me scream aloud, sending frightened birds flapping to the heights of the cliff. For there in the middle of the flower, surrounded by its wreath of yellow petals, was, clear as day, the image of the spying eye staring back at me mockingly. It filled me with dread to know it was not a dream, and although I thought I had it beat, as I had wrapped and hidden it away, the damage was done. I had lost my job and a chunk of my life. And now I began to fear that I was losing my mind as well. For even without gazing into it, it could still reach me, it could still see me, maybe even still control me with its dreamy hallucinations. I covered my eyes with my hands and hollered to the sky.

I was furious at the object that hung at my ankles wrapped in cloth. I cussed and cursed the very land it came from. Grabbing my shovel, I hopped over the stone wall that bordered my yard and headed into the cool shadow of the monstrous hill. I decided to rid myself of the thing that plagued me. I would bury it deep somewhere far from my backyard, where I had been so unfortunate to find it. I no longer cared about its age or its origin or what it could mean or what it might be worth. I had the rest of my life to ponder those things. I only wished to make it gone, out of sight yet, I feared, not necessarily out of mind.

I had not walked more than a quarter mile over the rocky terrain when a sight seized my footsteps. A sudden rush of excitement reverberated through me as I recognized the massive object I now found myself standing before. A smooth round stone, some forty feet in height, which was undoubtedly the same stone I had seen in a dream not long ago. Before I realized it, I was digging away at the wall to one side of the stone, the same way I had done in my dream. It was not my intention to bury the eye there in the wall, nor was it my will that I dig into the wall at all. Without any thought, I hacked away at the side of the cliff as if it were my plan. I had slipped into a dreamy, tingly, hypnotic daze, not unlike the state that overpowered me when I gazed into the eye.

Before long, a tunnel had become evident, and I went on digging as if I were reliving the dream. Suddenly I stopped. I came to my senses and realized what I was doing and wondered why I was doing it. Was it the dreams? Was it the eye that was controlling my actions and my mindless thoughts? My breathing was labored, I was pouring sweat, and I threw my shovel into the hole I had made in disgust. As the blade sunk into the dirt, I saw the handle of the shovel slowly turning upward. I could not believe what I was seeing, yet I stood and watched it rising still. Before I turned to flee, the reason for the handle's movement became apparent, for all at once I saw dirt and rocks raining down inside the tunnel. Dust came clouding out of the hole as the earth settled within.

When the dust settled, I peered inside, yet it was too dark to see anything beyond the tunnel. When I had returned with the candelabra, I lit the five candles and carefully crawled inside. Soon I had reached the end of the tunnel I had made, and the flickering light revealed an empty cavity of great volume. The cave I now found myself standing within was twenty feet wide and some fifty feet high. It stretched out and tapered into the thick, silent darkness before me.

Slowly I made my way down the colossal corridor, reluctantly inching my way farther and farther still into the bowels of the cliff. All was dreadfully silent save for my footfalls as I pressed on. I began to wonder what I was doing there, was it not the ill power of the mysterious eye that willed me within? The only other plausible explanation was my own curiosity. Yet as much as I wanted to satisfy it, I wished all the more to shut my eyes and find myself in the safety of my own bed, but still I walked on deeper into the dank passage. Suddenly I stumbled over an object at my feet. I did not fall, and gaining my composure, I knelt down and shone that candle's light upon it. It was with much delight I recognized the object at my feet. It was a beautiful dagger of ancient design. I was sure at first sight that it was old beyond belief. When I was done ogling and caressing it, the thought crossed my mind to pay close attention to the ground at my feet, and so I swept it slowly with the candlelight. Before long, I saw something shimmering among the dirt and scattered darkness. Although at first glance, I deemed it too good to be true, I found myself stooped over a small pile of gold coins! They were indeed ancient, and they looked as though at one time they were resting in a sack that had completely rotted away.

Gathering the coins and the candelabra, I continued walking down the immense earthen hallway. Now my mind was consumed with the thought of finding more coins. Even if I did not find any more gold, perhaps I might stumble on another dagger or another ancient relic. I walked with my head hung low, searching the ground with meticulous effort for quite some time without discovering anything else of value, yet soon I noticed that the passage abruptly ended at my feet and spilled downward into a colossal cave, whose ceiling hung high into the blackness above. I hung my candles down as far as my arm would reach, yet the faint small lights would not reveal much of what was lying in the moldy black mist beneath me.

Before I knew it, I was sliding down into the pit on my chest in total darkness, for the candles blew out as I descended. One hand dug itself into the dirt in a vain effort to stop my fall, while the other clutched the candelabra with all my might, for fear of losing my only light source. As I crashed upon the floor of the cave, I heard a peculiar sound. It was the sound of things dry and hollow clanging together. I was afraid to guess what it was, as I fumbled in my pocket for a match. One by one, I lit the candles and brought the holder close to the ground.

Bones! The ground I stood on was littered with skulls and bones! Rib cages, arm and leg bones, hip bones. I recognized some of them as the remains of animals. There were the skulls of goats, rams, and sheep, yet others were undeniably human, all of which were broken, mutilated, and scattered in piles of macabre confusion. My soul cringed, and my body trembled as I stood among them. The horned skulls of animals and the lower jaws and hands of many men stretched out in the darkness all around me, much farther than the candles' glow could penetrate.

My pulse was now slow, and my body still, for quite some time passed while I stood staring at the vast pile of jumbled remains that surrounded me. How long I stood gazing in disbelief I could only guess, for it wasn't until hot wax poured over my hand that I was shoved abruptly out of my hypnotic state.

As I waded through the bones, my mind abandoned me. It was as if it went to sleep for the same reason a body might mercifully faint when absorbing too much pain or terror. Mindlessly I wandered among the shattered skeletal remains as if it were merely a terrible dream. Then I heard the gold coins jingle in my pocket, and I wondered if there were more. And so I walked onward over and between the dry, dusty bones with no end of them in sight. I found no more daggers, no other weapons or tools, no more coins, only broken bones and smiling skulls.

Then I saw what looked to be a passage out of the massive den of death and dust. Without hesitation, I wandered into it. *Thank God*, I thought. What a blessing to feel only dirt beneath my feet. Slowly I walked down the earthen corridor deep within the cliff, holding my candles before me while my eyes slowly adjusted to the dim, shaky light within the pitch-black ever-night.

All at once I saw it. As I slowly rounded an abrupt bend in the tall, wide tunnel. At first glance, I thought it was a stack of bones piled neatly and high, like some wicked sculpture. But as my tortured eyes focused and my mind shook itself from its voluntary slumber, I saw all too clear that it was not comprised of human skeletal fragments, yet it was, without a doubt, bone. I trembled before it with the recluse of a madman eating away at my brain. The only sound I could hear was the thumping of my own heart pounding like a war drum, echoing in my head.

It was the rib cage I noticed first. A gigantic structure of parallel bones at least a dozen feet wide and rising over twenty feet above my head! Ten men could have easily fit in the space within the bony enclosure. Then I saw its hooves. Hooves like a goat yet so large that they could stomp a goat like a man might stomp a beetle. Then I noticed the horrible hands at rest beside them. Hands that resembled curled branches of a tree. Huge and powerful hands that consisted of only three appendages with tapered claws as large and as long as curved swords. The leg bones, as thick and as long as tree trunks, were folded into a sitting position, and still, the skeleton rose over twenty feet above me. But it was the skull of the beast that disturbed me the most, for as I strained my neck to gaze on it, I saw its mouth of tremendous teeth shining against the blackness. And I saw on its skull a massive horn jutting from the middle of its forehead. Between its ghastly jaw of teeth and its hellish horn was a single circular cavity in the middle of its giant skull. A hole filled with mystery and madness and the darkness of ages. A hole filled with dust and cobwebs, which beckoned me to fill it. Now it all made sense to me. The smooth, glass-like appearance and the red and blue dots. The ends of severed veins that were once attached to the brain of the monster. The petrifaction of the cantaloupe-sized organ of vision that rested for eons in the dirt of my garden plot.

Before I even thought about what I was doing, I grabbed hold of a parallel bone and began climbing the massive rib cage. I could not wrap my fingers round the bone for it was too thick, and the enormous skeleton did not budge a single inch with the weight of my body. Higher and higher I climbed the cage of bone, well over twenty feet into the thicker darkness above. The candles flickered beneath me as I pulled my way up to the gleaming teeth, which were as wide and as long as the dagger that hung at my waist.

Standing on the breastplate of the giant, I wasted no time cutting the cloth sack with my ancient dagger, for I could not wait to get down from the enormous beast and out of its silent, dusty lair. Carefully I took the eye from the sack, without looking into it, and placed it into the web-laden cavity. It was a perfect fit. I knew of the dangers of looking into the eye, and so I jerked my head away from it faster than the dust could rise.

When I was again standing before its colossal hooves, I reclaimed my candelabra and looked high above at the bony face of the thing looming above in the darkness. How horrid it looked with the eye back in its niche! How horribly it looked down at me through the candles flickering glow. How long we stared at each other I could not tell. I felt then as though I could never look away. Suddenly, the silence and the spell was shattered by a rumbling sound, which I could neither identify nor conceive. Yet I somehow recognized it as the terrible roaring I had heard in a nightmare I had suffered through not long ago. I kept expecting the humongous skeleton to move as the roaring commenced. There would be no rationalizing what I was seeing or the deplorable sound that tore at my ears. Reality was the scream that fled from my soul, never to be sought out or captured again. As the sounds of both my terror and the rumbling ceased, still I expected to see the thing stir and rise, yet it did not flinch.

The newfound silence woke me. I turned from the insane skeleton and dashed back down the darkened corridor. I don't know how I did not fall, for I had stumbled and tripped the whole way across the floor of bones and skulls. Upon the incline, I scampered with only one free hand to aid my ascent. Somehow I made it up with surprising agility. Past the spot I had found the dagger and the gold, I ran in the dim, jumping light.

Then I came face-to-face with a new horror I had not before seen. A heart-sinking sight that stopped me dead in my tracks. How abruptly my running came to a halt as I held the candles before me to view a wall of earth that had swallowed up a mile of tunnel. The roaring sound I had mistaken for the breath of the monster was nothing more than the rumbling of dirt and stone as the passage back out into the light caved in.

I could not stare blankly at the wall of dirt anymore. Nor could I stroll aimlessly among the smiling skulls and broken bones upon the floor. I knew that soon I would be joining them, and it was a fate I wished not to look upon, nor did I wish to be reminded of every second, as the candles melted down low. And so I sat before the bony monstrosity of nature and beheld the frightful sight until the last candle burned out and left me alone in total blackness with the thing. As horrifying as it was to be left in total pitch-blackness with all the horrors beside me, it was somewhat comforting to no longer be able to see what I knew all too well was towering before me. With nothing but time on my hands, I recalled then some of the creepy stories that my grandfather used to tell me. "Don't worry, boy," he'd say to me at the end of the tale. "Don't worry, it's only a myth," he'd say to me before I walked up the stairs to bed. "My grandfather used to tell me the same stories when I was your age, and they're only stories."

I sat there in the dank black cavern, contemplating the myth and its possible origin. Recalling all the chilling stories he had told me as a child and some of the disturbing nightmares that they had inflicted on me. I thought about how my life was over and how I'd never taste the delicious vegetables I had set out to grow or how I'd never feel the sun on my face again. Then, I could feel the undeniable presence of the great beast before me. Although this whole experience had been quite spellbound, dreamy, and insane, I knew without a doubt what was looming in the darkness before me. Then I looked up. Straining my neck, I gazed up, some twenty feet or more into the absence of light above. The claws of terror seized me as I found myself gazing back at the horrible eye! It glowed there in the darkness above. It glowed without candlelight. It defied all science and reason as it stared down at me. Yet this time, it did not look at me with contempt or anger. It looked on me rather pleasingly, almost as if it were trying to thank me for putting things back where they belonged. And I felt an odd sensation of comfort and contentment nestle within me as I began again to slip beneath the mystifying spell of the ever-spying eye.

THE MINIONS OF NEATH

It was a typical day of hunting. Hiding in the brush, waiting, listening, watching for some critter to hop by or fly overhead. Well over an hour had slowly drifted by as I sat drenched in anticipation and boredom. But all was not in vain, for even if I returned home with an empty sack, like I had many times before, I always went home feeling replenished in mind and spirit. The wilderness always had that effect on me. No matter what was troubling me at that time, it was nothing that Mother Nature couldn't fix.

Suddenly, my hopes were stirred like dust kicked up from the ground as I heard a rustling in the growth a short distance before me. I grabbed my rifle and aimed it at the movement among the vines and branches. Excitedly yet calmly, I peered down the barrel of my weapon at the disturbance in the moving leaves, wondering which sort of beast might emerge. My right forefinger slightly caressed the trigger as a tall black figure stepped into the clearing. My pulse raced madly at first glance, for I thought it was a black bear moving toward me on its hind legs. My itchy finger almost pulled the trigger backward with the sudden rush of fear surging through my veins. Luckily, I held my wits and did not shoot, for at second glance, I realized it was no bear. It was a man in a black hooded cloak, wandering slowly and awkwardly. I sat for a moment and watched him feel his way clumsily through the trees. He seemed helpless and lost.

Pointing the barrel at the mossy forest floor, I stepped out from the greenery that clothed me and called out to the man who seemed in need of help. "Sir, are you lost?" He stopped abruptly and slowly turned in my direction. For a second, my pulse again quickened as he exposed his hooded face to mine. His skin was a pale ash gray, and his lips were dark and cracked. But it was his eyes that chilled me so, for they were empty and white and completely devoid of color or dark pupils. The sudden shock was soon diluted as his ugly, dead eyes reached for me. *Get a hold of yourself, Lucas,* I said in my mind. *He's just a harmless old blind man lost in the wood.*

With a few slow and reluctant paces, I found myself standing before him. "Sir, can I help you find your way?" I repeated.

"Hmm!" He grunted somewhat arrogantly. "My friend," he spoke in a cracked voice, "long ago I found my way. Tell me, what is it you seek?"

The man has a strange way of conversing, I thought. *Perhaps he is mad.* "I'm out here seeking sustenance. I often fish and hunt to help feed my family, sir," I answered the black-robed man.

"But where is your mind when your belly is full? Are your mind and soul not starving for that which cannot be seized by an arrow, since with your eyes it cannot be seen?"

Now I thought for sure he was mad, and I wished not to stay and listen to his ramblings. Still I responded the only way I knew how. "Is that some sort of riddle, sir?"

He chuckled and said, "No, my friend, it is no riddle. What I mean to ask, and perhaps you'll understand me at the risk of using an old Christian cliché: man cannot live on bread and water alone. Tell me, do you survive on fish and fowl alone?"

"I've gotten along just fine so far without spiritual sustenance. And although you Christians think you have it all figured out, I feel that our true creator will guide me humbly through life as he has done since my birth. No offense, sir, but I have no desire to be converted to your faith. Good day, sir."

Before I turned to walk away from the strange old man, I was disturbed by his sudden expression at the taking in of my words. He seemed overly disgusted with me. "No offense!" he shouted abruptly. "No offense! You have indeed offended me deeply by assuming that

I am Christian! You should be careful with your words, sir," he said with a sarcastic emphasis on the word *sir*.

"I am sorry. I should not have assumed. I meant no disrespect. Now if you don't mind, I'll be on my way."

"You go then!" he shouted sternly. "You wander off into the darkness and hope that your maker will guide you through it. The truth is, with your pattern of thought, you don't realize it, but you are wandering alone. We are creatures of need, and we all need guidance. It's too bad, my friend, that you are too blind to see it."

His words gripped me. Suddenly, he did not seem mad at all. He seemed wise and focused. He did not speak like the damning Christians who had tried to convert me with fear, threats, and superstitions. He did not point his finger at me like they had done. It didn't feel like sink or swim with him. It seemed like he genuinely cared about my fate, yet at the same time, he wouldn't condemn me if I refused to believe him. "Where exactly is your faith, sir? Where does it lie?"

"It never lies!" he shouted. "My faith is submerged in truth. I don't get my knowledge from their Bible. The Bible has fooled many billions of souls for over a thousand and a half years. These poor people have devoted and wasted their lives in its name. The Bible is just a book, a work of fiction written by ancient madmen. A book which is filled with many contradictions and has claimed countless souls. And these impressionable fools sleepwalk their precious lives away in the name of their God. And they condemn in the name of their God. And they kill in the name of their God! You ask me where does my faith lie? My faith, my life is nestled in the colossal arms of the one true deity, and his name is Neath!"

I was stunned with his words. They were stern and flowing. Never before had I heard of this Neath, and yet it seemed strangely suicidal to deny his words as far-fetched, as some of them were. Suddenly, I found myself, without much thought, instead of walking away, squatting down to sit by his feet. He folded his body to join me on the moss and stared vacantly in my direction. "Tell me of this Neath," I begged.

"There is much to tell, my son, and it will consume much time to learn. I can tell you only some of him while we sit here, for it is not wise to speak of him in the outer world, and it is also forbidden to reveal his truths to strangers. Besides, it is not my job to teach."

"What is your job?" I asked with the curiosity of a child.

"It is my job to search the land for lost souls such as yourself and give them the opportunity and the choice to seek the truth."

"So you're somewhat of a recruiter?" I asked.

"Yes, I guess you could say that," he responded.

"So whose job is it to enlighten lost souls?" I asked.

"That responsibility is on the head of JWC. Some say he is an ancient man. Some say he is immortal, although he has never confirmed nor denied the rumor. I believe he is, for I was born into the wisdom of Neath, and as you can see, I am quite old myself. JWC has been the teacher as far back as I can recall. When I was just a young boy, he was a white-haired old man. I was twelve when I first heard the rumor, and many long-dead men, then older than me, spoke of how he was teaching Neath's word when they were young."

"What do his initials stand for?" I asked.

"No one knows his name," he responded. "He is a man of great mystery. He divulges only the information about himself which he wishes to share, which is only little."

"What do you call yourselves?" I asked.

"We are called the MONS, and unlike JWC, we do know what it stands for: the minions of Neath."

"It's funny that I have never heard of your faith. How long has it been in existence?" I asked.

"Eight thousand years before Christ the carpenter. Before the Druids, even before the sun god Ra! JWC has told us that Neath himself taught him. And he in turn has taught us all we need to know to move about in a world of darkness."

"A metaphor, I presume," I interrupted. He did not answer, yet he went on as if he was doing his best not to get angry with me and my questions and assumptions. "The world is full of darkness, as you no doubt have seen with your own fully functional eyes, yet you unknowingly stumble about in the blackness of ignorance. JWC will show you the truth… how to see what is real and that which are lies, if you are willing. But first, you must be willing to see without eyes, for this is the only way to truly see. You must also be willing to sacrifice."

At the utterance of this word, my spirit became chilled. "Sacrifice?" I muttered nervously.

He laughed. "Ah, not to worry, my friend, just more metaphors."

We talked for a while more, and somehow I allowed him to convince me to go back with him and hear the words of this JWC. I had no intentions of being converted to the mysterious MON religion or cult or whatever it was, yet I was all too curious about the whole thing. I had to see this odd man's world with my own eyes. I had to give it a listen. And so I walked beside him while his robe fluttered in the breeze. I walked in his shadow and watched him make his way through the trees and the thorny brush and wondered how he did it so effortlessly without vision. We did not walk far before he suddenly ditched into a thick mass of tall brush. I thought he lost his way until I heard him say, "Here we are, my friend."

I followed him into the middle of a circle of thorny bushes. The strange old man stood there in a clearing before a large flat rock that rested on the forest floor at his feet. He tapped the stone twice with a stick, paused, and then tapped three times more. He dropped the stick and straightened his frame. Suddenly, the rock began to turn on its side. Slowly it raised like a large door within the ground. To my astonishment, I noticed there were no hinges, and I gasped aloud when I expected to see a rope or a chain, yet I saw nothing save the stone itself and the darkness it had been hiding. It came to a halt when it was perfectly vertical, and that was when I turned my attention to the hole it was covering. The sunlight had poured into the hole, revealing a steep set of stone steps that spiraled into the darkness below. I did not wish to descend into that dreadful darkness, and I said to the creepy old blind man, "Down there? You expect me to go down there?"

"Do not be frightened, my friend. There are far worse fears to be dealt with in the light of day. Besides, down there is where the answers hide. Down there is where you'll find the truth." I stood staring down into the dizzying staircase. Down past the white spiral stones into the sleeping darkness below. I could not speak. It felt as if my mind was empty in that moment. Almost like a man might feel when he's watching enormous waves crash toward the shore or is hypnotized by a dancing fire. "Come, my friend, have a little faith!" he said, half-smiling.

"You first," I responded.

"Leave your weapon above, you'll have no use for it below."

When I agreed to go down there, it was only with the assurance that I had my rifle by my side just in case, and now he was telling me to leave it above. Great! I was hoping he had forgotten in his sightlessness. *At least I have my hunting knife,* I thought as I reluctantly jumped into the hole, landing on the first step.

Slowly and cautiously I followed behind the stranger. *I must be out of my mind!* I thought. Down we went quietly in a circular pattern of decent. Our footsteps echoing into the blind abyss was the only lonely sound that filled our ears. Slowly the faint light below revealed only more and more steps of stone as we went farther down. Within a moment, the small amount of suffocating light had been snuffed out as I heard the stone above shut us up inside the well. It rumbled and thumped as it sealed us in complete darkness. It was a darkness so thick I could almost feel it resting on my shoulders. As the complete and devouring darkness swallowed us up, my movements seized. I stood on the edge of a stone step, silently begging my open eyes to do their work. Yet as they searched in vain, the only thing I could see was that which rested like a burden on my shoulders—the dense, absolute absence of light. The pure nothingness I felt then piercing into my side like a hook through a squirming worm, and I could not continue downward. I could not even turn around and ascend the staircase, which was now my overwhelming will. It was all I could do to stand frozen upon the stone, too nervous to flinch.

"Hug the wall, my friend. Do not be afraid. Feel your way along the wall. Feel your way carefully with your feet. Remember what I said earlier: you must learn to see without eyes."

"I can't," I responded with a shaky voice. "There's no way."

"There is no other way!" he shouted, and his voice echoed like a faint, distant rumble of thunder. "You will find a way, for it is worse in the eyes of Neath to be in between. You either seek him and believe him, or you don't. There is only one thing Neath despises more than a nonbeliever, and that is one who will not choose. So stand there in the dark alone if you wish, but let it be known that Neath may seek you out and devour you where you stand. So come, my son. Slowly, carefully hug the wall. Embrace the darkness. Feel with your feet. Descend with me and learn. Learn to see without eyes."

For fear of being left alone on that step, I slowly felt along the wall. It was cold yet somewhat welcoming. I knew I could not move the massive stone that lay in my way back to the outside world. I began to feel the edges of the step with my foot. My heel slid slowly down the vertical surface of the riser until it came to rest on the lower step. Once I felt the solid stone beneath my feet, I gradually pressed my weight on it. In my mind, I pictured the spiral staircase of white stone and the curved wall that encompassed it. I listened for the steps of the blind man before me. Even if he was lying about, being sought out and eaten by his deity on the stairs, I did not wish to find out the hard way, nor did I wish to be left on that stair alone in the murky darkness. *I can do this,* I thought to myself. *I can do this.*

Down and down we inched our way through the dizzying depths. How many feet? How many moments? How many godforsaken steps? It felt like an eternity since I'd last heard a single word uttered by the strange old man who led the way down. And now as my foot rested on yet another stone and searched for its sharp edge, something didn't feel quite right. Forward and forward still my foot stretched, and I felt neither its edge nor end. Now I knew that my foot had snaked its way across twice the length of the other steps, and still I felt no drop-off. Blindly I patted my foot farther forward along the length of stone, hugging the wall as I went. Finally, the old man broke the spell of silence with a long boasting laugh. "Good job. You made it down, my friend. I had faith in you from the start. Now you're on your way to the truth."

Slowly we shuffled down a dank, earthen corridor. All the while I dragged my palms across the cold dirt wall while listening to the old man's feet. My feet were slow and reluctant to accept the weight of my body. Soon I felt an absence in the wall and halted. "Sir, does the path round a corner here?"

"No, it's perfectly straight. Don't mind those gaps in the wall. There are plenty of them along the way, but they're only three feet deep. Do not reach or step into them. Simply feel with your arms extended before you, and you will come in contact with the wall again. It is vital to stay on the path and keep up. Do you hear?"

"Yes," I responded. I did as he said, and sure enough, I felt along the edge of the path. I had no desire to reach in or wander off and become lost, so I obeyed the queer old man. I shuffled along the dusty path for what felt like an hour, in a blind, struggling pursuit of the strange cloaked man. All the while, his jaw was sealed, and with each cautious step, I began to feel more and more regretful of my following him down those never-ending steps of white stone. His silence spawned within me an eerie sensation of dread, which I could feel growing in my guts with each empty moment.

Suddenly I realized that I did not so much as know the name of the old man I was following, and so I decided to break the silence. "Sir," I spoke in a timid tone, "I just realized I don't even know your name."

"Names do not matter here," he answered swiftly. "Only the names of JWC and the mighty Neath himself are needed to know. In fact, most of the minions were never born with a name."

"Then how do you communicate?" I asked.

"How does the mother mole call a certain pup to her side?" he answered with another question. "How does she know that one of her large litter isn't getting enough milk when the stronger pups are bullying it? She just does. Neath has bestowed this natural instinct within all creatures great and small. And just like he has shown them how to see, live, and thrive, even communicate in total darkness like the ants and the mole, like the crawlers and the ones who slither on the deep, dark ocean floor, so too will he teach you the ways of his minions. They do not use speech to communicate, the same way they need not their eyes to see. As I've heard some of your kind say: it's all in the mind. Anyway, soon you will know. You will not feel the need to keep asking questions. If you accept Neath and are willing to devote your life to his ways, then it will all come to you at once, like a rising sun reveals a surrounding landscape. It will all make sense in a single moment like it makes sense to a newborn mole. You see, my son, all that needs to happen is you must show your willingness and accept the truth. Only then will Neath awaken within you the sleeping instincts he has planted in every man. In every man, there is good and evil. The evil is taught by man. The good is that tiny part of Neath inside you that you never knew existed. All you have to do is allow him to show you how to open that door that has been forever sealed. All you need to do is ask him to wake up that part of you which has been dormant since your birth."

I had no response. And although I had many questions, I kept my mouth sealed like that door he spoke of. Every time he answered one of my questions, he ended up raising a dozen more. Still I followed him deeper into the darkness, thinking about his words, which were more like riddles than phrases. Then I became aware of a distant commotion filling my hungry ears. It sounded like when you put a conch shell against your ear. A muffled and echoing sound almost like a billion ants crawling over each other. A faint clicking and clatter of numberless legs grinding and climbing, reaching and kicking. Like bubbles in foam popping in dying waves. It was then when I realized why I had blindly and trustingly followed him down. I wanted to hear the words of this Neath. I wanted to understand the logic of the strange old man. I grew more and more anxious to hear the speech of this JWC.

We walked farther down the never-ending hall. The sound slowly grew louder as we inched on. Again he finally spoke. "Ah, here we are, my friend."

"Where is here?" I asked as baffled as ever.

"Here is where you'll stay the night. Tomorrow I will wake you. I will come with sustenance. Then I will bring you to the great hall, where you will begin your enlightenment, for tomorrow JWC speaks to the masses. Until then, remain in your cavern. Do not wander about alone!" he ordered sternly. "Stay here until I come for you, do you understand?"

"Yes, of course," I promised.

"You will be safe here," he continued. "However, if you wander about in your current state, as a non-minion, you will not be recognized as one of us, and you will be devoured." His words tore through me as I stood before him. I could picture his rough, wrinkled face and his empty white eyes burning through me as he spoke. I could almost see his long white hair reaching out in all directions from the hood of his cloak. "I will be safe here?" I begged for reassurance.

"Don't second-guess me, you fool!" he hollered. "Listen once, and listen good! I hate repeating the same tired words over and over again. Life is too short to waste your breath on those who don't listen." It took much resistance to keep my legs from trembling. I did not want the old man to know I was intimidated by his sternness and knowledge. Without another word said by either of us, I heard him turn and wander away into the black. I stood listening until I could hear his steps no more.

I decided to explore my new confines. I began feeling slowly along the dirt wall. Reluctantly I reached out and slid my hand across the face of the cavern as he called it. Slowly it led me around in a short circle. The confines of the cavern were extremely claustrophobic. The chiseled out room could not have been larger than six or eight feet in circumference. Just enough space for a man to lay down and stretch his legs. The thought of sitting there, staring blindly out into the darkness, made me ill. I wasn't incredibly tired, yet I decided it would be best to try and fall asleep, so I lay down on the hard ground, burying my face into my elbow. The complete absence of light was toxic enough with the old man around, now alone it was tenfold worse. As I shut my eyes to rest them, a peculiar thought occurred to me. I realized that I could have had them closed the entire time I was down here, and it wouldn't have made the slightest difference. I lay there on the rough dirt floor, listening to the faint, rustling din. I wished that there was a door to seal me up.

I woke suddenly to a somewhat familiar voice. "Wake up, my friend, wake up!" My head was groggy, and my neck was stiff. I raised my heavy head, and my eyes toiled in vain to make sense of the nothingness before me. It took me a few moments to grasp the situation.

To realize where I was and why I was not lying in my comfortable bed, and it took a few seconds more to realize that I was not dreaming. "You must be hungry." The half-familiar voice spoke across the thick, cool air.

"Yes, I am," I responded humbly. "I haven't eaten since breakfast yesterday."

"Well, eat up, my friend," spoke the unseen figure before me. "Eat and I will return for you in a while."

"Thank you, sir, I appreciate it greatly, thank you," I said as he pushed an object against my chest. Wrapping my hands around what felt to be a cold, crudely carved bowl of stone, I thanked him yet again and listened to his feet shuffle off into the distance. Once the sounds of his feet were no longer present, a new sound aroused my ears. At first I dismissed it as the rustling sound off in the distance, which reminded me of the ocean, yet I soon realized that it was closer than the sound I'd heard before. In fact, it was right under my nose. The sound was slightly different than the one before. It was a wet, squishy, sloshing sound, and it was coming from the bowl!

How long did I sit silently before that bowl, listening to the gut-churning sounds it emitted? Finally I got the nerve up to reach down and touch its contents. Slowly my hand sunk down toward the edge of the bowl to feel, to touch, to realize what was to be my morning meal. My hand hung inches above the bowl, and I heard my stomach rumble, yet I could not force my hand to move. Several times I tried to sink it into the bowl to take a scoop of its sustenance, and each time I tried, I could not bring my hand to budge. Finally, my left hand grabbed my right hand and pushed it into the bowl with a will all its own. My right hand submerged in a cold, slimy substance and grabbed a palm full and ripped itself out of the bowl faster than it had been dunked in. As I stretched my balled fist out before me, I felt a moistness, which squirmed and tickled my fingers as it moved. I opened my hand abruptly and flung violently with my open hand what it once held. Swiftly I stood up and backed away from the bowl. Yet still I felt a faint tickle in my palm. With my left hand, I felt for it. My fingers stretched out to examine it, for my right hand would no longer move. Slowly the fingers of my left hand found the writhing thing in my palm and caressed it. From one end of its tiny, slithery body my forefinger was dragged. I had come to the realization of what it was in the bowl. I laughed madly at the revelation. But my laughter came to an abrupt halt when I realized what he was feeding me. Again, I heard my stomach growl.

It was quite some time before he returned. Whether hours or days had passed, I could not be sure. Without the sun, it was impossible to even tell the difference between day and night. It was then it dawned on me that down here, it is always night. I felt nauseous at the thought of not seeing the warm rise of the sun to reveal my surroundings. I was sure it wasn't just the worms that made me feel ill. "How was your meal?" he asked.

"Delicious," I responded nervously.

"Neath hates a liar!" He growled. "Don't waste your breath trying to deceive me. There is only one place for liars here, and that is within the belly of the great one. If you truly wish to learn the truth, you must be prepared to give up your old ways and tell the truth. There is no benefit in lying down here, for you will fool no one."

"I'm sorry, I only—" I began my pathetic apology, only to be cut off in midsentence.

"I understand, still, great or small, a lie is still a lie. Now, that being said, are you ready to hear the words of the wise one?"

"Yes, I am," I said eagerly. "Well, then, if you are ready to hear, you must first be willing to see, to see in total darkness. Only then will you be able to hear, for the words of Neath, spoken through JWC, cannot be heard with the use of ears. Only via the mind can the message be received, for his mouth emits no sound, yet the minions and I can take in every word. Are you ready to see, my friend? Are you ready to hear the truth?"

"I am," I responded without hesitation.

"Then let's begin," he said. "Here, put this on."

"What is it?" I asked. "It is a mask. Now put it on."

"Why must I wear a mask?" I asked.

"No more questions! If you want to understand, you'll do as I say without hesitation. Now here, take it and wear it proudly, if only for a moment." I had so many questions about the mask. Why did I have to wear it? And why would only wearing it for a moment appease him? Would the minions actually see the mask? Do they actually see through the thick dark veil that forever hung before them? If so, what was the purpose of concealing my face to total strangers? These and many more questions were surfacing in my brain like so many weeds in a freshly tilled garden plot, yet I knew better than to ask any one of them, and instead I reached out my arms to receive it. He rested it in my hands and told me it was facing the right way. He said not to turn it or caress it, just to put it on.

Slowly I raised the heavy object to my face. It smelled horribly of rotten shellfish and mold. The stench of the mask made me want to throw it down and back away from it like I had done with the bowl of worms, yet I still raised it closer to my blind eyes and wrinkling nose. I held it there, perhaps an inch from my face. I wanted to do as the strange man asked without question. I wanted to show my faith. Hell, I wanted to have some, yet I could not bring myself to press the mask over my face. "What are you waiting for?" He sneered. I did not answer. I only froze with the mask before my face, breathing in the fowl stench it emitted. Then I heard a slight sound that tore my spirit in two halves. It was a squishy sound like that I had heard coming from the bowl yet slightly different. And not only did I hear the disturbing sound, though faint as it was, I actually felt a slight vibration within the mask. Faith or no faith, I began to push the mask away from my face when I felt a sharp pain on one of my eyes. An intense, piercing pain that both stabbed into and sucked at my eye. Within a second, my eye and my brain, as well, were throbbing as I fought with all my strength to push the mask away. I screamed, "Help me! Get it off!" Yet there was no response from the old cloaked stranger. The pain was so bad now that it began to become numb as I fought to peel the mask away from my face. My mind was infested with horrible images undreamed as I tried to comprehend what was happening. My mind suffered in vain to understand what was ripping and pulling at my eye. I began in my struggle to feel weak and weary. I fought off the urge to black out many times. Suddenly, I felt the tickle of a moist thing on my other eye, and it was then that I summoned the strength to tear the mask away from my face in a final swift motion. As I pushed the mask away, I felt the terrible tearing of my right eye. I heard an awful snapping sound as my arms abruptly extended. My arms froze in that position, still grasping the mask tightly. After a moment, my mind began to come back to me. I tried desperately to understand what had happened. I did not have to see to realize that my right eye was no longer nestled in its socket. It was then I felt a disturbing tickling on my left hand. It was wet and slimy. Violently I threw the mask across the darkness. I felt blood pouring swiftly from my face and streaming down my neck. Quickly I ripped off part of my shirt and stuffed the fabric into the hole in my face to stop the blood. A powerful dizziness engulfed me, and I fell backward to the ground.

When I awoke, I was seated in a cold stone chair. My head as well as half my face was numb. The pain was almost nonexistent, yet it was still evident enough to remind me of the horrible incident, and it reassured me that it was no nightmare. Had I been drugged? Why had he done this to me? I wondered. And where was he now? Better yet, where was I? That seemed like a more crucial question. As I sat on the course stone, I pondered many questions, while my groggy head throbbed with white dots blinking and swirling like fireflies in my brain. Again I heard, repeating in my mind, one of the many threats from the old man of this Neath. Things about his mighty jaws, his gullet, and his belly. I was too frightened to budge. Slowly a slight sound became apparent. The more I listened, the more of it I heard. It was not like the first din I had heard before off in the distance; rather, it was much quieter, yet at the same time, I felt, without any doubt, that it was close. So close, in fact, that I was sure I was in the midst of it. At first it sounded like a slight rustling of clothing. Like the quiet grinding and twisting of cloth over flesh. The flesh of a great crowd that shifted uncomfortably in their seats, stretching their limbs in slow, scuttle movements. Then I heard distinctly another sound. The more I sat and listened, the more familiar it became. It was a low, faint wheezing sound. It was quiet yet altogether immense. I was sure after a moment or two that I was hearing the labor of many multitudes of lungs. The disheartening breathing of masses of strange, unseen souls all about me.

How long I sat there frozen on the cold stone bench with those sounds torturing my ears, I could not tell. Time did not matter down here. Nor did the fact that one of my eyes was somehow missing from its socket. Nor did the fact that I still had the use of my left eye, for there was nothing here to behold save for the dark. Sometimes I couldn't tell if my one good eye was open or shut. Anyway, it made no difference either way. Even the reason I ended up here no longer mattered. The so-called truth no longer concerned me. I did not wish to learn any longer; I only wanted out of the strange, ancient place of blackness. Suddenly a new noise arose. It was like the noise I'd heard when I first traversed the never-ending hall. Except this time, it was much louder, as I was among it all. In my mind, I tried to picture what was happening. It seemed as though the crowd had rose to their feet simultaneously and began to slowly shuffle out of the great room. A few times, something brushed against my leg, yet I sat unflinching.

It must have consumed an hour or more to empty out of the great room, for finally I could hear the last of them disappearing down the great hall. I sat and listened patiently to the silence returning. Soon, however, I was startled by a stern and an all-too-familiar voice. "Well, what do you think?" he asked.

"What do I think about what?" I returned the question. "About the words of JWC. Did not his mental enlightenment tickle your eardrums?"

"The only thing that tickled my ear drums was the wheezing of your minions, you old fool! Now if you'll be so kind as to lead me back to the surface world of light—"

Again he stopped me in midsentence only to return his own demands. "I'd be less reluctant to feed you to the one true god! The god which you've denied! You'll make but a morsel, but you'll do!"

"Wait!" I implored. "I have denied nothing. You have given me nothing to deny nor believe."

There was a brief moment of silence before he spoke again. "Are you saying that you have not heard a word of the sermon? That not one of his words reached your mind?"

"That's exactly what I'm saying."

"Hmm. Then you must not have worn the mask. You didn't put it on, did you? I was sure I heard it doing its work. You must have stopped it from finishing." I tried to respond, but before I could, he went on. "I have given you the choice. Now we will make the decisions for you from now on. I thought you were willing to see. I thought you displayed faith. Now we will force the faith into you. We will make you see, or make a meal of you! Exalted one, please bring forth the mask of enlightenment, while I restrain this blind fool." Before I could budge, he had me bound. My arms both behind me, twisted and bent past the point of submission, clearly displayed surprising strength in the old man's limbs. Then I could hear the footfalls of the silent stranger moving toward me. I tried to muscle my way out of his hold, yet it seemed useless to struggle. Closer and closer the footsteps advanced. Louder and louder the sound of his feet grew until they stopped before me. In my mind, I could only picture a faceless black figure swooping down over me, holding in his outstretched arms that horrible, living mask, which hungered for my only good eye.

Again, the wretched stench of rotten fish and mold wafted like an evil cloud around my face and slithered into my nostrils. I coughed and gagged as the vile stench choked me. Now I could feel the mask only inches away from my retracting face. Again I heard a wet, sticky, sloshing sound emitting from the mask. Soon I would feel the moist tickle upon my tightly closed eye. I tried again to rip my arms away from the old man's grasp; still it was of no use. Next, I felt the rough leather-like shell of the mask slightly touch my face, and in a last summoning of strength, I pushed with my legs against the floor, knocking my own body backward, as well as the man who bound me. The bench of stone made a terrible thump as it crashed to the floor. With my arms still bound from behind, I kicked blindly up at the stranger's face. I hit something, although I could not tell if it was his face I connected with, for I did not hear him grunt. I knew then that I had only kicked the mask. I listened for it to hit the floor. Within seconds, I knew all too well that it was still in his hands.

I knew he was still coming toward me. I tried to picture him in my mind, the distance, and his positioning. The stench again became intense. I struggled again to strip from his grasp in vain. I knew it was yet again upon me. I raised both my legs up and behind my head. Swiftly I used them both to kick somewhat like a mule. Once again I connected. I heard his body tumble awkwardly to the floor, but not before it rolled backward over a stone bench. Again I struggled to no avail. The old man's strength was unbelievable. It was a sad revelation to discover that I could not use my legs on him. Now our ears were pierced with the sounds of this JWC screaming. Screaming and calling out to my captor with deafening cries of pain and hopelessness. Before I knew it, I was free. I heard the old cloaked man demanding me to get off him. I gladly rolled to the cold ground, gasping for air, and tried desperately to gather my thoughts.

Although the complete and potent darkness rendered my one good eye useless, I knew and could almost see what had happened. With the first kick, which was more of an uppercut motion, I connected with the mask, not sending it flying from his grasp, yet only spinning it around in his hands. With the second kick, a more forward motion, I slammed the mask on his face! And as he writhed and screamed between the stone pews, I had another revelation. It was then I remembered that I had brought a friend down with me. I wasn't even sure if it was still in my possession, and as I fumbled around in the pocket of my jacket, I felt a coldness, which only warmed my spirit—the coldness of steel. I held the knife firm by its handle. I gripped it harder than a man had ever held an object in his palm. Slowly I felt my way to the screaming man and the strange old man who tried in vain to peel the mask from his face. "Help me save him!" he yelled. "Help me save the exalted one! It's your only hope," he pleaded as he struggled.

"I'll help him," I responded emotionlessly. "I'll help you both!"

I raised my right arm up and behind my head. I used the old man's advice to the best of my knowledge. I pictured them both there on the floor. I used his screams to close in on him. I made him scream one last time as I brought the knife down. "No! No! You fool! No! You fool!" he cried in disbelief.

"Tell me," I said as I stood over him. "Tell me, wise one, does he not bleed?"

"Of course he does not bleed, and he will not die! He cannot die! Do you hear me, he cannot die, you fool, for he is the exalted one! The voice of the mighty Neath! The immortal, exalted one! And you shall pay dearly for your evil ways." I wished I had a match or a candle. If only I could see what was happening, if he truly was bleeding and dying. Soon I could hear no more screams from his lips, and I was almost sure he was dead. Yet something kept telling me to expect him to rise and moan. To let me know he was still alive before he retaliated. "Does he not bleed?" I demanded. "He no longer screams, old one, but does he not bleed?"

"No! No, he does not, and he cannot, you fool! Look what you've done!" I heard him fold to the floor and whimper and moan in disbelief. I ran my finger along the blade. It was wet and sticky. A smile came over my face. "Minions! Minions!" The old black-cloaked man began screaming as loud as his lungs would permit. "Minions! Minions!" Quickly my blade silenced him as well, for at that point, there was no denying that he was lying. I had to find a way out.

As I felt my way past the never-ending rows of cold stone benches and out into another wide dirt tunnel, I thought of what I had done. I was a hunter and a family man. I had never been a violent man. I had never hurt anyone before now. I had killed my share of animals, but I never killed a man. I had to keep reminding myself that I had to kill them. I had to prove to the old man and to myself that they were wrong. That he wasn't immortal, and so I would know the truth. And now I knew the truth. The whole thing was a lie. Besides, they hurt me. That crazy old man lured me down here, why, I can only guess, but he lured me down here only to harm and deceive me. *They got what they deserved,* I kept telling myself. *Who knows what they were going to do to me. I am missing an eye because of them. They got what they deserved.*

Soon I felt again an absence within the side of the wall, and I stopped abruptly. What was the purpose of the spaces? I wondered. Were they pathways leading off into other directions? There were countless numbers of them. You couldn't take five paces without encountering another one. In my mind, I pictured a vast array of maddening tunnels, many connecting, yet others leading nowhere, like a colossal, incomprehensible, underground maze of darkness. An ill feeling of hopelessness began churning in my gut. *If they each were tunnels, I'll never escape,* I thought. But be they tunnels or not, I was too terrified to find out. I continued slowly onward after my hand felt again the moist dirt wall. *I hope it doesn't come down to finding out if they are tunnels,* I thought as I quickly shuffled through the ultimate blackness. I was careful not to extend my hand into the voids in the wall.

    I was lucky that the minions had not heard the old man's cries from the great hall or the screams of JWC as the mask ate his eyes. What evil creature, or creatures, dwell inside that hideous mask? Oh great god of mercy, the questions I pondered, the horrible images that crawled around my brain as I inched along the tunnel, feeling with cut-up hands and listening through the dreadful silence for evidence of pursuit. Gap after gap my hands slid past. Onward and farther I wandered through the endless hall. My head was light with confusion and disbelief. My stomach was rumbling for sustenance. I was weak and dizzy. I had no way of telling how long it had been since my last meal. Time was a torturer.

    Feeling yet another vacancy in the wall, I stretched out my arm to feel the wall's continuation. A few steps more, and still I felt nothing but black air. Sliding my feet along the ground, I moved ahead a few more paces without feeling the side of the tunnel. Finally, I felt before me a wall of earth. Soon I realized as I felt along the wall that the tunnel was bent to a right-hand direction. And so it began. Another endless hall laden with gaps on each side. Length after length, gap after gap, bend upon bend, I trotted on weary and half mad, dragging my sore, numb, open palm along the dirt and the rocks within. Then I stubbed my foot against some solid object, and slowly I knelt down to examine it with my hands. *Ah! A set of stairs, and leading up no less! Thank God!* I said to myself. A sensation of relief surged through my spirit, and I began crawling upward. But my hopes were short-lived, for soon the steps ended, and I found myself walking cautiously into some chamber or hall.

    Along the wall I felt as I traversed a great many paces. All the while it was solid and free of niches. It seemed slightly curved, as if it were a large round room. Suddenly, I felt a warmth on my face, and at the same time, I heard a slight, gentle hissing. I froze where I stood and gasped aloud. My body began to tremble. In my mind, I pictured a large snake looming in the darkness before me with its tongue slithering about, feeling for me. I waited there with my back against the wall and listened to the faint, constant hissing. Quite a few moments of terror had slowly drifted past until a thought came to me. It didn't all make sense at first, until I thought about the effect the darkness had on my vision. An instant of bravery arose in me, and I stretched out my hand toward the sound. "Ahh!" I hollered in immense pain. My fingers began throbbing, and I snapped them back. *It was true!* I said to myself. *It's fire!* Feeling once more, and with much more caution, I reached lower than I had before along the wall up toward the object. Caressing what felt to be the handle of a torch, I grasped it and pried it from its place of hanging. Light! Holy and blessed light! I thought. There is light down here after all. Now all I have to do is wait for my eye to adjust, and I'll have light enough to find my way out.

As I sat before the hissing torch, warming my hands and waiting for what must've been hours, slowly I began to see a slight blur of orange before me. I knew it would take more time before I could see again properly. Still, there was no time to waste, so I decided to feel my way around the room. Slowly I felt along in a half circle until I heard again the dull hissing of yet another torch. And without burning myself again, I found my way back to the stairs. There clearly was no other access to this chamber. My curiosity wanted to wait till my vision returned to scope the room, but this time, I was all the wiser. I made my way down the stairs with the torch in my left hand.

As I walked down yet another tunnel, my vision was slowly returning. The flame of the torch became clearer and clearer. It was one of the most beautiful things I'd ever seen. The darkness was still potent; however, I could now see a patch of dim, shaky light a short distance from me. I could now see the dim tunnel I was dragging my hand along. Suddenly, my feet came to a halt, although I knew not why I had stopped, the only thing I wanted to do was to keep moving. But for whatever reason, I found myself standing still in the corridor, listening to the hissing of the flame in my left hand. It was almost as if I got the notion that someone or something was drawing close to me, yet I heard no sound save for the torch. It was almost as if I could sense a presence close-by. By now I could see well enough that I no longer had to caress the wall to guide me, so I took the torch in my right hand. As I did, I realized that I was standing before one of the many cavities in the tunnel. Slowly my eye adjusted to the vacancy within the wall. Slowly an outline emerged from the darkness. It was about three feet wide, stood eight feet tall, and came to an arc at the top. The darkness inside was thicker, and I pushed the torch in closer to see if it was indeed a passage. All at once, I saw at eye level the sight of a ghastly face standing silently before me, only inches away. At first I thought it was a statue, yet as I gazed on it with my one good eye, I noticed to my horror that it was not made of stone. The decrepit face was a pale gray, whose lips were closed, and did not grunt or flinch. Both of his eye sockets were bare, and I found myself gazing, terrified into them.

My mind was swirling with madness and fear as I walked a few paces to the opposite side of the tunnel, expecting him to suddenly speak or move toward me, yet he remained silent and still. Here I found myself standing before another arced gap in the dirt wall, and I raised the torch up slowly. Again I saw the face of yet another pale gray-faced man with a solemn expression and holes where his eyes should be. He stood still and silent before me, like some macabre statue in a museum's cellar.

The next thing I knew I was running. Running down the hall with the torch outstretched before me, casting a faint, jumping light on the dirt floor. I could feel them all around me. I knew not if they were sleeping or awake or even if they were aware of my presence at all. I only knew they were standing silently like sentries in the countless darkened niches on either side of the tunnels. As the tunnel bent around a corner to the left, I halted yet again at the bend. I turned slowly around and gazed into the blackness before me. There I saw a figure moving out of the wall. A gray figure that silently and awkwardly lumbered in my direction. I heard the scraping of feet upon the ground, which chilled me to the bone. Running down the tunnel, I felt a body brush up against mine. I heard a grunting sound as I bumped it still it did not slow me down.

Then I felt a hand grab for my arm. For a split second, it seized me, but I managed to twist and pull myself away from its grip, and I kept on running. I could see more of them out of the corner of my eye as I ran past. Stepping out slowly from the walls as if they were simultaneously summoned by some unheard force. I could hear them moaning and grunting behind me and scuffing their feet across the dirt. Then, before I could halt, I ran directly into a crowd of them. I could feel a hundred cold hands on my body and face. A dark cloud of eyeless faces and cold gray hands gripping, groping, and pulling at me.

The next thing I knew, they were carrying me off down the tunnel. I tried to ward them off with the flame, but it was no use. Now the torch was in the grasp of one of them, and I heard not one English word spoken among them as they carried me. But soon, I did hear a word. A word that I recognized: "Neath!" One of them spoke it, and the rest of them began to chant it in synchronicity. Louder and louder the word was uttered. "Neath! Neath!" It echoed down the tunnel and within the walls of my skull. "Neath! Neath!" Down the corridor they carried me above their heads. I could still see vaguely before me for the torch was held close-by. We passed through an arc of stones and into an even wider tunnel. It was four times as wide as the others, and darkness hung thickly above, concealing the ceiling. Then I saw a massive stone that stood as wide as the entire passage and rose up into the darkness above. It slightly resembled a colossal door, yet I could not be certain. Suddenly, the chanting ceased, and we stopped before the great stone.

Then I noticed a hole in the stone about eight feet from the floor and three feet wide in circumference. Without a sound, they moved me forward and stuffed me headfirst into the hole. With a thump, I slammed on the ground and lay there in pain, as still and quiet as I could be. I heard a faint roar of flame as the torch was tossed in with me. I lay there and listened to the crowd make their way back to their holes in the walls. I lay there and contemplated my situation. What kind of horrors had I been tossed in with? I had confirmed the words of the black-cloaked man to be lies. His precious JWC was no more immortal than he was blind. And yet, I could not help as I lay on the cold dirt and listened to the awful silence but to wonder if there was any truth to the tales of this Neath. Maybe they keep venomous snakes in here to rid them of nonbelievers and to ensure the faith of the minions. Or perhaps there is something down here. Something that the surface world has never seen. Maybe some species of terrible beast that the people on the surface have yet to discover. I have experienced strange things down here that cannot be denied. What was in that horrible mask? These and many questions I pondered without closure. My own mind was working against me; it began to betray me. I was overwhelmed with terror as I lay there, listening, waiting for something to come for me. The anticipation was torturous, and the silence was dreadful as I lay on the cold ground, shivering and listening intently for the horrid sounds of something moving about. Finally I decided to rise. I gathered what was left of my wits and picked up the torch. I held it before me. I found the wall and started walking beside it. The room was vast. If there was something here, it was certainly enormous. Why would they go to such great lengths to carve out such an immense chamber unless it was indeed for housing something? As I walked cautiously on, I expected at any second to be seized by someone or something. I only hoped it would be over quick. I just wanted it to be over. By now, I had lost all hope of escape.

What felt like hours slowly drifted by. I had searched the massive chamber through and through. I found myself finally laughing aloud. There was no Neath! But still I felt the clutches of doom. It looked as if I was going to rot down here. The entire place seemed empty. I could find nothing to use to climb up to the hole in the rock. But I had plenty of time to think. Once I had gotten over my fear, my mind was clear, and I could focus on a plan. Finally, it came to me. I stood by the edge of the great stone and took out my knife, the same knife that would be useless against the hordes of minions that put me here. I began stabbing the wall by the edge of the stone, stabbing and digging at the wall of dirt.

It wasn't long before I was through and found myself again holding my trusty, hissing torch and walking quietly down the tunnel. But what was to stop it from happening again? There were countless cavities on either side of every tunnel, each one occupied by an eyeless oaf. If I could just sneak past them. If I could only find the staircase, then maybe I could dig my way around the stone. It was my only chance. Back down the corridor I snuck. Each recess in the wall made me cringe as I passed it, expecting them to crawl out at any second. Yet there was no sign of movement as I passed quietly yet swiftly from tunnel to tunnel with no specific direction in mind. I could not believe they weren't on to me. Were they sleeping or merely toying with me? I could not tell, yet every arced nook I passed without incident gave me the nerve to press on. Still I knew not where I was headed. I only knew that they were everywhere and that they could come for me at any second.

Finally, I came across a hollow in the wall that was much wider than the rest. I extended the torch before me to shed some light inside. Expecting to see another horrid, eyeless face peering back at me, I was surprised to see nothing but darkness. Slowly I crept inside to investigate. Three paces in, I stubbed my foot on a small object. I knelt down to pick it up. It was smooth and curved. It felt like it was made of stone. Suddenly, a revelation came to me. Clearly what I was holding in my hand was the very bowl that contained my previous meal of worms. Placing the stone bowl quietly back down, I left the chamber. Quickly I advanced down the tunnel, knowing all the while, for the first time, where I was going. It wasn't long before my eye beheld them, the beautiful white steps of stone shining in the small glow of the flickering torch.

Still, I knew the immense stone that blocked my way to the surface was too large and too heavy for one man to lift. If I only had enough time to dig around it before they were the wiser. As I stood before the staircase, I noticed a huge chain that stretched above into the darkness. *So that's how they move the stone!* I thought. It must take a lot of men to move that stone. Halfway up the stairs, I heard a commotion. I knew then that I would never have enough time to dig my way out. I heard them uniting and coming for me. Soon they would be upon me like ants on a caterpillar. When I finally reached the top, I could hear them gathering at the bottom of the stairs. Not a word could I make out of the confusion, only a muffled clatter. Without a second to waste, I stabbed into the ground above, tearing away at the dirt beside the huge flat stone. Dirt fell into my empty eye socket and threatened to blind me temporarily as it rained down on my face and over my squinting eye. Madly I dug, and I don't know where I got the strength from, for I was weak from a lack of sustenance. Before too long, a sizable hole was emerging, yet I could hear the minions closing in on me as they chokingly ascended the steps.

With almost lightning speed, I stabbed and tore into the dirt ceiling above me with an energy I could not explain, save for the fact that it was propelled by absolute fear. Suddenly I was blinded by a strong light piercing through the small hole above. I hacked away faster and faster. The hole grew larger as I stabbed the knife in over and over again, while dirt continued raining down on my face. Yet soon I felt a hand on my wrist as I cocked the knife back. The eyeless horde of freaks was upon me. They choked the stairwell with their numbers, and they gripped and pulled and seized me. I looked up at the beautiful ray of sunlight that was streaming down through the hole. Somewhere, the end of the sunray was lost within the crowd of snorting minions. I swung my blade half-blindly at the cramped crowd of arms and hands. I was sure I stabbed a few of them for I heard a couple screams. But quickly the blade was taken from me, and so was the torch.

How close I had gotten. How far I had come, only to be swarmed upon again by the great moaning, grunting crowd of blind, brainwashed minions. What would they do with me now? I did not want to wonder. I kicked and I writhed. I swung my fist, and still it was of no use. There were simply too many of them to count. I knew it was over. The gray eyeless faces went on sneering and grunting. The hands were everywhere, grabbing and tugging. Slowly they began to carry me back down the steps. Again one of them shouted out the word "Neath!" And they all started in the chant: "Neath! Neath!" It echoed like distant thunder throughout the stairwell as they carried me down.

I felt my mind letting go, slipping into madness. Perhaps it was just as well. Insanity can be merciful. But then I cleared my head. Above all the noise, the chanting, and the many footfalls on the stone. I emptied my mind. I thought about nothing, nothing at all. And for a brief moment, everything was all right. It was almost as if it wasn't happening. But I knew all too well that it was. Then I thought about how I got down here in the first place. About the strange old man and his words, and a last-ditch effort came to me. I pictured in my mind a great and terrible beast. The same beast I had pictured when I was thrown into the great room. The horrible and colossal monster that infested my mind and soul, while I lay upon the dirt within the massive darkened chamber. Then I pictured the great stone door. I imagined it crumbling down, submitting to an undeniable force. I pictured that terrible, humongous, hungry beast breaking out of its chamber and squeezing its horrid body through the tunnels. I pictured it crawling, drooling, snarling, and reaching through the darkness with terrible limbs.

Suddenly they halted. Abruptly and simultaneously they ceased the awful chanting. All at once they froze upon the steps of stone. They stood there for a moment with me above their heads, and all was wretchedly silent. I continued thinking my disturbing thoughts while being careful not to let my fears distract me. Before I knew what was happening, they put me down. They lay me down on the steps halfway and began to descend without me. Quietly yet swiftly they poured down the stairwell and down the corridor.

I saw the torch burning on the steps. The flames looked as beautiful as when I first saw them, yet I had no use for it anymore. I ran back up to the top of the stairs and, with my bare hands, tore the hole open till it was wide enough to permit me to escape. The light that poured in stung my one good eye. It blinded me temporarily as I pulled myself through.

FLICKER OF FEAR

THE STORE WAS CLUTTERED WITH dingy things, most of which I could not identify. The shelves hung high above my head and were weighed down with wooden tools and toys. Glass items; moldy old books; brightly colored linens and clothing that looked as if they once belonged to gypsies; odd, outdated gadgets; and dreary old paintings. Costume jewelry was piled high among other queer items. The phony gems tried vainly to shine beneath the layers of dust that encrusted them in the dim and gloomy aisles. The smell of mold was chokingly potent as my eyes shifted to and fro among objects both useless and unique.

"Shame, just not making enough money to keep the shop open," said Tex to my father as we followed him through the narrow corridors of the dark, junk-infested maze he called a store. No wonder he wasn't making any money. I'd imagine most of his would-be customers would be afraid to step foot in the place. Anyway, Tex, I never knew his real name, was a good friend of my father's. Yes, he did come from Texas. He wore a cowboy hat and all. He was a kind and humorous man, as I recall. A tall, slim white-haired old man who wore a white suit and hat on the day we paid him a visit. He told us he was closing up shop due to lack of sales, and he planned to return to Texas. He was taking with him only the most valuable and cherished things, as it would not be possible to take it all back with him. He had set aside quite a pile to give to our family. Things we could either keep or try to sell.

I remember how considerate he was in giving. He was not very familiar with the rest of our family, yet he kept us all in mind. I was delighted upon receiving some Indian memorabilia, which included colorful and intricately fashioned beaded headbands and belts of Navajo design. Just to possess these small items gave me a magical feeling of connection with the ancient ones. I would hold the fragile things in my hands and ponder over who had made them and who had owned them, and I wondered how old they were. My mother was given a bulk of clothing and costume jewelry. Fine furs and hats, silk robes and gloves that she sold for a fair price, mostly to other antique merchants. I was with her in many of those stores and witnessed many of those sales. My father was given many old tools and gadgets and a stack of old musty oil paintings. Quite a few old and beautiful pieces of heavy and intricately carved furniture, some of which he quickly sold. My brother was given a few old toys and other items I can't recall, but what sticks out in my mind most of all was not the elaborate furniture or the expensive furs. Nor the beaded Indian belts or any of the other odd things that were bestowed on our family. It was a single possession that was given to my younger sister, an old and ugly baby doll.

Indeed it was ugly. Perhaps it was not meant to be, perhaps it was its age alone that tarnished a softness and a beauty it may or may not have had at one time. It was not dirty or ripped, yet there was an unmistakable ugliness about it. Perhaps its ugliness was not exuded from its physical appearance at all, yet still there was an undesirable quality about it. It gave you a churning feeling deep in your gut when you gazed on it. There was an uneasiness about its very presence. I recall how all in the room became silent when one would look on it or pick it up. I remember feeling a strong negative vibe as I gazed into its faded gray eyes. The eyes! Yes, it was the eyes that gave it away. It was the eyes that were to blame for our discomfort. It was the eyes that silenced the tongue of the beholder. It was the eyes that captivated, hypnotized, and disgusted all who shared its space. It was its misty glass eyes that made grown men cringe. It made your stomach twist when you looked into its old, tired eyes that gazed back.

MIDNIGHT CREEPS

The very night that detestable doll was given to my sister, I had an awful dream. I remember standing in front of Tex's store with my sister beside me. She was pointing through the glass at the same doll she was now sweeping with. She was pointing and smiling, saying, "I want that dolly." Her face was solemn and frowning, disturbed and confused. And as I gazed at the doll, it only conjured up the same dreary feelings it had stirred up the day before. In my dream, I kept expecting the doll to flinch, yet it only lay still on the shelf. So too did I expect its clutching eyes to shift from side to side and to freeze again as they fixed themselves on me. Yet like the previous day in which we all, save for my sister, had peered back at it in disgust, somehow expecting its eyes to move, they did not. However, as I looked at its reflection in the glass, I saw not one but four faces, all of which were different. All of which were foul, miserable, and bespoke of evil. In one face, she was sighing and on the verge of tears. Another malign face grimaced at me with an open mouth full of pointy, sharp teeth and eyes full of fire. The other seemed frozen in a fit of maniacal and insane laughter, while the fourth face was distorted in a way I could not begin to describe with words. When I woke from the dream, I was wet with sweat and trembling terribly. I could not get back to sleep that night. Perhaps my subconscious wouldn't let me.

The next day, my brother and I helped my father in the garden. When the work was done, we had lunch and played in the fields beyond the stone wall that bordered our land. So many countless hours were spent there. It was a magical place. I was holding a praying mantis in my palm when I heard our father calling. It was a Sunday, I recall, a bright and warm spring day. Our father asked us if we would like to go for a Sunday ride, as we did every other Sunday or so. When we left, it was midafternoon and still very bright. We went for a long ride and decided to visit our grandparents instead of hurrying back. We ended up staying for dinner, and before we knew it, it was getting dark. I remember my sister sleeping in my mother's arms on the ride back. It was dark, and the stars were bright. I was glad she didn't bring that eerie doll along for the ride.

But as we slowly neared the top of the hill, our eyes at once became filled with an unbelievable sight, which abruptly seized our playful laughter. For a few long, dreadful moments, we stared silently at our house, which was ablaze with light at the top of the dark hill. Suddenly, my father whipped the horses, and they started racing up the winding path. Closer we drew, and the lights grew brighter, yet we knew without a doubt that the house was not on fire.

Soon the horses came to a halt before our house, and my father jumped from the carriage, grabbed his shotgun, and charged madly toward the house. As if he expected entrance to the house without keys, he pushed at the door, yet it did not yield. Fumbling for the keys in his pocket, he finally unlocked the door and ran inside. From room to room he searched, checking closets and under beds, any conceivable nook that might hide an intruder, yet no such person could be found. He checked the back door and was shocked to find it still locked. There was no evidence of entry into the house, for both doors were locked, and all windows were securely latched. Nor did we find a single thing missing or disturbed. Nothing out of the ordinary, save for one thing. Every single candle in every room, including the storage room, cellar, and attic, was lit up with dancing candle flame! And as you might recall, it was a sunny afternoon when we left.

My father sat on the edge of his chair, silent and astounded, with his head in his hands. We all huddled close-by, too frightened to speak. I remember staring intensely at a flickering candle on the fireplace mantle, wondering why and how it was lit. "That's it!" My father killed the silence and made us all jump. "The doll! That evil thing! The doll! It was the doll!"

My poor sister was crying her eyes out. She was oblivious to our fears and concerns, for she was too young to be inflicted by such supernatural torment. She had no idea why we were so freaked out by the house being so bright. All she cared about was that wretched old doll that she only had for a day, and she could not understand why her father was running out the door with it, his hands wrapped tightly around its scrawny neck.

When he returned, he was once again calm, although it took at least three hours of uneventfulness to restore a smile on his face. He told us that he took that ugly doll for a quick and short ride to the river, where he ripped off its nasty head before he threw both parts into the raging water.

Ever since he returned without that evil doll, our lives have been nothing but normal. Or perhaps it was something evil that resided within the doll that filled us with negativity and filled our dark house with a frightful light. Either way, as confused as we all were, there were a few things in which we could all agree on. It was an undeniable fact that no one entered the house and lit those candles. It was also a fact that we left in the day; therefore, there was no mistaking that we did not light them before we left. It was also unarguable that nothing odd happened before the doll was brought into our home, and upon my father's discarding of the thing, our lives have returned to normalcy.

Now that I'm a grown man with a family of my own, I still cannot forget the trauma of that awful night of horrid light. And although my daughter feels quite deprived, and she often stops me before shop windows and says with a smile as she points at some old doll on display, "I want that dolly, Daddy, I want that dolly!" My answer, although it breaks my heart to deny her, is always the same: "No, honey, you don't want that particular doll. Ah, ah… her eyes are the wrong color."

THE ORBS

How many times had I taken the shortcut back home through the lonely fields on the thistle-ridden path that ran adjacent with the winding brook? More than I could try to count, I imagine. And how much time did I spend sitting on the rock by the flowing water, soaking up the sun and watching the white clouds drift by? And how many nights had I sat on that same rock, gazing up to the black sky in awe of all the shimmering stars, wondering what might lurk behind them? These questions have no answer, and, there are many more countless questions of a deeper tone that also have not been answered.

It was but a minute after the sun had dropped on the day my eyes were opened. Since that day, I had never looked at anything the same way. The dwindling day was slowly passing into night, yet there was still a lot of light to behold. I remember looking back in lament on the events and being glad that a friend of mine had been walking with me at that time. And although I'd never been more frightened in my entire life, it was not for fear of experiencing it alone so much as for the fact that I had a credible witness with me, so that I could be sure of what I saw and that it was real. For reputable reasons, I had let many years pass before I finally decided to talk of the disturbing event, and although I could expect nothing more than any and every pair of ears to think me mad, I decided I could no longer keep quiet. Call me mad, I know you will. Lock me up in an asylum if you must; it won't wash the validity from my words. I'm sure of what I saw.

We were halfway down the path when I saw it. My friend, who was walking behind me, had finished a conversation we were having. A moment of silence had gripped us as we both searched our minds for something new to say. Yet another minute had slowly passed as we walked without either of us speaking a word. Suddenly, a shimmering object demanded the attention of my eyes. A silver-colored flashing thing that hung low in the early evening sky. All at once, the queer vision struck me as if an unseen entity had reached through my shell to molest my soul. Within seconds, I knew all too well that what I was seeing was not a fleeting flash of the sun's light, nor was it any other describable hallucination or misunderstanding. I knew what I was witnessing was unexplainable yet undeniably present, and it filled me with unfathomable terror.

As much as my horror-infested spirit felt frozen in time, my feet kept their course, and though they slowed considerably, they moved through the weed-choked path as if by their own will. Slowly I wandered beside the brook with my eyes fixed on the sphere-shaped object in the sky. The round metallic orb hung there mockingly, perhaps a mile above the ground. Then without warning, it moved. It jolted from a complete standstill at an alarming rate of speed. It darted across the sky perhaps an eighth slower than a flash of lightning. And after it had covered quite a distance, easily a few miles past the other side of the brook, it came to an abrupt halt. It stopped without slowing down at all as abruptly as it had set itself into motion.

Again it hung there as if it were dangling from an invisible string, and I watched it wide-eyed as my blood turned cold. The undeniable eerie feeling of being held under the scrutiny of unearthly eyes ate away at me like the pecking of a murder of crows on a half-dead varmint. Still, I could not look away. Then I watched as again it broke its stillness and rose diagonally into the sky until it was but a dot. Again I saw it stop without slowing momentum, as if a child had palmed a rolling ball. The fear in me was throbbing, reverberating through my mind and body. So much so that at first I had wholly forgotten about my friend, who still lingered silently behind. So much so that even when I remembered his presence, I was too afraid to speak. Onward I slowly stepped with my eyes to the sky, trying to bring the words to my tongue. I realized then too that he had been silent for some time. I had to know if he could see what I was seeing. It must have been a full two minutes before I could actually speak. It was almost painful to utter a single word, but somehow I managed to force out a few. And to my surprise, all I had the chance to say was "Mike, do you—" Before I could finish asking the question, he cut me off. I could hear the terror in his shaky voice as he said, "Yes!"

Neither of us spoke a single word after that. We just kept on walking and watching the absurdity in the sky above. Soon I noticed to an elevated state of fright that there were two of them. Both round in shape and metallic in color, both darting across the sky at unbelievable speed, in all conceivable directions, stopping with insane abruptness and hanging motionless in the sky. The fear in me had reached its peak when I realized that the two oddities we were witnessing emitted absolutely no sound. As low as they hung and flew across the sky above us, not a single sound could be heard. The silence of their motion was dreadful.

As high in the sky as we watched them climb, they were also hovering quite low above us at times. I fancied that the things were not of great mass, perhaps anywhere between fifteen to twenty-five feet in circumference, and it seemed when they hovered low, as if the vessels were expanding and contracting slightly, as if they were breathing, and as the sky grew gradually darker, bright-colored lights began to flash on the surface of the orbs. Red and green, yellow and blue lights began blinking on them as they hovered and speared across the sky. Presently the fear had somehow been washed away and replaced by awe and admiration. Perhaps I was too busy trying to explain and take in all we were seeing to be afraid any longer. I pictured a man in one of those orbs, racing across the sky at almost lightning speed. I remember thinking that his brain would turn to mush as the craft came to such an abrupt stop after such intense velocity. No man could handle that, I remember thinking. These ghastly visions could not be of this earth.

Before the sky was too dark to see anything between the stars, they both bolted off like fleeting beams of light as fast as they had appeared. It was then I noticed that the crafts left behind no trail of flame or smoke as they swiftly moved through the darkening sky. By now our sleepwalking feet had taken us up to the rock by the end of the trail. My friend was cold in manner as he said something like, "See you around." He walked off over the steppingstones, across the brook, and through the brush toward the road. "See ya," I called out with delayed response, and without much thought, I sat on the cold rock, listening to the singing stream. My eyes turned up to the darkened sky, watching as the stars twinkled brighter.

For a while, I strained my neck as I stared into space, half expecting to see the mysterious flying orbs again, but the sky was empty save for the countless stars. Suddenly, my head was light, and I became weak and dizzy. The stars all seemed now to be reaching out with euphoric beams that stretched across the vast solar system to caress me with their strange light. All at once, I felt drunk with pleasure, and my mind was not my own. I remember laughing before all went black.

When I woke, at first I was convinced that I hadn't woken at all. I looked all around me and thought that I was surely dreaming. No longer was my mind groggy with euphoric influence. I felt again as sober as I was when I walked with my friend along the brook. But now I began to cringe as I realized that I was no longer sitting on the rock beside the lazy flowing water. Nor had I made it back to my wife and my pillow.

The same awesome fear that I had felt earlier had again pierced through my every pore like an instantaneous and fatal disease, only now I felt the choking terror gaining potency by the second. I had been laid out on an uncomfortable flat slab, which felt smooth beneath my palms. The queer slab that supported me was inexplicably translucent, and upon caressing and tapping it, I came to the surprising conclusion that it was not made of glass. I had never before seen an object with such mysterious properties, and it was all the more disturbing to realize that the slab itself was not supported by chains or wall or base. And as I sat up and looked around, I felt my guts began to churn as I examined my confines. All around me stretched a dull silver-colored metal. The walls of which were not only disturbingly claustrophobic but extremely curvaceous. I found myself standing in a tiny circular room whose ceiling was no more than a foot above my head. The circumference of the chamber could not have been more than seven feet. A strange artificial light, whose source I could not fathom, illuminated the round room vaguely. It seemed to be slowly fading in and out of an even duller glow. And as my mind worked frantically to try to explain it, I only came to the conclusion that it was not emitting from a torch's flame or a candle's wick. And as the pulsating magic light began to torment my brain, I came to the nauseous realization that it produced no shadow at all on the sphere-shaped metallic walls.

The utter absence of sound, too, was maddening, and I listened for its break. And although I heard a faint ringing, I was sure that it was only between my ears, for I felt an immense pressure within my head. The silence, the tiny round metal room, the absence of my shadow, and the eerie flameless light was all too much to bare. Still one thing that hung on the curved wall stood between blurred reason and complete insanity, something that baffled my already seething brain. It was a circle but one foot wide, which clung like a black stain on the curvaceous metal boundaries. At first I fancied that it might be the opening of a tunnel-like structure, and I feared moving toward it. Even more so, I feared what might lie in wait beyond its passage and what might come crawling through it at any instant. Still, the blackness and emptiness of it beckoned me to its side against my fears. My curiosity for its mystery began to slowly overwhelm my fright.

After gazing almost mindlessly for some time, I suddenly jerked my head away from it. It almost felt as if it were slowly draining all sane and rational thoughts from my numbing brain. I had to look away. My next thought was that of the peculiar slab, and I sought to further explore it. What strange material could it be comprised of? Although it was translucent, it was clearly not made of glass. And most of all, I wished to understand how it hung there without support. When I turned to face it, yet another element of mystery was added to the pile, for I had not moved a single step, and the clear, strange slab that hovered at my right-hand side was but a memory. First I figured that due to the fact that it was made up of translucent material, that it was still by my side, it was simply too hard to see, but after feeling around for it for quite some time, I was sure that it had vanished entirely.

After coming to the frightful conclusion that the slab that I had woken up on was no longer in the strange round room with me, I began examining the bowed silver-colored walls. And as my palm slowly caressed them, an overflow of questions began to erode my brain. Each question only defied all reasonable yet imaginative explanation and only brought forth a raging river of yet more unanswerable questions. The wall was cold, and indeed it did feel like metal, yet as I raked my hand along it, I suddenly noticed that my fingertips were digging into it as if it were sand. As I slowly pawed it, I beheld the queer metal balling up before my fingers such as wet sand. Shocked as I was, I pulled my hand from the mysterious wall and watched in horror as the five raised clumps slowly sunk back down to the smooth, curved surface it previously displayed. So too did the five shallow grooves that my fingers had made slowly fill back in before my poor, wide eyes.

All at once, my hand was throbbing and tingling with pain, and I gasped as I saw peculiar red bumps appear rapidly upon it. Within mere seconds, the entire hand had sprouted so many red bumps that soon there were bumps protruding from other bumps, till my entire hand was red, swollen, and freakishly disfigured. As I knelt on the cool, mystical metal, observing closely the painful disfiguration of my throbbing hand, a disturbing sound beyond the wall made the tiny hairs in my ears uncurl, for I heard distinctly a shuffling of feet outside my confines. My attention was turned wholly to the scuffling beyond the curved wall, so much so that the throbbing pain in my right hand had ceased altogether. I listened for some time to an ill, disturbing silence, all the while watching the wall in the area where I had heard the noise. It was my heart that was throbbing now as I watched and waited for the source of the scratching to show itself to me. Perhaps it would come through the magical metal wall and lumber toward me. Maybe it would crawl through the black circle that hung there like the mouth of a deep, dark tunnel. I could feel the presence of someone or something only feet away from me behind the curvaceous wall. I could feel their eyes fixed on me like cold moonbeams. I could almost hear their thoughts as they stood there motionless. I could feel the eyes draining my spirit away slowly. I could not move. My only thoughts were of my observers and what they wanted of me. I knew I could not fool them with my silence and motionlessness. I was painfully aware that they knew of my exact position. I was somehow sure that they could see me through the queer metallike walls. Finally, I heard again the scuffling of feet, and with great yet temporary relief, I knew they were moving away from me. All was silent again, yet it failed to comfort me.

I found it quite odd how the pain in my deformed hand had stopped so abruptly. It was swollen to the point of uselessness, and it pained me to look at it. What sort of ailment or unknown, unnamed disease might be coursing through my fingers, I could only imagine. The abrasive red dots that piled on one another were no more explainable than the lifelike metallic walls that stretched around me. All at once I felt like a tiny lizard waiting to hatch from his claustrophobic egg, knowing all the while that larger, more powerful things were circling just outside, waiting for an easy meal.

The pressure in my head was now immense. My ears popped, and a dull buzzing sound echoed in my head, while again I found myself gazing at the dark circle on the silver walls. As terrified as I was by the thought of someone or something crawling through it to get in at me, the next thing I knew I was slowly walking toward it. With each step I took, I felt as if I were drawing nearer to the edge of a cliff on a moonless night, not knowing exactly where the edge was, yet all the while being sure it was close. Without letting my fear control my movement, I was soon standing before it, trying to understand it, while all the time expecting something to spring forth and seize me. Motionless, I stood before the black circle with my disgusting red hand dangling at my side. And for what felt like a great while, I stood there frozen, as if hypnotized by the thick black spot, trying to penetrate it with my vision like a stagecoach driver trying to guide his steeds through a foggy night.

Suddenly, a bright white light glowed from inside the circle, which was no longer dark or black. I flinched violently at first, but

I somehow stood my ground. I felt like turning and running, but I remembered quickly that there was nowhere to run to. So I stood before the circle, which now, within the glow of light that beamed beyond it, resembled a round pane of glass. Within an instant, I realized that I was gazing through a window and not into the mouth of a dark tunnel. With this new revelation, it dawned on me that there were no openings whatsoever in the room, and I wondered how I had gotten in the sphere in the first place, and I cringed as I wondered how I could possibly escape.

I stood before the window, gazing out at the strange, artificial light that tickled the great darkness outside the queer craft that undoubtedly I was aboard, and unwillingly so. I was greatly impressed with the powerful light and wondered of its source. And I marveled impatiently at the sights it might bestow on me. Yet it shone only upon the darkness as I watched with great anticipation. The darkness was thick and stingy with its secrets. Suddenly it dawned on me that I might never see my wife again. And that I might not ever wade through the tall grass again with the sound of the singing brook delighting my ears. I could not comprehend the power or the intelligence or the mystery of my captors or even of the strange vessel I was in. But I knew that I was far from my beloved earth, and I knew it was no nightmare. And as I stood before the round window, it suddenly dawned on me that I saw no twinkling lights among the pitch-black. And I came to the gut-twisting conclusion that perhaps we were moving through a strange, starless space, hurling past unimagined galaxies, past the existence of light and shadows, to a cold, blind space beyond the stars.

Then in an instant, in which I questioned my sanity as well as reality itself, the mysterious light revealed to me a great dark mass of what appeared to be stone. As we slowly drew closer, I saw that we were gliding alongside a great rock wall that I could not see the end or the summit of. Closer we neared to it as my mind raced to explain what my eyes were inflicting on me. A terrible chill froze the blood in my veins as two enormous red eyes glared back at me from a large cavity inside the wall. What this beast was, I could not fathom; I was only sure of its cyclopean girth, for its eyes alone were at least the size of the craft I was in, perhaps even bigger. The horror that seethed within me reached its peak as we drifted slowly past the huge red eyes; all the while, I expected the craft to be gobbled up like a grape. More and more eyes now were visible and glowed like tiny lights within the cliff structure. Some were a sickly yellow, while some were colors I could not describe. Some stared back in pairs of two, while single eyes were seen watching from within the rocks. And once, I fancied that I saw a creature with at least twenty eyes. Was it not a crowd of curious creatures gazing out, tightly cramped from a tunnel within the rock formation? Or was it a single freakish creature with many eyes on its vile head? I felt the weight of the strange and terrible eyes on me. I felt as minuscule as an ant among the feet of men or, worse, a crowd of strange giants that I could only see a fraction of and could not begin to recognize. Strange, indescribable titans that hid their masses within the shadow of mystery.

Then, with much relief, I realized that we were moving away from the wall, and I saw a great grayish plain stretching out into the darkness as I looked downward. I prayed that we were not about to touch down on this eerie, unknown land. Slowly we passed over it, and I saw no plants or trees, only a flat ash-colored landscape, which only vaguely reminded me of a desert. Then I saw what I could only describe as a giant patch of white on the ground some distance ahead. As we slowly got closer, I could see that it was made up of two separate bodies. Soon we were over them. Two gigantic, swollen, bright white grub-like beasts whose immense bodies were laden with sickly wrinkles and laid drunk-like on the ground, completely unconcerned by our presence. If they had eyes, they were not visible. And as for head, limbs, or tail, the front and rear of the strange and massive animals were undistinguishable. And as we drifted slowly away from them, I marveled at their disgusting, bloated bodies as they lay stretched out lazily on the flat gray ground.

As we passed slowly over more of that ashy ground, I realized that the atmosphere must be quite dense, for I noticed that it was full of tiny particles that hung in the air both high and low, and I wondered if there was such a thing as gravity in this galaxy unweened. Time passed by unmeasured as I scanned with heavy eyes over more and more empty gray land slowly slipping under the round window. Then without warning, the monotony of the barren region was broken. At first it looked like a snowy landscape lay glistening off in the distance. Cold snow and ice, if not warm white sand. But as we drew closer, I realized that in my ignorance, I was trying to explain to myself only with things familiar to me the things I could not fathom. For as we got closer, I could see again the dull gray ground stretching out beyond the great white mass, and I saw too that this mass was moving.

Soon we were above them. A massive, insane herd of unbelievable creatures that I could only attempt to describe as colossal beasts, half-worm, half-spider. They twinkled like broken glass as they scampered madly across the ground with impressive speed, and I watched with ill delight their many translucent crystal-like limbs kicking and stretching among a cramped cluster of deformed-looking, see-through bodies. There were thin bright-green lines running through them like veins, and although they seemed to have no heads, they did have two antennae protruding off their strange bodies, each supporting a black ball, which might have been eyes. They were the size of Clydesdales and displayed the multitudes of ants. There were literally millions of them, and they poured out from the darkness like a mad crystal river. And as we drifted away, a thought instilled yet a new fear within me. I suddenly wondered what they were running from.

Suddenly, my worries and fears became intensified as I heard yet again a distinct scratching sound behind the round silver walls. With my back to the window, I now stared eagerly at the direction of the scuffling feet and scratching just outside the cramped, curved enclosure. *How long will they torture me with their sneakiness?* I wondered. I stood there, waiting and listening to the pestering silence. *Why won't they just come for me and get it over with?* I wondered as I watched, expecting to see a cavity open up within the wall. But it was still and unyielding as I stood frozen in wait. I wanted to shout out to my unseen captors, to urge them to do whatever it was that they were going to do to me. The anticipation was consuming me. Still, I could not muster up the courage to urge them on. And so I waited, bathed in an ill silence that was finally broken with the sound of dragging feet moving slowly and awkwardly away. It was quite some time before I turned around to face the window again.

And when I did, I was again amazed and baffled at what I saw. Colors spread out as far as my eyes could see, vibrant, unbelievable colors. Colors I had never before seen or imagined. Colors I could not begin to describe. The once-lonely gray ground was now littered with large squiggly, oval-shaped growths, which bore an uncanny resemblance to brains! Some of the colors were so bright that they seemed to give off their own strange light. I got the feeling that they were harnessing immense amounts of energy. And within that moment, I felt distant from myself, as if I had left my shell entirely. An odd sensation of comfort tickled my soul, and I felt as though I were dreaming although I knew I was awake, and I knew without a doubt that all the oddities I was witnessing were frighteningly real. In that moment, I could form no solid thoughts. My mind was bedazzled by the beautiful insanity that my eyes were absorbing. All I could do was to gasp in awe and wonder, with my hands pressed against the glass as we slowly passed over the vast garden of colorful brains.

Be they animals or, more like, flowers, I could only wonder. The brain-like things, which glowed with fantastic and unimagined colors, most never seen by human eyes, stretched out in all directions as far as I could see. For the first time since I woke up on the transparent slab, I felt not fear or anxiety, only peace of mind and an illusion of contentment. For some time, I had completely forgotten about my situation and the intentions of the beings that had brought it about. My mind was wiped clean of all worry, paranoia, and negative thought. I only stared down on them with dreamy fascination as the indescribable colors worked their magic on my mind.

But panic and terror swiftly possessed me again as I watched in disbelief a black shadowlike mass pass quickly beneath us. A body so gargantuan that it was seemingly infinite. So incredibly vast was this beast that I could not distinguish its features from one another as it passed below. If it had limbs or eyes, I saw them not. If it had wings, it could have easily blanketed the entire white mountain range as it effortlessly glided over the queer and colorful garden, blocking out all the vibrant colors and light they emitted. Within one terrible moment of disarray, I watched as the immeasurable monstrosity loomed over the brains below like an unending thundercloud, blanketing the light and colors like an unthinkable shadow. All was dark below the great beast, yet the artificial light from the orb still shone down upon it, and I could see its dark figure still pouring out from the nothingness as it continued to spread its darkness and dominion over the once-bright and beautiful landscape.

The horror within me bubbled like magma in a ripe volcano as I watched it continually pour out from the darkness with still no end of the thing in sight. Before I knew what was happening, the orb was spinning violently, and as it spun, my backside clung to its curvaceous insides as dizzily and hopelessly as a bug inside a rolling fruit. Finally, we stopped spinning madly, and I found myself sliding downward along a curve till I came to rest below the round window. Before I could shake off the vertigo enough to stand again, I knew that we had been brushed by the great and terrible beast as it glided over the garden, consuming all its beauty and light. Then my ears were violated by a thunderous and piercing shriek, which was so unbearably loud that it commanded every muscle in my body to flex and cramp up, and I froze in an unnatural and twisted position on the curved floor of the craft. My ears rang, and I went temporarily deaf, yet I knew the awesome roar was still battering all ears that could still hear, for I felt the strange metal vibrating impressively beneath me.

Once again we were in motion, and within a brief moment, I could tell that we were moving upward. I could not tell how fast we were moving; I only knew that we were going straight up, for as we rose and rose, I could finally see a small patch of insane colors glowing faintly below on the edge of the vast, shadowy beast. And as I stood with my face and fingers pressed against the glass, I got my last glimpse of the wonderful madness before the light over the window was extinguished.

The darkness was gripping as we climbed higher and higher. All the time I wondered what would become of me. My mind was heavy. I was weary and hungry, yet I fought the urge to fall asleep. Several times I almost nodded off, but it was my fright that kept me awake and kept my mind throbbing with self-torture. My ears popped, and my head rang with an immense pressure as I stared into the darkness that filled the orb, and I prayed I would not soon feel a strange hand on my face. All was dreadfully silent as we rose. I heard not the tormenting scratching and scraping of feet or the whining of machines.

Suddenly, a faint light began to glow again within the orb, and, as we ascended, it gradually grew brighter, like the rising of the sun over the horizon before you actually see the burning ball of gasses. Weary as I was, I turned back to the window to see what I could. I was quite reluctant to look, although I was just as afraid not to. And as I turned around to face the window, I saw a wavy horizontal line stretched midway across the glass, the lower half of which was bluish green, and the upper half was a faint blue, which was mixed with a blinding light. Quickly I saw the level of the bluish-green line sink beneath the round window, and my eyes, half-blind as they were from the stinging light, struggled to see and makes sense of their blurry vision.

It wasn't long before my sight was returned to me fully, and now my reeling mind again struggled to understand what I was indeed going through. At first I thought to myself, *Wow! Maybe there is water on Mars, for there's an ocean teeming with alien life upon this strange and distant planet.* My next thought was to simply deny the evidence of the revelation as it slowly came to me. And I watched with newfound terror through the round window as we soared over the glistening waves of the churning, foamy ocean. And I watched with a warming heart green trees swaying on brown and gray cliffs. I watched confused as a lonely white seagull circled effortlessly below us. My mind throbbed as I looked down on a snake-shaped brook which, seemed as small as a vain.

I never saw my captors. Without actually touching the ground, the queer metallic orb came to a smooth halt and hovered silently, only a few feet above a field of waving weeds and thistle. They had, for whatever reason, brought me back to the same spot. Why they had abducted me in the first place, I knew not. All I knew is I was never more happy than when I saw a small circular opening appear within the shell of the craft that held me prisoner for so long.

As I watched the metallic orb dart off abruptly in a diagonal line, silently, up into the sky from whence it came, I exhaled with great relief. But the comfort and peace of mind was short-lived. For not only did I realize in that moment that the heavens were filled with beings and strange vehicles that transport them from strange worlds inhabited by things that make us cringe when we attempt to imagine them, but our own undiscovered world, the world that we think we know and understand, is not at all so familiar to us. And that there are great and mysterious things crawling and soaring and looming about in deep, dark places on our very own planet. Things some of which I have lived to only see their eyes. Things that stare from holes and tunnels in massive rock formations. Things that men have never dared to imagine, and for the sake of their own sanity, even if they had seen them, like I have, they would still try to deny. Things that sane and intelligent men of science could never fathom. Yet fathoms down, they swim and crawl and snap their powerful jaws at other unmentionable beasts. And as I sit on the cliff and gaze out at the churning sea, I am filled with a newfound, humbling respect as I think of the things I'm afraid to speak of. And as I look at my splotchy, swollen red hand, I wonder how I will explain it, if it does not kill me. And as I gazed at the stars as they twinkled, I thought of the mad herd I saw twinkling as it galloped swiftly across the ocean floor, and I asked myself what I feared the most, the darkened sky or the deep, dark sea. I knew one thing for certain, I would never look on the world, the churning ocean, or the sky above it and see it as I once had.

SHARK ON THE SHORE

It is bafflingly uncertain exactly how it happened. The foamy white sea and its rolling twelve-foot swells might have surely been a factor. It is known that some species of shark sometimes dare to go after pray in knee-deep water. And then there are the dolphins, who, like the killer whale, are notorious for purposely beaching themselves in order to snatch up a seal in their powerful jaws. Upon seizing their prey, they find themselves in the death-defying struggle of wiggling back into the water. Is this what happened to this poor animal? Did it beach itself purposely, or did it simply swim into shallow water and get pushed onto the sand by a tumbling wave?

Either way, there it was, lying on its sandy belly, its gills flapping as it struggled in vain to breathe. Its tail flopped and its fins slapped the wet sand in a sorry attempt to move its now-awkward body. One of its poor and piercing eyes gazed hungrily out at the swirling sea, while the other looked disturbingly on the blurry alien vision of a high dune, with its dancing grass atop it and its blowing sand rising high above and over its summit.

The poor fish out of water hadn't been lying on the sand for long when along came a young boy, perhaps the age of twelve. His face was wrinkled by the distortions of anger and discontent, and his hands, which swung at his side with a negative vigor, were both balled into fists. By chance, the miserable young lad was the first to stumble upon the shark as it lay there, hopeless.

Earlier that day was a day like so many before. His sweet and loving mother tried to get him to do his homework and a few simple and quick chores. But trying and pleading with her rebellious and ungrateful son, as she did daily, was of no use. She would beg of him the things that he was rightfully expected to do, and yet he would only yell back at her in ignorant defiance. Most of the time, he would run out of the house, ignoring his frustrated mother's commands not to go. Sometimes he would sneak in sometime after dark, when he knew his parents were asleep. Some nights he would not come home at all, but he would always return in time for breakfast.

Now little Timmy found himself standing before the huge gray fish, looking down on it as it gasped for air. Tim could not have moved the helpless shark back into the water alone. But he could have easily run for help, for not far off, there sat a small crowd of people who could have easily moved the shark with combined effort. But he did not call to them. Never once, in fact, did the thought of rescue or even mercy enter his head. Instead, we see him cocking his right leg back to kick the poor thing in the ribs. And when his foot began to ache with a dull pain, he found himself a large stick and beat on the defenseless ocean animal with a rage unprovoked and undignified. He beat it on the spine, and he whacked it on its long head, while it moaned and grunted in silence. So too did it scream silently, and with each contact of the driftwood on its rubbery skin, the poor shark wheezed with torture through its gills as more air was forced from its lungs. When the stick was broken in two across its bruised and bloody spine, he threw the short half down at its discolored body and laughed until his belly ached.

With his foot, he kicked the life from the big gray fish, and the soul of the shark silently cried out to the sea hag, and the sea hag heard her moan. For soon he began to feel a presence behind him, and each time he stopped and turned around, there was no one there. And every time he turned back and continued on his way, within a short time, again he would feel as if he were being followed. A few times he swore he heard the scuffing of feet on the dry sand, yet every time he stopped and looked back, all he beheld was an empty beach.

Now the feeling was all too intense, for it was almost as though he could smell and feel a foul and cold breath across the back of his neck, as well as the kicking of sand behind him. But this time he hesitated before he turned around and continued on. He stood there for a moment and stared across the empty beach. Who can tell what it was that compelled him to turn his gaze downward, but when he did, a horror infected his spirit with the swiftness of a cold and sudden wind as he looked down on the unmistakable sight of footprints that stretched out before him as far as he could see and ended abruptly beside his own. Once again, he turned around and pressed onward, never thinking to take the time to maneuver his footsteps around the many crabs that crawled on the wet sand. He would have laughed loud and long with each crunch he felt beneath his belligerent feet, as he had done so many times before, yet this time, he could not muster up a single sinister chuckle. For his soul was dampened by an unexpected fear. After a while, and a couple dozen more smashed crabs, he stopped and turned around again to check the ground behind him. Sure enough, the same footprints were indented in the sand. They stretched out before him, clearly beside his own tracks among the crushed crab shells and ended distinctly at his feet. He noticed too that most of the claws, as broken and mangled as they were, were still snapping and pinching at the air.

The disturbingly odd sight of the severed crab claws reaching out in vain to seize the subject of their senseless destruction and the horrific impressions of undeniable footfalls in the wet sand that followed behind him was enough to start him running off the beach. He remembered as he fled of the many times he had cut worms in half, which he had dug up only to watch each of the separate pieces wiggle around in pain. But never before had he seen this unorthodox behavior in crab claws whose bodies had been crushed or had been separated altogether.

As he ran, he listened for the sound of feet other than his own hitting the ground, yet the only thing he could hear besides the screaming gulls and the restless sea was the pounding of his heart throbbing in his ears and the strained labor of his own breath. Soon he had reached the fields beyond the dusty dirt road, which ran parallel to the shore, and without the sinking of his feet in the dry sand, he now moved swiftly through the tall wild weeds. When he was almost home, he tripped, and his body was thrown to the ground. When the air returned to his lungs, he stood up and turned around. He was quite reluctant at first to look down, but he had to know. And when he did, he could not see any distinct footprints, not even his own, for the grass was high and waving, and the wildflowers were so thick they blanketed the dirt. Now Tim found himself walking at an easy pace for he was close to home, and he could no longer feel or smell a cold and fetid breath across his neck. Nor could he see distinct footprints beside his own, and he started to dismiss the occurrences as a spawn of his wild imagination. *Surely it was only a breeze which tickled my neck,* he thought to himself. And there was no doubting that the beach at times was full of footprints and offensive smells.

For once, Tim was glad to be home, and his mother forgave him for his nasty behavior. She fed him a plate of goose meat, carrots, and potatoes and sent him to bed without doing his chores yet again. That night, Tim's slumber was defiled by a terrible dream. There he sat hungrily at the dinner table, while his mother worked her pots. And although he never saw her turn and place a hot plate down before him, there it was suddenly on the table, steam rising up in his face. But the odor that assaulted his nose was anything but appeasing, and when he looked down, he gasped and cringed at the contents on his plate. For looking back up at him were the sunken eyes of three scaly fish heads whose bones had been picked clean. In the middle of the plate was a hot, heaping pile of what appeared to be the entrails of some unidentifiable sea creature, and atop the gut-wrenching gray pile of slithery sustenance sat a purple urchin. Its now stiff and crunchy spines jutting out in all directions like some flowery garnish. And placed neatly in a circular row around the rim of the plate lay steaming crab claws, all of which were snapping and pinching at the pile of curious entrails! As he looked up from his plate of unmentionable morsels and turned his wide eyes on the back of his mother's head, who was still stirring a bubbling pot, he screamed to her, "You wretched witch! Have you lost your decaying mind? How dare you try to feed me this hellish vomit!" Without a word in response, she dropped her big wooden spoon into the cauldron. She stood there silently and began to tremble as if overwhelmed with a boiling rage. After a moment, she turned around swiftly to face her outraged son. But the old gray eyes that pierced through his own were not the warm brown eyes of his loving mother. And the tangled white hair that hung down, dirty and wild, was not the wavy brown hair that he saw his mother brush so many times before. And the teeth that made up her ghastly grin were nothing like his mother's welcoming white smile. For some were yellow, some were green, and many were missing altogether. And it was somewhat of a foggy blessing that the matted gray hair was covering most of her horrible face, for it was jaded and distorted beyond belief. Her ugliness was destructive to mind and soul, and her eyes seemed to grip him with a fear he had never known. For his body as well as his thoughts seemed to be held in a state of frozen suspension as her malign eyes bore into his own. Then, mercy reached out to shake him, and he woke in the night with a scream that set the neighboring dogs into a frenzy of howling.

It took Tim a good hour or so to slip back into the unpredictable clutches of the dream world. Yet he lay down trustingly in its arms, not knowing if it would hold him with a mother's caress, or if it would slowly curl its long vine-like fingers around his neck to strangle him. But the dream world was merciful to him, for the rest of his slumber was quite uneventful, as far as he could recall. Yet even so, his first waking vision was of the strange, malign old face aiming her nasty grimace at him. And all through the day as he played in the field, smashing spiders and beetles, that disturbing face kept flashing back into his head. And each time, his young mind was disturbed by that vision. His pulse quickened, and his belly ached. And each time it happened, he found himself dropping what he was doing to stand up and look all around him. But only the lonely weeds waved back, yet still there was an eerie electricity in the air as if there were a storm awry.

What Tim enjoyed even more than cutting worms and smashing bugs and laughing at the sound of each crunch as he stomped another crab was another disturbing pastime of his: using birds as target practice. Tim got quite a thrill from throwing rocks at birds, especially when he hit one. And he only stopped torturing the poor bugs when he heard a few seagulls screaming above him. There were three or four dirty white winged targets circling in the salty air above him, and all about his feet were colorful beach rocks that had been deposited there years before by incredible waves. It's not easy hitting a moving target, yet with all the years of practice Tim had, he was pretty good. With only about a dozen hurls, he had come quite close a few times, and once he even grazed a wing of one of the gulls.

Tim had little doubt that he'd be able to knock at least one of them out of the sky if they'd only keep hovering above him for another minute or two, and he smiled as he squatted down to fill his left hand with more rocks. He studied their flight patterns for a bit before he grabbed a choice round rock and cocked his arm back once more. And just as he hurled the rock upward, a sudden mad commotion above made his eyes bulge, and as he stood looking up, trying to fathom what his wide eyes were looking at, his head became quite dizzy. Slowly his hand went limp and opened up, dropping the rocks on his foot. For within a split second, the whole sky above was thick and littered with the gray-and-white seabirds. There were thousands upon thousands of them flapping their dirty wings, circling and swooping in a frenzy. A vast and awesome storm cloud of feathers and beaks, of claws and wings whirling in a cluster of confusion and rage swirled noisily above him. Some were banging into each other as they shrieked and defecated down on him. As he ran, his mind was scrambled, not only by the unexplainable phenomenon that blotted out the clouds, but mostly by the high-pitched din that pierced his ears with an overwhelming and maddening treble. His ears were ringing now. Although his hands covered them as he ran, the shrieking was still painfully unbearable. Some of the birds were swooping down and biting his back as he fled. Some were pulling his hair with their beaks and scratching his neck with their filthy claws.

If Tim had ever ran faster, it was the day before, when he ran off the beach, and soon he had reached his home. He fell on a patch of flowers in front of the steps and covered his head with his hands. Although his ears were still ringing and his hearing was now muffled, he realized as he lay there with his face buried in the garden that he could no longer hear the piercing clamor of the gulls. After another moment of silence had slowly passed, he rolled over to witness the sky. There was not a single gull circling above, only puffy white clouds. For a second, he wondered if he were going mad, until he saw the white-spotted mess on his clothes and felt a pain on the back of his neck that colored his fingers a sticky red.

Of course, Tim told his parents of his terrific ordeal, yet they dismissed the outlandishness of his story for his wild imagination. At first, Tim was surprised by his mother's lack of sympathy, but then he remembered the time when she caught him throwing rocks at birds. She cleaned up his scratches, fed him a hot plate of chicken with peas on the side for dinner, and sent him to bed again without doing his daily chores.

And when the moon was bright and high, and when a barn owl cried out through the rafters, Tim's body began to twitch in his slumber. For there came slithering forth a blackness on the midnight air that was darker than the night itself, and soon his impressionable mind was infected with its power and negativity. For now Tim was no longer lying in the comfort of his own bed. Now, in his mind, he was out walking the beach. The sun was dull for it was masked by swiftly moving clouds, and the air was thick with a salty gray mist. Yet there was enough visibility to see that the sand on which he trod on was littered with dead fish. Their sharp bones and shiny scales shimmered 'neath the struggling sun, and millions of dead, dull eyes looked up solemnly at him. The fowl stench was overwhelmingly miserable. It was so pungent and thick that he continually gasped and choked as his bare feet sunk deep into the mounds of rotting fish. Many times he had to stop to dislodge a bone from one of his feet. His walk seemed to never end, for instead of running off the beach like he would have in reality, he just kept on walking slowly, parallel to the water, all the while sloshing through the sea of dead fish, only stopping to pull out a bone splinter or to bend down to vomit.

The next thing he knew, he was awake again. Still he was not sure he was off the beach. For as he crouched on his hands and knees, waiting for the vomit to come, his nostrils were filled with that same vile stench that he had smelled in his dream. Beneath his knees and palms, he felt a soft, moist heap that he could not begin to identify without a lighted candle. His belly convulsed as he coughed and gagged with dry heaves. With his mouth stretched open wide, Tim felt something fall out of it, and at first he thought he had finally vomited. But as he crouched there with his jaw wide and his hands sunk within a damp pile of what he could not see, only feel and smell, he dry heaved and gasped for breath. All the while, this slippery thing hung from his mouth to the slimy floor, yet he could not spit or purge it out. After much struggling and sweating, he finally grabbed hold of it and gave it a tug. But it did not come out of his mouth as he tugged at it harder, and he could feel a pulling at the back of his throat. Now Tim began to panic as he pulled again at the thin rubbery thing that seemed to be lodged in his throat and that swung from his open mouth. He yanked and pulled until it finally came free. But not before Tim heard and felt an unmistakable snapping at the base of his throat, as if it were connected all along. As if it had grown there in the night, like some freakish tongue. And as he held it firmly within his grasp, mercy blessed him once again, and he fainted on his back.

    But the sting of the morning sun did not bring him the same blessings, for his nightmares, it seemed, had bled through the night and seeped into the light of day. For he woke, lying on his back, not in his bed, but upon the floor. At first he felt a slimy thing in his hands, and he held it before his face to examine it. All at once, he recognized it as a piece of seaweed he had swam with so many times before. The long brown seaweed, whose edges were ruffled like lasagna noodles. The same long seaweed he had nicknamed dragon's tongue. Next, he noticed a stench that reminded him of the beach, only it was tenfold worse. The smell was so thick he gasped with each attempt to breathe, and soon an unsettling moistness became apparent beneath his arms and legs. Abruptly he stood up, flinging the dragon's tongue across the room. And as he stood, he felt his feet sinking into the moist pile of fly-and-flea-infested slop in which he had spent the night lying on. For indeed, there was no doubting that it was no nightmare he had been tortured by, for neither his tired mind nor his unbelieving eyes could deny the plain and simple fact that his bedroom floor was entirely covered in deep, stinking piles of seaweed.

That morning, Tim and his mother had a terrible fight. Of course, there would be no convincing her that it was not Tim who brought all the nasty seaweed into his room. He could not begin to explain it away, and she could not force him to clean it. His mother was quite disturbed by the heaping piles of stench on the floor. She had been concerned by her son's attitude and unusual behavior for some time, but all this was too much. Why would anyone do this to their own bedroom? She asked herself. And what great lengths he must have gone through to do it. He must've been up all night, carrying buckets off the beach. And as she heard the door slam as he ran outside again, she sighed heavily and hung her head as she thought to herself, *What am I going to do with him? And how am I going to clean this up?*

And while Tim's mother spent her day doing just that, Tim spent his hunting for frogs in a state of anger and confusion. And when he had captured one, out came his penknife. For Tim loved to gently slice the poor frog's bellies. It was always a shallow and careful incision, for it was too easy to merely stab and kill a frog. He would peel back the skin as the poor little creature writhed and kicked in pain. He would strip most of its skin away and then throw the frog back into the pond, laughing maniacally as he watched it float and twitch on the algae-laden ripples. Then Tim noticed bubbles rising from the depths of the pond and wandered over to them. Perhaps it was a turtle, he thought. But soon, there were hundreds of them rising and popping at the surface. *If it's a turtle, it must be huge,* he thought. But hundreds soon turned to thousands, and Tim noticed that they were rising faster and faster. Now he knew it was no turtle expelling the bubbles, for now they were rising at an astounding speed. These bubbles rose faster than he ever saw a bubble rise before, and he knew what he was seeing was not normal, for the bubbles were shooting upward faster than they would in a boiling kettle. So fast, in fact, that they were losing their sphere shape, for now they were stretched out like cylinders. This went on for a moment or two, and he stood and watched with fascination until it all stopped abruptly. And when it did, he found himself gazing down at his reflection, and for a split second, he swore he saw fish eyes staring back at him from his own frightened face. He gasped and twisted his head away. His first instinct was to run, but he stood his ground and looked back down. This time, his reflection was normal, and he chuckled with relief. Still, he had a sickly feeling about standing there, and he moved away from the pond.

Tim sat on a rock in the lonely fields. He watched the rabbits hop by and the birds peck at berries. He was sickened by the thought of returning home to his parents. But his stomach rumbled, and the sun hung low. And he knew deep down that his mother would forgive him, and so he headed back reluctantly. His feet dragged slowly as he walked toward the old red house at the foot of the hill.

By the time he had returned, his room was clean, although it still reeked of red tide. His parents were gone, and he found some cold meat in a pot on the table. He ripped off a few chunks and ate them on his bed. Although Tim knew he had no part of the mess in his room, he also knew his mother was furious with him, and he wished not to face her, so he went to bed early. But all through the night, they tortured him. For as he lay in his bed, his body twitched somewhat like the poor frog had on the thick green pond. In his mind, he saw darkness that was thick and black, and out of that shadowed realm stretched the pinchers of many large crab claws, all reaching and snapping out at him as he squirmed in his bed. He never saw a whole crab although there were a multitude of claws and spiderlike legs bending and crawling on their pointed tips. Flashes of their faces continually appeared to taunt him. He saw their beady black eyes watching him from atop their antennas. The rapid movement of their hairy flaps over their rectangular mouths disturbed him so. Perhaps a bit more than the abominable claws that reached and pinched and snapped at him, trying to nip at his hide.

The nightmare persisted until the cock crowed, and his head was heavy as he opened his eyes to stare at the ceiling. His body felt rested, though his spirit was ill and unsettled. As he lay there resting, a faint sound filled his ears. It was a sound that he could not identify.

It sounded almost like the rustling of a hundred dry, hollow branches scraping against each other in a silent breeze. It was a disturbing sound, the likes of which he'd never heard before, and it did not make him think of anything; it only suggested a slippery movement of some kind. Now he was fully awake, and the sound summoned him to swiftly rise. Tim sat up in his bed and swung his feet to hang off the side. But he did not rise to stand on the floor. Instead he rose swiftly and stood on his bed, for he now could see that his floor was moving! For it was covered with grotesque large brown crabs, which crawled upon themselves, snapping their abnormally swollen claws at the air. Each crab was easily two feet wide, and they had strange bright-crimson-colored markings that were tear shaped on their shells. Tim slapped himself in the face, but it only confirmed that it was no dream. For the floor was still littered with the large, bloated, ugly things, as they struggled to climb atop one another, breaking one another's limbs off and pinching at the empty air. Quite clearly Tim could also see many detached claws still nipping at the air, some blindly grabbing hold of other crabs' pointed limbs. Next he called out to his mother, and soon he heard her stomping down the hall. What relief the sound of her feet brought him was little at best, and soon he saw his door was being pressed on. But as she called out to him to open the door, he could only respond, "I can't!" As she rammed the door with her shoulder repeatedly, it only opened but a crack, for the large brown crabs were thick and heaped high.

Again and again she pushed at the door while calling out to him, and while this was going on, Tim was undoubtedly convinced that he was not still dreaming. And when his mother finally forced the door open, he saw not the beady eyes and brown pinchers piled high but only the wet, smelly floorboards. His mother was half-awake and in a panic as she came charging in, only to slip and fall on her back. Without complaining, she rose to her feet to tend to her son's needs. "What, Timmy! What's the matter?" What could he say? Could he tell her of the things that haunted him so as they crept across his bedroom floor? He thought about it for a second. He knew she would never take him seriously, for she was quite convinced that it was he who brought in the seaweed the night before. "Sorry, Mother," he whined. "I had such a horrible nightmare."

It had been a while since Tim went for a swim, and he thought of heading down to the water as he walked out of the house. It was a hot summer day, but the beach now seemed such a loathsome place to him now. So instead, he wandered around in the fields, looking for snakes in old stone walls and climbing trees. He also collected bugs. He gathered up spiders, earwigs, and beetles. He liked to put them in a jar together and watch them fight one another. After a while, he grew bored with his ill games and went for a long walk out of the fields and into the thick and shady wood. He walked for hours 'neath the tall trees and the twisted, hanging vines till his legs grew weary. He soon came upon a clearing and sat down on a soft patch of moss to rest.

It was getting late in the day, and Tim was hungry and thirsty. He wondered what his mother was preparing for dinner as he swatted a butterfly that hovered before his face. When he had rested enough, Tim stood up and started back. He took but a few steps to the edge of the clearing to where the path back was. Just as he had reached it, he could not help but notice a peculiar object hanging at eye level from a tall maple tree. A bolt of fear ripped through him as his eyes fell on the disturbing sight of a fishbone hanging from a vine. There was no doubt that it was not there when he walked in, for it hung in the middle of the narrow path, and he would have had to duck so as not to feel it rake across his face. And it worried him even more when he thought about how he did not hear or see anyone nearby. Tim stood there before the white fishbone and watched it sway only inches before his face. He stood mindlessly for a while in the grip of fear and confusion, till finally he turned around without quite knowing why. Now his fear was seething within him as his gaze fell on yet another fishbone hanging from a tree on the edge of the clearing. As he swung his head slowly to either side, he saw more and more of them gently swaying and twisting in the breeze. He soon realized that there were a number of them and that they all hung in a circular pattern on the edge of the clearing.

He wanted nothing more than to leave that place; in fact, for a second, he wished he had gone down to the shore, but still he did not move. It was as if something or some unseen force were holding him there against his will. As he stood there, his eyes remained fixed on a single hanging fishbone as it turned side to side with the leaves. His limbs began to tremble. From the corner of his eye, he saw something shimmer on the dirt, and so he swiftly turned his gaze down at the movement to see his jar, which was on a level surface, tip over without explanation, and he stood and watched all the bugs slowly pouring out. Again he found himself staring at a hanging bone, while the bugs crawled away. The breeze that twisted the hanging bones was a gentle one. In no way could it be blamed for the overturned jar, and if it were a critter, Tim would have seen it scamper away. And as he stood frozen in eldritch awe, he felt something tug at his pant leg, which snapped him out of the trancelike state he was in. Swiftly he looked down at his feet and saw a large brown crab, the same strange and ugly kind from his dream, with one of its huge, swollen claws clamped tightly to his hem. He tried to kick it off, but its grasp was firm. He kicked and kicked at the air, but it would not let go. Tim was too horrified to grab hold of the thing, so he turned back and fled down the trail with the crab dangling at his right foot. He ran with great speed till he could run no more, and he finally stopped and collapsed against the trunk of an enormous oak tree to catch his breath. Looking down, he was extremely relieved to find that the crab was not still clinging to his leg, and as he took in deep breaths, he wondered what a crab might be doing so deep in the woods.

Tim wanted to tell his parents of the strange happenings, but as he reached his house, he knew he'd be better off to keep his mouth shut. He knew they'd never believe him, and besides, he wanted to forget about it anyway. He promised himself he'd stay out of the woods as well as the beach. As he opened the door, he heard his stomach growl, and his nose caught hold of the sweet smell of his mother's cooking, though he could not quite identify the aroma. Soon he was resting at the dinner table, and his mother put a steaming plate down before him. On the plate was a pile of brown rice next to a large chunk of fish. When Tim's mother saw the look of disgust on her son's face, she asked him, "What's wrong, Tim? You love codfish."

"Ah, sorry, Mother, I'm not very hungry tonight." Tim ate the pile of rice, and when his mother had left the room, he scraped the fish back into the pot and helped himself to another pile of rice before he went to bed.

And in the still of the night, just as the tides began to shift, Tim's heavy mind became saturated with the poisons of a dream. For as he lay in his bed, a crack began to slowly widen in the doorjamb. It whined and it creaked as it opened halfway. The dark silhouette of a woman's ghastly face and long scraggly hair poked in through the opening. Two sharp gray eyes stood out among the dark room and gleamed with the glow of a crescent moon, which shone dully through the window. With the palm of her open right hand, she pushed through the opening and held it flat before her face. In her overturned hand sat a pile of finely ground powder, and she whispered a rhyme through her cracked, salty lips: "With ingredients three, all gathered from the sea. The ancients 'neath the waves and their children, who should be let be. Creatures which crawl, slither, and swim with the anemone. With the crushed claws of crabs shall all be set free." With that, she blew the powder from her palm, and it shot out in a stream across the darkness of the bedroom. But it did not fall to the floor. Instead, it moved through the air like a sea snake squirming, and instead of falling or running into the far wall near Tim's bed, it curved to the left and continued stretching out in a long dusty stream till it made a complete circular rotation around the borders of the chamber. Around and around it circled madly through the stuffy, still air of the room, turning left as it reached a corner, all the while slowly picking up speed. Suddenly within the circular stream of floating dust, a fish did appear, which swam in the stream as it circled over Tim's sleeping body. Three times around the room it did swim, till behind it another fish did appear and began to swim closely behind the first fish's tail, all the while bending to the left to follow the circular pattern. Soon, another anomaly appeared behind the second swimmer. It was a fish that had no flesh! The clean bones of a long-dead fish now followed closely behind the two other fish, and the sharp bones shimmered in the moonlight as it swam.

Soon, a squid appeared behind the fishbones, and its body was white and bright against the darkness as it joined the freakish sea parade. One by one, sea stars began to appear among purple urchins, whose quills jutted upward as they slowly moved across the floorboards of Tim's room. In the center of the floor sat an ugly large clam whose swollen, foul-looking meat began to slowly ooze out of a crack between its shells. From one side of its hinges, a tonguelike appendage began feeling around the air of Tim's room, which once again reeked like red tide and rotten fish. Slowly it did slither as it stretched out halfway across the room. The long, slender muscle extended, hanging in midair, feeling and sniffing around, till it was now but a foot from his bed. And when the heaps of horrid brown crabs began crawling among the sea stars and urchins, she laughed quietly yet maniacally as she pulled shut the door.

Behind the illuminated squid appeared a jellyfish whose long, thin purple tentacles dragged some three feet behind as it followed the other sea creatures in a circle pattern, which turned slowly and insanely around Tim's room. More and more fish appeared to join the pattern, and soon there slithered through the night air with them the monstrous, ugliness of a moray eel. Its long teeth jutted from its open jaw as it swam through the room, while its cold, dull eyes sought a potential meal. As it slithered behind the ugly fish, one last huge gray fish appeared out of the night air to close the nightmarish circle. Its large tail whipped to and fro as it moved through the air. Its dorsal fins stretched downward as it moved, and its malice-filled eyes gleamed by the light of the moon, as did its mouth full of jagged teeth. Round and around they circled above his bed and the crawling crabs on the floor.

All at once Tim's eyes jerked open, yet they did not wash the nightmare beasts away. For as he sat up in his bed, his eyes fell on them swimming in a circle only some feet above his head. The scales, the fins, the teeth, and the eyes all stood out against the darkness with the aid of the moon's rays. In a sorry attempt to escape them, he fell awkwardly from his bed, only to find himself crawling around in a heap of crabs, which pinched at his limbs and held him down. Round and around they circled above. The eel, the fishbone, and the shark, till the fear within him was untamable.

Tim wanted to scream, but he knew he could not, for he held his breath and flapped his arms and kicked his legs, not only to break free from the claws that pierced his hide, but in a desperate attempt to swim away. But it was of no use. No matter how hard he tried, he could not swim upward. Now he began to panic as he held his breath and watched the creatures slowly descending in a circular pattern toward him. Closer and closer they drew, while the crabs pinched at him and crawled over his squirming body. Round and round and downward they swam, till Tim felt the slippery and rubbery hide of the shark brush against his shoulder. Now the fear had reached its climax, and he could hold his breath no more. As he gasped for breath, he felt the salty water rushing in, and the last thing Tim saw was the vicious gray eyes of the circling shark gazing back at him.

The next morning, Tim's mother called him to the breakfast table. After a while, before his eggs got too cold, she walked down the hall to his room. As she opened the door, she heard the high-pitched cries of an enormous horde of seagulls hovering above the roof. It was so disturbingly loud her ears rang, so much so that she could not think. And when she screamed as she opened the door of her son's room, within an instant, this scream of the mass of gulls halted altogether, and an eerie silence was all that followed.

Tim's mother stood in the doorway, while her sanity began to evaporate through her ears as she looked down on the mess that covered Tim's bedroom floor. The stale stench of the sea slapped her in the face as she beheld dozens of sea stars and thorny urchins blanketing the floorboards among heaps of seaweed. And she gasped in horror as she beheld the piles of freakish, ugly, large brown crabs that were pulling the guts of her son through his picked-clean ribs with their detestable, swollen claws.

IN THE CHAIR OF NIGHTMARE

When I rapped on the door, neither my partner, Officer Banes, nor I were surprised when after a moment of silence, no one answered. Still, I grabbed hold of the large brass knocker and continued to make our presence known. Once again, after a minute or two of waiting to no avail, we resorted to peering into the windows from the porch. I found myself staring into the kitchen. Almost expecting to see the place in complete disarray, I was once again surprised by the apparent order and cleanliness of the house. Copper pots hung from nails on the walls. The kitchen table was free of debris. Only one neglected, dirty glass was left on the counter, which was otherwise barren. The only thing I saw that made me think was a small house plant that hung from a great wooden beam. It disturbed me slightly, for all its dangling leaves were brown and crusty.

It was our mission on this windy day in early November to check up on the owner of the house. His name was Christopher Winthrop, and it was reported that he had not shown up to his place of employment in well over three months. It seemed peculiar too that he had not even shown up to collect his pay for the last week he had worked. It was a relative of his who finally contacted the police department, his niece Gertrude, who became quite concerned when she hadn't received a letter from him in such a while. Nor had she received a response from any of the letters she had sent. It was normal that they kept in contact through letters at least once or twice a month.

MIDNIGHT CREEPS

And so we stood on Mr. Winthrop's porch, contemplating beating the door in, when a gust of wind whipped across our feet, sending a heaping mass of leaves up and over the railing and spiraling toward the sky. Now I found myself looking down at a group of full and neglected milk bottles that were clattering like an eerie song in the chilly wind. Banes and I both looked at each other, and without a word said, we began to batter the front door. Soon we were standing in the den, and we began shouting out the name of the homeowner. But we were greeted with no response. Once again we called out to him, and once again only silence answered back. As we walked through the house, we noticed nothing out of the ordinary save for the sorry sight of some dried-up houseplants, until I spotted a small hanging cage in the back room that housed a rigid parakeet, which was lying in a pile of seed casings and its own excrement. It lay on its back, and its poor little claws were fixed in a permanent curl.

One last time I called out the name of Mr. Winthrop just before we ascended the staircase. It was only procedure, for by then we expected no response. At the top of the stairs stretched a long, lonely hallway, which we slowly passed down with precaution and stealth. We passed many rooms with open doors, all of which were empty and neat, till our eyes fell on a door at the end of the hall that was shut tight. I rapped on the chamber door, and once again, only a creepy silence tickled our ears. So slowly I turned the copper knob and pushed open the creaky door. Upon hastily entering the room, we were confronted with the ghastly sight of the man in question. He was sitting peacefully in the embrace of a great and intricately carved chair with fine red velvet cushioning and large claw-and-ball feet. Although I could only guess of its actual age, it was obvious at first glance that it bestowed great antiquity. And there he sat, shirtless, with his fingers hunched over the end of the chair's arms, his feet flat on the floor, his posture straight, upright and stiff. Although a thick band of flies buzzed noisily around his head, we could not help but notice that his eyes were open and wide, and they stared blankly at the opposite wall. Being a policeman, you must be brave, have a strong stomach, and you cannot be squeamish. I fit all these requirements, but I must admit that every time I come face-to-face with a corpse who has wide and open eyes, something sickly reaches down through my skin, muscle, and marrow and touches my very soul and starts it squirming.

Presently, I loosened my collar and pulled my shirt up over my nose for a pungent stench hung in the thick, stale air of the shut-up room. Banes was sneezing and coughing as we quickly moved about the chamber to pull open the windows. Not unlike the rest of the house, we could not say that anything in the bedroom was unorthodox. There were no visible signs of foul play or anything out of the ordinary to speak of as we inspected the contents and the condition of the room. Everything seemed in order and was neat and clean, save for a distinct layer of dust. And so we turned our attention away from the room and its furniture and found ourselves once again face-to-face with Mr. Winthrop and the cloud of flies that relentlessly tortured the face of his corpse.

I touched his arm. It was rigid and cold. My partner and I found ourselves in a debate about how long he had been dead, and soon the wager of a beer and burger were at stake. But food and drink were suddenly the least of our concerns when the corpse in question flung wide open his jaw and released upon the world of crumbling sanity a scream so loud, so deplorable, so shredding that we both simultaneously fell to our knees and clamped our palms over our horrified ears. That terrible cry lasted for a solid minute, and when all the air was expelled, he gasped deeply for a breath. And as he did, we both watched in absolute disbelief the entire horde of buzzing flies funnel into his open mouth as he drew in a huge breath. Upon the closing of his dry, pale lips, we saw that not one single fly was left to circle his face. So too did we notice that upon the drawing of the fly-laden breath, he swiftly returned to his corpse-like state. His body was stiff and frozen. His feet remained flat to the floor. Neither his arms nor his fingers flinched. And his eyes remained as they were, wide and open and staring blankly at the same empty spot on the far wall.

After a moment of mental adjustment, we began once again to call out his name, yet as many times as we screamed it in his face, it drew forth no response. My partner resorted to lightly slapping him in the face to conjure such a response, yet to no avail. I felt for a pulse. At first I was only swayed, yet finally I felt the slow and tired throbbing of an ill and weary heart. I took him by his bony shoulders and shook him side to side in his chair, yet only the parts of him that moved were the ones that I made move. He was absolutely unresponsive in every way. So I began the task of pulling him from his chair in order to prepare him for a short trip to the doctor. This too proved to be an inconceivable task, for pull as I may, the stiff frame of Mr. Winthrop would not give. We could not spark a response or movement no matter what we did, and no matter how hard I pulled, I could not peel him from the chair. As I tugged at his stiff limbs with no effect, Banes continued his investigation by focusing his attention to the backside of the subject. "Stop!" he suddenly commanded. "Stop pulling!" The look of horror and disgust in his eyes had reached its climax, and soon I discovered why. As I slowly walked around the side of the carven chair, I saw what my partner was shouting about. The sharp thorns of horror pierced me, for the pale, sickly flesh of his back was undoubtedly infused with the soft red velvet cushioning of the great chair. And as I stood beside the half-dead man in a state of surreal confusion, mulling over the whys and hows of the fact that the flesh of his back was one with the back of the chair, I was finally pulled back to reality by the sound of Banes vomiting in the corner.

Upon a thorough examination by two separate doctors, both of them were left completely baffled. They could not explain why he was so rooted to the chair. They could only agree that it was an excessive amount of time in which he spent sitting in it without moving a single muscle, which only raised more unanswered questions. They could not understand how he had survived in his state for so long. However, they were both in agreement that Mr. Winthrop had not taken a bite of food or a single drop of water in well over three months. "I can't wrap my brain around it," one doctor exclaimed. "The only thing that I can state with absolution is that this man should have been dead three months ago!"

The poor, unfortunate Mr. Winthrop was sent to a hospital where doctors could access his unorthodox situation and commence rehabilitation. After only the passing of a single day, I followed my curiousness and concerns to the hospital to check up on him and to see if I could get him to speak. Sadly, all further investigations would leave me once again in the dark, for the nurses and doctors had the same luck in getting him to come around as Banes and I had. The doctor whom I spoke with said that he would be bedridden for the rest of his life at best, for he had not used his muscles in such a long time, and all hope was fading in getting him to move a single muscle or to even stimulate a flinch from his torpid body. His eyes, both by day and night, remained open wide and vacant, and every attempt to spoon-feed or to rehydrate him had miserably failed for he would swallow neither food nor drink. Every attempt to pour liquids or protein mash down his throat ended up in discouragement. The only bodily movement he would ever make was the painful struggle to spit out all vital substances. One distraught nurse was brought to tears as she held out a shaking spoon and watched as the pureed food dripped from his lips and down his neck. That very next morning, he was found dead, but bafflingly, not in the hospital bed. Doctors and nurses alike could not understand how he summoned the strength to be found sitting upright and rigid in a visitor's chair.

    The events of Mr. Winthrop's untimely and unexplainable passing would not let me rest. I found myself losing sleep as I could not forget or explain away all that I had witnessed. My partner, Banes, was so disturbed by the strange happenings that it began to affect his work, and so the captain ordered him to take a two-week vacation to get his head together. One day, a week and a half after the burial of Mr. Winthrop, I found myself mindlessly wandering well off my sanctioned beat and ascending the steps of the deceased. It bothered me all the more when I saw a small group of moving men emptying the contents of the house. Upon reaching the porch, I saw two men carrying the large kitchen table through the front door. I stopped and turned around to watch them load it onto a wagon. When I turned back to face the door, two more men were carrying the old carven chair across the threshold.

    As they passed by, the fetid odor of a rotting animal polluted my nasal passage, and my eyes fell on the sickly sight of the late Mr. Winthrop's frayed back flesh still encrusted upon the red cushion, and I cringed as I saw much of it dancing and flapping in the breeze. But they did not carefully descend the stairs with the beautiful and awful chair; instead I saw them carrying it to one side of the long porch, and both struggled to heave it up and over the railing. "Wait!" I yelled abruptly. "Wait, men!" I quickly mustered. "That chair is a key object in a police investigation. Do not destroy it!" They agreed to set it down gently on the ground, where they intended to smash it to pieces, and later that night, I came back with my buggy to retrieve it. Although it smelled horribly, and I knew I could never rid my mind of the horrible events that lent it to my possession, I knew that I could have it properly cleaned and deodorized. I could not watch that exquisite antique be destroyed. And although a small fraction of me wanted to see it in pieces on the tall grass of the Winthrop estate, my love and appreciation of antiquity could not let it happen. Within weeks, it was returned to me, professionally cleaned and smelling as normal as a dusty old relic could. The price was more than fair, and I soon found myself in possession of a chair that was literally fit for a king. I pondered happily of its origin and of its value and, most importantly, of its actual age. I could not bear to have witnessed that beautiful chair be tossed atop a pile of unwanted things such as withered house plants, broken bottles, and a dead bird inside a smashed-in cage.

One day, I returned home after a long day of walking the beat. My legs were weary, and for the first time, I sat down and sank into the red velvet cushioning of the antique chair. I could not recall within that moment ever feeling more comfortable. My aching arms stretched out lazily across the arms of the exquisitely carven chair, and my fingers dangled over the lionlike paws. I drew in a long, slow breath, and I felt the stress of a long workday begin to evaporate away from my mind. Before I knew it, I was slipping into a dreamlike state, and just before I fell asleep, I shook my head the way a dog does after it emerges from the water. I did not wish to fall asleep in the chair, for I had not yet eaten dinner, and I did not want to wake up in the chair with a stiff neck. So I found myself fighting the urge to fall asleep, and just before I made a move to rise from the chair, I felt a change in my emotions. No longer was I content in my relaxation. Within a moment, my mood had changed from the comfort of contentment to a restlessness that only seemed apparent in my soul. For my body was happy to remain within the chair, yet my thoughts and desires were solely to depart from its comforts. And then I felt it: a tenebrous sinking in my gut. My mind began to dwell on only negative aspects of my daily life. I felt my face twisting into a drooping frown, and it was then that the feeling of contentment and comfort completely vanished. Presently, I felt the cold embrace of a maddening force soaking into my skin, and once again, my weary mind began to wander. I felt cold and colder still as I began again to drift off into slumber. Once again, I snapped out of it only to feel yet again the overwhelming sensation of discomfort and the chilly confines of an ill embrace. Somehow I fought the potent desire to succumb to my sleepiness, and swiftly I rose and stood before the chair. Slowly my thoughts cleared, and I was soon thinking of what I would prepare myself for dinner. Some pork and rice would suffice, I thought, and made my way to the kitchen.

As tired as I was that night, I yet again had trouble sleeping. I was certain that I would drift off into slumber quickly, but as I lay in my bed, all I could do was think of things I'd rather forget. I found myself yet again thinking of the poor Mr. Winthrop and how only five people attended his funeral, and I thought of how sad it was that Banes, the priest, and I were three of the five. And as I lay with my eyes closed, I mulled over the strange events of his untimely passing. I thought of how he managed to survive for so long without sustenance or water, and I pondered about how he amazingly moved his withered, jellyfish-like body into the visitor's chair. Then I found myself picturing the ancient, carven chair that he was found stuck to. And I cringed as I pictured it as it now was, standing against the wall in the darkness of my living room in between two hanging spider plants, adjacent to the fireplace. It was at least four hours before I finally fell asleep.

The following morning, the chief was handing out assignments, and he asked me to stay behind as the other officers funneled out of the conference room. "You look tired, Ben, even troubled. Have you been getting your sleep?" he asked.

"No, sir," I answered. "This whole thing with the Winthrop case won't let me rest. I don't know why it's still disturbing me so, it's not like I haven't been exposed to ghastly sights before. I've seen many corpses, and I've witnessed the tragedies of the bleeding and the dying, but I've never seen anything like the horrific case of Mr. Winthrop."

"Well, I can't say that anyone has ever been through anything remotely close, Ben. It disturbed Banes a great deal, and I figured you were okay, but it's affected you as well. Go home, Ben. Get some real rest. You take two weeks like Banes, and get your head together. I can't have tired officers walking the streets with cluttered minds."

So I went back to my lonely old house and jumped into bed. The thought of having the next two weeks free really relaxed me, and before I knew it, I was dreaming of normal and familiar things again. I slept soundly for a good five hours. When I woke, it was just past 1:00 p.m. I felt refreshed for the first time in quite a while. I made myself a sandwich, and as I ate at the kitchen table, I realized it was getting cold. Afterward, I carried in some wood, and soon I was warming myself by the crackling fire, and when the room was warm, I felt my feet aching under the weight of my body. So I sunk down into the soft red velvet cushioning of the antique chair and watched as the flames curled and twisted mesmerizingly.

It felt sublime to rest my bones and clear my mind in the warmth of the heated chamber, but my contentment was short-lived, for suddenly I felt a cold chill slither through me, and an undeniable sensation of sorrow and gloom coiled itself around me with its heavy and constricting embrace. Soon all the feelings of contentment and peace of mind were squeezed out of me, only to be replaced by a damp, dark cloud of negativity. I found myself thinking of things I'd never thought of before. Things of a gory and macabre nature. One by one, all the sickly and disturbing sights that I had lived through and had since long forgotten had invaded my mind with their deplorable visions. The crying victims of rape and brutality. The bloody victims of both accidents and violence. The cold, dead eyes of the murdered and even the indescribable and evil odors of the long dead, which were abandoned or forgotten. One by one, they all returned to my mind to spook and torture it. My soul felt like a cold, deep, dark pit of despair and gloom. And as I sat and watched the fire and tried to ignore the horrid and uninvited visions to no avail, I came to the realization that although the fire was still burning strong, I could no longer feel its heat. And I trembled slightly for I felt a coldness in my bones.

Then I felt it. As if some malevolent force was seizing my body and manipulating both my mind and my spirit. In my mind, I now pictured a shadowy figure standing against the wall behind me, silently watching me, feeling me out. Again, chills jolted through me as I felt the potent strain of a maniacal presence looming over me from behind. I continually tried to convince myself that it was only in my mind as I watched the fire die out. But I could not escape the overwhelming sensation of a hodgepodge of negative and ill emotions. And as I sat in the chair like a drunken man, the diseased feelings of horror had their way with me.

The next thing I knew, I was lying on my back in a hospital bed. I was weary and drained. I was extremely hungry and confused. I felt empty, and as I stared at the ceiling, the room began to spin, and I expelled a long and agonizing moan. "You're back!" cried a familiar voice. "You're back with us, old pal!" It was the friendly voice of my partner, Banes. There was a painful soreness in my neck as I strained to turn my head in the direction of his call. He was rising from a chair in the far corner and wearing a smile wide and bright. "Welcome back, Ben, we were all so worried about you."

"What happened?" I asked. "Did I have an accident?"

"Well, Ben, I think it would be best to wait and explain it after you're fully recovered."

"Recovered from what?" I begged. "What's going on, Banes? Tell me, tell me now!" I hollered.

"Calm down, Ben, relax and I'll tell you, but not until I watch you eat a good meal and wash it down with as much water as you can put down," he responded. Without hesitation, I agreed, for I could not recall ever being so parched or so hungry.

When I was done eating probably the best meal I'd ever consumed and when I drank more water than I can tolerate, the nurse gave me pills, which, of course, required even more water. And when she was done running a few tests on me and she left the room, I said to Banes, "Are you ready to tell me now?" Banes had a troubled look on his face as he dragged the visitor's chair to my bedside and slumped down in it. He took a long, deep breath before he began. "You were as troubled as I with the Winthrop case, right, Ben?"

"Yes, I suppose I was."

"And the chief sent you on vacation for two weeks the same as he'd done for me, right?"

"Yes," I agreed, having no idea what he was about to reveal.

"Well, Ben, a few days after I came back to work, you were also expected to return. I believe it was on a Wednesday, and when Thursday morning rolled around and you still hadn't shown up, the chief sent me to check up on you. I banged on your door till my knuckles were raw. I called your name till my voice was hoarse, yet you did not answer. So I kicked in the door and yelled out for you again with no response. Ben, it's hard for me to say this, harder still to believe, but I found you in that horrible chair, Ben! I found you staring up with wide, empty eyes at one of your brown, withered spider plants, smelling like hell and looking the same. You were as unresponsive as poor Winthrop. I almost had a mental breakdown, and I think the thought of saving you was the only thing which brought me back from the brink of insanity. Ben, it's a wonder you're still alive. The doctor said that you hadn't eaten or even drank a drop of water in over two weeks."

"Oh god!" I responded. "My god, that monstrous chair! Why couldn't I have just left it to the garbage heap? Oh my god!" I exclaimed again. We both were silent for a moment or two, and when I finally looked back at Banes, I imagined that the disturbed look in his eyes only mirrored the same in mine. And as I remembered the state Mr. Winthrop was in, I cringed as I was too afraid to ask a new question. And although I hesitated a while, I finally managed to ask. "Banes, tell me, were there flies?"

"No, Ben, no flies, thank God, and don't worry, I went back and cleaned up my vomit."

Of course, now my vacation had to be extended. I spent the following eight days in the hospital, recuperating. Slowly, as I ate, took my medicine, and rehydrated my body, I began to regain my strength and health as it was before I was carted here. It took over a week of physical therapy training before I was able to walk again, for my muscles were stiff and weak from over two weeks of not using them. How this all happened to me, I could not fathom, but I had a lot of time to lie around and think about it. Even after I was well enough to return home, I was not yet seen fit to return to my place of employment. And so the chief granted me an extra week to relax and recuperate. I was ordered by the doctor to walk a few miles a day to strengthen my leg muscles. It was fine by me, for I did not wish to spend much time alone in that house with that dreadful and mysterious chair. I found myself thinking of different ways to rid myself of it. At first I thought of taking it apart with an ax and burning it in my fireplace, but even though I came to loathe its presence in my home, my love for things of antiquity and fine craftsmanship led me to alternative solutions. *Perhaps I should try to sell or swap it. After all, I had spent a bit to have it cleaned and deodorized. Perhaps I could get my money back and then some. That old thing has to be worth something,* I thought.

That very day, I placed an ad in the *Daily Tribune*. I described the chair as best as I could, yet I could not leave a listed price for I had no idea of its value, and so I left the price to be negotiated. Three days went by without a single response. Three days of moving about my house without once stepping foot into the living room. Three long nights of lying in my bed, waiting for sleep to come as I pictured that dark old brown piece of furniture collecting dust and casting horrible shadows on the floor. The next morning, there came a rapping at the door, and upon answering it, a short, skinny man in a black suit and hat was standing on my porch. "Are you here about the chair, sir?" I inquired.

"Oh yes, I am here about the chair. That awful, evil chair! That damnable thing killed my wife!"

"My chair killed your wife?" I responded with apparent confusion. "I beg your pardon, sir?"

I offered him some tea, and as we sat at the kitchen table with the rain tapping at the windows, he began to tell his story. "I saw a disturbing article about a certain Mr. Winthrop a while back. I must say it disturbed me greatly. For it was not unlike the way my poor wife was taken from me. You see, I don't have to actually see the chair to know that it's the very same one which I found my wife half-dead in a year ago. The way you described it… it is the same exact vision which haunts me nightly. Not a day goes by that I don't think of it, and not a single night has passed since that I don't have horrific dreams about it. If only I had listened to my instincts and not bought the thing for my poor wife, who coveted it so. I bought it because she wanted it so badly, and I knew also that it was worth much more than the seller was asking. I had a feeling that it was too good to be true. I kept telling myself that the owner was unaware of the chair's antiquity and therefore its true value as well, and so I took it home. That very night, I received a telegram that my mother was severely ill back in Virginia, and so I made arrangements to see her. I spent a week and a half tending to her needs, and it helped if only little that I was at her side when she passed. But I had no idea that when I returned home that my horrors were not over, and when I found my beloved wife in her dilapidated condition in that vampiric chair, I was faced with the birth of yet a new and unexplainable horror."

The poor man began to tremble as he stopped explaining his woes. I noticed him pinching himself, perhaps to prevent the tears, which were welling up in his ducts, from falling before me. "I will tell you no more," he went on abruptly. "But I will tell you this. That chair is… well, sir, it's alive! I know you think me mad, and I don't care, but that awful chair is alive, and it is evil! Do not sell that chair. For the good of mankind, you must destroy it. Destroy it now while you still have a prayer. Do not sell the chair. Do not even give it away, and for your own good, sir, do not sit in it. Whatever you do, do not sit in that goddamned chair!" The man was clearly too troubled to be questioned, and I knew enough as not to argue with him. Our strange and tense conversation ended with a long, firm, and emotional handshake and a promise on my part not only to remove the ad from the newspaper but to destroy the chair altogether. Before he left, he made the sign of the cross on his chest, and he said to me, "Bless you, sir, for you have a good soul, and you know what is right. I'd bless this house too, but it would go unheard, for the disease within it has four legs and the claws of a mad, hungry, insatiable lion. And until you rid this house of its evil spell, you will find neither peace nor sanity. Good day, sir, and don't forget your promise."

"I will not," I assured him as I watched him turn and slosh through puddles beneath the pouring rain.

Not long after the strange man was gone, I threw on my coat and went for a walk. I felt like staying in my dry house, but the library was only a short distance away, and I could not bear to be alone in the dark house with that vindictive thing they call a chair for another minute. I thought too, as I maneuvered my way around puddles, that the chances of finding what I was looking for were slim at best, but I had to try. I had to have the answer to this perplexing, macabre mystery. My plan, be it a shot in the dark as it were, was to search in old newspapers for anything tragic or unexplainable that somehow involved a great carven chair such as the one waiting for me in my den. Perhaps another person besides Winthrop or the poor man's wife was found dead or in an inconceivable state in a large carven chair and would shed new light on the strange case.

Hours went by as I painstakingly mulled over stacks upon stacks of dusty, brittle old newspapers till finally a headline from seventy-some years previous caught my eye. The headline read, "Corpse Spooks Landlord to Death!" It was a shocking and unbelievable story of a landlord who, after not receiving rent for four months from his tenant, finally hopped a train and traveled over fifty miles to knock on the door of the deadbeat tenant. After knocking without response, the man used his master key to enter the home. Later, the police were alerted to the home for worried neighbors noticed that the front door had been ajar for several days. When the police arrived, they were struck in the face by a pungent odor, and they soon entered the room where the landlord was found sprawled out on his back with a look of horror frozen on his face. As they knelt over the man whom they say died of a heart attack, they heard from behind them a dull, weak moaning. They slowly turned around to see a man sitting in a large chair, a man who looked as if he were dug up and pulled from his grave. His eyes were empty and gray, and his skin was a sickly white, the same as a bloated body pulled from the ocean. His hair had fallen out and was seen in a pile on his lap. His arms, skinny as a corpse, hung limply off the sides of the chair, and his legs were rubbery, useless appendages. His chest and belly were sunken in, and his ribs in several spots were sticking out through small, gaping absences of flesh on his abdomen. It was disturbingly clear that his body was well in a stage of decomposition although the man was somehow still alive. There was even a large cloud of flies swarming around his tortured head, and many more of them were eating away at his deteriorated muscles. Some were even seen crawling in and out of the voids in his flesh, and ants carried pieces of him away!

Upon my reading of the article, I noticed that my hands began to tremble. I wondered how many more poor victims such as this had not managed to make the paper. The article moved me terribly as I thought of how more intense this story was as compared to mine or even Mr. Winthrop's. So too did the article mention that the half-dead man had to be cut from the chair as he was somehow attached to it. And I felt like vomiting as I thought of how, after all that, someone gained possession of the chair and cleaned it and brought it into his home just as I had done.

My eyes were getting weary, and my mind was swollen with fright and worry. Still I thought of going home and being in the same house with that chair, and so I continued with my search. And as I sifted through more and more stacks of even older newspapers, focusing only on headlines and article titles, I began to wonder about how I would destroy the chair. I was not only afraid to sit in it or to be in the same room where it stood and waited for me, I was now even afraid to be in the same house where it was harbored. Another two hours of relentless and mundane flipping through old newspapers and my tiresome investigations had finally paid off once again, for a headline article in a paper stood out among all the rest the way the last one had, yet it chilled my troubled spirit tenfold. It was in a paper that was over 150 years old! The words leaped into my face like a slimy frog from the murky greenish-gray depths. It was a paper from 1633. It was titled "In the Chair of Nightmare!"

It was a story that began with the arrest of a woman who was accused of the crimes of brutality and torture on her own son. Eventually, she was sent to the insane asylum for the story she told could not be believed by a soul although she swore her word was the truth. She did admit to the accusations of brutality and torture on her own son, which baffled police as the rest of her story was so surreal and unbelievable. She told them of how her son, against the wishes of his mother, would sneak out constantly and spend hours in local cemeteries, writing macabre stories and drawing devilish creatures and unfathomable landscapes. Her son's behavior was unacceptable and, even more so, blasphemous in her eyes for she was an avid churchgoer and could not tolerate her son's dark and twisted interests.

One night, he did not return home, and the following day, he still was not heard from. It seemed the mother was unconcerned with her son's disappearance; however, questions were raised at his school after two days of absence, and soon a search party was scouring the land. The mother told them of his eerie haunts, and it wasn't long before they found him in the oldest and most neglected boneyard on the island. After spending two days and two nights among the tall weeds and moss-covered slabs of the old cemetery, they found him alive yet incoherent and in a state that none of the large search party could ever dream of finding him or anyone else in. For they found him lying on his back, only a fraction of the young man he once was. For his limbs were all severed and were never found. Not a single trace of blood was discovered, and they soon realized that all his wounds had been cauterized. And it shocked the search party viciously when his eyes opened, and he began moving his head about. It seemed that he had made several attempts to scream, although nothing save for long soul-squeezing moans were expelled. It seemed that this horrible act was later blamed on his mother, although she continually denied any responsibility. She said it was hell's demons that inflicted the wrath of God on him, to put an end to his ill desires and blasphemies. After she had admitted to torturing him later on, it only baffled the authorities because she would not admit fault to the strange happenings in the graveyard. They summed it all up as extreme mental illness.

They could not accept the outlandish story from the victim's own mouth when they finally got him to talk. He told them that he was attacked by a large black hairy beast with the head of a wolf, which not only walked on its hind legs, but which also was wielding an ax whose blade was glowing red. He spoke of how he was preoccupied with his writing in the last dwindling light of the sun, which had already set, and before he saw the beast, it had already lopped off his writing arm. As he tried to rise and run away, the creature hacked off his legs and then his left arm as well. He said that the hairy beast then bundled up his severed limbs like so much firewood and bayed victoriously before it turned away into the night. And he watched as the red glow of the ax head disappeared between the shadowy tombstones.

Of course, no one took his story seriously, save for his mother, who believed it was a hellhound and her heathen of a son got what he asked for. Later on, when she was finally discovered torturing her son, who at this point was an old man, they blamed her for the dismemberment in the graveyard as well. When asked why she was doing horrible things to her own son, she replied, "I'm only carrying out the work of the good Lord. I'm only finishing the job that the hellhound left undone."

When they found the poor dismembered old man, he was perched upright in a large and intricately carven chair of Gothic style. They soon came to the disturbing revelation that his mother had stitched the end of his stumps to the red velvet cushioning of the chair to keep him from slumping out of it. It seems he had spent most of his long and tortured existence stitched to the chair, never bathing or lying down in a bed. The poor shell of a man was severely dehydrated and malnourished. It seemed that the mother fed him just enough to keep him alive so she could punish him further for his ungodly sins. It was revealed later as well that many times the man spat out the food as his mother tried to force it upon him. He wanted to die, but she would not let him. Oddly enough, however, as doctors finally arrived and severed a single stitch with a small pair of scissors, the man began twitching and shaking his head violently. He began screaming and jerking his torso about till the chair began to rock to and fro. Then suddenly, he stopped moving, and his eyes froze open wide. He was dead. Later, they realized that the sight of the scissors was what made him flip out. "My god, it must have brought back memories of being tortured!" one officer said while wearing a spooked look on his face. Upon a search of the house, the officers found a strange black suit made up of potato sacks with animal fur glued to it in the kitchen closet. They also discovered a mask that resembled the head of a wolf. Upon further investigation, one officer found an ax out back by a woodpile. The top of the handle was black and charred.

It was late when I returned home. It had been dark for hours, and the rain had stopped. If I didn't know better, I wouldn't have believed a word that I just read from the dusty old newspapers. My mind was reeling with fascination and terror as I stepped across the threshold and lit some candles in my kitchen. *No more will I live in fear and dread to be in my own home. Maybe when the deed is done, the nightmares will cease,* I thought to myself as I hung up my coat. But presently, I felt that the horror within me had grown out of control and swelled into a confused mass of vindictive and negative energy. Again I pictured the great chair in the cold, dark, and neglected chamber. All the new revelations were now turning over in my head, and they seemed to seize me in my tracks. I stood there silently at the mouth of the dark hallway, just trying to summon the courage to do what had to be done. It had been some time since I had been in the same room with that abominable antique that I once coveted.

In my mind, one by one I thought of all the victims it had claimed over the years. I wondered again how many never made the paper. I thought about that poor man's wife, then of Mr. Winthrop, and about how I was almost a victim myself. And yet again, I wondered if I could face the inanimate object once more. Then I turned from the hallway and ran out the door. Before I knew it, I was back inside and was moving down the hallway with a flickering candle in one hand and my ax gripped firmly in the other. I took a deep breath before I entered the chamber and wasted no time lighting the candles on the fireplace mantel. Soon, the room was aglow with jumping candlelight, and I turned to face my enemy.

Now I held the ax firmly in both palms and raised it above my head. "Destroy it! Do it now!" a voice echoed in my head. My legs as well as my arms began to tremble, and I knew I'd lose my nerve if I hesitated. Sweat began to trickle down my forehead and sting my eyes, and my limbs began to tremble more violently. *I'll lose my muscle control,* I thought. *I must do it now.* Again I heard the voice repeating in my head. It was an unfamiliar voice indeed. "Do it! Do it now!" Again I took a deep breath and swiftly brought down the ax with all my might. But something was terribly wrong, for before I knew what had happened, I was sprawled out on the floor. I thought for certain that the first blow would do considerable damage, and it did, but it seems that the damage was suffered by myself alone. Apparently I had struck the chair with a blow so swift and strong that I misjudged my swing, and instead of splintering the dark-stained wood, I hit the back cushion, which only sprung the ax back at me, and I smashed myself in the head with the blunt end of my own axe.

Now I found myself lying on the cold floorboards, half-unconscious, with a ringing in my throbbing head. And as I lay there, gazing at the chair, fighting off the desire to succumb to slumber, I felt blood pouring from a gash in my head. I was too disoriented to move, my muscles were awkward and limp, and my head and limbs began to tingle. I tried several times to rise, but it was as if I were paralyzed. I felt my mind beginning to fade into darkness. I knew my only chance was to rise from the floor, which was now wet, warm, and sticky with my blood. I knew I'd bleed to death for certain as I tried one last time to rise to no avail. And as I lay there, leaking on the floor and gazing at the ancient carven chair, I knew that it had beaten me. I knew this time that I would not survive its fiendish clutches, and I was all the more disturbed by the fact that it would go on surviving and existing and that I failed to destroy it. I knew that the next owner of the house would only cherish it and would sit and rest their weary bones upon its plush red velvet cushions.

I sighed as I knew that it would live on to continue its evil and malign ways. I knew that the hellish nightmare would continue. And as I began to fade into oblivion, I could feel his maniacal presence more than ever before, even more than when I was a captor of its parasitic embrace. And I could almost see him there, where his tortured soul resides, still stitched to the red velvet cushioning of the great, mysterious antique chair. Hiding in silence with the patience of ages long past. Waiting with a hunger both wild and mad. Waiting for the next poor soul to sink down into its cold, ill comforts. Waiting there in the flickering candlelight to slowly drain the life force from his lazy, mindless victims.

A DAY ABOVE GROUND

"Oh, bloody hell, Jay, what are we gonna do now?"

"I don't know, Rat. I'm sorry about this," I said with a sigh.

"They just had to take your horse too, those damn bastards. Now what are we gonna tell our wives, Jay?"

"We're gonna tell them the truth, Rat, the awful truth. You know, I've had old gray forever, she was a good girl."

"I know. Those scumbags don't deserve a horse like her. They don't deserve any of it."

"You're right, my friend, and nor do we deserve this, but we'd better stop sitting around, moping. You know this old road. We could sit stranded on it for a week without another traveler passing by, and then if you see someone at all, it might be some ruffians like we just had the pleasure of being robbed by."

"Yeah, but where to?"

"Well, Rat, we could abandon the wagon and walk eighteen miles or so back to town, or we could stray off the road and try to find some help somewhere closer, maybe find a farmer who would be willing to sell us a horse. I've got some cash left."

"I have a bit too. Good thing we stashed our money in our boots. Let's go, Jay, just don't get us lost."

We started out across a long and barren field and walked several miles through tall brush and thorns with no sign of civilization. We were both quiet most of the way. I kept thinking about my poor horse and how she would be treated in the hands of those rotten thieves and about how I was going to tell my wife and kids that we'd lost everything we bought in town. Although the path we walked was quite winding, I tried my best to keep in a somewhat straight line. The last thing I wanted was to add to our hardship by getting us lost. Seeing as how we were not only outnumbered but ambushed as well, they had taken our guns. I kept thinking about the coyotes and wolves that ruled the night and how we now were unarmed. And although we still had quite a bit of daylight left, there was no time to waste, for we did not want to get lost out here, especially at night. I hadn't eaten since breakfast, and my belly was rumbling. I had a cupcake in my jacket pocket that my daughter had made and given me for the ride into town. I wanted to eat it, but it was all we had between us. Half a cupcake would give us a bit of energy, but it wouldn't go far.

After another mile or so of weaving in and out of shrubs and trees with hanging vines, I saw an old stone wall stretching out in the distance. "Look, my friend, a sign of humanity."

"All right!" exclaimed Rat joyfully. "Let's jump that wall." At first, my hopes were high, but when I squeezed through a border of tall bushes and jumped down onto the other side of the wall and looked around, I knew we would find no help here. Far off in the distance stood the ruins of an ancient stone house that was covered in ivy, and most of the old walls were now mere heaps of stone and mortar around and within the base of the foundation.

"What now?" Rat asked.

"Let's cut through the yard, maybe there are some newer houses nearby." Soon we were walking in the shadow of one of the few existing walls. Twisted, rusted metal debris was scattered among the piles of rubble. Everything that was made of wood had long since rotted into worm-eaten dust. Just as we were about to leave the remnants of the ancient house behind us, a bluish gleam sparkled among the rubble, which I barely saw from the corner of my eye. "Hold on, Rat, let me check this out quick." Carefully I trotted up the crumbling stones and metal scraps while trying not to trip. Soon I was squatting over the sparkling blue thing that had commanded my attention, and I began to carefully brush away the debris that blanketed it with my hands. I was happy to find that it was exactly what I expected it was, and I was even more delighted to find that it was still all in one piece despite the rocks that sat atop it. I stood up again and held the antique medicine bottle before me and read it as it gleamed in the sunlight. I could only guess how old it was and thought it would be a fine souvenir. It would look good on my fireplace mantel, I thought as I slipped it into my pocket.

As I turned around and began walking back toward my friend, I slipped on the rubble, falling forward and crashing down on the remnants of a wall that was only standing two feet high. The air was forced out of my lungs as my belly slammed into the stones, and I choked as a cloud of dust rose around my face, for the force of my fall had knocked down the remainder of the wall. I lay there for a moment, trying to catch my breath and coughing madly as I breathed in the ancient dust. Soon, my friend was helping me to my feet while shouting questions of my condition. "I'm fine, Rat, just a little shaken," I said after I filled my lungs with fresh air above the settling dust cloud. I thought the bottle would have surely shattered in my jacket pocket; however, I was quite surprised to find it unaffected by my fall. "You're lucky you didn't break a rib," Rat said as I put the bottle back in my jacket. "Let's go, Jay, times a—" He suddenly stopped in midsentence, and I saw him gazing at the rubble when I looked at him. "What do we have here, Jay?" he asked excitedly. I lowered my gaze down to what caught his eye and noticed the corner of a well-rusted metal box still mostly concealed by the stones I had knocked over. He pried it out of the rubble and dusted it off with excited eyes. He held the box for a solid moment of quiet anticipation before finally lifting the lid. And when he did, he gasped. He lifted his head and hollered to the heavens before turning his eyes back to the contents of the corroded box and burst out into a fit of crazy laughter. Before he stopped laughing, I was peering over his shoulder into the box. I must have gasped as he did, for it was a while before we spoke a word. We just stood there in shock as the sparkling colors entranced our awestruck minds. It was the most surreal moment of my life, and I found myself flicking the sides of the metal box to assure myself that what I was seeing was real. There was no doubt; it was no daydream. I was not knocked on the head when I fell. It was no mirage. The beautiful rubies, emeralds, diamonds, and gold jewelry inside the box was as real as the stones I had fallen on. As real as the old medicine bottle in my pocket. As real as the summer sun above us that made them sparkle and gleam before our wide and frozen eyes.

Finally, my dumbfounded friend slipped from his spell and spoke. "There's a fortune in this box, Jay, a bloody fortune!"

"Two fortunes, my friend!" I responded. "A good, solid two fortunes!" After marveling over the contents of the box for a time, my friend got the idea to place the box on the grass and begin sifting through the rubble to see if there was anything else to be discovered. As if we needed to look for anything more. The contents of that box would make us both wealthy for the rest of our lives, never mind replace all we had lost in the robbery. I tried to talk him into leaving, for the presence of that box was making me uneasy and anxious to leave. All of a sudden, I felt a sickening sensation of being watched. All I wanted to do was to get out of there and find someone to sell us a horse so we could ride home. All we had to do now was to get that box home safely, and all our troubles would be over. But something made my soul squirm as I watched my friend frantically searching among the rubble, pushing stones aside, and kicking up dust like a madman.

I sat down beside the box and wiped the sweat from my forehead with my sleeve and watched as my friend, who now seemed somewhat possessed by the demon of greed as he pawed at the pile of crumbled walls like a hungry animal. To my surprise, it was not long before I heard him yelling, "There's something here, Jay! There's something—" Again he stopped in midsentence, and an eerie silence misted down over us as I rose to my feet.

"What did you find?" I asked. He did not answer, and I watched the dust around him settle as he froze in a squatting position. *More jewels?* I wondered. There couldn't possibly be more. *Maybe he found a box of coins?* I thought as I walked over to him. But it was no rusty box, nor was it another antique bottle. Nor was it anything to smile or laugh happily or insanely about, for my silent and disturbed friend was holding in his grasp the bones of a human hand!

"My god!" I yelled. "Rat, let's get out of here!"

"Wait," he muttered. "Look, there's the rest of it!" He placed the hand beside him and began again to take the heap of stones apart. Soon, he had uncovered the ribs and legs of a human skeleton, and he worked quickly to expose it entirely. Before too long, the legs were uncovered, and he began removing the debris that covered the arms and skull. Soon, the hollow eyeholes were gazing back at us, empty, yet they seemed full of curiosity and despair. The last part of the poor skeleton Rat uncovered was the left arm, and we both were stunned to find that there was a hand at the end of the arm, as well as the right one. "Bloody hell, Jay, there's more than one body here!"

All I could do was stand and watch in confusion and silence as my friend dragged the skeleton out of its unhallowed resting place and sat it up neatly against the remainder of the foundation. Without making eye contact or saying another word, he bent down again and began sifting through the piles of the crumbled old house. I cannot say what it was that came over me then as I stood up and opened the rusted box and removed one of the many diamond and gold rings. How many of these were wedding rings? I pondered as I walked half-hypnotized toward the old skeleton. Without a rational thought in my head, I bent down to place the ring on one of its dry, brittle fingers. And I found myself gazing into the empty eyes of the long-dead man or woman that sat so peacefully before me with a sparkling ring wrapped around its slim finger bone.

I don't know how long I stared into those empty eye sockets. All I can say is that my feet began to throb. And I don't know how long my friend delved in the debris, which seemed to consume his every thought and movement. But the next thing I knew, he was calling my name, and when I turned round toward him, he was standing before me with glazed eyes that were soaked with madness. His arms were both outstretched, and in one hand, he held a leg bone, and in the other, another skull. At his feet among the crumbled stone were two piles of twisted and intertwined skeletal parts. "There's an army of people buried here!" he said in a voice I could not recognize. I shuddered at the strange sound of his voice, for it was much deeper and so guttural that it did not resemble his in any way.

"Let's go, Rat! Let's take the box and go now!" I commanded. I did not wish to spend another second there, nor did I wish to see another bone. It must have been the reference to the box that snapped him out of his strange behavior, for he dropped the leg bone and the skull and rubbed his eyes with his dirty hands. "Yeah, let's take the box and go," he muttered, disturbed and shaken as he was. His voice was again familiar, and it slightly set my soul at ease, until I looked back down at the macabre pile of bones. And as I handed him the box of jewels, something else at our feet caught my attention, and I looked down to see a silverfish that was half-crushed, perhaps from my friend disturbing the heaps of stone and rubble. I don't know why, but for a moment, I could not take my eyes off the poor bug as it writhed in the stone dust, half-crushed and twitching.

"You're right, Jay, let's go. What are you waiting for?" he asked.

"Yeah, we should go," I responded. But before I took a single step, I looked back down at the dying silverfish, and I watched it squirm until it stopped.

"Jay! Jay, what's wrong with you? You wanted to leave, so let's go." But something held me there, and I kept staring down at the dead bug. It was then that a wave of horror crashed over me. A horror a hundred times worse than the discovery of those old bones had brought me. For as I looked down at my feet beside the dead silverfish, I could not help but notice that the bug had neatly and undeniably spelled out the letters d-i-g-e-r as it writhed. There was no mistaking it. It was no stretch of the imagination whatsoever. The letters, hell, the word, although it was missing one letter, was spelled out clearly in the dust at my feet.

"Unholy hell!" I hollered. "Come look at this, Rat!"

He stooped down to get a good look. "What the hell?" he responded with confusion. "What does it mean?"

"I think it means digger!" I answered nervously.

"No," he said. "You're imagining things. It just looks like a word. Anyway, it's spelled wrong. Do you honestly believe that that bug spelled out a word?"

"I know where you're coming from, Rat, but you can't deny that those are letters that form a word."

He looked down at it for a time before he spoke again. "Christ, Jay! I think you're right. If I hadn't been watching you the whole time, I'd be sure you scratched that with your finger in the dust, but I know it's no prank. Something strange is going on here. Let's move. It's getting late in the day, and we still have to find a horse."

"Yeah, Rat, let's go."

We started off again through the wild weeds of the property. All the while, the gems and jewels clanged against the sides of the rusty box as my friend walked. I felt my stomach churning, but it was not from hunger. The sight of those bones and skulls were infesting my mind, and several times as I walked, I thought I'd have to stop to vomit. An eerie silence seemed to put up a wall between us as we walked, and I wondered what was going through my friend's head. Soon we came upon a stone wall in the shape of a large square, which was itself bordered by tall evergreen trees, and before long, I found myself standing before an opening in the wall beneath an arc, which was formed by the intertwined branches of two massive dead cedar trees. Through this arc, I gazed at many weathered and slanted tombstones of a family that had long since passed. And as I stood there, staring, the arc above me began to creak in a manner that was both chilling and threatening, for I found it quite queer to hear those eldritch sounds above me since there was not a hint of the slightest breeze to be heard or felt. I ignored my friend as he called out to me, and I stepped into the family cemetery, and as I did, I felt the warm summer air flee from around me, and it was replaced by an odd, icy coldness that penetrated my bones. Presently, my limbs began to tremble till my teeth began to clatter as I stood before the white marble stone with a weed-laden mound of dirt beside it and a curious pit before it.

Matt followed me in and stood by my side, and we both stared quietly and solemnly into the hole. Finally he spoke, "Damn! That's one deep grave, Jay!" We could clearly see while the sun shone in that it was much deeper than a usual grave, for the sun shone down at least fifteen feet or so into the pit before the darkness began. Rat placed the box down at his feet and fumbled in his pocket for a cigarette. I couldn't take my eyes off the deep, dark hole, nor could I respond to my friend. I only stood there, shaking. "It's awful cold all of a sudden, huh, Jay? Goddamn, it feels like winter!" Rat went on talking, of what, I had no idea. For some reason, I was no longer paying attention to him, and his voice was distant and muffled. Suddenly I felt groggy as I gazed down into the pit. It was as if a hypnotist were beginning to cast a spell on me, and I stood at the edge of the deep hole on wobbly, trembling legs and stared mindlessly through entrancing patterns of smoke swirling in the unusually cold sunlight above the pit. The next thing I knew, I was coughing and gasping for air. I was suddenly snatched away from the clutches of the spell, and I found myself crouched down several yards from the pit, filling my lungs with fresh air and again feeling as though I might vomit. "Sorry, old pal, boy, those cigarettes really get to you." I heard Rat say now loud and clear. It seems that I accidentally inhaled a good puff of smoke, and when I coughed, I came back around.

But before I had recovered to a normal state of mind, I looked up to respond to my friend, and as I did, I saw him turn his head from my gaze to the space beside him, and I saw his eyes light up with fear, and his mouth opened wide as if he were about to scream, yet only a slight and horrific groan emitted from it as his half-smoked cigarette fell to the ground. In another split second, I saw the subject of his panic. The figure of a frightfully ugly woman stood before him and leered at him with piercing eyes. Her long gray hair was flowing wildly about her decrepit-looking face without the aid of wind, and a silvery glow danced about her frame. After my friend expelled his sickening groan, he began to gasp as if there were no fresh air to breathe, and I saw him take two short and clumsy steps backward, away from the terrible woman, which only made him trip on the box of gems he had placed down moments before, and it was all I could do to watch my friend as he fell backward into the deep grave pit.

There was no doubt in my mind that the woman was a ghost, and I was sure my friend knew as much. I cannot deny that I was as frightened as he of the gruesome-looking spirit in the stained long white dress. Still, I tried to ignore her presence as well as my own horror, and instead of fleeing, I crawled to the edge of the pit and called out to my poor friend. I was only answered with silence as I gazed into the intimidating gray eyes of the terrible woman. Again I called and listened with no response. "Your friend is done for!" she said with both vigor and threat. Her voice shot through me like a streak of lightning.

"No!" I shouted to the sky before I stuffed my face into the mouth of the pit and yelled out my friend's name again. This time, I did hear something, but it was only the sound of my own voice echoing back up at me.

"It's of no use. Your friend is gone, and now you must worry for yourself alone," she said as I clutched the tall grass at the edge of the pit with my closed fists. Though I wished it were not so, I knew then that he was gone, and so I stood to face her. I then realized that my hands were still clenched tightly, and long grass and weeds swayed like flower stems in my palms. "You'd be better off to willingly join your friend, Rat, then to carry that box home with you!" she said, both surprisingly and disturbingly. "Still, know that it is not my intention to deceive you. You see, digger, I want nothing more from you than to take it far from here."

"But I—" I muttered only to be cut off before I could plead with her.

"You'd be wise to only listen and to remember that if I need a response from you, I'll provoke one. Besides, I already know enough about you, for I can hear your thoughts! I see that you appreciate and love life. I can tell, for you cling tightly to the life that grows above and not to the dead dirt it emerges from. I can read you like an open book, but I already know all I need to know about you. Now you must listen to our story and judge for yourself what you must do." I wanted to run, but I could not. I had completely forgotten about the rusted box and what was within. I wanted to run like my legs were on fire, but the next thing I knew, I was sitting down cross-legged at the edge of the pit. I was not sure if it was her awful presence alone or some powers she held over me that sat me down; all I knew was I could not move, and so I sat and stared back unwillingly into her dreadful eyes and listened as her cracked and sunken lips spoke again.

"We were a normal family once, like most. My Erwin was a good, honest man at first. He was a farmer and did well for himself. I was charmed by his kindness when I met him, and we soon married and raised a family. What I loved about him most was he was happy and content. We never had a ton of money in the early days, but we did well. There was always food on the table and smiles all around it. Till one year, we suffered a terrible drought. All the crops withered before they had a chance to grow, and we had none to sell or eat. Still, we had our livestock, but they, without crops to eat, also began to wither away. We ate what animals we could. Some of the meat was rancid. Still, it was better than nothing. I remember pawning some jewelry for grain to keep the chickens alive. We practically lived off eggs for a year. We grew so tired of them! It destroyed me, but it came down to selling my wedding ring to buy more grain. It was a horrible time. Eventually, the malnourished chickens stopped producing eggs altogether, and we were left with a few scrawny birds to eat. Erwin also did lots of hunting, but it was a long, cold winter with lots of blinding snow. The game was scarce, and so was the ammunition, for it soon ran low, and we couldn't afford to buy more. Things looked like they couldn't get any more grim.

"One day, a small group of seafarers showed up at the door, hungry and cold. We took them in and gave them some of the last chicken meat we had. They were grateful to have a warm place to spend the night and to have full bellies. They had bottles of rum with them, and we stayed up late, drinking by the fire and listening to tales of their oceanic adventures. It was a good night, for we hadn't been able to afford drink, nor had we any company in quite a while. In the morning, they set out again for the coast, but not before showing their gratitude for our hospitality. The captain handed my husband a small satchel and shook his hand with a smile. Erwin waited till they were almost out of sight before he emptied it into his hand. The family gathered round, and all our eyes lit up as he poured the contents into his large leathery palm. I remember almost fainting, for he held in his hand a pile of gold rings, coins, and many precious gems. My legs wobbled as I watched them sparkle. Emeralds, rubies, diamonds, pearls, and gold necklaces. It was a small fortune.

"That very day, my husband rode into town and sold some of the jewels. He returned with a pig and chickens, sacks of grain, and plenty of vegetables, not to mention a pocketful of change. We ate like pigs that night and laughed like lunatics as we did. It was a lucky break. Godsent, I thought at first. And to make matters even better, spring was on the way. We thought our troubles were over, and for a long time, it seemed as if they were. But soon the contents of the sack were depleted, and all the food it had bought us was used up, but by then, it was midspring, and our crops were growing nicely, and our livestock had been replenished to a degree. But just when things were feeling normal, the rains again vanished, and the blistering sun beat down upon the crops till the leaves again withered and the stalks dried up and browned. It seemed we were doomed to suffer the same trials as the previous year. Months went by without a single drop of rain, and the only moisture to be found was the morning dew dripping from the brown and brittle grass. Once again, our livestock suffered as we, and our situation was grim at best, for we had three hungry mouths to feed besides our own and another on the way. And just as it seemed things could get no worse, the seafarers were again seen wading in the tall dead weeds towards our house. This time, they did not seek a place to spend the night, nor did any of the three complain of hunger. Instead, the captain wished only to speak with Erwin, and so they walked alone to the barn. I noticed he was carrying a large metal box. I didn't know at the time what they discussed that hot day in the barn. When I asked, my husband looked at me with piercing eyes. 'Never mind, Elizabeth!' he shouted. 'Things are looking up, and only concern yourself with that. Don't ask questions. I'm on my way to town, love, do you need anything?'

"This time he returned with his wagon loaded beyond its weight capacity. The horses were drained of energy, and the wood creaked terribly beneath the weight of a feast for both our family and the livestock. Things began to turn around for us at that point, and I noticed that the captain and my husband frequently met in the barn, at least every other month. Erwin kept me in the dark about his business endeavors, and soon I stopped inquiring altogether, for it wasn't long before I had an even bigger ring on my finger, and we hired a crew of carpenters and masons to put a rather fancy addition on our house. For once in our lives, the children and I were able to build up a fine wardrobe, for we found ourselves wearing the finest silk garments, which were imported from East India and the Orient. It began to feel as though we were wealthy, prominent figures of society. Hunger and poverty were all but a bad memory we'd rather forget, and forget we did, that is, until the seafarers stopped visiting altogether.

"Before long, the money was drained, and although the renovation of our home was almost complete, the roof was unfinished, and the workers needed to be paid. Sick with worry, my husband climbed into the carriage and rode away. I knew he had no gems or jewelry left to sell, yet I dared not ask him what he was up to. I remember the awful look in his eyes as he whipped the horse to set him in motion. It was a look I'd never seen before. I remember being frightened by his eyes, which were blank yet full of worry. When he returned, to my surprise, he had a heap of goods in his wagon, and the next morning, he paid the crew in cash for the completion of the job. I was too terrified to ask him how he was able to do this, and so I kept my questions to myself, and instead, I prepared the meal he had brought us. Years went by without the visit of the captain or his men. Years of neglect was bestowed to the crops and livestock. Erwin spent many a night out with his horse and carriage. Never did he speak of his strange activity, nor did he explain exactly how he now put food on our table, yet we were living a life of ease. People in town, as well as our neighbors, still called Erwin a jeweler. But it concerned me greatly for I knew that his seafaring source had long since run out. All the while, I felt as though we lived in the shadow of impending doom for I knew something was not right, and one day, my suspicions were confirmed.

"For one hot summer day, a terrible rapping was heard at the door. It was a disturbing sound, which strangely made the medicine bottles on the table tremble and clang together. When I answered the door, I was face-to-face with a furious woman who wore the queerest garb. There was a multicolored cloth wrapped around her head, and she was weighed down with jewelry which I was sure was made of glass, crystal, and worthless metals. Before I could ask for her name, she yelled to me, 'I curse you and your children for your husband's evil deeds! I have already cursed him, and now I damn this house as well as the ground it stands on!'

"I asked her what she meant, what Erwin had done, but she only answered, 'If you don't know what he's been up to, how he buys his bread, you're a fool, woman! I am not so convinced of your ignorance.'

"'What have you done with my husband?' I screamed. 'Did you harm him?'

"'I laid not one finger on his heathen head, though I could have killed him with ease, the way he slaughtered my innocent granddaughter for her golden amulet! But I only spared him, for I wish him to suffer a fate tenfold greater than death.'

"'You're a liar! My Erwin would never, could never...' I pleaded, but her eyes swelled as she stared me down, and she said, "think, woman, think about it". Have you asked him where he goes when he goes and what he does while he's away? Have you ever asked him how he makes his money now that the pirates' skeletons have long hung dry? You cannot deny the fact that your dog has eaten your neighbor's chickens when he has been out through the gate and out of sight. There, I have said my peace, yet I have not come to bring it. I have only come to deliver the curse, and I leave it at your doorstep, and it shall slither up your legs and worm its way into your hearts, and your tongues shall feel as though they've been cut out every time you bite into the blood-soaked, ill-gotten bread your murderous husband has set down before you.'

"Then she turned and walked away, and the door slammed shut behind her unaided, and I was left alone to ponder her words. Soon I remembered all the times I saw him fetch a shovel and walk out into the darkness and sometimes the pouring rain. And then I recalled how just before the masons were done with a dividing wall in the cellar, he fired them and finished the work himself. I also remember how he banned us from entering the cellar and how at times terrible smells would emit from it, though he could not explain them.

"I did not confront Erwin when he got back. He seemed disturbed though I did not ask him how he was. We went on living as we normally had, or at least we tried, but things were never the same. For every bite of food we took, no matter what it was, always tasted like a mouthful of dirt. The children no longer laughed or played, and the whole family seldom spoke. Before long, we started to become ill, and the doctors could not tell us what we were suffering from. I knew it was the curse, though I spoke not of it, and one by one our children died painfully and mysteriously. One night as I laid dying in my bed, I thought I was losing my mind for I could hear the cries of my poor children as they lay in their graves! Those dreadful sounds were the last thing that tortured my ears before I too succumbed to the curse. And till this very day, all these lifetimes later, the curse still is potent and unforgiving, for I still am tormented by those cries, screams, and awful moans that I hear nightly. So, digger, I beg of you, take the damn box. Take the fortune that still festers within. Take it and go now, and God willing, you'll take the bloody curse with you."

With that horrid revelation and the end of her crazy ramblings, she turned and pointed at the cedar arc, and I watched her decrepit image dematerialize before me. I had never seen a ghost before, never mind had a conversation with one, but I believed in them. For I had heard the shuffling of footfalls on the creaky floorboards of an old house many times, and I've even heard faint whispering and mumbling round the foot of my bed, but what I had just experienced was too much to endure. I stood up and looked all around me, but I no longer saw her, and for a moment, I started to doubt everything I had just seen and heard. Even if that story came from a living woman, I would only dismiss her as mad, and I began asking myself if what I had witnessed was merely a vivid hallucination. Had I banged my head when I fell over the rubble of the old Clayton estate? I felt my head for bumps. It didn't hurt. Then I saw the box at my feet and realized that I had forgotten about my poor friend. It was then that any speck of doubt was washed from my mind as I pictured him as he tripped. He saw her too and was so terrified he practically jumped into the pit. I knelt down beside the hole and called again to my friend. After a dozen times without response, I made the sign of the cross on my chest and said aloud, "God rest your poor soul, Rat. I'll miss you, old friend." I then tucked the rusted box under my arm and headed out of the graveyard.

As I neared the arc, the gloomy creaking sounds grew louder, and again I cringed, for I felt not the slightest breeze on my face. And as I began to pass beneath it, the sounds grew louder till the creaking changed to the sounds of cracking and splitting of timber. And before I could run, I felt the onslaught of branches beating me down to the ground, and I lay there stunned, sprawled out on my chest with my face in the weeds. At first I was sure my back was broken, and the thought of dying slowly 'neath the huge cedar limb at the gateway to a haunted cemetery made my skin squirm. But as I lay there in a senseless daze, the pain began to slowly dull, and I began to wiggle around. I exhaled a sigh of relief, for I could not believe that I was not paralyzed by the falling limb. But I could not stand, for the limb was about four feet from the ground, held up by many branches, which jabbed into the dirt as it fell. I was lucky I wasn't crushed, I thought, but as I began looking all around me, my hopes began to erode, for I saw that the branches were all deep in the dirt, and even worse, they were all too close together to allow me to squeeze through. As I crawled, I looked all around me, and I could not find a space between the branches more than a foot wide. *It's okay,* I thought to myself and began to calm down for I knew that the tree was dead and I was certain that I could break my way out. But try as I may, I noticed that I had underestimated the strength of the branches. They were surprisingly solid, and I only bruised my hands as I beat on them. And when my hands hurt too much to strike another blow, I lay on my back and kicked at the limbs with both feet. One by one I kicked at every branch, to no avail. I was tired, and my legs, feet, and hands were battered past the point of further assault, and I lay there in pain, breathing heavily, while my limbs throbbed. I searched my mind for a way out. I felt like an animal in a cage, and worst of all, I realized that the sun was now quite low in the summer sky.

My last resort was to dig beneath a few of the branches so I could tunnel my way out, but all I had to dig with were my hands. Luckily, the soil was quite soft for it had rained a lot in the past few days, and though it worsened the pain in my pummeled hands, I went on clawing and tearing at the moist soil in surmounting agony. When I thought I could dig no more, I found a flat stone and used it to scrape away at the earth around the branches. The use of a stone was much more effective than pawing at the dirt with bruised hands, and it hurt a lot less, and just as I began making progress, the sun had sunk down below the tree line, and the shadows of the branches as they stretched out on the ground resembled prison bars. The darker it grew, the faster I scraped at the soil. Like a desperate madman, I worked in the dwindling light, and presently, I heard myself grunting and groaning like an overexcited wild animal on the verge of a fight.

By now the sloppy hole I had made was about three feet deep, and still the tips of the branches were buried. I wondered how far down they had sunk as I scraped and pushed the dirt behind me. By now it was dark, and the crescent moon blessed me with a faint light when it was not partially covered by thin white fog-like clouds. What I'd been dreading now was all around me, a cold and strange darkness that seemed to imprison me as the branches had. I had failed miserably in my frantic race against the coming night, and so I stopped for a quick rest. I sat there in the pit, relaxing, while my arms and hands throbbed and ached, and my labored breathing slowly began winding down. I sat there and gazed upward past the dirt, through the branches, and watched as the dreamy clouds passed before the sliver moon. After a few minutes, I picked up the flat stone and continued scraping at the dirt around the branches. Though I moved quickly, my attempts were not as frantic as before, for I was weary and weak, and anyway, the night was already upon me. Now it was not a race against the dark, only an effort to escape. Then I thought I had heard a scraping sound beneath me, and I stopped and listened. The maddening sound of crickets was all that filled my ears, and I went on scooping up the dirt. Before long, I heard it once more, and I stopped again to listen. *You're losing your mind, Jay, get a hold of yourself. You're only hearing the echo of your own labor bouncing around in the hole,* I told myself. But just before I continued scraping, I heard it a third time, and this time, I was sure it was not of my own origin.

I dropped the rock and stood up. I could hear a muffled scratching below my feet, and my terrified mind raced in a sorry attempt to explain it away. *It's only a mole,* I kept telling myself. *A mole or a very large rat.* As I tried to convince myself not to panic, I could not recall if I had only thought those words or said them aloud. I crawled back up to the surface and stared down at the commotion in the hole. Now I saw dirt moving and churning in the shadowy base of the pit. I watched in paralyzing horror as the soil began to sink farther down as it moved, and soon, a round white thing was seen emerging from the earth. I clasped my gritty hands over my eyes. I told myself that what I was seeing was not real. I tried to convince myself that when I looked again, it would be gone. But I could look away no longer for it was even more frightening not to see, and when I uncovered my eyes, I saw the figure of a young girl in a filthy dress, which looked as if it was once white, crawling out of the hole. She stood up in the hole I had made, and I could not see her face for she wore a bonnet on her head. A moment of eerie silence tortured me as we both froze 'neath the worm-laden cedar prison.

Just then, the moon was obscured by the clouds, and a swift and threatening voice, which was unbelievably guttural, tore through me. "Where do you think you're going, you dirty digger?" And as the dark silence that followed continued to toy with my soul, I could not answer. I was speechless and horrified beyond explanation. "You are a bad man, digger! How dare you!"

I tried to speak but only choked on my words and coughed till finally I was able to say, "No, I am not. I'm a good man, an honest man."

"Liar!" she shrieked back at me. "You're a dirty thief and a liar! You're stealing my daddy's jewels. Everything we have is in that box. How do you expect us to make a living?" I could not answer. All I could do was tremble. Tremble and tell myself it was all a nightmare. "Still searching your mind for a believable answer to deceive me, ha? Well, it's of no use, you can't fool me. Don't waste your time, thief. Your best bet is to return the jewels to my daddy, for if you ever make it out of here alive with that box, you and yours will suffer a hellish fate far worse than death."

"I promise," I pleaded. "If I ever get out of this hole, I'll return the jewels."

"To my daddy?" she demanded reassuringly.

"Yes, to your daddy, and him alone."

"Okay then," she said. "For your own sake, you'd better."

Suddenly, she moved toward me slowly, and as she did, the clouds dispersed, and I couldn't help but notice that, as the moon's rays shone beneath her stained bonnet, her nose and eyeholes were packed with dirt. However, her face was turned right in the direction of mine. I could not fathom how it was possible, but there was no doubt that she could see me. After another torturous bit of silence, she changed her threatening tone and was now calm. Her voice was still uncharacteristically deep, but I could now also hear a hint of squeaky, girlish sweetness mixed in. "My name is Ivy, if you were wondering, Jay," she said, and before I had a chance to respond, she continued. "I haven't had a cupcake in a while," she said suddenly, as if she could smell it in my pocket. I cringed as she spoke my name for I could not understand how she knew it. Then, without much thought, I pulled it out of my pocket and unwrapped it.

"Here," I said. "Take it and enjoy. My daughter made it just this morning. She's about your age."

"Liar!" she snapped again. "I am much older than your daughter. I'm much older than you!"

"Either way, they're the most delicious cupcakes in the world." With filthy and trembling hands outstretched, I said again in a timid and terrified tone, "Here, Ivy, take it and enjoy." Slowly and reluctantly she took it and held it in both her dirty hands. She held it for a while before her face as to relish in the fact that she was about to indulge in a tasty treat that she hadn't tasted in ages. Finally, she bit into it. Slowly she savored it before she took another bite. After the third bite, however, she suddenly threw the half-eaten cupcake down into the hole she had slithered out of.

"Liar!" she barked again. "You said it would be delicious. But it tastes like dirt! Everything tastes like dirt! You'd better return that box to my daddy, for your own sake, digger!" Then she came out of the shadows and moved slowly toward me. "Do it or you'll end up worse than your friend, you filthy digger!" She then lunged for me, and I felt her bony fingers wrap around my arm before I felt her teeth sink painfully into my forearm. I snatched my arm away from her, and she stood before me, unyielding. "You taste like dirt too, digger!" she said and began laughing hysterically. When she was done laughing madly, she turned and dove headfirst into the pit. I stood, staring down into the dark pit as the silence seized me. I kept expecting the dirt to churn, to see her dirty bonnet emerging from the hole once more. I was too mortified to move a single muscle. I froze there for several moments in a state of shock. Finally, I snapped out of it. I checked my arm. She broke the skin, but it wasn't bleeding much. I slowly climbed back into the dank hole and fumbled around till I found my flat stone. Once again, I continued scraping away at the soil in a terrible frenzy. Faster than my race against the setting sun, I tore at the earth like a madman. All the while, the dirt was falling into the hole at my feet, and every few seconds, I had to stop and look down to see if she was coming out again. I pushed a large amount of dirt into the hole, yet it kept disappearing down into it.

Soon I was thrilled to find that I had finally reached the bottom of two branches, and I began tunneling beneath them. Then an alternate idea came to me. Instead of digging upward on the other side of the branches, now that I had freed the tip of the branches, maybe I'd have the strength to pull them till they snapped. I grabbed hold of a branch and pulled at it with all my might till it broke, and I fell backward into the hole I had dug. Before I could catch my breath, I was squeezing through a tight gap between two branches, with the cold metal box in my outstretched hands before me. And just before I was out, I felt something grab at my pant leg and seize me. I pulled and kicked, while I clawed at the tall grass, trying to pull myself forward. Finally, I pulled my leg free only to discover that it was part of a branch that snagged my pants. I held the box in my filthy, trembling hands, and I recalled the specter's words telling me to take it, then I thought of the promise I had made to the little girl in the pit. I had a decision to make, but I did not ponder it for very long.

I ran faster than I had ever run before. The trees whipped by as I ran, and the clouds manipulated the moonlight from bright to a faint glow as I listened to the contents of the box clanging against the rusty metal. I do not remember how I found my way home. All I know is that I did not return with my good friend. The memory of my run home was a confused state of artificial drunkenness. I remember feeling hopelessly lost the whole time I ran, and not once did I stop to rest or ponder my location or direction. As I finally reached the trail that led to my house, the sun was rising. It was then that my arm began to burn and throb. I stopped running and examined it. There were teeth marks on my forearm, and it reassured me that no part of my surreal and nightmarish experience was a dream.

After a long nap, I awoke. It was late in the afternoon, and the sweet smells of supper had aroused me from my slumber. My first thought was of the rusted box that I had tucked beneath my bed. How our lives were going to improve, I thought. *Things will be easy from now on,* I said to myself with a smile. As I stood up, my arm began to throb with a numbing pain, and I thought, *I can afford a doctor's visit and any medicine he can provide to cure me.* "Our worries are over!" I said aloud. I knelt down beside the bed and looked beneath it. It was still there. I smiled as I descended the stairs and thought about how hungry I was. When I sat down at the table, I saw that my wife had prepared my favorite meal. It smelled so good. My stomach was rumbling as I breathed in another whiff of steak, potatoes, and corn. I cut off a chunk and started to chew, but something wasn't quite right. At first I thought she must've overcooked it, but it was soft, and as I cut the next piece, I could see that it was prepared just as I liked it, tender and juicy. So I popped it in my mouth, and as I chewed the second piece, a horror seized me, and I felt like spitting it out for it distinctly tasted like dirt!

ABOUT THE AUTHOR

LITTLE IS KNOWN ABOUT THE author. It is said he was a bit of a recluse. He was born in Newport in 1971. Jeff lived in several houses on Aquidneck Island and claimed that many of the locations were haunted. He had many such stories and loved to recite them. Some say he was a tortured soul, constantly plagued by spirits both good and evil. He swore to have seen a few UFOs; it's no wonder most took him for crazy. Jeff always had a powerful and vivid imagination, with which he was either blessed or plagued. As a youth, he was fascinated by space, the deep blue sea, and the supernatural. He loved reading, often books that were filled with ghost stories. Soon he was writing stories himself, mostly science fiction and horror. As a young boy, he knew he wanted to be a writer, well, that and, of course, an astronaut and a pirate. As a young man, he discovered alcohol and drugs and fell in love with intoxication. He also loved nature and would spend much of his time in the woods, writing short stories. Around this time, he became mesmerized with music and realized that he wished to leave his scar on the world of rock and roll, for one day he heard strange music playing in his head. It was always a full band, which often involved unexplained melodies from invisible and unimaginable instruments. The writer began penning down poetic verse to the phantom orchestrations that began playing in his head randomly. He spent seven years writing lyrics, which he described as miniature stories, many of which had a macabre nature. He often wondered where the strange music came from, and one day, it all stopped.

Sometime in his thirties, he suffered a mental breakdown. It is not known what brought it about. Some blame his drinking and drug use, while others claim he spent too much time delving into the darkness of the supernatural realm. Jeff began hallucinating and wandering around, speaking gibberish to himself. People swore he was having conversations with an imaginary entity, and the author began questioning from where his ideas were spawned in the first place. His friends came to understand that he was now convinced that he lived in a time a hundred and a half years in the past. For example, when a car went by, he would see a horse and carriage, and one time, he swore he had burned himself with his torch when he was carrying a flashlight. The afflicted author began complaining of an invisible haunt, which he called the Garghoul, which would often perch on his right shoulder and whisper strange words in his ear, which he would somehow translate to English on paper. Now Jeff understood where the ideas came from.

There is a rumor in which he was committed to Butler Hospital. Some say he mysteriously vanished while under their care. However, there is no proof of his incarceration. Either way, the author was never seen or heard from again. Some speculate that he might have returned to his beloved woods and died out in the elements. One rumor that persists is that he regained his dwindling sanity and is now living in Italy with his wife and pet, Homunculus. One can only hope that he is still alive and is still penning down chilling and macabre stories that threaten to deliver both writer and reader to madness.

CPSIA information can be obtained
at www.ICGtesting.com
Printed in the USA
FFOW03n0746080917
39725FF